RED LINE

A DCI ROBERT KETT NOVEL

ALEX SMITH

RELENTLESS
MEDIA

RED LINE

Published Worldwide by Relentless Media.
This edition published in 2024.

Edited by Hanna Elizabeth

17.0.03

www.alexsmithbooks.com
relentless.media

ALSO BY ALEX SMITH

The DCI Robert Kett Thrillers

Paper Girls

Bad Dog

Three Little Pigs

Whip Crack

Run Rabbit Run

Stone Cold Dead

Every Mother's Son

Sweet Briar Rose

Jaw Breaker

Knock Knock

King Rat

Knuckle Bones

Lucky Number Seven

Unholy Saints

Truly Madly Deadly

Every Last Devil

Red Line

Cold Iron Kills

Other Books

Six Days, Six Hours, Six Minutes

The Harder They Fall

For Avalon,
The coolest girl I know.

PROLOGUE

Saturday

As far as parties went, this one was banging.

Kieran Spicer could hear the music from a mile away, even over the rumble of Jonah's battered Fiesta. It was as if the night had a pulse, like it was coming to life around them. When they reached the end of the deserted lane and Jonah cut the engine, each concussive charge of sound from the other side of the woods made the car's windows rattle.

Kieran clutched his rucksack to his chest like his life depended on keeping it safe.

Because his life *did* depend on it.

"Nice," said Jonah, nodding to the beat. He turned his weed-cooked grin to Kieran, his pupils dilated. He was almost drowning in his bright red Ralph Lauren puffer jacket. "Fancy it?"

"Allow it," said Kieran, checking the clip on the rucksack to make sure it was still sealed. "Be the last party we ever go to."

He got out of the car, the night brutally cold, the music

pounding inside him more violently than his own heartbeat. It had stopped raining, which was a small mercy, but the air was so icy it made his face hurt. He slung the big, blue rucksack on so that it covered his stomach, cradling it like a baby in a carrier.

The moon was up, watching him as he walked to the wall that surrounded the estate. Part of it had crumbled away, just like Niko had told him it would be, and he scrambled over the loose bricks.

Ahead was a woodland, darker than sin. The skeletal trees had been stripped of their leaves, shivering in the cold. The sound of the wind cutting past them was like faint violins, as if an orchestra of ghosts had assembled to welcome him. The thought of it made him shiver—or maybe it was the cold air and the damp. It was almost midnight, after all.

Almost midnight. He needed to get a move on. He'd memorised the instructions that Niko had given him earlier that evening—*one delivery, midnight, at the back door. Don't be early, don't be late, don't say a word, and whatever the fuck you do, don't go inside*—and he'd planned the route so that he'd get there right on time.

He had to stick to the rules, because this was a good job. The Masques only came this way for a couple of weeks of the year, and they were big business. This was his one shot at not messing up.

Although he'd already messed up, because Niko had given him another rule: *go alone.*

"Fucking bricks," said Jonah as he tripped over the broken wall. His jacket was the brightest thing in the night; it could probably be seen from space. "Fucking shank you."

"You'll shank a brick?" said Kieran.

"Yeah," said Jonah.

He was fumbling with something in his belt, and Kieran knew all too well what he was hiding there. He'd seen the carving knife earlier—nine inches long and wicked sharp. It was far too big to be useful. He was more likely to stab himself in the bollocks with it.

"You staying with the whip?" said Kieran.

"No," he said. "I'm coming too. Not giving you all the Ps, am I?"

Kieran wasn't too upset about it. The truth was, he didn't fancy going into those woods alone, even though he knew a few hundred people were dancing their hearts out on the other side. It wasn't like anyone was watching them.

He set off up a shallow hill, his trainers struggling in the wet soil. He sank up to his ankles in places, like the ground was performing a citizen's arrest. Each step took him deeper into the prison of the trees, and he had to keep reminding himself why he was here.

Money, baby. Ps. This job was worth an easy four bills.

Kieran tugged the straps of his rucksack to make sure it was safe, then began his journey down the other side of the hill. He slipped onto his arse halfway, the impact knocking the wind out of him. He jumped up, panicking that he'd damaged his cargo. There was no way of knowing for sure, because that rule had been drummed into him before any other.

Never open the bag.

Not that it was much of a mystery, of course. Niko thought he was Al Capone or something, but he was a mid-level dealer in King's Lynn. Kieran couldn't work out how him and his gang of twats had even managed to get a job delivering to the Masque.

"Fuck off!" said Jonah.

He was caught in a string of brambles, looking like a fly

in a web as he struggled to escape. Kieran had to scan the dark trees to make sure a giant spider wasn't about to scuttle out of them, red-eyed, its fangs dripping.

"Oi," he hissed, as Jonah continued to moan and groan. "Shut up, somebody will hear us."

"Not if I fucking shank them in the ear, they won't," said Jonah.

He finally pulled free, something tearing as he scampered over. He inspected his jacket, his face miserable.

"Bloody torn it."

"You should have stayed by the whip," Kieran said. "Should have kept watch like we talked about."

"Kept watch for what? Badgers? Nothing out here, it's—"

Something cracked behind them, as loud as a pistol shot. Every single muscle in Kieran's body seemed to contract, punching a grunt of air from his lungs.

"What was that?" he asked, just a whisper.

"That was the sound of Kieran Spicer shitting his pants," said Jonah, but there was fear in his face too.

They both stared into the moon-drenched trees, seeing nothing, but hearing the crack of another branch beneath somebody's foot.

"Fuck this," said Jonah, sliding the knife out of his pocket. There was just enough moonlight to glint off the blade. "Somebody followed us."

"Put it away," said Kieran.

"Yeah?" Jonah lifted the blade so that the tip hovered in front of Kieran's nose. "Who made you the fucking king? Who said you should even be holding the bag, eh? Why don't you pass it over, let me take it. Less likely to be a little light that way, innit?"

"Fuck off," said Kieran, turning away so that Jonah

wouldn't see his cheeks blaze. They'd been friends for years, but right here, in the middle of the woods and with a lot of money on the table, he wasn't sure he trusted him not to plunge that blade into his back.

He pushed on, ploughing through the trees. The machine gun crack of snapping branches followed them—running now.

"Move!" hissed Jonah.

Kieran did exactly that, because if one of the other gangs had followed them here, or if it was the cops chasing them to the house, then they were both fucked. That rule was the most important one, so obvious that nobody even needed to say it.

You lose the bag, you're dead.

They couldn't be far from the party now, the music like liquid thunder. Kieran's adrenaline spiked, and he moved as fast as the woods would let him, grabbing trunks and branches to pull himself along. After a couple of minutes, he spotted a harsher glow to his right. He changed course, climbing another shallow rise until the top of a house appeared. Even if he hadn't been out of breath by the time he'd got to the top, he would have had to stop.

The house was enormous. Not just a mansion, but one of those stately homes, like Downton Abbey or something. There had to be a dozen windows on this side alone, and all of them were lit up. Kieran could see people through them, most in skimpy clothes and masks. They danced to the pulse of the music, each beat making the air shake.

"Shit!" said Jonah as he came to a halt beside him. "This place is on fleek, man."

He set off towards the house, but Kieran reached out and grabbed him before he could take more than a couple of steps.

"No chance, Joe," he said. "You wait here, like we said."

"And miss that?" said Jonah, shaking his head. "No way. Place is raging. Look at the *skets*."

"Niko said I have to go alone," said Kieran.

"I've been with you all the way, and nobody has shot us or anything," Jonah said, his attention still on the blazing windows and the people within. "So it's fine. Come on, we can find a mask, they'll never even know we're in there."

He tried to pull away, but Kieran held tight.

"No," he said. "This isn't a joke. You don't piss about with these people. You go in there and you won't come out."

The truth of it must have been written in every line of his face, because after a handful of seconds Jonah shrugged.

"Pussio," he said, but there was no conviction there.

"Wait in the trees, yeah?" said Kieran. "I'll come back this way."

He moved away, grateful for the wide lawn and the blazing spotlights. He didn't know which side of the house was the back, but he was guessing it was the end with all the outbuildings—hunkered shadows that reminded him of security guards. He reached them in seconds, basking in the dark while he removed the burner phone Niko had given him.

11:57. He couldn't have timed it any better.

He slipped it into his pocket then pulled the rucksack from his shoulders, checking the clips. This was definitely the back of the place, there were fewer lights on and he couldn't see any people through the windows. He could hear the rumble of generators, though—big ones, like at a carnival—and the air was thick with cigarette smoke.

He glanced back, Jonah nowhere to be seen. He wondered if he'd sulk off home and hoped he wouldn't, because he needed the ride.

It took him a while to find the back door in the origami-like contours of the building, and when he finally reached it, another glance at his phone told him he'd missed his delivery date by a minute.

It didn't matter. He was here.

He knocked, the heavy door barely registering the sound. There was no bell, so he tried again, the pain rolling up from his knuckles into his forearms. It was no wonder they couldn't hear him, the music was literally deafening.

He knocked a third time, the panic leeching the last of the warmth from his bones. He'd been standing here for at least two minutes. What if they told him he was late? What if they blamed him? He'd—

A bolt slid back on the other side of the door, and it opened a crack. Light flooded out like it was trying to escape, the music close behind. Somebody stood there, a silhouette with a face as twisted as the trees he'd just walked through. It was so grotesque that Kieran had reeled back before his eyes had adjusted and informed him it was just another mask.

"Shit," he said. "Sorry."

He thrust the bag towards the door like there was a bomb inside it—which, for all he knew, there could be.

"Delivery," he said, a mouse's squeak. "Your food."

The man—it had to be a man, he was as big as the door—didn't react. His mask was like something from a carnival, the nose too big, the ears jutting out on either side, the eyes as dark as a devil's. It was bright red.

Kieran grinned nervously, hoping the guy couldn't read his mind.

"I, uh..." he started, proffering the bag again. "I..."

He didn't know what to say. Was he supposed to just leave it here? He leaned over to place the rucksack on the stone step, stood straight, then bent down again to give the bag a little pat, like it was a dog.

"Sorry," he said, his face on fire, every nerve in his body jangling. "I brought a deliv—"

"You're late," said the man, a deep voice muffled by the mask.

"No," said Kieran. "I mean, yeah, now I am. But I wasn't, I was here right on time, I just don't know if you heard me knocking, it's quite—"

"Move along," said the guy, and he slammed the door in Kieran's face.

"What?" he said. "Move where? Hello?"

He picked up the bag and backed away, feeling sick with confusion. It was so dark he couldn't see anything, so he pulled out his phone again and switched on the torch.

There was another door a few yards away, this one open. He walked to it, shining his torch through the gap to see a set of stone stairs leading down into a pool of shadow. A red ribbon had been tied to the metal handrail, he saw, the loop dangling like a coil of intestines.

"Hello?" he croaked. "Is anyone there?"

Kieran waited for a reply, hearing the music, and—even louder than that—the wet thump of his heart.

"Hello?" he said again.

He moved to the top of the stairs, almost screaming when he saw that somebody was standing at the bottom, drowning in the dark. Whoever it was, they were wearing a long, flowing robe, their face concealed by a red mask and a wide hood.

"Uh, hi?" said Kieran, shouting to be heard over the drum and bass. He held up the bag. "I got your food."

The person walked away, vanishing through a door, their robes trailing behind them.

"Yeah, it's only a big bag of really expensive drugs," muttered Kieran. "I'll just take it home with me, shall I?"

He wondered if he was meant to follow, but the memory of Niko's voice held him back.

Whatever the fuck you do, don't go inside.

"Hello?" he said, just a whisper. "Please? I don't know what I'm supposed to be doing."

You do, he told himself. *You need to grow a new pair of bollocks, Kieran, and take the bag inside. Because if you mess this up then Niko's going to remove your original bollocks and fry them for his breakfast.*

And it wasn't just that. If he could deliver food to the Masque, then Niko would give him more, and then he'd be a made man.

He took a step towards the door, and at the same time something crunched behind him, the scuff of feet on gravel.

He turned in time to see a figure running from the shelter of one of the outbuildings a dozen yards away—sprinting towards him. They weren't wearing a mask but they may as well have been: mad eyes, a cruel smile, all drenched in shadow.

In their hand, something glinted.

"Wait!" Kieran cried out.

The figure screamed, a noise that rose above the music and stripped every last trace of warmth from his body.

Kieran turned, bolting through the door, forgetting the steps. He put his foot down and found nothing but air. He snatched at the handrail, grabbing the ribbon only to feel it come loose in his hand.

The monster behind him screamed again.

Then he was falling into the pool of crimson light, a fist of stone waiting to catch him at the bottom.

CHAPTER ONE

Sunday

"You ever shot anyone?"

DCI Robert Kett wasn't sure if the person who was asking the question was a child or a scarecrow. He couldn't have been more than twelve years old, his broomstick-like limbs poking out of a tracksuit that looked about four sizes too small for him. His spotty face was almost entirely covered by a curtain of lank, greasy hair, as if he'd grown up inside a chip fryer. He had to keep tilting his head so that he could see.

"Huh?" said Kett, who was only half paying attention.

It was hard to think straight over the cacophony of alarms and whistles and music that was being blasted from the speakers all around him. He was standing in the middle of Joyland, one of Great Yarmouth's most popular attractions—a collection of dilapidated rides on the seafront that literally hadn't changed since Kett had ridden them four decades ago.

"I said, have you ever shot anyone?" said the scarecrow. He shuffled uncomfortably in his ancient trainers, picking at the spots on his face. "With a gun."

"Uh, no," said Kett.

The kid looked disappointed.

"Have you ever run anyone over?" he asked after a moment's thought. "With a car."

"Uh..."

Kett rubbed his face, wondering for the hundredth time why he'd agreed to help Superintendent Clare out this weekend. Joyland was currently hosting the annual '*Norfolk Constabulary, Getting To Know You!*' publicity drive, which was about as awful as the name suggested.

The front end of the amusement park was draped with police tape and banners, plus an IRV, while a handful of stalls offered free drinks, hot food, merchandise, and activities for the kids. Kett stood in front of one of these stalls, a paper flag in one hand and an untouched custard cream in the other. The place was mobbed, mainly with uniformed coppers who looked just as confused about being here as he was.

"Like, smooshed them into the road?" the kid went on, demonstrating it with his hand. "Smoosh."

"Have I ever run somebody over with a car?" Kett said. "I mean... probably? I can't remember. A little bit, maybe. Not a full... *smoosh*."

The kid grinned.

"Cool," he said. "Have you ever landed a helicopter on somebody?"

"I can't fly a helicopter," said Kett.

The kid's face fell.

"Do you get to carry a bazooka?" he asked, perking up.

"Uh, no," said Kett, waiting for the roller coaster to rattle past overhead before continuing. He offered the flag. "But we do have some cool merch. Cool stuff, for the cool kids."

The boy looked disgusted.

"I'm sixteen," he said. "What am I going to do with a flag?"

He sloped off, the hands in his pockets the only thing stopping his tracksuit trousers from hitting his ankles. Three almost identical kids stepped up in his place.

"Do you guys want a flag?" Kett asked hopefully.

"No," one of the boys squeaked. "But I do have a question."

"Yeah?" said Kett, sighing. "About guns?"

The kids sniggered as they shook their heads.

"Go on then," said Kett. "Do your worst."

"We want to know if you've ever shit yourself on duty."

The boys snorted their laughter into their hands.

"No," said Kett. "Not really. But the shifts can be pretty long so I'm not going to lie, there are times when it's been close. Can you guys excuse me for a moment?"

He walked away before they could answer, pushing through the tangle of coppers and civilians and eating the custard cream as he went. The morning was icy, and a mist of rain had started to fall, coating everything like dew. Nobody seemed to mind, the chatter light-hearted, the laughter louder than the rumbling tracks.

A platoon of younger children swarmed past him, almost knocking him over as they careened towards the snail ride. Kett followed them, spotting his own girls in the queue. They were champing at the bit as they watched the mechanical snails clatter around the bumpy track and drop over the low hills. Billie stood next to them, rubbing her lower back with both hands.

"How many times have you been on?" Kett asked when he was in earshot.

"About five hundred," she replied, wincing. "I think every bone in my body has been shaken to dust."

"Dad!" said Evie, spotting him. "Can you come on with us?"

"Yes, that's a great idea," said Billie. "It's definitely your turn."

"I would," said Kett. "But my old body won't cope. It's broken enough as it is."

That wasn't a lie. The pain in his spine was worse than ever, to the point that it was starting to affect his work. Some mornings he could barely tilt his head.

"They're only snails, Dad," said Alice, rolling her eyes. "They don't even go that fast."

As if on cue, a little red snail thundered down the slope, a child whooping with joy, while her mum grimaced in pain. They whipped around the corner so fast that Kett thought he heard the crack of the woman's vertebrae separating.

"You know, you don't need a grown-up to go with you," he told them. "You're old enough to ride by yourselves."

"If they ride by themselves, those snails will be driving into traffic," said Billie. "They'll be on the road back to Norwich."

Kett laughed, and together they shuffled up the line. He spotted DC Savage walking over, PC Duke by her side in full uniform. A gaggle of teenage boys followed them, all ogling Savage.

"Fans?" asked Kett.

"Yeah, something like that," she replied. "The snails! I used to ride these when I was a kid. Proper back breakers."

"Can you come on with us?" asked Moira, jumping up and down. "Please, Kate?"

"Oh, I would," she said. "But... but I'm on duty, I'm not allowed. Sorry, girls."

"Nice excuse," said Kett.

"But *you* can come, Dad?" asked Evie. "Right?"

"Oh, no, Kate's right," he told her. "I forgot, we're not allowed to go on the rides when we're working."

"Can you come, Aaron?" said Evie, grabbing Duke's hand. "Can you sit with me?"

"That's a superb idea," said Kett. "Duke can go."

"He'll be perfect for it," added Savage.

"I'm working too!" said Duke.

"Yeah, but it's not the same thing," said Kett. "Go on, mate."

"Oh, right, sure?" said Duke, adjusting his Taser. "They don't look too bad."

Savage threw Kett a knowing grin as they reached the front of the queue. Moira and Alice charged for the next available snail, fighting to get in. Despite the growing size difference between them, Moira won out—aided by a powerful thump to her older sister's arm.

"Ow!" yelled Alice, her hand clamped to her bicep. "Moira just hit me!"

"I *barely* hit her!" Moira shouted, jiggling in her seat. "I gave her a fifty percent punch. Next time she'll get a hundred percent and she'll go into space."

"That's..." Kett shrugged. "That's actually great maths, Moo-moo, well done."

"Brilliant maths," said Billie, turning to Alice. "And to be fair, she gets the punching from you."

Alice stared at them in outrage as she climbed into the snail, still rubbing her arm. The attendant fixed the safety bar in place and the cart trundled off into the first bend.

The next snail stopped beside them, and Duke got in. Or at least he tried to. The rides hadn't been designed for a six-foot-five berserker, and it was a little like watching a polar bear trying to climb into a shoe box.

"I'm not sure if I'm going to fit," he said when he was halfway down.

"You'll fit," said Kett.

"Jiggle your hips," added Savage. "That's it."

Evie was doing her best to help, pushing on Duke's leg.

"Just a little more," said Savage. "Get that thigh in."

Duke twisted his body and dropped into place with a solid crunch. Kett wasn't sure if it was the big PC that had broken, or the snail. He filled the entire seat.

"There's no room for me!" Evie protested.

"Ow, wait," said Duke, trying to escape. "I'm not sure about this, can I—"

The attendant slammed the safety bar onto Duke's lap and he screamed like a prepubescent girl.

"Wait!" he said. "Sir, I don't think—"

Then he was off, howling his way around the bend.

"Is he okay?" asked Billie. "Those sound like real screams."

"Yeah..." said Savage, a flicker of concern crossing her face. "They do."

"Mummy," said Evie, holding out her hand to Billie. "I don't want to go on my own."

"Sorry," said Kett, flexing his neck as if trying to prove that he wasn't fit enough to ride with his daughter.

Billie pulled a face as she stepped into the snail, and in a heartbeat they were out of sight too.

"Back still bad, sir?" asked Savage.

He didn't have time to answer before the group of teenage boys skulked over, all swagger and Nike and Lynx.

"Have you decided about that date yet?" said the cockiest of the bunch. "I'll be happy to show you my truncheon, Officer."

His eyebrows wiggled. Savage sighed, glancing at Kett for backup.

"Hey, lads, she's taken," he said. "The big copper with the beard. I wouldn't push your luck, he can be scary."

A cry for help rose from the track, and everyone watched as Duke rolled over the top of the first hill. He looked like he was crying.

"Well, just saying," said the boy. "If you want a real man, come find me."

He grabbed his crotch, then skulked away.

"Ew," said Savage.

"Ew is right," said Kett, and he was about to go on when a roar cut him off.

"Oi!"

It was Superintendent Clare, cutting through the crowds like Godzilla.

"Run," said Kett, and Savage just managed to cover her laugh with a hand.

"Oh, you think this is funny, do you?" said Clare. His clothes were damp from the rain, and Kett could swear he saw steam rising from them. "You've neglected your post, Kett. What are you doing over here?"

"Oh, uh..." Kett swallowed. "I ran out of flags, sir."

"Likely story," said Clare. "And you, Kate, I didn't think I'd have to reprimand you today."

"Me, sir?" said Savage.

"Yes, you. Can you please stop flirting with the teenage boys?"

"Really *not* flirting, sir," said Savage.

"Can I tell you what else you're *not* doing, Kate? You're not *working*. Where's the walking wardrobe?"

"Sir?" said Kett.

"The hairy portaloo?"

"Duke?" said Kett.

"Yes, Duke! I need him. He better not be pissing about back here."

"He's, uh..." Savage started.

Duke's snail rolled around the corner and juddered to a halt. The PC made a valiant effort to get out, his face warped with pain. Clare's eyes bulged when he caught sight of him.

"Duke, get out here right now, you beef-scented haemorrhoid cushion."

He was trying to get out, but the safety bar was wedged so tightly over his lap that the attendant couldn't release it.

"Sorry," said the guy as the line of snails grew longer behind him. "You're clogging the ride. You'll have to go again."

"Don't you dare go again," said Clare.

"I don't want to go again!" wailed Duke as he clattered around the bend.

"Forget about him," said Clare. "I need you two over at the refreshment stand. There's a problem."

"A problem, sir?" asked Savage.

"Yes, Kate, a problem. Somebody's poisoned the tea."

Clare marched towards the ride attendant, bellowing like a horny buffalo.

"Poisoned the tea, sir?" said Savage. She looked at Kett, and they both understood the problem immediately.

"Porter," they said together.

Sure enough, by the time they'd navigated the crowds and arrived at the front of the park, an argument was in full swing. A small mob had formed beside the drinks stall, all of them shouting at once.

DI Peter Porter stood alone in the shadows of the stand, looking just like Dracula before his castle was stormed by pitchfork-wielding peasants. Kett walked a little closer to try to work out what they were saying.

"... then what are the white bits that are floating in it?" yelled a man who was almost as big as Duke, dressed in shorts and a string vest despite the fact it was November. "Eh? You should be ashamed of yourself, you tea pervert."

"It's not... I didn't..." Porter looked exasperated. "It's special milk."

"He admits it!" screeched a woman. "He's spunked his special milk in our tea!"

"No, it's *pea* milk," said Porter.

The outrage of the crowd swelled, two of the men looking like they were about to drag Porter over the counter.

"Pea!" Porter was shouting, an effort that wasn't helping at all. "Pea!"

"Jesus Christ," said Kett, pushing into the back of the crowd. "Alright, everyone, that's enough. Move away."

"He's trying to poison us with his dirty pee milk," said the same woman. "Arrest him!"

Kett reached the stall and turned to face them.

"As much as I would love to arrest this man for crimes against tea-making," he said, "and believe me, this isn't the worst of them, you've got the wrong idea."

He glanced at the nearest cup, seeing the slightly yellow tinge to the tea, and the creamy lumps that floated on the surface.

"At least, I *hope* you've got the wrong idea. Pete, what's going on?"

"It's pea milk," said Porter, holding up a carton. "We ran out of dairy, it's all we've got. It's made from yellow split peas, it isn't poisonous."

"There," said Kett. "Split peas. Not... not whatever you lot thought it might be. If you don't want it, you can get your money back."

This seemed to diffuse the situation, and Kett retreated while the angry punters moved in for their refund.

"Porter's got a new nickname then, sir," said Savage, unable to stop the smile. "Tea pervert."

"Suits him," said Kett.

The last of the customers slouched away and Porter changed the sign to *closed*. He appeared from the side of the stall, his cheeks blazing.

"Bloody hell," he said. "I thought I was a goner."

"You did put pea milk in their tea, Pete," said Kett. "What are you doing behind there anyway? Don't all tea-making facilities have a restraining order out on you?"

"You're not allowed to be mean to me, sir," said Porter. He rubbed his shoulder, where three months ago he'd been stabbed by Aggie Clegg. The wound hadn't been deep, and he'd been back at work after a few weeks, but he'd been using it as an excuse ever since. "Molly needed the loo. I said I'd hold the fort for five minutes."

"Better clear off before she gets back, sir," said Savage. "You've put her out of business."

"I haven't..." said Porter. His brow wrinkled. "Actually, you're probably right, we should go."

They skulked off into the crowd, only to freeze when they saw Clare advancing once again. His cheeks were mottled in the way they only got when he was truly furious, and the subject of his ire was apparent in the way he jabbed a long finger towards them.

"Run," Kett said again.

"You lot have truly Ketted this up," Clare bellowed, attracting the attention of everyone in the vicinity. "Duke's on his fourth trip around the snail track and he's still wedged tight. We're going to have to call out the fire service."

Porter snorted out a laugh that was cut off when Clare turned his attention to him.

"You've had four official complaints from people who think you've squirted toss in their tea," he said.

"It was pea milk, sir," muttered Porter. Clare pulled a face.

"Same thing, you bloody tea pervert."

Porter frantically rubbed his shoulder.

"You're not allowed to be mean to—"

"Stick a dick in it, Pete," Clare roared.

He swung his finger to Savage.

"You're a bloody pervert too, so you can shut up. I've just had to tell the mum of a teenage boy that you didn't offer to polish his helmet."

"What?" gasped Savage. "I... *what*?"

Kett gave them all a smug grin, but even that didn't last long.

"You can wipe that smile off your face as well, Kett," said Clare.

"I haven't done anything, sir!" he protested.

"Tell that to your children. Because one of them almost shot a man in the crotch at the archery stand."

Kett had no idea what to say to that.

The Superintendent rubbed his face.

"I should have known better than to bring you lot here,"

he said. "But at least I've got an excuse to send you away. Call came in while I was watching your fiancé piss about on the snails, Kate. We've got a body."

"Who?" said Porter.

"How the hell should I know?" Clare was literally foaming at the mouth. "That's your job, you fart-flavoured camel toe."

Porter grimaced.

"It's out near Dereham," said Clare, gesturing to the exit. "So grab your coats and toss off."

CHAPTER TWO

THEY CROSSED THE COUNTY IN RECORD TIME, SAVAGE following the scar of the A47 all the way from Yarmouth to Dereham before cutting south. She navigated a spiderweb of tangled, narrow roads, nothing on either side but barren fields stripped of their harvest. Nobody lived out here except the cows and the crows, all cowering beneath a sky that was as heavy as concrete.

"Bleak," said Porter from the back seat.

Kett couldn't argue. The rain hammered the windscreen, the cold leaching into the car even though the vents were blowing hot air.

"Still better than hanging about in Joyland with the boss, though," Porter went on. "Right?"

"You're not wrong," said Kett, nodding. "I think this might be it."

There was an IRV up ahead, blocking a junction, its blue lights cutting through the dull morning. A constable sat in the open front door and she clambered out when she saw them approach, gesturing to the main road ahead until she saw who they were.

"Oh, sorry, sirs," she said when Savage had rolled down her window.

"Where are we going?" said Kett.

The constable stood straight, pointing to the right.

"It's a quarter of a mile down there, sir," she said. "You can't miss it."

"How bad?" he asked.

The woman took a breath but couldn't find an answer.

"Bad, then," said Kett when Savage had pulled away.

They drove for a few minutes, another IRV appearing like a beacon ahead. It sat in a small patch of land that might have been a car park. Two more uniformed constables hung around, stamping their feet and breathing plumes of breath like cigarette smoke. Gravel crunched beneath the tyres as Savage pulled the car up next to the others. When she turned off the engine, silence fell like a bag over Kett's head.

He opened the door, groaning his way out into the cold. The rain fell like wet gauze, coating his skin and making the wind feel much colder than it was. He shivered, pulling up the collar of his coat as he crossed the patch of barren land. At the end of it was a small playground ringed by a low wooden fence that was littered with crows. There wasn't much here: a slide, a set of monkey bars with a swing at one end, a basketball hoop and, right at the back, a merry-go-round.

Kett observed the landscape as he walked. They were at the top of a hill here, more or less, fields sloping down on every side except one, where a stunted woodland grew.

He stopped by the fence, nodding to the PCs who had gathered there.

"Definitely a body?"

They looked at each other as if they'd rehearsed what to say, but in the end none of them answered. One opened the gate for Kett and he walked through, Savage and Porter treading on his shadow. The crows hopped from one foot to the other, shoulder to shoulder as they watched.

The body waited on the merry-go-round. It sat with its back to them, its head covered by the hood of a thick, black Canada Goose jacket, its hands casually resting over the bars. From this angle, there was nothing dead about it. It looked like somebody who had come here for a play, and who was enjoying a moment of quiet—an illusion that lasted until a crow landed on its head, its strangled cry the loudest thing in the world. It bent down as if it meant to peck at the hidden face and Savage ran towards it, clapping her hands.

"Shoo!"

It flapped off in a panic, and so did the others, a storm of noise that disappeared into the trees.

Kett made his way past the slide, scanning the ground as he went.

"Blood," he said, nodding to a small, dark stain on the woodchip. "Watch your feet."

There was a little more blood next to the merry-go-round, and he gave it a wide berth, his back scraping the fence as he shuffled by. It was a good job the fence was there, because when the front of the body came into view he almost tumbled backwards, the wooden support the only thing holding him up.

"Fuck me," he said.

The face was lost in the shadows of the hood, but the horror of it was obvious. It was crimson, as if the skin had been peeled away. One of the eyes was gone, the socket gaping. The other peeked from beneath a drooping lid, staring past the fence and into the woods as if trying to work out where the crows had gone.

"Dear God," said Savage, her hand to her mouth. She

glanced at Kett, her eyes wet from the wind, or from what she saw. He could read her thoughts as easily as if they were his own.

It never ends.

"Kid?" asked Porter, leaning against the fence, his face hollowed out by the cold.

It was hard to tell. The body was dressed in a black Nike tracksuit that had been torn in at least six places. The trainers had been white once, but they were now caked with dirt and blood. The hands poked from the sleeves, too grey, surely, to have ever been real. There was blood between the fingers, more black than red.

"Hey," Kett yelled to the constables. "Who called it in?"

"Some woman," replied the PC who'd opened the gate. He pulled out his notepad, scanning it. "Fi Hogan. She was driving up the lane at about nine and spotted what she thought was a kid on the roundabout thing. Said she wouldn't have thought anything about it except the crows were all over him. Didn't stop, she called us when she got home, just in case."

Kett nodded.

"What time did you lot get here?"

"After ten, sir," said the second constable. She wiped her nose, shivering in the cold. "We were on the way out earlier but we had to respond to a domestic up the road."

"And you didn't see anything?"

Both constables shook their heads.

"Nobody's been up here since you arrived?"

"Just you, sir," said the man. "And *them*."

He nodded to the fence, and Kett looked back to see that the crows had returned—so quietly that he hadn't heard them arrive. He did his best to ignore them, taking a couple of steps towards the body and crouching in front of it.

He breathed a sigh of relief. The face hadn't been skinned at all. It had been wrapped in what looked like red cloth. The single eye seemed to watch him, the illusion so powerful that he wondered if the body was actually alive. The jolt of adrenaline that tore through him almost sent him sprawling onto his arse.

"Fuck's sake," he muttered, bracing one hand on the ground.

"Sir?" asked Savage.

"Nothing, Kate."

He studied the face, the cloth that had been wound around it. It had a shine.

"What is that?"

"Ribbon, sir," said Savage. "I think."

"Ribbon," Kett echoed. "There's a lot of it, and it's neat. That would have taken time."

His leg was threatening to cramp in the cold and he pushed himself up, the pain in his back making him reel. Savage took hold of his arm to steady him, and he pulled away a little harder than he'd meant to.

"I can fetch you a chair, sir?" she said, entirely serious.

"I don't need a bloody chair, Kate."

"Sure about that, sir?" said Porter. "You look like you need a *push*chair."

Kett ignored him, accepting a pair of gloves from Savage and doing his best to work them onto his numb fingers. He patted the body's pockets as gently as he dared, first the trousers and then the hoodie. The merry-go-round must have been in good nick because even his gentle touch spun it on its axis, the noise like the shriek of nails down a blackboard. He used the back of his hand to bring it to a halt.

"Can't feel any ID," he said. He called out to the coppers at the gate. "You lot searched the park?"

"No, sir," said the woman. "We didn't want to make a mess."

"Didn't want to do any work, more like it," grumbled Kett. "Pete, can you do a quick whizz around, see if you can find a phone?"

"Sure, sir," said Porter. "Any phone?"

Kett gave him a look.

"No, Pete," he said, pointing to the corpse. "*His* phone."

"Oh, right," said Porter. "Yeah."

He lumbered off, ducking low to check beneath the slide. Kett moved as close to the body as he dared, trying to make sense of the scraps of skin he saw beneath the ribbon. He wanted to pull the hood back but he didn't want to risk disturbing the scene.

"Why would you kill somebody, then wrap their head in ribbon?" he asked. "Why go to that trouble?"

"Maybe they were ashamed of what they'd done?" said Savage. "Couldn't bear to look at it."

"Maybe," said Kett. "But if that's the case, you use a bag, right? You don't take minutes to wind a reel of ribbon around them. That seems more... I don't know, ceremonial."

"Personal," said Savage with a nod. "They're trying to hide what they've done, but they don't want to insult their victim by rushing it."

Kett breathed out slowly.

"What else are you seeing?" he asked her.

Savage thought about it for a long moment.

"Definitely murder, sir," she said. "A violent one. Look at the cuts to the tracksuit."

Kett had already spotted them, and from this angle, he could see that it wasn't just the clothes that had been mauled. He could make out the ravaged flesh beneath, hacked and split. There was blood everywhere, but it was almost invisible against the dark fabric of the tracksuit.

"Can't have been killed here, sir," Savage went on. "There's blood on the ground, but nowhere near enough for all those cuts. There's at least seven of them. Machete, maybe? Or a big axe. I don't know."

"I agree," said Kett. "Can't have happened here unless they used tarps, unless they came prepared. But..."

He turned slowly, taking in the surrounding countryside.

"What is this place, Kate?"

"Sir?" asked Savage.

"This place, what is it?"

"Playground, sir," said Porter, wandering back over.

"Yeah, Pete, I know that. But what's it doing all the way out here? There are no houses, no schools. Just fields and woods. Why build a park all the way out here?"

"I don't know, sir," said Savage. "But it must be popular, there's enough parking for about twenty cars."

"You couldn't fit twenty people in here," said Kett. "Don't you dare."

He directed these last words at a crow, which had flapped its way off the fence and onto the ground by the corpse's feet.

"I will punt you into the middle of next week if you don't piss off."

The crow thought about it for a second and decided it was a battle it couldn't win. It took off, landing in the field on the other side of the fence and jeering loudly.

"Bastard things," said Kett.

A gust of wind cut up the hill and the merry-go-round moved another few inches, screeching like a banshee. The corpse's feet dragged on the ground but it stayed put, the body as rigid as a Halloween decoration.

"Why here?" Kett said. "Why like this? Why not bury it in the woods?"

"Feels like they're sending a message, sir," said Savage. "It would have been risky, bringing a body here, propping it up like this. And..."

She leaned in for a closer look.

"Must have been dead a while, sir," she went on. "Because there's no way you get a fresh corpse to sit up like that. It would fall off. The arms are locked tight, rigor mortis. They must have just hooked them over the bars."

"Sending a message," said Kett, nodding. "But what's the message?"

His phone buzzed in his pocket and he pulled it out, seeing Cara Hay's name on the screen. He passed the phone to Savage.

"Can you do it?"

Savage took the phone, answering it as she walked away.

"You find anything in the park?" Kett asked Porter.

"No phone," the DI replied, shaking his head. "But you might want to take a look at this."

I really don't, Kett thought as he followed Porter to the slide. It was a metal one, the kind that got hotter than a skillet in the summer. He bent over to take a closer look, the pain in his spine like crushed glass.

"What?" he asked.

"You can't see it?" said Porter.

"I obviously can't see it," Kett told him. "Where am I looking?"

"There, sir."

Kett followed Porter's finger to the steps. They were red,

which is why he hadn't spotted the bloody smudges that went all the way to the top.

"Shit," he said, walking around and seeing another crimson smear going all the way down the slide—this one being slowly washed away by the rain. "What the hell is that?"

"Somebody used it," said Porter with a shrug. "Somebody went down the slide, covered in blood. There's more on the swing, too."

"That doesn't make..." Kett started, the words faltering.

He walked to the swing, which was moving gently in the wind as if an invisible child was playing there. Sure enough, there was another stain on the wooden slats, unmistakably blood. He checked the ropes, but they were clean.

"That doesn't make any sense," he finished. "They brought the corpse here and then what? Played for a bit?"

Porter shrugged again, wiping the rain from his red nose.

"Or maybe it was the corpse who was playing," he said.

"Hay's on her way," said Savage as she walked over. "Half an hour tops."

She frowned at him.

"You okay, sir? You look like you've seen a ghost."

Kett glanced again at the body as the merry-go-round turned another screeching inch. He couldn't stop himself from imagining the corpse cavorting around the park in the dead of night, scraps of ribbon snapping in the wind, that one eye burning.

"Maybe I have," he told Savage, a shudder tearing through him. "Let's wait in the car, yeah?"

CHAPTER THREE

The little park filled up fast, and it was fitting company for the lonely dead.

Seven technicians, dressed head to toe in white, surrounded the corpse like angels, their movements slow, their heads bowed. Their overalls fluttered in the breeze, echoing the flap and stutter of the ribbon and the snap of the cameras.

Cara Hay busied herself with the body, anchoring the merry-go-round with a car jack, of all things, before examining every inch of the miserable scene. Kett watched from the other side of the fence, Savage leaning against him, Porter a little further away, lost in his phone. For what felt like a lifetime, nobody spoke.

Then Hay turned to them, pulling down her face mask to reveal an expression mired in sadness.

"I have what I need. I'm going to uncover the head now, if that's okay with you?"

Kett nodded, and Hay went to work. Two of her technicians supported the body while she pulled back the hood, revealing a crop of sandy hair that was slick with blood. Kett heard Savage gasp, and it took him a moment to notice what she had: the deep gashes visible beneath the hairline, a glimpse of skull.

"He was *butchered,*" said Savage.

The head was mummified in ribbon, from the top of the ears down to the collarbone. The ribbon was red, and darker in some places than in others. Kett didn't need to be a forensic technician to understand why.

"Christ," he said, wanting to turn away but holding his ground.

The dead deserved to be seen.

"I think we've got a male," Hay said, feeling the man's neck with her gloved hands. "No grey in the hair, skin is supple. They're young."

She ran her fingers over the face, skirting that single, bulging eye.

"Definitely ribbon," she said. "Looks like the kind you get anywhere, satin finish. It's secured with a safety pin. Two, actually, one at the top, one at the base of the neck."

"They were prepared," said Kett. "They didn't just tie a knot."

Hay didn't reply, fiddling with the safety pin until it came free. Another technician held out an evidence bag and she dropped it in.

"Did the killer leave the eyes exposed?" asked Kett.

Hay considered the question while the wind whipped through the park, a storm of sand and rain.

"I wondered that myself," she said. "I don't think so. The ribbon is tight, but it's still just ribbon. I think the crows helped themselves."

In the field beyond, the birds hopped and cawed as if protesting their innocence.

"I think they pulled the ribbon away from one eye so

they could remove it. The bandage was tighter around the other, but I can see marks where a beak has punched into the flesh of the eyeball."

Kett winced.

"Maybe a blade, though," Hay went on. "Franklin will be able to tell us."

She began to unwrap the body like a gift, unwinding the ribbon in ever-growing circles while feeding it into another open bag. The face beneath appeared like a slowly developing photograph, a wide forehead, a small nose, a mouth that was so distorted by terror it could have belonged to a melting waxwork. By the time she'd removed the last of it and stood back, there was no denying who sat in front of them.

"He's just a boy," said Kett, feeling the familiar sting of anger as it boiled through him.

The kid couldn't have been older than fifteen, his plump cheeks still carrying the memory of childhood and boasting nothing more than a fuzz of blond hair. One side of his face was lost beneath a mask of dry blood, a gash stretching from his ear—or the place where his ear should have been, Kett realised, because it had been removed—to the tip of his chin.

"Somebody attacked him with..." Hay shook her head. "I don't even think 'fury' is a strong enough word. Maybe there is no word. He's been struck repeatedly with a very, very sharp, heavy blade. I can see bone."

She pointed a gloved finger to his neck. Kett leaned over the fence to see better. There was another cut along the front of the victim's throat, this one so severe it looked as if somebody had tried to behead him.

"I think this is the one that killed him."

"Can you check his pockets, Cara?" asked Kett, his voice hoarse. "I had a feel, but didn't go in."

She took her time, rummaging in the boy's clothes until she suddenly flinched, drawing her hand back.

"What?" asked Kett.

Hay pushed her fingers back into his trouser pocket, then gently pulled them free. Kett couldn't make sense of what she was holding until she turned around and lifted her hand.

It was an ear.

It was *his* ear, caked in blood.

Nobody knew what to say. Kett's body fizzed, pins and needles in his fingers. He watched as Hay dropped the ear into another evidence bag, then she took a few steps back, sucking down fresh air. She looked rattled, and it wasn't often you could say that about Cara Hay.

"Franklin can do the rest," said Kett, wanting to put her out of her misery. "Take a minute, Cara."

"Any minute I take is a minute less we have to find who did this," she said, meeting his eye.

Kett nodded.

"Can you guess a time of death?" he asked.

"Body's cold, I don't know any more than that. It's hours, though."

"You've seen the stains on the slide? On the swing?"

"Blood," said Cara. "Although obviously we don't know whose. I'm confident our victim was dead when he arrived here, which means either his killer was drenched in his blood, and still took the time to play on the equipment or..."

She didn't finish, as if the wind had stolen her voice.

"Or they carried the victim's body up the stairs and pushed him down the slide," said Kett. "They sat him on the swing."

"And they turned him on the merry-go-round," Hay finished, nodding. "One last trip to the..."

She choked back a sob, her eyes glassy.

"One last trip to the park," said Kett. "Your boy's about this age, isn't he, Cara?"

"Both of them," she said. "That's why I... I'm sorry, I shouldn't..."

"Go," said Kett. "Find out whose blood that is, leave the body to us."

Hay nodded, taking a moment more to study the dead boy. Her lips moved in silent prayer, and her sigh was a cloud of breath that rose over her head as she made her way to her van.

"This feels personal, sir," said Savage. "Right? The care the killer took with the ribbon, the fact they brought him here to the park, that they might have... I don't even know how to describe it."

"He's like a toy," said Kett. "The girls take their teddies to the park sometimes, put them on the swing, push them down the slide. It feels like that."

Savage nodded.

"But why?" said Kett, looking at the boy. "And more to the point, *how*? Kid's young, but he's still got to be, what? Ten, twelve stone? That's a hell of a weight to push up some steps."

"Unless you're not doing it alone," said Savage. "Two killers, maybe more. We've seen it before."

"So a bunch of people kill a kid and bring him to the park?" said Porter, wandering up. "That's even weirder than one person doing it."

Kett puffed out a cloud of breath, wishing it was cigarette smoke. The cravings were always worse at the start of a case.

"Kate, can you have a drive around?" he asked, turning to Savage. "I don't know this area at all. See if you can find some cameras, anything that might have caught the killer on their way here."

"Sure, sir," said Savage.

"And see if you can figure out why there's a park in the middle of nowhere," he added. "Pete, can you take a look in the woods over there?"

Porter looked like Kett had asked him to eat a shit.

"The woods?" said the DI. "Can't Kate do that? I'll drive around. I like driving. I *hate* woods."

"I know," said Kett. "That's why I'm sending you."

Savage smiled, but only for a moment. Porter massaged his shoulder, pouting.

"I'm still in a lot of pain, sir, you have to be nice to me."

"I'm being nice, Pete," said Kett, in the tone of voice he used to tell his kids that the argument was over. "A gentle walk in the countryside will be good for you."

Porter grumbled away, muttering obscenities at the crows.

"What are you going to do, sir?" asked Savage.

Kett considered the question for a moment as the cold wind cut up the hill.

"I'm going to call Clare and hand in my notice," he said. "Then I'm going to go home, climb into bed with the hot blanket on and a nice cup of tea, and read a book."

Savage nodded sympathetically.

"Yeah, right," she said.

Kett breathed a quiet laugh through his nose. Savage headed for the car, resting a gentle hand on his shoulder for a moment as she passed.

He pulled out his phone, calling DS Alison Spalding back at HQ, then hanging up when he remembered it was

Sunday. He tried Clare instead, the Super's phone going straight to voicemail.

"Hi, sir," he said. "It's Kett. Body's a young man, around fifteen, no ID. He's been..."

He couldn't think of a better word than the one Savage had used.

"Butchered. Head is wrapped in ribbon. Dead a few hours, according to Hay. I'll check mispers, see if we can figure out who he is, and the sooner we can get him to Franklin, the better."

He paused a moment more, staring at the body that sat on the merry-go-round. Tugged by the insistent wind, he moved gently, as if trying to eke out one last spin. The hungry crows were advancing again. They knew nothing of who this boy had been, knew nothing of his history, of his voice and his laughter, of his dreams, his fears, his loves—the unfathomable complexity of all his collective days.

All he was to them was death, and a fortunate meal.

"He's just a kid, sir," Kett whispered into the silent phone.

Then, with nothing else to say, he hung up.

CHAPTER FOUR

"Please tell me you're not still on the snails," said Savage as she crunched across the car park towards the parked Audi.

Duke's sigh made the line rattle. Behind it, Savage could hear an obnoxious buzz that might have been an angle grinder. And behind that, a sizeable amount of laughter. She shifted her phone to her other ear as she opened the door, then slid into the driver's seat.

"They can't get me out," Duke said, the misery in his voice perfectly audible even from fifty miles away. "I'm literally wedged in. And everyone is watching, Kate. The whole of bloody Yarmouth has turned up. I..."

The scream of the angle grinder grew even louder.

"Wait, that's too close! That's too close!"

"Too close to what?" said Savage when the noise had quietened.

"What do you think, Kate?" Duke said. "They're cutting away the safety bar on my lap, it's right next to my... Wait, *stop*!"

The roar of the grinder rose again.

"Kate, if I don't make it, remember I love you," said Duke.

"You're not going to die, Aaron," she told him. "Call me when you're out."

He wailed her name as she ended the call, and she felt more than a little guilty about it. Throwing the phone onto the passenger seat, she started the engine, pulling slowly out of the car park. A welcome gust of warm wind puffed from the vents, slowly thawing her fingers and toes.

"Right," she said, pausing for a moment while she looked one way and then the other. She didn't know this area too well either, mainly because there wasn't much here. Half a mile north was the village of Shipdham, and another mile past that was Dereham. But in every other direction, as far as she knew, there was nothing but farmland.

And maybe a killer.

She turned right, heading south. A lone figure stumbled over the field that flanked the park, heading towards the distant woods. Porter must have felt her watching, because he turned and shot her a glare—and possibly a middle finger, too, although he vanished behind a bush before she could be sure.

She drove on, keeping her speed low as she scanned the landscape. Other than the hill where the park sat it was almost perfectly flat here, the barren fields resembling an ocean as they stretched towards the grey horizon. Oak trees penetrated the sky like lonely ships, floundering beneath storms of crows. And the rain did its best to wash the whole scene away.

Porter was right. It really was bleak.

She spotted a road on the right and took it, the lane so narrow that the high verges tried to snatch the car as it passed. For four minutes she bumped over potholes and edged around tight corners until, finally, the track widened and she spotted a building ahead.

Although *building* was putting it a little strongly, she realised, as she parked the car on a stretch of broken concrete beside it. It was a wooden barn, one wall bowing out and the roof sloping dramatically. It looked like a gentle breeze might knock it over.

Savage exited into the cold air, pulling her coat tight. On the right-hand side of the road, past a scraggly row of hedges, was the field that sloped gently up towards the park. She couldn't see the playground from here, but she could almost make out the fringe of woodland that Porter was exploring.

The barn was open and she walked over, peeking into the dark to see a couple of ancient tractors that were little more than metal skeletons. A dozen or so plastic boxes littered the floor, and a chemical smell filled the air: part petrol, part something else that she couldn't identify.

She walked along the front of the barn, finding a path down the side of it. The place looked long forgotten, the weeds growing through the cracked concrete path almost reaching her knees. She fought her way through the overfamiliar hedges until the path opened up into a yard that was empty of anything other than a clothesline. On the far side of the yard was a small farmhouse, the windows cracked and broken. The door was open.

Savage held her breath, listening for any sign of life. It was impossibly quiet here, she couldn't even hear the crows. She cleared her throat, called out.

"Hello? Is anyone there? It's the police."

Only her own voice replied as it echoed back from the flaking brickwork. She walked a little closer, putting her hand on the wall and leaning through the door. It felt ten degrees cooler in there than it did outside, as if the building was refrigerated. It was dark, too, darker than it should have been considering none of the windows had curtains. The short corridor ended up ahead in what looked like a kitchen, two doors peeling off to the side.

"Hello?" she said. "It's the police. If anyone is home, can you let me know?"

Something chirruped up ahead in the kitchen, followed by a soft slap—alien sounds that made her skin crawl.

"Hello?" she said again.

A small, furry shape appeared in the door, masked by shadow. It miaowed, and the fear that had locked Savage's body melted away. The cat sauntered up the corridor, rubbing itself against the walls, its purr as loud as a generator.

"Who are you, then?" said Savage as the cat—a massive ginger tom with dirty white feet—wound its way between her legs. It chirruped again, looking up with enormous yellow eyes that might have been cut from glass. It was an ugly thing for sure, a snaggle-tooth pinning back its bottom lip and one of its ears torn in two, the scar long healed.

Savage bent down and offered a hand, which the cat eyeballed suspiciously before headbutting. She gave it a little scratch on the scruff of its neck.

"Don't suppose you saw anything weird last night, eh?" she asked it. "Over at the park? Maybe some—"

The cat bit her, faster than a rattlesnake. It bolted back down the corridor before she even had time to stand straight.

"Ow!" she said, pulling her hand to her face, the fire throbbing down her finger into the meat of her palm. "You little... What was that for?"

The bite was a deep one, droplets of blood pattering to

the filthy wooden floor. She put her finger to her mouth, sucking deeply, tasting copper as she followed the cat down the corridor.

"I'm going to have to get a jab for this, you little git," she said.

The door on the right led into a toilet, the ceramic bowl shattered. To the left was a living room with an awful patterned carpet and a single sofa that looked like it carried every disease known to humankind. There was an ashtray on the coffee table, overflowing with cigarette butts, and a minefield of empty beer bottles.

She made it to the kitchen, hearing another innocent chirrup from the bastard cat. It was nowhere to be seen amongst the pine units. She ducked to see if it was waiting for her beneath the table, but there were only dust balls there, as big as mice. Another door led out of the room, and she was halfway to it before she understood that there was another sound beneath the drum of her heart: a soft hiss.

There was a kettle on the stove, the gas hob lit.

She swore beneath her breath, backing away. The cat miaowed from beyond the other door, a much louder sound.

And somebody answered.

"Alright, alright."

A shadow rose in the door, and before Savage could even open her mouth a man walked into the kitchen. He was shorter than she was, somewhere in his sixties, his portly body stuffed into a lumberjack's shirt and blue jeans that were almost black with dirt. He was holding a cardboard box, and was so engrossed in its contents that he didn't see Savage even though she was standing almost right in front of him.

"Uh," she said. "Hi."

The man screamed, the box jettisoning from his hands

with such force that it hit the ceiling. Vegetables rained to the floor in a hail of dirt, the man's shriek continuing as he staggered back towards the stove.

"I'm police!" Savage yelled, but the man was lost to his terror, his eyes like pickled eggs.

He reached behind him and found the kettle, the same scream still punching its way from his gaping mouth.

"Don't!" Savage said.

The man hurled the kettle at her. The lid flew off, a cascade of water cleaving through the air. Savage threw up her arms, feeling it spatter over her skin, in her hair—hot, but not boiling. By the time she'd looked again the man was running at her, something gripped in his hand—*still screaming*.

"I'm police!" Savage shouted, backing through the door. "Police!"

The man charged, oblivious, reaching her in an instant. He thrust whatever he was holding at her face—a flash of bright orange—and she jerked back, grabbing his arm.

"Stop!" she roared.

She bent his wrist as hard as she could, the weapon falling to the floor. The man's shriek rattled into a gargled grunt as she twisted the arm even further. She stuck a foot behind his leg and gave him a shove, almost losing her balance.

"Fuck off!" the man roared, pushing her back with surprising strength. "Get the—"

Savage jammed her elbow into his gut, then pushed again. The man tripped, falling back, and she landed hard on top of him.

"Stop fighting me," she said, straddling him, struggling for breath. "I'm police!"

He seemed to hear her this time, his bloodshot eyes bulging, his movements slowing.

"Police?" he said.

Savage nodded, still sitting on him.

"Fuck are you doing here?" the man asked, his accent pure Norfolk. "Scared me half to death."

He looked Savage up and down, licking lips that looked like undercooked steak.

"Half to..." he repeated, and he suddenly clutched a hand to his meaty chest. "Christ," he said. "It hurts."

"Shit," said Savage. "You okay?"

"My... heart," the man said, writhing beneath her. She slid off him, kneeling next to him. "Help... me."

He bucked once, then lay still, bubbles of spit leaking from his open mouth.

"Shit," said Savage. "Shit shit shit."

She pulled out her phone, calling 999 before laying it on the floor. She felt the man's fleshy neck, searching for a pulse, then she braced both hands on his chest and pushed hard. He grunted, his brow creasing. She did it again, the phone still ringing.

"Come on," she said.

The cat wandered through the door from the kitchen, purring. It sidled up to them, rubbing its head on the man's face, on his arm.

"Not now," said Savage, still pumping the guy's chest.

The cat reached the man's hand, sniffed his finger.

Then it bit him.

"Argh!" the man yelled, sitting up like Dracula in his coffin, almost knocking Savage over. He lashed out at the cat, which skipped deftly away, then he pulled his wounded hand to his chest. "You little prick!"

Savage sat against the wall, nursing her own thrashing heart.

"You okay?" she asked again.

The man turned to her, sweating despite the cold that washed in from the open front door. He licked his lips again.

"If I lie down, will you keep giving me CPR?" he asked.

Savage pulled a face.

"Uh, no," she said.

The man turned his rage to the cat, which was licking its arse by the door.

"You little shit! I was about to get mouth-to-mouth!"

Savage stood up on wobbly legs, picking up her phone as she went and hearing the operator's voice.

"Sorry," she said. "False alarm."

"You're sure?" said the woman on the other end of the line. "Are you in trouble and can't speak?"

"I'm police. DC Kate Savage, Norfolk. I thought somebody was having a heart attack."

She glared at the man who lay at her feet.

"Turns out he was just a pervert."

"Sadly no cure for that," said the operator. "Call us if you need us."

"Pervert?" said the man as Savage hung up. "You're the bloody pervert, coming in my house, spying on me, wrestling me to the floor and... and *touching* me all over my chesty parts. I should report you."

He struggled into a sitting position, panting hard enough to make Savage think he might *actually* have a heart attack. His shirt had ripped open, the flesh beneath the texture of a Cornish pasty that had been left in the sink. She offered him a hand but he shook his head. He looked like a child as he studied the bloody wound on his finger.

On the floor beside him was the weapon he'd attacked her with.

It was a carrot.

Savage pulled out her warrant card, holding it out even though he didn't look up.

"DC Savage," she said. "I'm sorry, the door was open, I thought the place was abandoned."

"Well it wasn't, now, was it?" he said.

She slid the wallet back into her pocket.

"Can we start again?" she asked. "What's your name?"

"Jim," the man said, slapping his hand into his lap and glowering up at her. "Prescott."

"And who's that?" asked Savage, nodding to the cat.

"That's Cunty Fuckface the King of Shit," he said. "He bite you too?"

Savage showed him her hand. It had stopped bleeding but the pain swelled with every beat of her pulse.

"Well, you deserve it," said Jim. "Arsehole comes after me every day if I don't do what he asks. Thought my wife was bad afore she passed, but at least she didn't bite."

The cat walked past Jim, its golden eyes full of insolence. He shied away from it like he was scared, only relaxing when it had vanished into the kitchen. He sighed, staring once again at the teeth marks in his hand. He was literally covered in bites and scratches, Savage saw.

"You can always get rid of it," she said, feeling a little sorry for him.

"He's not even mine," said Jim. "Bloody thing just turned up one day and won't leave."

He sighed again, then stretched a hand towards Savage.

"Help me up, will you? Hips are shot to shit."

"You seemed pretty nimble when you came after me in the kitchen," said Savage, grabbing his hand.

It took four attempts to get him on his feet, and on two of those she almost ended up on top of him again. He looked disappointed when it didn't happen.

"You want your weapon?" she asked, scooping up the carrot.

Jim laughed as he limped into the kitchen.

"Didn't exactly give me time to get my gun," he said. "You're bloody lucky I keep it locked up."

She *was* lucky, she realised. This was the countryside, after all, and most of the farm folk owned shotguns.

She dropped the carrot on the table and proceeded to pick up the other vegetables that had been scattered, throwing them back into the cardboard box.

"You live here by yourself, Jim?"

"Uh-huh," he said, slumping into a chair. "Barb's long gone, kids fucked off, don't even come back for Christmas now. Just me and the cat."

There was no sign of the tom, and Savage was grateful for that. She placed the box carefully on the table and collected the kettle from where it had fallen. That was another thing she was grateful for, that the water had only been halfway to the boil.

"Sorry about that," said Jim. "Scared me, is all."

"It's my fault," she said, putting the kettle on the stove and turning off the hob, which was still burning. "Stupid of me to just come in. I did call out."

"Hairy ears," said Jim, turning his head to demonstrate. He wasn't wrong. It looked like the arse end of a squirrel.

"You want me to make tea?" Savage asked, although she couldn't see the lid of the kettle anywhere. Jim shook his head.

"Need a bloody rum after that," he said. "Under the sink, help yourself."

She opened the door, seeing a collection of glass bottles. None of them had labels. She pulled out the one that looked closest to rum and began the search for a glass.

"Just give it here," said Jim, snapping his dirty fingers.

She passed him the bottle and he swigged deeply, half of it raining onto his shirt. When he finished, he kept hold of it, using his free hand to wipe the liquid from his chapped lips.

"I need to ask you a couple of questions," Savage said. "And don't worry, you're not in trouble."

He nodded, taking another drink.

"You're familiar with the playpark up the road? The one on the hill?"

He nodded again, his eyes glazed.

"Can you tell me anything about it?"

"Park," he barked. "What do you want to know? Slides and shit. For the kids."

"Are there any kids around here?" Savage asked. "I don't see any houses, or schools."

Jim shrugged, sitting back in the chair.

"Have you ever seen anyone playing there?"

"No," he replied. "But I don't go around spying on kids in parks, now, do I?"

"Fair enough," said Savage. She took a breath to steady herself. "Jim, we found a body in the park this morning. A young man. A *boy*, really."

He gave her a side-eye, like he was pretending not to look.

"Body?" he said. "Dead one?"

Savage nodded.

"I didn't do it," said Jim.

"Not accusing you. I just need to know if you saw

anything strange between last night and now. The field across from you leads right up to the park."

"Big field," said Jim. "Can't see nothing from down here."

"But you might have noticed somebody driving along the lane in the night? A car, a van, anything."

"Nope," said Jim, lifting the bottle to his lips again.

"A light in the field? Torches?"

He drank like a parched man.

"Nope," he said again when he'd finished.

"Did you hear anything, Jim? Screams? Laughter? An engine? The sound of somebody playing, maybe?"

He gave her another side-eye, then shook his head.

"Out like a light every night," he said. "Like most men what do proper work. Don't hear nothing."

The cat miaowed from the other room, a clatter of feet as it chased something. Jim winced like he might come under attack.

Savage pulled out her wallet again and laid a business card on the table, using her index finger to push it towards him.

"If you happen to think of anything, please call," she said. "He's a child, Jim. Somebody killed him and left him up there. We need to find whoever did this. You're a father. This person kills children."

"Mine aren't children anymore," he said, turning to the wall, his eyes glazing again. He lifted the bottle, but Savage gently grabbed it, holding it in place.

"Call me if you remember anything," she said, and she kept a tight hold of the bottle until he nodded. When she let go, his arm jerked so hard that a glug of rum spilled over his lap. He muttered something that sounded a lot like a word she didn't like to be called.

"What?" she asked.

"Nothing," he said, putting the bottle to his lips. "But if you don't mind pissing off now, that would be great."

She was more than happy to oblige, retreating. Only the sound of the cat meowing made her turn back. It had emerged from the far door, skittering over the tiles as it chased imaginary mice. There was something in its mouth, fluttering—something that looked so much like a living thing that Savage ducked down, ready to pry it from the creature's murderous jaws.

The cat stopped moving, clutching its catch.

Not a living thing at all, she saw.

It was a ribbon, maybe two-foot long and the colour of blood.

"Oh shit," she said.

CHAPTER FIVE

Porter struggled across the field, rubbing the mostly healed stab wound in his shoulder as he went.

It hurt. Not as much as it had when Aggie Clegg's ceremonial blade had gone in, of course, but still enough to make him miserable. It had penetrated a little over an inch into his deltoid, requiring a dozen stitches and a lot of rest. But it hadn't done lasting damage, and the doctor had labelled him fit for work after six weeks—even though Porter had asked her not to. It hadn't helped that Allie had come to the appointment with him and stated, quite emphatically, that he was 'perfectly healthy and needed to get out of the house before he drove everybody mad.'

Still, it wouldn't have hurt anyone to be a little nicer to him.

He tripped on a ridge of muddy soil, his arms wheeling as he tried to stay up. The burn in his shoulder grew, the sensation like he was literally on fire, and he rubbed it a little more. He shot the ground a murderous look as he went, glaring so intently at it that he tripped again.

"Prick!" he roared.

However bad the field was, though, he'd take it over the woods any day. He'd almost reached the line of trees, which held their arms out to him like kidnappers reaching for a child. They were dancing gently in the breeze, their crowns crimson as the last of the leaves clung on. Between the crooked trunks, the shadows shifted and sighed, and he lifted both middle fingers in defiance.

"You're all pricks too," he said. "Stupid woody bastard arsehole pricks."

He stopped by the closest tree, resting his foot on a root before looking back. The park seemed too far away, just an ugly sketch on the top of the hill. He thought about the boy that sat on the merry-go-round, and pictured his killer setting about him with a machete or an axe or a sword.

Then he thought about Bobby, the way he tried not to when he was working a case, but the way he found himself doing more and more these days: Bobby on the ground pleading for his life, Bobby filled with terror, Bobby slowly bleeding out from a cut to the throat. And a wave of fear and panic and grief almost consumed him.

Somebody had killed that boy.

They'd dismantled him.

"Prick," he said again, and he stepped into the trees.

The air changed almost instantly, the cool breeze giving way to a funk of damp, rotting air. The noises from the park surrendered to a silence that felt unearthly. Porter scanned the gaps between the trees, seeing nothing but green. He opened his mouth to call out and before he could make a sound a dozen birds exploded from the branches overhead, scattering into the sky. The words lodged in his throat, his heart palpitating.

He coughed, tried again.

"Hello? Is anyone here? It's the police."

Yeah, just one police, he found himself thinking, and he wondered if he should go back and grab a constable. For all he knew the same person who'd sliced up the kid was right here, waiting with bated breath behind a tree, a blade clenched in their hand.

His shoulder throbbed in sympathy, the fear of being stabbed again making him hesitate.

Only for a moment, though, before he moved forward, holding onto the low branches to stop himself tripping. As much as he hated it, it was worth the effort. Killers loitering around the scene of the crime wasn't just something you saw on the TV. It was true. Still, he wished they'd have a little more consideration than to hang out in the frozen woods—

A dry crack from up ahead interrupted his thoughts and he stopped again, cocking his head. He could hear the warble of a pigeon somewhere to his right, but he couldn't see anything. He glanced back, planning an escape route if he had to leg it, but he couldn't even see the field anymore.

"Prick," he said quietly, directing the word at the trees. Their leaves rustled like laughter. "And you're a prick, and you, you too. All pricks."

He set off in the direction of the pigeon, only because he didn't have any better ideas. There was less undergrowth here so his progress was faster, and it wasn't long before he caught a whiff of something over the tang of rotting leaves.

Smoke.

He turned slowly, sniffing, trying to work out where it was coming from. It wasn't just smoke, there was the meaty scent of something cooking, and his stomach growled in response. He pushed through the trees like a hungry bear, following the scent past a wall of thick bushes and seeing a clearing ahead.

Two men had gathered around a small fire, their backs to him. One was tending to the flames, poking them with a stick. The other sat on a camping chair tapping his foot restlessly. Both were wearing green duffel coats, their hair a tangled mess, their trainers caked in mud. To the right, past the fire, was a small tent and a rack of clothes laid out to dry.

Propped up next to the flap of the tent was a long, curved knife.

Shit, thought Porter.

He looked back again, no idea which way he'd come. He pulled out his phone, writing a text to Kett—*men in the woods, two, with knife*—and pressing send before he realised he had no signal here.

Shit, he thought again, considering his options.

The men hadn't noticed him. If he retreated now and headed back to the park, he'd be able to return with some backup. The danger with that was that the men might bolt. He could sneak around and grab the knife, but there was no way he'd be able to get close enough without being spotted—and what if they had more weapons?

Or he could move in with force, a lot of blood and thunder, scare them into submission. He had a set of cuffs in his pocket. If he could subdue one, the other might give up. Or run.

That was a big if, though. He wasn't in the best shape of his life after months of rest, and the thought of being stabbed again—

"You gonna stand there all day, pal, or do you want to join us?"

It was the man by the fire who had spoken. He dropped his stick into the flames and turned around, looking right at Porter. He was probably in his late-twenties, his face almost hidden by his dark, tangled hair and a wild beard. His Scottish accent was plugged by a thick cold, and he wiped a hand over the tip of his nose.

The other man turned as well, revealing the unmistakeable features of somebody with Down's Syndrome. He was younger, his cheeks covered with little more than fluff. There was no sign of fear on his face, and when he saw Porter in the trees he smiled—just about the biggest, most welcoming smile he'd ever seen in his life. He lifted a hand and waved.

"Stand there all day, then, is it?" said the first man, whose expression was wary. "You'll no' find much worth staring at."

The man glanced at the tent, and at the knife, as if remembering it was there.

Porter stepped from the trees, his hands up.

"Sorry," he said. "I'm police."

The smile on the younger guy's face fell away, and he tucked something into his jacket—too quickly for Porter to see what it was. The men looked at each other, and Porter could read the panic there as easily as if they'd shouted it.

"I'm not here for you," he said, advancing a little further. He pulled out his warrant card and opened it. "I didn't even know you guys were in here. My name's DI Porter. Call me Pete. I'm here because of something that happened in the park over there."

He put his warrant card away and pointed a finger into the trees, although he had no idea if he was pointing in the right direction.

"You know it?"

"The park?" said the first man.

The second guy said something too, a misshapen word Porter couldn't make sense of. A smile appeared through the first man's beard, although his eyes were still guarded.

"No, Freddy, we're not going now," he said.

"You play there sometimes, Freddy?" Porter asked.

The younger guy smiled again, nodding so enthusiastically he almost fell off his chair.

"Park," he said.

"It might be out of bounds for a while, sorry," said Porter, moving a little closer to the fire if only to warm up. The smell of the sizzling rabbit was incredible. "Lunch?"

The first man nodded, watching Porter like he was waiting for something.

"I couldn't care less," he said, understanding. "I have zero problem at all with you guys being here, okay? You live here?"

"Passing through," said the man. He'd relaxed a little, but not much.

"You know who owns the land?" Porter asked.

He shook his head.

"Well, we've had no complaints, no calls. Far as I'm concerned, you can stay as long as you like."

Freddy lifted both hands in the air, then slapped them onto his legs, still grinning.

"Can I ask your name?" he asked the first man.

"You can ask," he replied. He took a breath, wiping his dripping nose again before heaving a sigh of resignation. "Ben."

"You got any ID?"

"Why?" he said. "Not done anything."

"I just need to see it," said Porter. "We found a..."

He glanced at Freddy, who was still smiling at him.

"Can we chat somewhere quiet?" he said. "It's not pleasant."

"He's a grown man," said Ben. "You can say it here."

"We found a body this morning," he said. "In the park. A teenage boy."

Ben frowned.

"We think he died last night sometime," said Porter. "He was killed."

Freddy put his hands to his ears, rocking in his seat. Ben glanced at him, then walked over to Porter. He smelled like somebody who hadn't washed in a long while, and Porter saw the grime beneath the collar of his jacket, his black fingernails.

Ben opened his mouth to speak, and Porter knew what was coming.

"I'm not accusing you of anything," he said before the man could start. "I was in the woods looking for any sign that somebody had been here, that's all."

Ben chewed on it for a second or two, then nodded.

"Because I wouldnae kill anyone," he said. "And if I did, I wouldnae be daft enough to pitch my tent next to where I'd done it."

"Exactly," said Porter. "Were you here last night?"

Ben hesitated before nodding.

"All night?"

"Been here a few nights," he said. "Caught a brace on Thursday and it's seen us through."

"Did you see anything last night?" Porter asked. "Anything at all. Lights, cars, people."

Ben looked at the ground, scuffing the dirt with the toe of his trainer. There was a hole in it, Porter saw.

"Didnae see nothing," he said. "Cannae even hear the road from back here. Peaceful, like."

Porter sensed there was more coming, but the man didn't offer it.

"You two related?" he asked, looking at Freddy. The

younger man still had his hands to his ears, his body hunched over.

"Aye."

"Brothers?"

Ben nodded.

"How old is he?"

"Twenty-two," he said, turning to Freddy.

The young man dropped his hands into his lap with another loud slap. He smiled again, and Porter found himself smiling back before he even knew it.

"You don't have to tell me," said Porter, keeping his voice low, "but what are you doing out here? Weather's turning, it's cold. You got anywhere else to go?"

"Plenty of places to go," said Ben.

"I mean places with a roof," said Porter. "Running water, heat, a toilet, some decent food."

"You no' smelling that?" Ben said.

It was a valid point. The scent of the roasting rabbit was divine.

"You know what I mean," said Porter. "It's no life for you, and it's definitely no life for him."

"Fuck are you to say that?" said Ben. There was anger in his expression but his voice was a whisper. "We're fine."

"I'm just saying, we can help," said Porter. "We can find you a place."

Ben sniffed, his nose leaking, his beard caked in snot. He closed his eyes for a moment and the exhaustion almost took him, his body teetering before he found his balance.

"We dinnae need anyone else," he said. "Do we, Freddy? Me and you."

Freddy said something, stretching out his arms and jabbing both thumbs into the air.

"That's right," said Ben. "You see that? He's fine."

"Still going to need to see that ID," said Porter.

Ben looked like he was going to argue again.

"One look and I'm gone," said Porter.

"Fuck's sake."

Ben walked to the tent, dropping onto his hands and knees while he rummaged inside. Porter took a second to pull out his phone, zooming in on the curved, serrated knife and snapping a quick photo. Freddy watched him, rocking gently back and forth on his chair.

"Smells great," said Porter, nodding to the fire. "You hungry?"

Freddy rubbed his stomach.

"Good lad," said Porter.

"Here," said Ben, returning. He held out a driving licence and Porter took it. "Out of date, but it's me."

Porter had trouble believing it. The man in the photo—Benjamin Rawling—was years younger, no beard, his hair neatly trimmed. His mouth was the same straight line you found in every official photograph, but there was a light dancing in his eyes, the defiant energy of youth. He looked like a man with everything ahead of him.

"That's you?" asked Porter.

Ben's face seemed to crack—just for an instant, then he pulled everything back into place. The expiry date on the licence was earlier this year, and the address was somewhere in Kirkcaldy. His date of birth put him at twenty-seven.

"You need to get this replaced, mate, if you're driving."

Ben took the licence back from Porter, his hand shaking. He shoved it into his pocket like he wanted nothing more to do with it.

"My advice is move on," said Porter. "We have no idea

who killed the boy, and whether they might come back. Find another place to stay tonight, yeah?"

He pulled a business card from his wallet and held it out.

"I mean it. We're here to help."

"And I meant it too, we're fine," said Ben. He sneezed violently into his hand, closing his eyes for a moment and rocking on his heels. When he opened them, the card was still there.

"Please," he said. "Just leave us alone."

Porter nodded, his hand withdrawing. He walked to Freddy, who looked up at him with wide eyes. He was still holding something inside his jacket, cradling it protectively. Porter offered him the card and he took it.

"Got something else for you, too," he said, reaching into his pocket again and pulling out a silver Parker ballpoint. He passed it to Freddy. "That's my lucky pen. You look after it, okay?"

Freddy held it tight, studying it intently.

"And you look after your brother," he said. "He looks like he needs it."

Ben stood by the fire, his shoulders slumped. Porter nodded to him as he turned to leave. He'd made it into the trees before he heard Ben call out.

"Hey."

He looked back.

"Look, we don't get involved," said Ben. "We just don't. Better that way for everyone. But... You found a kid there?"

"Yeah. A boy. Fifteen, maybe."

Ben sighed.

"Never saw anyone in that park who wasn't dealing," he said. "Been there the last couple of nights, four or five of 'em. Hoods. Bags. Cars stop, but only for a few seconds."

"Did you see a boy about fifteen, sandy hair, black tracksuit?" Porter asked.

"Wasnae close enough," said Ben. "And they all look the same, don't they?"

"You happen to get a look at any of the cars?"

Ben glanced at his brother, but just for a second.

"No."

Porter met Ben's eyes again, saw the exhaustion there, the pain. He thought about offering once more to help, but he knew it wouldn't do any good.

"Stay safe," he said.

Then he set off into the trees.

CHAPTER SIX

THE IRV CAREENED AROUND THE BEND SO FAST THAT IT almost couldn't stop in time. The constable slammed his foot on the brake, bringing them to a halt just inches from the rear end of Savage's car.

On the side of the road was a lopsided wooden barn, and past that was a path that led through a parade of overgrown bushes.

"Move," said Kett, climbing out.

Savage had called him a few minutes ago, claiming that she'd found a red ribbon inside a farmhouse after a man had attacked her. There was no sign of the house here, so Kett jogged down the path, slapping wet fronds of vegetation out of his way. The two constables from the car followed close behind, one of them armed with a Taser, the other as compact and ferocious as a pit bull.

"Kate?" Kett called out. "Where are you?"

He emerged from the path to find a small courtyard ahead, and past that a farmhouse that had seen better days. Several of the windows were cracked, the paint peeling off the walls. The door was open, nothing but darkness inside.

"Kate?" Kett said as he stepped up to the door. "You in there?"

The house reeked of old age, its bones crumbling, its foundations riddled with damp. The hallway led to a closed door, and Kett thought he heard a clatter from behind it, a strangled cry.

"Go!" he said, moving out of the way to let the constables through.

The smaller constable reached the door in an instant, shouldering through in an explosion of dust and splinters. The second followed, his Taser out.

"Police armed with—" was as far as he got before something shot out of the room, a streak of orange fuzz that vanished through the open door on the left.

"Grab it!" yelled Savage, pushing past the constables. "Where did it go?"

"Where did what go?" asked Kett.

"The cat!"

Kett pointed to the living room and Savage flew into it, the constables giving chase. By the time Kett had caught up, all hell had broken loose inside. Savage was kneeling on a sofa trying to look down the back of it while a PC did his best to haul it away from the wall. The second constable was still holding the Taser.

"What..." said Kett, then he heard a noise from the room that Savage had run out of, following it into the kitchen.

A man was sitting at the table necking something from a clear bottle.

"Who are you?" said Kett.

The man swallowed a deep swig.

"Who are *you*?" he asked.

"Sir!" yelled Savage from the living room. "Close the front—"

Kett looked back in time to see the cat leg it out of the house, skittering across the courtyard.

"Door," finished Savage, panting for breath as she appeared. "Where did it go?"

Kett pointed outside and Savage groaned.

"Kate, what is going on?"

"Ribbon, sir," she said, moving down the corridor. "Red ribbon, in the cat's mouth. Same kind we saw on the body."

"And him?" said Kett, nodding to the man.

"Just don't let him out of your sight."

Savage bolted through the front door, the two constables in hot pursuit—one *still* gripping his Taser. Kett shook his head, bewildered, before returning his attention to the man in the kitchen. He was about to take another drink from the bottle, but Kett grabbed it, depositing it onto the counter.

"Oi!" said the guy, pushing his chair back like he was going to stand up. He was a solid bloke, carrying a lot of weight, but it was a look from Kett that sent him crashing back down.

"You're the one who attacked my officer?" he asked, looming over him.

"She was in my house," he replied, his voice slurred. "I didn't know she was no officer."

"What's your name?" said Kett.

"Jim," he said. "But you lot can call me Mr Prescott."

Kett did a quick circuit of the kitchen, opening a couple of cupboards to find nothing but broken crockery and grime. Food crunched on the floor beneath his boots, tiny bones amongst the crumbs. The entire place was festering, and when he studied the man he saw that he was too, his skin the colour and texture of uncooked dough.

Jim held his eye for a moment then let his head fall.

"Can you tell me where you were last night?" Kett said.

"Why?" he replied, asking the question to the table. "I was here, obviously. Where else am I gonna go? Buckin'am Palace?"

"You weren't up the hill at the park?" asked Kett.

"No. I wasn't, and I didn't have anything to do with that boy you found up there."

Kett waited.

"An' afore you say shit, your woman police officer told me about him," Jim went on. "Already asked me a load of questions. I got nothing else to tell you unless I got a lawyer with me."

Kett heard footsteps, and a few seconds later Savage walked into the room holding an evidence bag. The other two coppers were nowhere to be seen, but a thump from upstairs let him know they were searching the house.

Savage slapped the bag on the table, and sure enough there was a length of red ribbon inside it, maybe a foot long. It was mottled with a darker shade of crimson, although in the weak light of the kitchen Kett couldn't be sure if it was blood.

"Managed to get it out of the cat's mouth, sir," she said, holding her arm up to reveal a nasty cut. There was another one on her finger. "He resisted arrest."

"That's Cunty Fuckface for you," said Jim. He was looking at the ribbon. "Nothing to do with me."

"You've never seen this before?" asked Kett.

"Like I said."

Jim glanced across the room to the open door opposite, so quickly that Kett almost didn't notice it.

"What's in there, Jim?"

"None of your fucking business."

Kett walked away from the table, listening to Savage continue the interrogation.

"The body we found up the hill was wrapped in red ribbon," she said. "Just like this."

"I never saw it before," Jim protested. "Oi, stay away from there."

Kett reached the door, using his knuckles to open it all the way. On the other side was a small larder lined with almost empty shelves. Past them was another open door, this one leading into the back garden.

"Because I don't think it's a coincidence, Jim," Savage went on. "I think you've got this ribbon for a reason."

Kett probed the handful of boxes he found on the shelves, spiders and woodlice scuttling to safety. The second one he tried contained what looked like a sewing kit, safety pins nestled in with the needles and thread. He searched the others to no avail before stepping outside. The drizzle was still falling, the overgrown garden like a jungle.

"I said don't go out there," barked Jim, appearing behind Kett. He was short, and there was no mistaking the violence in his posture, the way his meaty fists were clenched. He reeked of rum. "I ain't got nothing to do with that kid in the park and you know it. Harassment, this is."

"That your sewing kit on the shelf there?" Kett asked him.

Jim looked genuinely bewildered.

"What?"

"The ribbon on the body was fastened with safety pins," said Kett. "Like those ones."

"Fuck you," said Jim, advancing until the bulge of his belly almost touched Kett. "Get out of my house."

"Sir?"

The bigger of the two constables stepped into the kitchen, squinting against the light of the day.

"Got two shotguns upstairs, plenty of shells."

"What the fuck?" roared Jim, wheeling around. "Who said you could go up there?"

"And some interesting reading material," the constable went on. "Didn't want to touch it, sorry."

"You piece of—"

Jim hurled himself at the constable, managing to trip on the doorstep as he ran over it. He fell in a heap in the little larder, hard enough to knock two of the boxes from their shelves. He struggled to get up again but the constable kneeled beside him, planting a hand between his shoulder blades.

"Put some cuffs on him," said Kett.

He waited for the constable to do as he'd asked before stepping over Jim's thrashing body and entering the kitchen again. It seemed even darker in here than it had before, the shadows bleeding from the corners, filling the claustrophobic space.

Savage was waiting for him at the bottom of the stairs, and she led the way up to a short, narrow landing. The bulb was on, but it was so caked in cobwebs and dirt that the gloom followed them up. The ceiling was so low that Kett had to bend his neck to stop himself from being scalped.

The second constable had holstered his Taser, and stood to attention beside the door.

"In here, sir," he said, shuffling out of the way.

Kett could still hear Jim howling his rage downstairs, and when he ducked beneath the lintel and saw what waited there for him, he understood why the man was so upset.

In the middle of the dark room was a double bed, and lying there, secured to each of the four posts with a length of rope, was a...

"What the hell is that?" Kett asked, clicking on his torch.

"I'm honestly not sure, sir," said Savage who had squeezed in next to him. "A body?"

It *looked* like a body, dressed in a grey tracksuit and white trainers. But the clothes weren't wrapped around skin and bone, they were stuffed with what looked like sheets and blankets, a pair of gardening gloves attached to both sleeves. The head was a round yellow cushion that was wearing some kind of wig, and fastened to the front of it was a photograph of a young man's face.

"Right," said Kett, puffing out a breath.

"The photo's from one of those," said the constable, pointing to the floor beneath the bed.

"Do I want to see it?" Kett asked.

He lowered himself painfully onto all fours and peeked beneath the rumpled bedspread. A carpet of magazines had been left there, most of them so weathered by age and use that Kett could barely make out the titles.

The images on the covers, however, left no doubt at all what they were.

"Wow," said Kett, pushing himself back up. His back twinged, almost a full spasm.

"You okay, sir?" Savage asked.

He nodded.

"But I might need somebody else to pull those magazines out," he said.

Savage ducked down, but he hoiked her up again.

"Not you, Kate," he said. "And whoever does it will need a hazard suit and about fifteen pairs of gloves. There are a lot of tissues under there."

"Ew," said Savage, scrubbing her hands on her trousers even though she hadn't touched anything. "Porn, sir?"

"Yeah, a lot of it. Looks like it's mostly, but not exclusively, young men."

He nodded to the lump of fabric on the bed. The printed face grinned back.

"Does this look like a guy to you?"

"I mean, no, not really," said Savage. "But maybe it does to him. A lot of coincidences, right? About the ribbon, the safety pins, and then this."

Kett nodded.

"Too many to ignore," he said. "Nothing illegal here, though, far as I can see. And you've got to be an idiot to leave all this for us to find if you've just murdered somebody."

"I can tell you already that Jim Prescott is an idiot, sir," said Savage. "He tried to stab me with a carrot."

Kett breathed out a laugh, too quiet for anyone else to hear. He pictured the young man they'd found in the park, wrapped in ribbon and slung over the merry-go-round like some kind of trophy. It wasn't a million miles away from this, was it? From this effigy of a boy tied to the bed.

"Yeah," he said. "Too many coincidences. Bring him in, but just for a chat."

He walked to the curtains and tugged them along the rail. Daylight showed absolutely no interest in entering the room, loitering like a frightened teenager in the clouds of dust that had been shaken from the curtains. Kett used a fist to smear a circle in the greasy glass, seeing the back garden laid out before him. It looked less like a jungle from up here, a square lawn surrounded by a fringe of bushes, and past them a row of neat flowerbeds. Only one of them had been recently weeded, a small patch of soil turned over between two tangled rose plants.

Kett frowned.

"Kate," he said. "Get over here."

He waited for her to join him, listening to the continuing tirade of fury from the room below. He tapped on the glass.

"What does that look like to you?" he asked.

"The flowerbed, sir?"

He nodded, and she blew out a long sigh that steamed up the window, hiding the garden from view. It didn't matter, though, she'd seen the same thing he had.

"Looks like a grave," she said.

CHAPTER SEVEN

Up close, beneath the oppressive sky and in the cruel chill of the day—serenaded by yet more crows that danced manically in the trees at the end of the garden—it looked more like a burial plot than ever.

The flowerbed was rectangular, maybe five foot long and half that wide. Two rose bushes grew at opposite ends, only a single white flower remaining, its velvet petals browning. The bed was conspicuous only because nothing else in the garden was tended, everywhere covered in an armour of thorns and creepers. Whoever worked this land, whoever tilled and levelled the soil, who trimmed the bushes away from the edges, only seemed to care for this coffin-sized rectangle of dirt.

"Weird, sir," said Savage as she shivered by Kett's side.

"Weird how?"

"Weird that Jim was carrying a box of vegetables into the house when I first met him. Carrots, onions, and a bunch of potatoes. I assumed he'd just dug them up from somewhere, but I don't see a vegetable patch."

"And there's nothing planted here," said Kett. "Nothing living, anyway. Can you see a spade anywhere?"

"I'll check," said Savage, heading off towards a weary-looking shed in the corner of the plot.

Kett made his way back to the house, kicking the mud from his boots before ducking beneath the low door. Jim Prescott had been moved to an IRV—in cuffs, because he'd made it clear he wasn't going without a fight. Kett could still hear him howling his fury from the distant lane.

Two uniformed coppers wearing latex gloves were rifling through the kitchen drawers and Kett nodded to them as he passed by. Another was stomping miserably down the stairs, pulling off a pair of gloves.

"Sir," she said when she spotted him. "We've investigated the bedroom."

The shudder that passed through her was visible even in the gloom.

"The magazines under the bed are all pretty standard, and all legal. He's got, er, broad tastes. Found a couple of scrapbooks there with what look like favourites."

"Favourites?"

"You know, favourite faces, and other... parts."

"Oh, right," said Kett. "And the sex... object?"

"The bed thing?" she asked. Kett nodded. "It's just clothes and bags and pictures cut from the magazines. Plus some..."

She hesitated, making strange sounds in her throat. Kett wondered if he should put his fingers in his ears before she finished, but he was too slow.

"Some raw chicken, sir."

"What?"

"I think that's what it is. I'm not going any closer. Raw chicken breasts. They look fresh."

"In the..." Kett said, gesturing downwards with his hands.

"Yeah, in the..." said the constable, imitating him.

"Right."

"But there's nothing illegal. Guns are registered, no blood, no sign that anyone has come to harm here."

"Apart from the chicken," said Kett.

"Yeah," she said, shuddering again.

His phone started ringing as he walked out of the front door—Porter's name on the screen—but he didn't answer it because the DI was halfway across the courtyard.

"Oh," said Porter. "There you are, sir."

"Here I am," said Kett as they both slid their phones back into their pockets.

"Franklin's up at the park," said the DI, wiping a film of rain from his face. "Said she couldn't wait any longer. She wants you there, if you're not busy."

"Not busy at all," said Kett, rolling his eyes. "How'd you get on?"

"Yeah, quite a lot of discomfort, actually," said Porter, rubbing his shoulder. "Tough going in the woods, think I might have opened the wound again."

"I mean did you find anything?" said Kett.

"Oh, right. I did, actually. Two guys are camping out there. Brothers, in their twenties. Tent, campfire, they're living off a brace of rabbits."

"Yeah? What's their story?"

"I honestly don't know," said Porter. "They wouldn't say. I got the feeling they were running from something, or hiding. Younger one's got Down's, sweet guy. Older one's looking out for him but..."

Kett waited while Porter searched his thoughts.

"Got the feeling they're at breaking point, sir. Offered to help but..."

He shrugged his big shoulders, then winced, putting a hand to the wound.

"You get their names?" asked Kett.

"Yeah."

"You like them for the murder?"

Porter shook his head.

"Wasn't sure when I first got there, but I'm not getting those kind of vibes at all. Good news is they said they saw people at the park a few times in the three days they've been here, kids selling drugs. Lot of traffic. People pull in, do their thing, then leave."

He paused for a moment to listen to another caterwauling from the road.

"Who's the fat fella in the car?" he asked.

"Jim Prescott," said Kett. "Lives here. Tried to stab Kate when she turned up at the door."

"Seriously? She okay?"

"He stabbed her with a carrot," said Kett. "I can't figure him out, but he's got some kind of..."

He didn't know how to explain it.

"You have to see it for yourself, Pete. But it's clear he's into young men."

"Sexually?" said Porter.

"No, Pete, artistically," said Kett. "Yeah, of course, sexually. He's got a little... perv shrine thing going on, in the bedroom. And Savage found some red ribbon in the mouth of his cat."

"What?" said Porter. "An actual cat?"

Kett stared at him.

"Yes, an actual cat. What did you think I meant?"

"Just sounded weird, sir."

"The whole bloody thing is weird," said Kett. "Oh, and there might be a grave in the back garden."

"You've collared him?"

"No, not yet," said Kett. "Doesn't make a lot of sense that he'd shit in his own backyard like this. But I'm not ruling him out. He's clearly..."

He paused, and for a few seconds they listened to Prescott's shouts from the road.

"Clearly, sir," said Porter. "Stopped at the other houses I saw on the way over, just three of them. Only spoke to one person but she corroborated the fact the park's mainly used by dealers. They've called us a hundred times, apparently, but nobody's managed to stop it."

"They say why there's even a park there, in the middle of nowhere?"

"Nope," said Porter. "Nobody knows."

"Weird," Kett said again. "Okay, I'll head over to the body. Can you give Kate a hand in the back?"

"Sure, sir, what's she doing?"

"Gardening."

Kett gave Porter a gentle slap on the shoulder, completely forgetting about the wound there. Porter groaned like he'd been stabbed all over again.

"Shit, sorry, Pete," he said.

He walked off, heading around the dishevelled barn where more coppers were conducting a search, before arriving back at the road. Two more police cars had joined the queue, blocking the lane, and it wasn't hard to spot the one with Jim Prescott in the back. The entire car was moving with the force of his fury, and his shouts had steamed up the window. Two constables stood outside the open driver's door, chatting quietly.

"What's the hold up?" Kett asked.

"He's spitting," said the woman. "Waiting on a van."

"Fuck's sake," grumbled Kett.

He reached the car and ripped the back door open so hard that the man inside froze like a frightened deer. His hands were cuffed behind his back, his cheeks so mottled that he looked like he was wearing makeup. He'd managed to coat himself in his own spit, a strand hanging off his chin and swinging like a pendulum.

"Pack it in," said Kett.

Jim started to reply, but Kett loomed in.

"Right now, you're not under arrest. But that can change in an instant, you hear me? We've found your..."

Again, he struggled for a way to describe it.

"Creepy sex mannequin, and—"

"That's not mine!" roared Prescott. "You planted it there!"

"Yes, that's right," said Kett. "I always carry a... a home-made, chicken stuffed hump pillow with me just in case I want to frame somebody for... for whatever you do with one."

"I don't do nothing with it!"

"I don't care," said Kett, pressing in even further and forcing the big man to lean back. "There's nothing illegal about it. You're entitled to do whatever the hell you want in your own house, as long as nobody is getting hurt. And that's what I want to know, Jim, whether you've hurt somebody."

The anger seemed to drain out of the man, leaving him with a profound tremor.

"I haven't," he said. "I wouldn't. I don't want to hurt nobody, I'm just... it just gets. I..."

His sagging face was like a mask slipping free.

"You don't understand how lonely it gets out here," he said. "Lonely without Barb, but..."

His tongue was a slab of meat that rolled over his lips. His wet eyes blinked in the shadows of the car. Kett felt his throat tighten at the sheer misery of the man, a lifetime of pain that seemed to have been etched into every pitted hole in his face.

"But so lonely with her, too. You don't get it. You'll never get it, but I didn't hurt that boy. Never hurt nobody."

"So who's buried in the garden?" asked Kett.

Jim could only hold his eye for a moment.

"Nobody," he said, just a whisper.

"We're about to dig it up, so now's your chance."

The man shook his head, licking his lips again. Kett leaned back a little, just to get away from the ripening smell.

"Did you know they were dealing drugs up in the park?" he asked.

Jim stared at the seat in front, his shoulders rising and falling in a shrug.

"You ever see them up there?"

The man must have used the last of his energy during his tantrum, because he slumped even further into himself, defeated.

"You going to shout anymore?" Kett asked him.

Jim shook his head.

"Spit?"

He shook his head again.

"Because if you give them any more trouble, I'm going to tell them to put you in the boot. Understand?"

Jim nodded, a man defeated. Kett blew out a long breath, another wave of pity rolling over him, strong enough to make the goosebumps rise on his arms.

"And I meant it," he said. "You're not in trouble for the..."

He waved a hand in the air.

"Sexy meat thing. If that's all this is, you'll be home before the end of the day."

He stood straight, closed the door, and nodded to the constables.

"He's all yours."

CHAPTER EIGHT

It was only after he'd watched the IRV do a fifteen-point turn in the narrow lane and rumble out of sight that Kett realised he should have asked the constables for a lift back to the park. He decided to walk, pulling the collar of his jacket up against the cool wind and the relentless drizzle and slogging his way to the main road.

It took him longer than he'd expected to make his way up the hill, and almost twenty minutes had passed before he spotted the car park ahead. Emily Franklin's bright blue TVR straddled the three spaces next to Hay's forensic van, along with two more IRVs on site. White-suited technicians and uniformed constables were dotted over the scene like chess pieces, although nobody looked like they were winning.

Somebody had erected a series of screens around the front of the park, blocking it from the road. They whipped and snapped in the increasingly agitated breeze, loud enough that Kett couldn't make any sense of the voices he heard until he'd stepped past it. There, he saw the young pathologist standing shoulder to shoulder with Cara Hay, both studying the corpse of the young man on the merry-go-round. A forensic tent had been set up beside them, the flaps open to reveal a workbench.

They looked up together, their faces gaunt.

"Hi, Emily," said Kett. "I thought we were bringing him to you."

"You know me, Robbie," said Franklin, brushing her disobedient hair out of her face. She was wearing her usual outfit of brightly coloured dungarees—these ones bejewelled with gems that caught the meagre light and winked—and a ridiculously oversized puffer jacket. "I'm an impatient girl. And I was out this way anyway visiting an old friend."

"A four-legged friend," said Hay.

"A donkey," said Franklin. "I grew up not too far from Dereham and we had a donkey a few fields away. I called him Sheepy."

"Sheepy?" said Kett.

"I was too young to know the difference. He was lonely, I was lonely, we struck up a... friendship."

"Right, uh..."

Kett shrugged, no idea what to say.

"I still see him from time to time," said Franklin. "We have a cuddle, exchange war stories. You know how it is."

"I'm not sure I do," said Kett. "Anyway..."

He gestured theatrically to the body.

"Yes," said Franklin. "I did notice him. Poor lad. I was about to start a cursory examination, we were just waiting for the screens to go up. Not that anyone has driven past. Has anyone asked why there's a children's playground in the middle of nowhere?"

"Yeah," said Kett. "Although nobody's been able to answer it yet."

Franklin nodded as she approached the body. She

ducked down, opening her bag of equipment. Kett watched as she took the young man's temperature.

"Can you help me get him in?" she asked, gesturing to the tent.

It was the last thing he wanted to do, but Kett moved forward and took hold of one of the boy's arms, hooking his other hand beneath the angle of his knee. Cara took the other, and together they hefted the body from the merry-go-round. Kett marvelled at how light he felt, as if the body had already dried to a husk. The boy kept his shape as they carried him, his arms like folded wings, his legs bent, looking like a child playing in his parent's arms. In the twenty seconds or so it took them to lay him on the bench, Kett's heart seemed to break a thousand times.

"Safe to say rigor mortis is well and truly underway," said Franklin. "That and the body temp leads me to think we're around twelve hours into death."

Kett checked his watch to see that it was after midday.

"Midnight," Franklin confirmed. "Give or take. And the place of death wasn't here, was it, Cara?"

"Definitely not," said Hay as she closed the flap of the tent. There was barely enough room in here to move, and Kett felt the familiar strangling panic of claustrophobia as he shuffled around to make space for her. "There are tracks where the body has been dragged over the ground, and of course the presence of more blood on the slide and the swing. He was brought here after he died."

"It isn't hard to work out what killed him," said Franklin, examining the wounds on the boy's head, his missing ear, the cavity where his eye had once sat. She traced a gloved finger along the cut to his cheek, then down his neck. "Multiple strikes," she said. "All done with force. This isn't a case of somebody working up to a killing blow, the tentative attack of a person who is uncertain of their actions. Each of these dealt enough damage to kill, and indeed he may have died after the first."

"Small mercy," said Kett.

"Of course, he may not have," Franklin added. "He might have felt every single one."

"The ear was severed during the attack?" asked Kett.

"Or before, or after, yes," she said. "It's recent."

"It was stuffed in his pocket."

"The ear?" said Franklin, her eyes shining.

Kett nodded.

"What about the eye?" he asked.

"Did you find that in his pocket, too?"

"No."

"Then I think you have the crows to thank for that," she said. "I can see beak marks on the other one too. Greedy little horrors. Can somebody help me with his coat?"

It was a struggle to get it off, like undressing a mannequin. Beneath the substantial Canada Goose jacket was a plain T-shirt that had once been white. The boy's torso had been sliced up with as much force as his head. His left forearm had almost been severed at the wrist. Kett put a trembling hand to his face, swallowing down a throat that felt sandpaper dry.

"Christ," he said.

"Seven, eight, nine," Franklin said, counting the injuries. "Ten, eleven, twelve. Thirteen here, and more on the back."

"But *why*?" said Cara, shaking her head. "The killer must have continued to attack him long after he was dead. Why would anyone do that to a child?"

Franklin found a scalpel and delicately severed the boy's T-shirt, peeling the bloodied fabric away from the mess of his chest. Kett saw the ivory nub of a rib before he turned away, forcing himself to stare at the canvas wall of the tent until his eyes stopped burning. The smell of rent flesh was unbearable in the small space.

"He wasn't just killed," said Franklin, leaning in for a closer look. "He was obliterated. They wanted to... I don't know, *destroy* him, I guess. But it's interesting, look at the angle of the wounds."

Kett didn't want to, but he did. The deep gashes criss-crossed the body, bisecting each other, overlapping in a tapestry of violence. Franklin lifted her hand as if she was holding a weapon, then brought it down. She did it again, twisting her arm unnaturally. She moved around the body for a third strike, bustling into Kett. He stepped to the side, colliding with Hay. It felt like the tent was shrinking around them.

"What are you getting at, Emily?" he said, a little snappier than he meant to.

"Most of these wounds are cut into the flesh from an upright position," she said. "The blade—I'm thinking machete or sword, they're too narrow for an axe—slices into the body and moves downwards. That's the case for the majority of these injuries."

She turned, swiping the blade of her hand down and slapping Kett's arm hard enough to make it sting.

"Ow," he said. "So the kid was standing up when he was attacked, is that what you're saying?"

"That's exactly what I'm saying," said Franklin. "But that's strange, right?"

"Not really," said Kett. "People don't tend to lie down when they're being murdered."

"No, but imagine this was a machete."

She sliced her hand down onto his arm again, harder this time.

"Ow!" Kett protested, stepping back and knocking into Hay again. Franklin came at him a third time, her eyes wide with deranged aggression. "Don't—"

She slapped him on the shoulder this time, like a karate chop, and he toppled backwards. Only Hay's hands under his arms stopped him from falling on his arse.

"Fuck's sake, Emily, stop hitting me!"

"But you get my point?" she said, backing off. "I'm a delicate young lady tapping you gently with my fragile lady hands."

"Wasn't that bloody gently," said Kett, his shoulder smarting.

"And you still ended up on the floor," she finished.

"I wasn't on the floor," he said.

"But somehow this boy managed to withstand upwards of fifteen strikes to his head, limbs and trunk without falling over?" Franklin said. "How?"

"He was tied up?" Hay offered.

"Maybe," said Franklin. "But I don't see any bruising suggestive of being restrained—except one, which I will come to in a sec. No, I think this is something else. Multiple injuries, all sustained at the same time, or certainly within seconds of each other."

"There was more than one killer," said Kett.

Franklin beamed at him.

"Bingo," she said. "Two, at least, maybe more, and possibly each with more than one weapon, each one unleashing a sequence of attacks simultaneously."

She lashed both arms repeatedly through the air, thankfully not aiming at Kett this time. In three or so seconds she'd managed twice as many powerful strikes.

"It's the only thing that can explain the angle of the cuts," she said. "He must have been hit a dozen times before he even thought to fall to the ground. It was a frenzy. I've never seen anything like it."

She drew a deep, shuddering breath, then pointed a finger at the kid's severed throat.

"This is different. This isn't a slash, it's a cut. Slower, more considered. I think it was done last, when the boy was almost certainly already dead."

"A guarantee," said Kett. Franklin nodded.

"They wanted to make sure."

They stood there for a moment, as silent as the dead. Kett wished Franklin would close the boy's remaining eye, but she didn't. He stared up in horror like he could still see his killer above him.

"What were you saying about restraints?" Kett asked, breaking the quiet.

"Oh, right," said Franklin. She pointed at the boy's shoulders. "There, between the cuts, can you see what looks like bruising?"

Kett couldn't make out anything past the sheen of dried blood.

"Not restraints," she went on. "They look like the marks that are left when you carry a heavy bag. A rucksack, maybe. You didn't find a bag here?"

Kett shook his head.

"I might be wrong," said Franklin. "There's a first time for everything, I suppose. There's also some grazing on his elbows here, a slight bruise. Looks like he fell."

Hay had picked up the boy's coat and was making her way out of the tent. Kett waited until she'd gone before speaking again.

"Can you tell me anything else?"

"Nothing you don't already know," she said. "I'd guess fifteen or sixteen, in good shape. He's used to a fight, though."

"Yeah?"

Franklin lifted the boy's right hand, trying to turn the stiff limb around.

"Swollen knuckles," she said.

"Did he fight back?"

"Maybe, but these are old injuries, sustained over a long time. I'd say he was a boxer, but he doesn't have the nose for it, or the physique. Maybe he just likes hitting things."

She held onto his hand for a moment more, frowning.

"What is it?" asked Kett when she didn't speak.

"I'm not sure," she said. "What does this look like to you?"

Kett put on his glasses and leaned in, breathing through his mouth so as not to lose himself to the smell. There was a dark red mark on the boy's wrist, maybe five inches long and perfectly straight, stretching from his pulse point towards his elbow.

"Scar?" he asked. He'd seen them before, on suicide survivors.

Franklin shook her head, and he moved closer.

"Looks almost like pen," he said. "Or a..."

"A tattoo," Franklin finished for him. "It's a tattoo. Still wet, no sign of scarring. I think it was made after he died."

"A tattoo of what?" asked Kett.

"Just what it looks like," said Franklin, letting go of the boy's arm. "A red line."

CHAPTER NINE

"Shouldn't we be getting them to do this?"

Porter rested on his shovel, nodding towards the constables who had gathered at the back of the house. He was seven scoops into the grave-sized patch of soil in Jim Prescott's garden and he was already out of breath, his shoulder aching from the effort of moving the heavy dirt.

"I'm injured," he went on, speaking louder than he needed to so that the idle coppers would hear. "Stabbed in the line of duty, if anyone remembers..."

They continued to ignore him, and so did Savage, who worked the earth like a machine. She dug deep, grunting as she hefted a spadeful of dirt onto the growing pile beside her. She seemed to notice that he'd spoken, looking up at him.

"What?" she asked.

"Nothing," grumbled Porter, going in for another load. He grimaced as the spade crunched against a stone, jarring his back. "Bloody hell," he said, using the spade to lob the soil a little further than he needed to, scattering it at the feet of the constables. He wasn't sure if they retreated because of this, or because of the murderous look he shot them. "I hate this job."

"Just sit over there and be quiet then, sir," said Savage. "I'll do it."

Porter shot her a look.

"I'm fine, Kate," he said.

He wasn't fine, though. His shoulder was bad enough, but even worse, his Cleverleys were filthy. He used the back of his hand to brush the dirt from the Italian leather, wondering when he'd learn his lesson and wear cheaper shoes to work. By the time he'd picked up his spade again, Savage had stopped.

"What's that, sir?" she said, pointing the tip of the shovel at a tattered strip of blue cloth that was drowning in soil.

Porter leaned on his spade, squinting.

"No idea," he said. "Vegetables?"

"*Blue* vegetables?"

Savage dropped to her knees, using one hand to scrape forensically at the dirt. Gradually, that strip of cloth grew longer.

"Is that a belt?" said Porter.

"I don't think so, sir," she said, using the back of her hand to scratch her nose. "Looks more like a strap of some kind."

She gave it a gentle tug and a larger section of soil started to lift, as if something big was pushing its way to the surface.

"Do you think we should wait for Cara, sir?" she asked, looking up.

"Nah," he replied. "Get it up."

Savage pulled the strap again, and a moment later a rucksack emerged from the ground like the undead rising from a grave. It was bright blue. She let it fall onto the flowerbed, and they both stared at it.

"Shit," said Porter.

"You want me to open it, sir?" asked Savage.

He blew out a long breath.

"I'll do it."

He knelt next to the bag and wiggled the zip, but it was caked with so much muck it wouldn't budge. He delicately probed the side pockets instead, then turned the bag onto its front.

"Oh!" he said, letting go like he'd found a bomb inside it.

A gloved hand gripped the other strap, loose fingers tangled around it like they meant to pull it back beneath the ground. The hand was connected to an arm that was still buried, a glimpse of a black jumper.

Porter stood, his entire body bristling like an earwig had scuttled up his sleeve.

"Was not expecting that," said Savage.

"Really?" said Porter, scrubbing his hands down his trousers. "Creepy grave-sized patch of earth outside a weird man's sex dungeon and you didn't expect to find a body?"

Savage shrugged, her face gaunt.

"Cara?" she asked.

Porter nodded.

"Give her a call."

KETT THREW himself out of the forensic tent so hard he almost brought the whole thing with him, one of the flaps wrapping itself around his neck like a cold hand. He shuddered his way free, almost colliding with Hay in the process. She was holding the dead boy's jacket in one hand while she rummaged through the pockets with her other.

"Sorry," he said, his heart thrashing in his chest. "You find anything else?"

"I think so," said Hay. "I did not get a proper look when he was wearing it. There's a residue of some kind inside the breast pocket."

She dug her gloved hand into the coat and pulled out a pinch of dirty white powder that looked almost like sugar. She delicately sniffed it, then held it out for Kett.

"What do you think?"

He moved closer and inhaled through his nose, recoiling when the stench of cat piss seared its way into his sinuses.

"Powdered meth?" he said. "Smells like ammonia."

"That's what I think. I'll take it back and run some tests to find out."

There was a jaunty tune from her pocket, and she passed the jacket to Kett while she searched for her phone.

"Hey, Hay," she said when she answered it. The muffled voice on the other end of the line sounded like Savage. "Okay, Kate, I will be right there."

Hay hung up, her brow furrowed.

"They've found another body," she said.

KETT DIDN'T fancy another walk, so they got one of the constables to run them back down the hill in an IRV.

"And when they were up, they were up," he sang, the nursery rhyme stuck in his head. "And when they were down, they were down. And when they were only halfway up..."

He stopped when he noticed that Hay was looking at him weirdly.

At Prescott's farmhouse, a constable steered them down the path to the back garden. Porter and Savage were standing beside the plot of dark soil, which looked more like an open grave now than ever. They were both filthy.

"A body?" said Kett as he walked over.

"I'm not sure, sir," said Savage. "Did a bit more digging, and... well, see what you think."

He crouched at the edge of the flowerbed, taking a moment to examine the arm that emerged from the dirt, the gloved hand, the blue rucksack. Part of the corpse's head had been excavated, but it was covered by some kind of hessian sack.

"Why aren't you sure?" he asked. "Looks pretty dead to me,"

"Give the hand a squeeze, sir," said Porter.

"What?"

"Squeeze it."

"I don't want to squeeze it," he said.

"I will," offered Hay, kneeling down beside him. She took the body's fingers in her own. "It's not a hand," she said after a moment.

She felt the corpse's arm, and gently pulled back the sleeve to reveal the slim limb of what could only be a mannequin.

"Plastic," she said, giving it a tap with her nail to be sure.

"Check the head, will you Cara," said Kett.

She tugged on the sack and it came away in tattered strips, rotten through. There was a collective release of breath when the dead-eyed grin of a shop dummy emerged. A photograph of a young man's grinning face had been glued to it.

"That is so weird, sir," said Savage. "Why would somebody bury a mannequin?"

Kett didn't have an answer for her. He turned to the rucksack instead.

"You looked inside?"

"Not yet," said Porter.

Kett's joints played a percussive tune as he stood up. He moved out of the way so that Hay could move in. She tugged at the zip a few times.

"Jammed," said Porter. "We couldn't—"

Hay managed to free it, opening the main pocket of the bag.

"Just needed some elbow grease, Pete," she said.

"I'm injured," he muttered.

Hay peered into the bag, her expression serious. After a few seconds, she held it open for Kett.

"Looks like drugs," she said.

She wasn't wrong. Hundreds of little white baggies filled the bottom of the bag, each one containing a small amount of powder or a bundle of pills.

"Franklin said the boy in the park might have been wearing a rucksack," said Kett. "She found meth in his pocket as well. You think this is his bag?"

Cara tilted the rucksack, studying it. Then she opened it up again and looked inside.

"I'm not sure," she said. "The clothes on the mannequin are riddled with damp, and the fungal growth you see here takes weeks to grow. But the bag seems fresher. No fungus, no mould, no insect activity, just fresh dirt."

"Find out what you can, Cara," Kett said. "Something

tells me there are more secrets to be dug up in Prescott's garden. Pete, stay and help."

"Do I have to, sir?" Porter replied. "It's cold, and I'm in—"

"Kate, you're with me," Kett went on before Porter could get started. "We need to find out who our dead kid is."

CHAPTER TEN

Thankfully, somebody had turned on the heat at HQ, a hug of warm air welcoming Kett back. He shivered with the relief of it, rubbing away the goosebumps as he made his way to the open-plan offices of the Extreme Crime Task Force.

The relief was short-lived, the way it always was now. Although half of the building had been closed off since August so that the damage from the fire could be repaired, the smell of smoke still permeated the walls and the carpets, a constant reminder that good police had died here.

That *Porter* had almost died.

HQ had once been a fortress, one of the few remaining secure places in an increasingly dangerous world.

Now it was just another reminder that nowhere was safe.

Kett held open the door for Savage and they made their way into the bullpen together. It was quiet, a couple of Major Investigation Team detectives chatting quietly by the photocopier, and DS Alison Spalding sitting at Kett's old desk by the radiator, chewing on a pencil as she studied her computer. She didn't look up.

There was no sign of Superintendent Clare.

"So much nicer in here when the boss isn't about," said Kett as he crossed the room to his desk. "Right?"

"Doesn't feel quite so much like entering a minefield, sir," Savage agreed, shrugging off her coat.

"A minefield of toss," Kett said, laughing. "Where one wrong footstep can—"

"I can hear you, you buffoon!" came a roar from the Superintendent's office.

Kett almost took off, his body contracting painfully.

"Jesus Christ," he said, glaring at Spalding. "You could have given us some warning."

Spalding pulled the pencil from her mouth.

"Super's back," she said, with the smallest of smiles. "Serves you right, sir, for bringing me in on my day off."

"I didn't bring you in!" said Kett.

He shuffled to the Super's open door. Clare sat at his desk, watching him approach with one eyebrow raised.

"You shat yourself, Kett?" he asked.

"No, sir. Of course not. Why?"

"Because you're hobbling around like a goblin who's mired his breeches."

"Oh, uh, it's my back, sir."

"You want to sit down, then?" said Clare, and Kett was halfway to the chair on the other side of the room when the Super slammed his fist on the desk. "Tough titties. Only detectives who are doing their job get to park their arses on my chairs. You're not doing your job, are you? You're limping about with soiled underwear doing absolutely fuck all."

"I haven't shat my—"

"Where are we, Kett?" said Clare, looking positively demonic. "Who's our dead man?"

"Boy, sir," Kett said, leaning on the wall. "Franklin thinks he's about fifteen or sixteen. No ID, but there is some drug residue in his jacket. No distinguishing features except for a tattoo on his wrist, a red line, possibly made after death. The park where we found him is a hotspot for dealers. There's not many houses round there but locals report a lot of traffic, plenty of teenagers hanging out. I'm thinking the kid's part of it, possibly slinging meth."

He had to pause to collect his breath. Clare gurned at him.

"He was executed, sir, by more than one killer. Machetes, probably, and sharp ones, too. They set about him while he was standing up, and he was probably dead before he hit the floor. That was last night, around midnight, and he was killed somewhere else before his body was brought to the park. Franklin thinks there's bruising on his shoulders where he was carrying a bag, or where a bag was pulled from him. We found a rucksack buried in Jim Prescott's garden, not sure if it's connected."

Clare steepled his fingers like Sherlock Holmes, resting his chin on them.

"Feels like it might be a gang thing, sir," said Kett, shrugging to show that he didn't really know. "Kid's carrying meth, gets set on by an armed group, gets his gear stolen."

He paused again.

"Here it comes," said Clare. "Everybody get ready for Kett's hideous butt."

"*But,*" he went on, "whoever took the boy's corpse to the park carried it to the top of the slide. They sat him on the swing and pushed it. They set him up on the merry-go-round."

"He was definitely dead?" said Clare.

"Yeah, there's not enough blood for him to have been alive by the time he reached the park. He was pretty much drained. Somebody took him there and... played with him."

"Doesn't sound like a typical gang hit," said Clare, frowning. "And I worked narcotics at the NCA for years."

He pursed his lips, his eyes scrolling.

"Don't tell me you've got a massive butt too, sir," said Kett.

"I don't have a butt," Clare snapped back. "*But*... gangs commit murder for a number of reasons, and it's sometimes to strike fear into their enemies. If they killed the lad to make a point, there's nothing to say they didn't mess about with his body. I've seen gangs dress their dead like clowns, put face paint on them, string them up in weird positions to humiliate them. They video it, release it online for other gangs to see. If people think you're crazy, they're less likely to mess with you."

Clare wiggled his eyebrows like he was making a point about himself. Kett chose to ignore it.

"So they dragged his body about the park as some kind of statement," said Kett, nodding. "To mark their territory, maybe. If the victim was a regular there, this might have been a warning to anybody he associated with."

"That's what I just said," barked Clare.

"I know, sir. I was agreeing with you. Anything from missing persons yet?"

"I don't know, do I?" said Clare. "I've only just got back from Yarmouth, thanks to your fat-arsed, snail molesting friend."

"How is Duke?" asked Kett.

"How the hell should I know? Last I saw, he was being

loaded into an ambulance complaining about a crushed bollock."

"Oof," said Kett, squirming.

"I told him he needed to stop moaning," Clare went on. "Doesn't matter if one's crushed, does it? He's got two of the bloody things."

"Not sure that's how it works, sir," said Kett.

"If it's a drug thing, you want to speak with a CI called Willy Boyle."

"That cannot be his real name, sir."

"Why?" said Clare. "Perfectly good name. He's got his fingers in everything, lives in the city. Narcotics will have his current address on file."

"I'll go see Willy Boyle then," said Kett.

"Spalding's been working missing persons," Clare said, flapping his arms at Kett like he was a fly. "Go bother her for a change."

Kett didn't need to be told twice. He closed the door behind him, crossing the bullpen to Spalding's desk. Savage was approaching from the other direction, three steaming mugs of tea in her hands. The smell of it almost blew Kett's head clean off.

"Have I ever told you how much I love you, Kate?" he said.

"Not enough, sir," she replied, setting the tea down on Spalding's desk. "There was no sugar left, sorry, Sarge."

"Don't worry," said Spalding, her face as sour as always. "I'm sweet enough."

Kett lifted a mug, holding it to his chest like a hot water bottle. The heat radiating from it was like a blast furnace.

"You got the photos of the vic?" he asked Spalding.

She nodded.

"Doesn't match any current misper files, sir," she said,

leaning back in her chair. "Got four teenage boys missing across the region. Two are seventeen, one's thirteen, one's fifteen. First three have been missing for weeks, the last one was called in on Monday. But he's black, so it isn't our guy."

"If our victim only went missing last night, nobody might have noticed yet," said Savage. She sipped her tea and pulled a face. "Too hot. Tongue's gone fuzzy."

"I've checked the logs, no calls came in last night from anyone concerned about a teenage relative," said Spalding. She picked up her own mug and set it down again immediately. "Bloody hell, Kate, what did you use to make this tea? Lava?"

"Sorry, Sarge," said Savage.

Kett risked a sip of his own, instantly regretting it.

"You're right, though, Alison," he said.

"About what?" Spalding asked.

"There has to be a way of cooling your tea more quickly. Why has nobody invented that yet?"

"I can pop it in the fridge for a bit, sir?" said Savage, entirely serious.

"I'll be okay," said Kett. "You find anything else?"

"Yeah," said Spalding, tapping the screen with her pencil. "Your playpark, you know anything about it?"

"I know it's in the middle of nowhere," said Kett.

"Weird, right?" said Spalding. "It's been there for twelve years. Planning permission was put in back in 2010."

"Who by?" asked Kett.

"Not who, *what*," Spalding answered. "Juniper Homes Ltd, a building company based in North Walsham. They're defunct now, owner went bankrupt. Carl Blowers. He wanted to build twenty homes on the hill but the locals told him to bugger off. So he built the park as a way of softening the blow. To show he was willing to give back to the community."

"Can't have worked," said Kett. "There are no houses."

"Right," said Spalding. "The locals accepted the park, then rejected the application. Council vetoed it anyway, because of the damage it would have done to the woods, and the lack of drainage, all the fun stuff. Blowers gave up the fight after a few years, and he actually gifted the land the park sits on, for free, if you can believe it. It's been owned by the local authority since 2021."

"But nobody uses it except for the dealers?" said Savage. Spalding nodded.

"There are a dozen complaints on record from residents in the area that kids are dealing up there. That's why nobody uses the park anymore, because families were finding needles and all sorts. Dereham police told me they send a unit out there every now and again, but it's hopeless because it's at the top of a hill and the kids can see an IRV coming from a mile off, they just scatter into the woods. Had cameras for a while but they kept getting destroyed. They know it's a problem, but it's at the bottom of a very big list of problems."

Spalding pulled out a notepad, flicking through the pages until she found what she was looking for.

"Good news is they've got a list of offenders they've arrested there over the years. It's a small one, but it's a start."

She slid the note across the table and Kett studied the three names written there.

"First two were released with a caution back in 2019, the third spent eight months in Norwich prison last year for PWITS, Class C. None of them have a registered address, I have no idea where you'll find them. But this guy..."

She tapped the second name, Aaron Tidswell.

"Owns a Nova that's registered to his old foster home, and it pinged a cam on the A47 a couple of days ago. Looks like he's still local."

"Thanks," said Kett, picking up the note. "That's good work, Alison."

"Well I'm not just a pretty face, sir," she said, batting her eyelids in the most unflattering way possible. She tried to pick up her tea again but couldn't. "I don't get how it's still so *hot*."

"Sorry," Savage said again. "I don't know how to make the boiling water any less boiling."

Kett carried his mug to his desk, setting it down. He passed the note to Savage.

"You happy to try to find these guys?" he asked.

"Sure, sir," she replied, scanning the names. "I worked out Dereham way a little when I was in uniform. I've still got a couple of friends there."

"See if any of them can ID our boy," said Kett.

"What are you going to do, sir?" Savage asked.

Kett pulled out his chair and collapsed into it, the pain in his back like a fast-spreading fire.

"Just going to rest up for a bit," he said, leaning back and closing his eyes. "Take a painkiller or three."

"Sounds good," said Savage.

She headed off, and Kett gave the mouse a nudge to wake up the computer. The face that greeted him was the same face that had greeted him every single day he'd come to work for the last three months: a grainy snapshot of a man in his fifties wearing an expensive suit. It had been taken from a distance on a residential street, the man's head tilted to the side as he prepared to enter a car. The malice seemed to radiate from him—a single dark eye staring back at the camera over a smug smile.

It was the only photo they had of Joseph Maynard.

"Fucker," said Kett beneath his breath.

Maynard was a member of the Hollenbeck crime group who'd managed to escape on the night that the King Rat case had ended. Hollenbeck—a collection of wealthy psychopaths who had made a sport of recruiting, training and sponsoring serial killers—had been dismantled after Kett had escaped their clutches. They'd been all but destroyed.

Except for Maynard.

Everyone had assumed he'd gone on the run, that he'd fled the country. But he hadn't. He was still somewhere nearby, still revelling in demonic bloodshed and brutal murder. Under the alias Jasper Homandy, he'd corrupted Agnes Clegg and her father in the summer, leading to the catastrophic series of events that had almost killed Porter and two innocent teenagers.

And who knew what else he'd been up to since then.

But Maynard had vanished, he'd slipped underground. Nobody knew where he was, nobody had the slightest inkling where he'd show his face again.

Or who he'd kill next.

"I haven't forgotten," Kett told the man in the photo, trying to ignore the frustration and the fear. "I'm still coming for you."

On-screen, Maynard grinned back.

CHAPTER ELEVEN

Savage was pulling the Audi out of HQ when her phone started to ring. She answered on the hands-free, recognising Duke's voice immediately. He sounded exceedingly sorry for himself.

"Can you come and get me, Kate?"

"Now?" she asked, pulling onto the roundabout, then flooring it onto the A11.

"Yeah."

"I'm on my way out to Dereham," she said. "You want to come with?"

"I want to go home," he said. "But anything's better than here. Can you pick me up on the way?"

"Sure," she said, checking the time. "I'll be there in ten. What's up?"

"I can't say," he whispered. "I'll be outside."

Savage swung around the city, pulling into the enormous hospital car park thirteen minutes later. True to his word, Duke was sitting in the bus stop, still in uniform, staring at his phone like somebody had just died. She pulled up beside him and honked the horn, the sound of it almost knocking him off his seat. When he saw who it was, he broke into a smile, looking like a kid who's seen his parents after getting lost in the woods. He eased himself up, waddling to the car like John Wayne.

Savage leaned over and opened his door.

"How's you?" she asked as he gingerly sat down.

"Not good," he replied.

"How's, uh, *Little* Aaron?"

Duke stared at his crotch.

"I don't know," he said. "I didn't want anyone to look."

"What do you mean?"

"I mean the nurses wanted me to pull my trousers down, and then the doctor did too, but I didn't want to."

Savage raised an eyebrow.

"There were like thirty people in the room," he said. "They were all looking. It was like they were at the circus or something."

"Okay," said Savage. "So you haven't shown anyone?"

Duke shook his head.

"Do you want me to have a look?"

He shook his head again.

"Have *you* had a look?" she went on.

"Everything's still attached," he said. "There's no blood. But I was so scared, Kate, I thought I was going to lose them. The bar cut off the circulation to my entire lower body, I didn't think I was going to walk again."

He was so serious that Savage couldn't stop the laughter from bubbling up. She covered it with a hand, but it was too late.

"It's not funny, Kate," said Duke. "I could have been horrifically injured. I could have *died*."

"I can see the headlines now," Savage said, still laughing. "Hero cop castrated to death on children's ride."

"Kate!"

"Squashed privates spell the end for the beloved Yarmouth snails."

"It really hurt!"

"Sorry," she said. "But you're okay, yeah?"

Duke shrugged.

"Everyone was taking photos," he said. "I'm never going to live it down."

Savage checked her mirrors as she pulled onto the road, heading for the exit.

"Aaron, it's a much bigger deal in your head. Nobody is going to remember it."

"OH MY GOD, it's Bollock Cop!"

They had only just got out of the car when they heard the words hollered across the street. Two teenage lads were strolling up Market Place in the middle of Dereham, both smoking vapes and howling their laughter through clouds of sweet-smelling smoke.

"What?" said Duke, almost choking.

"It's not him," said one of the boys. "No way."

"It is!" said the other, holding out his phone. "I was literally just watching it."

The two lads stared at the phone and howled with delight.

"It is him!" said the second one. "Holy shit, how's your bollocks, Bollock Cop?"

"Flat!" said the first, and they were almost on the floor.

Duke looked for a moment like he was about to shout something back, but his head dropped. If he had a tail, Savage thought, it would be well and truly between his legs.

"Pack it in," she told them. "I don't know what you're watching, but it's not him."

The kids must have heard the steel in her voice because they scuttled off without another word.

"My life is over," said Duke. "I can't be known as Bollock Cop."

"It'll blow over," said Savage.

"You promise?"

"I promise," she said.

Her phone dinged in her pocket, a text from Porter.

It's on the bloody BBC News page!

The text included a link, and she clicked on it expecting to see a photograph of the crime scene they'd found that morning. What she saw instead was a close-up of Duke on the snails, his face warped in pain as half a dozen firefighters crowded around trying to free him from the safety bar.

He had his trousers around his ankles.

The headline read: *Norfolk Policeman Rescued From Children's Ride.*

"Oh God," she said.

"What's that?" asked Duke, leaning in. She quickly swiped the page away.

"Nothing."

He squinted suspiciously at her.

"Forget it," she said. "We have a job, remember?"

He spluttered out a sigh.

"You have any idea where to start?"

"Kind of," she said, heading south.

The town was packed with Saturday shoppers, swarms of teenagers circling like sharks, while older folk clogged the pavements with shopping trolleys and motorised scooters. The road was jammed with drivers trying to cut through, the air thick with fumes. Even though it wasn't far past three, the skies were darkening.

She hated this time of year.

"When I worked here, the youths all hung out round the back of the library," she said, marching south through the crowds. "Always told them they'd be better off *inside* the library, but you know what it's like."

Duke wasn't listening. He was looking at the passers-by like they were all part of a conspiracy. It might have been her imagination, but people did seem to be looking at him weirdly, and she thought she heard the phrase 'Bollock Cop' spoken more than once before they reached the end of the road.

Luckily, it was quieter when they turned into the alleyway that led along the side of the library, just a handful of people loitering in quiet groups, drowning in cigarette smoke. Most moved away when they saw Duke coming—even with the pout on his face and the limp he still looked imposing.

The alley opened up into a giant car park that was hemmed in on all sides by drab brick shops and lifeless new-build flats. The leafless trees that grew between the spaces were stunted by a lifetime of fumes, looking more like skeletal hands than greenery.

Sure enough, some kids were skateboarding on the far side of the car park, seven of them in all. A couple had caught sight of Duke already, and before they'd got halfway to them, they'd all stopped what they were doing, as alert as a group of gazelles who sensed a lion.

"Wait here," she said. "Act less... *liony*."

"What?" said Duke.

Savage walked the rest of the way alone, her hands up.

"Nobody's in any trouble," she said. "I just need some information."

The kids—four boys and three girls, all around twelve years old—glanced at each other, their bodies tense. None of them knew what to do, which was evidence enough that they were harmless. If they'd ever been in trouble with the police before, they'd have scattered as soon as Duke had walked around the corner.

"How're you all doing?" she said. She nodded to the skateboards that two of the boys and one of the girls were holding. "Nice rigs."

"Thanks," said the girl. "It's alright, I guess."

"Better than the one I had when I was your age," said Savage. "We couldn't afford one, so my granddad screwed some trolley wheels to a plank of wood. First time I went on it the whole thing went shooting out from under me like a missile and he ended up needing stitches in his forehead."

She laughed at the memory, and a couple of the kids smiled too.

"Never skated again after that," Savage went on.

"You want a go?" said the girl, holding up her board.

"That depends," said Savage. "Do you want stitches?"

Their laughter was more genuine this time, but two of the lads were stone-faced.

"I'll be gone in a second," she told them. "I just need to ask you if you know a guy by the name of Aaron Tidswell."

She studied their faces, but didn't see so much as a glimmer of recognition on any of them. She pulled Tidswell's mugshot from her pocket, holding it up.

"He's eighteen, lives in the town. Got arrested a while back for drugs."

Still nothing, although one of the scowling lads had started scuffing the floor with his battered trainer. He wasn't looking at her, he was staring at Duke. A couple of the other kids were taking sly photos of him on their phones.

"You haven't seen him around here recently?" Savage asked.

Nobody replied for a few seconds, then the boy nodded across the car park.

"That the cop who got his nuts squashed?" he asked.

"How on earth did you hear about that so quickly?" said Savage.

"TikTok," he said. "He's a meme."

"Does he know he's famous?" asked the girl with the skateboard.

"Uh, no," said Savage. "So none of you know him? Aaron Tidswell, this guy?"

"I might," said the lad. "I mean, not him, but I know where he might hang out."

"Yeah?"

"Yeah."

He left it hanging, and Savage shook her head.

"I'm not paying you," she said, knowing she didn't have any cash on her.

The kid looked disappointed. Savage puffed out a couple of breaths, trying to work out what to do. She could threaten them, but that would be more likely to scare them off. And it wasn't like she could appeal to their sense of civic duty.

She glanced at Duke, who offered her a sad little wave. Then she turned to the kids again.

"You want a photo with..." she lowered her voice to a whisper so he wouldn't hear. "With *Bollock Cop*?"

"For real?" said the girl, grinning.

"You tell me what you know," said Savage, "and I'll make it happen."

"Photo first," said the lad.

Savage called across the car park.

"Aaron, come here for a second, would you?"

Duke waddled over, his face still screwed up with pain.

"Hey," he said, nodding to the kids. They all snorted with quiet laughter.

"These guys would like a photo," said Savage.

"With me?"

"Yeah. They, uh, they saw you on the news, back when you were Britain's Bravest Copper."

"No, it's—" started the boy, and Savage shut him up with a look.

"Britain's Bravest Copper," she said again.

"Sure," said Duke, managing a smile. "All of you?"

He stepped into the middle of them and they assembled around him. Savage took the girl's phone and lined up the shot. It was a small mercy that Duke was so busy posing for the photograph that he didn't notice every single one of the kids was grabbing their crotch and pulling pained expressions.

Savage took a couple of photos, feeling terrible.

"Done," she said.

"Can I see?" asked Duke.

Savage passed the phone back.

"No time," she told him. She turned to the boy. "Right, deal's a deal. Tell me what you know."

The kids had crowded around the phone, all laughing their heads off.

"Hey," Savage said, a little louder.

The boy looked up, scratched his nose.

"All I know is Aaron's brother hangs out at the Stag," he said. "Whole crew of them there, but I don't know 'em. Don't want to."

"The Stag," said Savage. "One more question. You know if anyone around here went missing last night? A boy, about fifteen or sixteen. Anyone looking for somebody like that?"

The question fell on deaf ears, the kids laughing again as they looked at the phone. Savage thought about showing them the photos they'd taken of the victim that morning, see how funny they found it then.

But they were just children. And images like that would scar them for life.

"Thanks," she said. "You lot be careful, okay?"

She turned and walked away, Duke limping by her side.

"Nice to know I'm still a little bit famous," he said.

"Sure, Aaron," Savage replied, patting him on the arm. "Come on, it's this way."

CHAPTER TWELVE

Kett bumped the Volvo onto the kerb and switched off the engine, taking a moment to enjoy the canned heat before cranking open the door.

The cold dragged him out like it meant to beat him up on the pavement, and he shuddered his way down the street of terraced houses until he found the one he wanted. He hammered on the door and stood back, doing a jig to try to keep warm. When nobody answered, he knocked again.

"Willy, if you don't open the door I'm coming in the hard way," he yelled. "It's too cold out here to mess about."

He heard a bolt being drawn, and the door opened—just wide enough for a beady eye and a nose that looked like a potato.

"Fuck you want?" said a voice so thick with phlegm that he could have been standing underwater.

"I want to come in," said Kett. "Before body parts start dropping off."

"You don't want to come in," said Willy. "They won't like you."

"Who won't?" said Kett, leaning closer to try to see

through the gap. All he got for his trouble was a noseful of something awful.

"*They* won't. They'll hate you. They'll probably try to bite you."

"Who's in there with you?" Kett asked. "Tell them if they bite me, I'm biting back. Now open the bastarding door."

He didn't wait any longer, shouldering his way into the living room. It was barely big enough for the two of them and the ancient leather sofa. The carpet had been beige at one time, but it was now a highly suspicious yellowy-brown colour. Willy was dressed in a pair of moth-holed tracksuit trousers and a Led Zeppelin T-shirt with the armpits cut out. His bulbous nose was streaming, his upper lip red raw and his eyes the same colour. He closed the door and slid the bolt back across.

"Christ, man, what *is* that?" Kett said, putting a hand to his face against the tidal wave of piss stench that rolled over him.

"Them," said Willy, running the back of his hand over his suppurating nose. "They won't stop going on me carpets and eating me furniture."

"*Who?*" Kett said again.

"You sure you want to know?"

Kett wasn't sure about anything, and Willy must have taken that as a yes because he crossed the damp carpet in his bare feet and opened the kitchen door. Almost immediately, something rushed through it—a streak of furry lightning that zipped behind the sofa before Kett could identify it.

"What—"

A dozen more creatures surged into the living room, tearing across the carpet towards him so fast he screamed.

One of them launched itself onto his leg and began to climb, needled feet in his skin.

Kett shrieked again, falling back against the wall as the creature—a ferret, he realised—reached his stomach, still climbing. He swiped at it, but the thing had the reflexes of a snake, and before he could say another word it was clinging to his chest and he was face to face with the bloody thing.

"Miriam, down!" Willy yelled. "Bad girl!"

Kett grabbed the ferret, which coiled and squirmed in his hands. There was another one scaling his trousers and he lifted his leg up, hopping on one foot.

"Get them off!" he shrieked.

"Bernard, I told you," Willy shouted. "You can't hump the guests!"

Kett dropped the first ferret to the floor so that he could concentrate on the second one. But it was the *third* one he needed to worry about, because this one was climbing his leg too, but *inside* his trousers.

"Christ!" he said, collapsing onto the sofa. "No, no! Get it out, get it out!"

Willy kneeled beside him, grabbing at his waistband.

"You have to open your belt," he yelled. "Or it will chew its way out through your leg."

It squirmed its way up, almost at his knee. More ferrets were closing in from all directions, squeaking their heads off. Kett unfastened his belt, jiggling his hips until the ferret's face appeared in the dark.

"Out!" he ordered, and it must have understood him because it tore its way free and scuttled over the top of the sofa, vanishing.

"Behave yourselves!" Willy roared, back on his feet and spinning in wild circles. "You're embarrassing me!"

The ferrets had lost interest in Kett, busying themselves

on the carpet as they foraged for food. He did up his belt, then leaned over and tucked the hem of his trousers into his socks. His heart was fizzing, fireworks exploding against the walls.

"You could have warned me," he said, catching his breath.

"I did bloody warn you!" said Willy, crashing on the sofa next to him, close enough that their elbows were touching.

Kett pushed himself up, not because he didn't want to be near the man—although that was certainly a motivating factor—but because the sofa felt wet through. He stood in the middle of the room until his pulse was back to normal.

"I hate the bloody things," said Willy, watching the ferrets. "Make my life miserable, they do."

"Then why do you have so many of them?" Kett asked.

"They keep having babies!" he wailed. "I can't get 'em to stop."

Kett rubbed his face, taking as deep a breath as the fetid air would allow him.

"I need to ask you some questions," he said.

"About the ferrets?"

"No, Willy. Not about the ferrets. I need to ask you about the gangs."

Willy shrugged. Two of the creatures had climbed onto his lap and wound themselves around each other, looking like a blanket. He tickled their heads and the chirrups they made were almost cute. Willy's nose was running even more furiously, like somebody had turned on a tap. He screwed up his face, then sneezed so hard he almost left the sofa.

"Don't know you, though, do I?" he said when he'd recovered. "Got my contact, don't want to complicate it.

Risky enough without you lot turning up whenever you like."

"This is different," said Kett. "We found the body of a teenage boy in a park just south of Dereham. Killed last night, probably by more than one attacker. They basically cut him into pieces."

Willy's face scrunched up in disgust.

"Don't know nothing about—"

"We think he was dealing," said Kett. "But we're not sure. Whoever killed him displayed him like some kind of trophy on a merry-go-round. You know any of the gangs who would do that to a kid?"

Willy shrugged again, accepting another two ferrets onto his lap. One climbed his T-shirt and sat on his shoulder, looking up at Kett and licking its little pink nose.

"County Lines gangs are bad right now," he said. "Got one lot of lads up from London, made some kind of deal with an outfit in Norwich and one in King's Lynn—proper Silk Road to the north, that—and they're pushing bare food: meth, coke, MDMA and PCP. Heroin, too. Nasty bastards. Proper hard bastards, old school. Cutting up folk left, right and centre, if you believe what you hear."

"You got names?"

"They go by the Fulham Crew, mostly. But your lad don't sound like them. County Lines gangs don't leave their dirty laundry out, they tidy it away."

"How?" asked Kett, poking his toe at a ferret that was creeping towards him.

"They feed the bodies to the pigs, or they drown 'em with weights, or they burn 'em. That's what they promise you, if you fuck them over. You're merked. You disappear, nobody ever sees you again. That scares folks more than the thought of being found dead."

"They don't kill people as a warning?" Kett asked.

"Sure, they do," said Willy, scratching his potato-shaped nose. "Sometimes. Can't think of anything recent, though. They don't want the kids to be shook, you know?"

"The kids?"

"Yeah, that's the only reason they're up here, *int'it*? They recruit kids to carry the drugs, make 'em think they're going to be fucking millionaires or whatever. The only way they can keep the mules interested is if they think they're going to be safe, if they think there's not much risk in it. Soon as the kids think they're in danger, soon as they know they're slipping, they back out, they say no, they won't do it. Don't make no sense for anyone to murder a kid like that, leave them in the open."

He sneezed again, then wiped the snot on the back of the nearest ferret.

"Little bastards," he muttered. "Allergic to 'em n'all. Boy have a name?"

"The victim? We don't know. No ID." Kett shrugged. "He was white, about fifteen, sandy hair, Canada Goose jacket. Wasn't much about him that made him stand out. Oh, except for one thing."

The ferret was sniffing his boot and he took a step away. Two more were closing in, all of them watching with rat-like eyes.

"You think we could put them back in the kitchen?" he asked.

"You can try," said Willy. "But they won't be happy about it. 'Sides, I was wrong; they like you."

"You sure about that?" said Kett, taking another step back and hitting the wall.

"Well they ain't bitten you yet," he said, wheezing out a laugh. "Day's still young, though, I suppose. What was it?"

"What was what?" said Kett, all his attention on the animals as they gathered around him. There had to be about twenty of them in the room now.

"The thing that made him stand out."

It took Kett a moment to find his way back to the conversation.

"Oh, right. It was a tattoo, on his wrist."

One of the ferrets made a run for it, beetling up his leg. He screamed again, the noise out of him before he could stop it.

"Jus' relax," said Willy. "Can't be shook by a little thing like Petunia."

Kett forced himself to stay calm, letting the little creature climb onto his arm. It stretched upwards, sniffing his face.

"Hi," he said. "Please don't bite me."

The ferret replied with a squeak.

"See," said Willy. "You made a friend."

"Not my friend," said Kett.

He realised Willy was still waiting for him.

"A tattoo," he said again. "On his wrist. A red line."

The atmosphere in the room changed instantly—enough that the ferrets picked up on it. The puddle of fur on Willy's lap dispersed, starting a stampede as the creatures retreated to the kitchen. The ferret in Kett's arms actually kicked itself free, almost flying. It hit the floor and scampered into hiding, and Kett scrubbed away the goosebumps it had left behind.

"A red line?" said Willy, just a whisper.

"Yeah," said Kett, holding his hands six inches apart. "This big. I thought it was a scar, at first."

"It is," said Willy. He was pushing himself back into the

sofa like he wanted it to swallow him, his bare feet kicking at the carpet.

"A scar?" asked Kett.

"Of sorts," said Willy. "I don't know nothing, not really, but I heard about it. You got the red line, you've given your life to them."

"To who?" said Kett.

"I don't know. Nobody does. But everyone knows the line, they know what it means."

Kett waited until Willy had found the words.

"Follow the red line," he said. "You do that, they've got you forever."

He suddenly lurched forward, pushing himself to his feet. He stood in front of Kett, hunched, trembling. His bloodshot eyes blinked hard.

"You see the red line, you turn the other way and you keep running."

He pointed a finger at Kett.

"You turn the other way, and you get the fuck out of my house."

CHAPTER THIRTEEN

The Stag had always been a festering wound on the edge of Dereham, but in the five or so years since Savage had last been here, it had grown worse than ever. The entire front of the building seemed to have crumbled away, the brickwork exposed, the windows peeling. Somebody had ripped the T from the gold lettering on the wall, replacing it with a hand-drawn L, and the sign was missing from the bracket over the door.

"Nice place," said Duke as they crunched their way through the empty car park.

"Always was a craphole," she replied. "Hardly a weekend went by that somebody wasn't stabbed or glassed or pineappled in here."

"Pineappled?" said Duke.

"You don't want to know."

She pushed open the door, a gust of cold air billowing past her like it was trying to escape. At the end of a short corridor that stank of urinal blocks was the bar, which resembled a cave thanks to the tiny windows and the fact that no lights were on. A handful of punters hid in the shadows, nursing beers, their eyes like gimlets as she and Duke crossed the room.

"Rozzers!" came a gruff shout from the corner.

"That's not very nice, mate," said Savage. "You know that Rozzer comes from the word pig, right?"

"Rozzers!" the man yelled again.

"Oi, that's enough," said Duke, resting a hand on his Taser.

"Rozzers!" he bellowed for a third time, and Savage was on the verge of marching over when the door behind the bar opened and a woman appeared. She had to have been eighty if she was a day, dressed in blue mechanic's overalls, her bright pink hair glowing.

"I'm coming!" she said, her voice so weak she was gargling. She didn't seem to have the strength to lift her head properly, her face hidden beneath thin wisps of hair, but Savage recognised her immediately.

"Roz?"

The woman tilted her head like she had a stack of weights resting on it, her rheumy eyes taking a moment to find Savage. When they did, her mouth curled into a smile.

"Blow me down," she said—something that could probably have been achieved with a single breath. "Kate Savage, as I live and breathe. Don't look so savage out of uniform, though."

"Roz Perkins," said Savage, and she realised that the man in the corner had been calling her name. She looked back. "Sorry, thought you were insulting us."

"Was trying to help you," the man replied. "Bloody pig."

Savage let it go, turning to the old woman as she propped herself against the bar.

"I heard you died," she said.

"I did!" Roz replied, vomiting out a wet laugh. "Had me

on the table for about eight hours while they fixed my leaky brain. Nobody thought I'd be back, but who else is going to run the place? Duane? Sack of shit couldn't find a barrel of beer if he was lying under it."

"How is your son?" Savage said.

"In bed, the lazy prick," said Roz, pointing up. "Stays up all night on his CB, chatting to who knows who, about who knows what. He's sixty next year, and he's never bloody left."

She raised her voice, aiming it at the ceiling.

"Never bloody left!"

"Well, it's good to see you," said Savage. "Business okay?"

Roz actually spat on the floor in disgust.

"What do you think? This is about as good as it gets these days."

She spotted Duke for the first time, her eyes widening.

"And who is this chunky monkey?"

"PC Duke," said Savage.

"Duke, eh?" said Roz, licking her lips. "You two bumping uglies? Because if not, you should be."

She leaned in, whispering.

"If you're not, I might!"

Savage laughed.

"No," she said, because it was easier to lie. "Look, I just need to ask you some questions, is that okay?"

"Thought it was a personal call," said Roz, and she looked genuinely disappointed. "You want to wet your whistle while you ask?"

"Wish I could," she said. "But it's pretty urge—"

"I'll take a Ribena, if you've got one," said Duke.

Roz ogled him.

"A Ribena?"

Duke nodded, rubbing his throat like he'd been stranded in the desert for a month.

"You want that full strength?" said Roz, and she hurled out another laugh.

"He's fine," said Savage, shooting Duke a look. "I'll get him one from the shop. Listen, a little birdie told me that one of the Tidswell boys drinks here. Aaron's brother?"

"Lot of little scrotes drink here," said Roz. "Always have."

"Because you'll serve them even if they're underage," said Savage, remembering all too well.

Roz shrugged.

"Not my fault I can't read the dates on their passports," she said. "I know Scott Tidswell. He's always in here, him and his mates. Seen Aaron a few times too, although not recently. What's he done?"

"You ever catch them dealing in here?" asked Savage.

Roz waved the question away.

"Dealing to who? Geoff over there? He wouldn't know drugs if there was one on the end of his nose."

"Shut up, woman," came a reply from the corner. "Do loads of drugs, thank you very much."

"He's full of shit," said Roz. "He about fainted once when he accidentally snorted some talcum powder. Nah, they don't deal in here, but I know they deal other places. Always heaps of cash in their pockets. I ignore it. So long as they're paying, who cares where the money comes from?"

"Nice to see you're as morally grey as always," said Savage.

Roz shrugged weakly.

"You don't get to my age by being a goody-two-shoes, Kate. What's this about, anyway? Your breeches are too big to be chasing toerags like the Tidswells."

"I'm not chasing them," said Savage. "We found a kid a few miles south of here this morning. Teenage boy. He was murdered, left in the old playpark near Shipdham."

Roz's face fell, a genuine look of grief.

"We're trying to ID him," she said.

"You got a photo?" asked Roz.

"We do," said Savage. "But it's... He was mutilated, Roz. It would be hard to recognise him. I don't want to put you through that."

"Is it worse than when Jimmy Freeman got pineappled?" she said.

"Yeah," said Savage. "It's worse."

Roz held out her hand, doing her best to snap arthritic fingers. Savage pulled out her phone, reluctantly cycling through the crime scene photographs she'd taken that morning. She couldn't bring herself to look at the poor kid they'd found, so she slid the phone across the bar instead. Roz slipped on a pair of reading glasses and picked it up. Her gasp of shock seemed to echo around the pub.

"You know him?" asked Savage.

She studied it a little longer.

"I think that's Maggie Spicer's little boy," she said. "Kieran."

When she looked up, there were tears in her eyes.

"Who did this to him?"

"I don't know," said Savage. "Not yet. You sure it's him?"

Roz didn't seem to want to look again, and Savage didn't blame her. The woman handed the phone back with a trembling hand.

"How old is Kieran?" Savage asked.

"Must be sixteen," she said. "He had his exams this

year. I thought he was a good kid, though. Maggie's always boasting about him, about how well he's doing at school."

She shuddered.

"Might be wrong, though. Might not be him."

Savage put the phone back in her pocket.

"Please don't share this with anyone," she said, although she knew that in a place like this, that was an impossible request. "You know where Maggie lives?"

"Down Toftwood someplace," she said. "I only see her on the market, or up the school if I'm picking up my granddaughter's boy."

"You know if Kieran was ever involved with the gangs? If he ever dealt drugs?"

"He's a teenager in a small town," said Roz. "What do you think?"

Savage nodded, tapping the bar a couple of times.

"Thank you, Roz," she said. "I appreciate it."

"You make sure you get them," said Roz, her eyes fierce. "Get them, and don't bother locking them up, either. Prison's too good for scum like that."

There was nothing else to say, so Savage crossed the bar and escaped the pub. Duke closed the door after them. For a moment they both stood there in the growing dark, then she pulled out her phone and called Kett.

"Hi, sir," she said when he answered. "I think I've got a name."

CHAPTER FOURTEEN

Kett closed the door of the IRV and stretched the vertebrae in his back, the pain like a knife sliding between his ribs. He leant on the car for support, but the constable who'd driven him out to Dereham was already pulling away. By some miracle, he managed to stay on his feet, muttering silent curses at the PC until the car vanished into the evening.

"Sir!" came a shout from behind him.

He turned to see Savage stepping out of an Audi parked further down the road, illuminated by a streetlight. Duke was extracting himself from the passenger side even more slowly than usual, pain etched into every line of his face. There was a kid-sized bottle of Ribena clenched in his giant hand.

"How's your, uh?" Kett asked him, nodding towards his crotch. "You know."

"Swollen," said Duke. "They look like a couple of bulging—"

"Actually, I really don't want to know," said Kett,

holding up a hand. "This job has scarred me enough. Shouldn't you just go home?"

"He's fine," said Savage, closing her door. "I got him a Ribena, he should stop moaning."

Duke opened the cap of the tiny bottle and took a delicate swig, looking like a gorilla sipping from a thimble.

"A Ribena?" said Kett.

"You want a bit?" said Duke, holding the bottle out.

The truth was, he *did* fancy a bit. He was parched. But he shook his head, turning instead to the street. Even in the dark, he could tell it was one of the nicer parts of the town. The big houses were nestled in wide driveways beneath blankets of old-growth trees. Golden light spilled from a few of the windows, pooling on stone porches and in well-tended flowerbeds. Some even had their Christmas lights up, even though December was a couple of weeks away. The cars were the upper end of affordable, BMWs and Audis and the occasional Jaguar.

"Kieran Spicer, right?" said Kett, reminding himself.

Savage had told him everything on the phone, and Spalding had messaged him a few photos she'd found on social media. It was hard to tell, of course, because he'd been so badly disfigured by the attack, but the living boy he saw on his screen wasn't a million miles away from the dead one they'd found in the playground.

He prayed, as he always did, that he was wrong.

"Yes, sir," said Savage. She nodded to a house across the street. "It's that one."

Past two crumbling brick pillars sat a red-brick Georgian semi-detached house with sash windows and a wide, purple door. Most of the building was lost beneath a wisteria plant which still, incredibly, held most of its flowers. Fairy lights had been wrapped around the oak porch, blinking merrily.

It looked like home, thought Kett, and the last thing he wanted to do was knock on that door.

But that was the job.

He'd only just started up the driveway when a shout drew his attention. A man stood at the gate of the next house over—the other half of the Spicers' semi—somewhere in his seventies and vastly overweight. He was wearing brown tracksuit trousers and a white shirt that had been buttoned wrong, barely hiding the swollen mass of his stomach, plus a pair of ancient tartan slippers. He held onto a stick with one hand and the pillar with another.

"Oi," he said again, waving the stick at Kett even though he already had his attention. "You police?"

Kett glanced at Duke, who stood there in full uniform, then nodded.

"We are," he said. "Who are you?"

"Morris Gough," said the man, coughing wetly. "You hear about that little shit next door?"

"You're going to have to be more specific," said Kett.

"That little oik, the teenager. The Spicer lad. You here for him? It's about time."

"Why are you asking?" said Kett, walking up to the man and taking a look at his house. It was a mirror image of the Spicer place next door, but it couldn't have looked more different. The woodwork was painted a dull shade of constipated brown, and so was the door. Parked on the driveway was a classic car half-hidden beneath a tarpaulin. In the dark, it looked the colour of shit.

"Because he should be arrested, that's why," said Morris. "He should be arrested, then taken away, then shot."

"Hey," said Kett, giving the man a hard stare. "That's enough."

"Yeah, that's about right," said Morris with a snarl. "That's Norfolk Police for you. Threatening upstanding citizens like me, protecting the scum of the earth. He's a drug dealer, you know. You look at the kids around here who're overdosing, choking to death on their own puke, and tell me shits like him shouldn't be executed."

Kett took a couple of steps towards the man, enough to make him stagger away.

"You sound like you want to hurt this boy, Mr Gough," said Kett. "You want to tell me where you were last night?"

"Why?" he replied, still retreating. "What's happened?"

"If you want me to explain it to you, then I'll happily take you to the station," Kett told him. "Or you can go back inside your house. Your choice."

The man harrumphed, wheeling around like a drunken elephant before struggling back to his front door.

"You're all the same," he shouted as he went. "You're as bad as the criminals."

"That wasn't suspicious at all, sir," said Savage once he'd disappeared. "You want me to talk with him?"

"Maybe," said Kett. "But not right now."

He returned his attention to the Spicer house, taking a deep breath.

"I think I'm going to need all the help I can get in here."

He walked up the gravel driveway, his boots crunching out a warning. He was close enough now to see that although the wisteria plant was real, the blossoms were fake, dozens of plastic flowers tied onto the stem. There were voices inside the house, children yelling at each other, the pounding of feet.

As he passed the living room window, the light came on,

as if it hoped to catch them out. A boy ran in, maybe six or seven, throwing himself onto the sofa. Another followed, a couple of years older, screaming about something. They were both oblivious to the three police officers who walked by in the dark.

Kett waited for Savage and Duke to catch up before rapping his knuckles on the glass. He was answered by more shouting as the boys continued to argue, the crash of something being thrown. He counted to ten, and tried again, but the hurricane of noise from inside could have drowned out gunfire.

"Can you do it, Kate?" he asked, standing to one side.

Savage pounded on the door the way only she could, the house trembling. It did the trick. Kett heard a shout from somebody older, and a moment or two later a blurred shape appeared in the marbled glass.

A lock turned. The door opened. A woman stood there, in her early forties, wearing a green dress and a red spotted apron. Her cheeks were flushed, her fair hair plastered to a sheen of sweat. Wedged between one hand and her waist was a baking tray full of uncooked potato waffles, and she was using a shoulder to pin her mobile phone to her ear.

"... yeah, on Tuesday," she said, giving Kett an apologetic look. She almost dropped the tray, using her other hand to steady it. "I've already told you. Look, can I call you back? Something's up."

She turned, as if looking for somewhere to put the waffles.

"You need a hand with that?" asked Kett.

She held out the tray and Kett took it.

"I will," she said, still speaking to whoever was on the phone. "I'll call you back."

She slid the phone into the pouch of the apron, studying

Kett with a look of apprehension that grew more pronounced when she spotted Duke standing just outside of the porch.

"Is everything..."

And her face crumpled like it was buckling beneath some horrendous pressure. It crumpled the way a woman's face always did when three police officers showed up at the door. Because mothers *know*. That ancient intuition, that unbreakable connection to your child that is part blessing and part curse.

"Please," she said, as if that would make any difference at all.

"Are you Margaret Spicer?" asked Kett.

She shook her head, but it wasn't a denial of her name.

"It might be easier if we come in," he went on. "Do you mind?"

She looked back as if somebody might be able to tell her what to do, then stepped out of the way, almost tripping on a toy garage that had been left by the stairs. She took hold of the newel post to balance herself, clinging on with both hands as if the building was falling apart around her.

"Take your time," said Kett, entering the house, the tray of waffles still in his hands. It was hot enough in here to cook them without an oven.

One of the boys from the living room appeared in the doorway to the left, the older one. He looked at Kett, his quizzical expression darkening when he turned to his mum, when he saw a look on her face that he'd probably never seen before, one he never would have imagined she was capable of wearing. The younger one appeared, squeezing under his brother's arm.

"I'm starving!" he yelled. "Who are they?"

"We're police," said Kett. "But don't worry, okay?"

"Why did you call the police?" asked the older lad, and the worry was right there.

"To cook dinner," said his little brother. "Obviously."

"Shut up, Peanut," said the older boy.

"You shut up."

It looked like they were going to start throwing punches, so Kett intervened.

"He's right," he said to the older boy. "We've brought our finest officer. He turns up when he senses that people might be hungry. He's like Batman, but with... waffles."

He turned to Duke, proffering the tray.

"Can you deal with these?"

"Sure, sir," said Duke, taking it from him. He beamed at the kids. "Waffles are my speciality. You got beans and cheese?"

"Gross!" said the younger kid. "Only weirdos eat beans."

"I eat beans," said Duke.

"Case in point," said Kett. He turned to the mother. "Have you got somewhere we can talk?"

It took her a moment to remember how to nod.

"Go into the kitchen, Jay," she said.

The older boy shook his head, but his mother gave him another look, one he seemed all too familiar with.

"*Now*, Jay, and take Peanut with you."

He resisted quietly for a handful of seconds before pushing himself off the door frame and following Duke into the kitchen. His little brother chased after them without a backward look.

"I can grate the cheese!"

The silence that fell when they'd moved out of sight was somehow even louder than the chaos. It felt airless, too, as if they'd all been plunged underwater.

The woman walked through the door the boys had appeared from, leading Kett and Savage into a living room that looked as if it had been hit by a tsunami. There were toys everywhere, teddies and cars and plastic guns and playing cards, all thrown into sharp relief by the overhead light. Opened board games lay like corpses, their guts spilled across the two sofas, the coffee table and the varnished wooden floor. It was a struggle to get past them without stepping on something.

Photographs lined the walls, most of them showing three boys in various stages of their lives. Two were the boys he had met just seconds ago.

The third was older, and there was no denying the similarity to their victim.

"I'm sorry," the woman said, that ubiquitous apology that parents always made for something that was never their fault. "I do ask them to tidy."

She staggered to the window, shouldering up the stubborn wooden sash to let in a welcome breeze. She drew the curtains across as if she'd only just noticed it was dark.

"They keep turning the heating on," she said, tripping her way around the edge of the room and standing in the far corner, as if she meant to hide behind the lamp there. "I keep telling them it costs money, but..."

"I know," said Kett, finding a clean space by the sofa. "They never listen. Can I just confirm, you *are* Margaret Spicer?"

She nodded, chewing on a fingernail as she waited for the inevitable.

"You've got a son called Kieran?" Kett went on.

Margaret closed her eyes and tilted her head towards the ceiling. Kett could almost see the prayer she was firing towards the heavens.

"Is this him?" he asked, pointing to a photograph of Kieran in skiing gear on a snow-capped slope.

"It's him," Margaret replied.

"Can I ask you when you last saw him?" Kett said.

"Yesterday," she whispered. "In the morning, before he headed out. Is he..."

She couldn't bring herself to say it, Kett knew. To *jinx* it.

"We're not certain of anything right now," said Kett. "You didn't see Kieran after he left yesterday morning?"

Margaret shook her head.

"He lives here?"

"Most of the time," she said. "Sometimes he's with his dad down the road, because Mike'll drive him places. I haven't got a car. It's hard here for Key sometimes, being here, especially the nights. I have to give so much time to the little ones, because we don't get any help. Peanut never sleeps through, always jumping on his brothers first thing. Good for Key to get some peace and quiet."

"He was supposed to stay here last night?"

Margaret shrugged.

"He's old enough to do what he wants. I don't pressure him. He's a..." She paused, her entire body shuddering like a broken engine. "He's a good kid, he's sensible, he's never in trouble. I trust him. If he's not here, I trust him to be somewhere safe."

She thumbed away a tear, looking directly at Kett for the first time since she'd opened the door.

"He's not safe, is he?"

"We don't know," Kett told her. "Like I said, we're trying to work out what happened. Do you remember what Kieran was wearing when he left the house yesterday?"

She pushed her knuckles into her eyes, shaking her head.

"Just the usual stuff, you know?" she said. "A tracksuit, his trainers."

"And what about a coat?"

"Yeah, he's got a coat," she said.

Don't say it's a Canada Goose, Kett thought.

Then he cursed *himself* for jinxing it.

"Big black thing," said Margaret. "Expensive, it was, but it was a present for his GCSEs this year, because he'd done so well. He's always wanted one. It's a Canadian Goose, got the badge on the arm."

Kett tried not to let it show, but when Margaret lowered her hands and blinked at him, she read it on his face as easily as if he was holding up a placard.

"He's dead," she said, every single muscle shaking. "Isn't he?"

Kett took a breath, wiping the back of his hand over his sweat-streaked forehead.

"We found the body of a boy this morning, in a park just south of here," he said. "It matches Kieran's description, but we—"

Margaret's body collapsed like a house of cards, knocking over the lamp. Savage ran to her, toys cracking and snapping beneath her feet as she crossed the room.

"Mrs Spicer?" she said, ducking down, one hand on the woman's shoulder. "You're okay, just breathe."

The door opened and the older boy, Jay, lurched in like he was ready to attack everybody there.

"What did you do to her?" he said. "Mum?"

"She's okay," said Kett. "Don't worry."

"Mum?" said Jay, ignoring Kett and running to Margaret. "Mum?"

He put a hand to her face, then stroked her hair, an act of tenderness that pushed a fist-sized lump into Kett's throat. The touch worked, because her eyes opened, finding the boy.

"Are you okay?" Savage asked. "Can we call anyone for you?"

She helped Margaret up, practically carrying her to the nearest sofa. She collapsed there, her hands curled into fists beneath her chin. Kett could hear her teeth chattering from where he stood. Jay sat next to her, his body folded into hers. His expression was defiant, like he was *daring* them to do any more damage.

"Can I get you some water?" Kett asked the woman.

Her arm unfolded in lurching movements, finding its way around her son's shoulders, pulling him so tight he winced. She shook her head so hard her hair tumbled over her eyes.

"I'm sorry, Margaret," said Kett. "Like I say, we don't know anything for sure. Do you know if..."

He glanced at the boy, wondering if he should ask him to leave and knowing he wouldn't.

"If Kieran had any dealings with criminal gangs? Drugs? Anybody who might have wanted to hurt him?"

"Drugs?" she said, using her free hand to claw her hair out of her face. "Of course not. He wouldn't ever. He's a good kid; didn't you hear me say that?"

"Where's Kieran?" asked Jay, turning to his mum.

"He didn't hang out with anyone else who might have been into that?" Kett went on.

"Where is he?" the kid asked again, this time to Kett.

"He wouldn't do any of that," said Margaret. "It's not him. It can't be him, if that's what this is. You've made a mistake."

"Mum, where is he?" said the boy, desperate now.

The youngest brother walked through the door, a plate grasped in both hands that was overflowing with cheese.

"Look how much I grated!" he said, staring at the plate like there was nothing else in the universe that mattered. Duke stepped up behind him, offering an apologetic look.

"That's amazing," said Kett.

"Look, Mum," he said.

It must have been the hardest thing in the world to do, but Margaret smiled.

"You're a superstar," she said.

The boy beamed.

"Margaret, do you mind if I have a quick look in Kieran's room?" asked Kett. "It would be really helpful. Kate and Aaron can stay down here."

She didn't answer, her eyes locked on something only she could see. Kett nodded to Savage, then squeezed past the youngest boy and Duke.

"Wait," came a shout from behind him. It was Jay. "Kieran won't want you up there."

Kett stopped at the foot of the stairs as the boy ran through the door.

"Don't," said Jay, and the warning there was clear.

"I'm sorry," said Kett. "I know you love your brother, but this is important. We need to find out what's happened to him."

"He's fine," said the boy. "Just go, and he'll be okay."

Kett sighed.

"I can't do that, Jay," he said.

"Then I'm calling Dad," said the boy. "He's going to come, and you'll be sorry."

"You do what you have to do," he said.

Then he grabbed the banister and hauled himself up.

CHAPTER FIFTEEN

The house was as cluttered upstairs as it was down, a hoarder's paradise of old toys and books and bin bags full of clothes. The landing was nicely decorated, but the wallpaper had been peeled away in places by bored fingers, the skirting boards covered in scribbles. All the lights were on, and the heat up here was almost unbearable.

Kett peeked through the nearest door to find a bedroom, but the decor was too young to belong to Kieran. As he was retreating, Jay pushed past him, heading into the big bedroom at the front of the house. The door slammed shut.

The next door led into what could only be Margaret's room, even though there was barely space for a single bed, a dressing table and a small wardrobe. Past the bathroom was another bedroom, this one with JAY written on the door in big, black letters.

Kett made his way to the front bedroom and tried the handle. The door opened an inch or so before hitting something.

"Jay?" he said. "I really need you to let me in."

"No," came the reply.

Kett heard the thump of something falling to the floor. He pushed the door with a little more force and whatever was behind it gave way. Squeezing through the gap, he saw Jay on the far side of the room beside a chest of drawers. The top one was open, its insides hanging over the edge. The kid glared at Kett. He had his hands in his pockets and his cheeks were roaring—nothing to do with the heat.

"You need help with something?" Kett asked.

No answer.

"You love your brother, right, Jay?"

The kid glared at him, his bare feet scuffing the boards.

"I could do with your help," Kett went on. "Can you tell me about him?"

"No," said Jay, and he bolted, barging past Kett with surprising strength. He vanished into his own room across the landing, the door crunching shut.

Kett tugged at his collar, the sweat rolling down his neck. This was the master bedroom, a big bay window looking down onto the street. It was decorated for a younger kid, but the posters on the walls—mean-faced wrestlers and mainstream metal bands—were thick with dust and wrinkled with age, peeling at the corners. There was a TV bracket mounted on the wall, but no TV, and the overhead bulb didn't have a shade. The curtains—floral ones—were open, the windowsill cluttered with old toys and the night lurking right outside.

A double bed had been pushed into one corner, the chest of drawers opposite, and next to that was a desk that was littered with books and stationery. The space in the middle of the room held a weight bench, dumbbells of all shapes and sizes scattered around it. There was another one by his feet where it had been used to block the door. A punchbag lay on the floor next to the bench like it had been defeated in the ring, the strap along the top ripped away.

Kett started at the desk, rifling through the paperwork to see essays and notes, mostly history and geography. He didn't understand most of what he was reading, but there were comments from teachers, and it wasn't hard to see that Kieran was doing well. Kett counted more than one '*Brilliant work!*' on the pages.

There was nothing in the drawers other than a tangle of old headphones and some ancient DVDs, and not much beneath the desk except a pile of dirty laundry. There was more of that under the bed, too, and stuffed down the side of the chest of drawers—the magical washing baskets that all teenagers seemed to possess. He rummaged through the open drawer of the dresser, finding nothing but socks and underwear. The other two drawers held clothes as well.

And that was it.

Kett left the room, switching off the light behind him. He could hear voices downstairs, raised with emotion, but he didn't head back just yet. He knocked on Jay's door, listening for an answer. When he didn't get one, he tried the handle. Just like before, it opened a fraction before colliding with something.

"Go away," said the kid.

"I'm going," Kett told him. He thought about the way Jay had been standing next to his brother's dresser, his hands wedged in his pockets. "But I need to know what you took out of Kieran's room."

The few beats of silence that followed told him everything he needed to know.

"It's important, Jay. I want to know what happened. I don't care what it is, I don't care if it's something he shouldn't have, even if it's illegal. I just need to know."

"I don't know what you're talking about," said Jay. "Leave me alone."

Kett gave the door another push, but it didn't give, and short of battering it down there wasn't much he could do.

"Alright," he said. "But if you change your mind, we'll be here."

Jay answered, but he was speaking to somebody else—on the phone, most likely. Kett made his way to the stairs, checking the photographs on the walls as he went. Kieran smiled back at him from several of the frames, a snapshot of the boy's life: on his bike, holding one of his younger brothers as a baby, up a tree with a friend, maybe eight years old. Like the posters, the photos were crusted with dirt and cobwebs, forgotten. But that's what happened, wasn't it? Life had no time for good intentions, especially when you had kids.

Kett spotted the same friend in another photograph halfway down the stairs, him and Kieran standing outside the gates of one of the high schools in Dereham. They had their hands folded over their chests, their fingers flicking Vs, looking like a pair of wannabe gangsters. Kett worked the frame off its nail and carried it downstairs with him.

He poked his head through the kitchen door to see Duke sitting at the table with the youngest brother, both of them stuffing their faces with waffles and cheese. Duke swallowed painfully when he saw Kett staring at him, almost choking.

"You eating Jay's dinner?" Kett asked.

"Was hungry," he said, ramming a fist against his chest to dislodge whatever had stuck there. "I didn't think he wanted it."

Kett walked to the living room to see Margaret still on the sofa, clutching a glass of water in both hands. Savage was perched next to her, her face a knot of worry. They both looked up as Kett walked in.

"How are you doing?" he asked Margaret.

There was no answer she could possibly give to that.

"Thanks for letting me look upstairs. Kieran's room's the one at the front, right? The big one?"

Margaret seemed to wind herself up like a clockwork toy, her head nodding.

"He, uh..." She licked her lips. "He asked for more space, because of school stuff. A place to get away from his brothers. It was too big for me."

She took a sip of water, everything rattling.

"That's what you do, isn't it?" she said. "You give them what they need."

"You give them the air in your lungs if they ask for it," said Kett, making his way carefully across the room and sitting on the coffee table. "He's doing his A-Levels, right?"

Margaret nodded.

"Doing well?"

The nod continued.

"He's smart," she said, sniffing. "Wants to go to university. Wants to be a solicitor."

"Yeah?" said Kett, feeling her every word like a sledgehammer to the stomach. "That's great. Does he have a job, too? There's a lot of clothes in his room."

He'd done his best not to phrase it as an accusation, but Margaret still gave him a look.

"You can blame his dad for that," she said. "Buys him anything he wants. Always has."

"Is this Jay's and, uh... Peanut's... Wait, Peanut, is that right?"

"Peter," she said. "Jayden and Peter. But he was tiny when he came out, so we always called him Peanut."

"They've all got the same dad?" Kett asked.

She gave him another look, and it was clear enough what she thought of the question.

"Not my business," he said. "It's just good for us to know."

"Same, yeah," she said. "But Kieran's Mike's golden child. Firstborn, oldest son, you know how it is."

"I've got three girls," said Kett, nodding. "Your boys are close?"

She took another sip of water.

"Close as kids ever are, when they're in the same house. Always fighting, always arguing. But yeah, they're close."

"They look out for each other?" said Kett.

Margaret nodded, but she was frowning.

"Why?"

"Nothing," said Kett. "It's just Jay ran past me right now, before I could get to Kieran's room. I think he might have taken something, something he didn't want me to see."

The woman's frown grew, the lines cut deep into her forehead.

"He wouldn't do that," she said. "He's a good kid, like his brother."

"I might have read it wrong," he said. "Sorry."

He held up the frame so she could see it.

"I've seen this guy in a few pictures around the house. Is he a friend of Kieran's?"

This drew a soft smile.

"Jonah," she said. "Yeah, you could say that. Separated at birth, those two."

"They're still close?"

Margaret nodded, staring at the photo for a moment more. The smile slowly fell away.

"Why?" she asked after a moment. "Has he got something to do with..."

The horror seemed to hit her all over again, as if she'd managed to forget it.

"Have you got an address for Jonah?" Kett asked. "It might be good for us to speak to him."

"He's just across town," she said. "Kennedy Close, round the back of the Millwright's. His surname's White."

"Do you know if they saw each other yesterday?" said Kett.

"I don't know," said Margaret. "Probably. They used to go to school together before the summer, and they mainly hang out at the weekends now. Key never tells me where he's going."

"And you—"

There was a knock on the living room door, and Kett craned his neck back to see Duke there.

"What is it?" he asked the PC.

"I was wondering if there was any pudding?" said Duke.

Kett glared at him.

"Not for me!" Duke protested. "Peanut was asking. Honest."

"There are some..." Margaret put a hand to her face, burrowing into it. "Uh... I think there are some Mini Magnums in the freezer."

"Yes!" said Duke, vanishing down the hall.

"Sorry," said Kett. "He's... uh..."

He couldn't think of an appropriate way of finishing, so it was just as well that there was the sound of a car door closing from the street, followed by a shout. Margaret flinched like somebody had come through the window, her back suddenly straight, her eyes wide.

"Did you call him?" she asked Kett.

"Who?" he said.

Somebody tried to open the front door, the bolt doing its job. They pounded on it instead, their voice like thunder.

"Maggie? Maggie! Open the door."

"I'm guessing that's Mike?" said Kett, staring at the shape in the glass. "I heard Jay on the phone upstairs. He lives close?"

"Next street over," said Maggie. "Likes to keep an eye on us."

"Maggie, where's Kieran? Let me in for fuck's sake."

"You want me to talk with him outside?" said Kett.

Margaret shook her head.

"You won't be able to keep him out."

"We will," said Kett, heading for the hallway. "Duke, get the door, mate."

Duke walked out of the kitchen with a Mini Magnum in his hand and a splodge of ice cream on his nose. There was no time to tell him to drop it, the big PC sliding the bolt across and opening the door.

The man outside was in his late forties, wearing tracksuit trousers and a black T-shirt. He was in good shape, his arms covered in tattoos and another one stretching up the side of his throat. His hair was halfway to grey and deliberately messy. He was tall enough and strong enough to push past Duke before the PC could get a word out.

"Fuck's going on?" he said, walking up to Kett and standing an inch or two taller than him. Duke shut the door. "Where's Kieran? Maggie?"

"Hold up," said Kett, planting a hand on the man's chest as he tried to barge past. "Mike, right?"

Mike eyeballed him, pushing against his hand with no small amount of aggression.

"Who're you, then?"

"My name's DCI Kett," he said, pulling out his warrant card. "I'm with the police."

"But why are you *here*?" said Mike, stepping even closer. He reeked of aftershave. "In my house?"

He moved away before Kett could answer.

"Mags? Where are you?"

Mike walked into the living room, kicking a stuffed dog out of the way and staring at the toys that had been strewn over the floor.

"Christ, Mags, what've you done to this place?"

Margaret leaned back in the sofa like she wanted it to eat her. Savage stood up, positioning herself in front of the woman and giving Mike a hard look that stopped him in his tracks.

"You a copper n'all?" he asked, jutting out his arms to make himself as big as possible. "Maggie, I'm going to ask you one more time, mate, and then I'm going to lose it. Where's my boy?"

"Oi," said Kett, his voice filling the room like a gunshot. "You're going to sit down, Mike, and *calm* down, or I'm going to get Duke here to take you outside."

Duke was standing in the living room door, still eating the Magnum. Mike scoffed at him, but it didn't last. His brow creased, his eyes bulging—not with anger, Kett knew, but with panic.

"Sit down, so we can make sense of this," said Kett. "Okay?"

After what felt like an eternity, Mike nodded. He sat on the other side of the sofa, his elbows on his knees, his body jittering so much that Kett wondered if he'd taken something. He looked sideways at Margaret.

"Mags?"

"They found a kid," she replied. "A boy, in the park. Dead."

The jittering stopped.

"Not Kieran," he said. "Can't be."

"You've seen him today?" said Kett, and he could barely keep the hope from his voice.

"No, he..." Mike stared at the floor, looking for something amongst the toys. "He said he was going out last night, him and Joe."

"Out where?" said Kett.

Mike licked his lips, shaking his head.

"Just out," he said. "In town. Never saw him after, assumed he'd come back here, or gone to Joe's place."

Kett heard footsteps thundering down the stairs, and a second later Jay ran into the room. He tumbled onto the sofa and sat next to his dad, but Mike didn't even seem to see him. Margaret tried to take hold of the boy's hand, but he pulled it away, staring defiantly at Kett.

"Kieran and Jonah don't hang out at the park near Shipdham, do they?" said Kett.

"Too old for a park, isn't he?" said Mike. "He's sixteen."

"He never went there for other reasons?"

"What are you saying?" said Mike.

"They think he was doing drugs," said Margaret, wiping away the tears.

"We don't know that," said Kett. "We're just—"

"Wrong kid," said Mike, shaking his head. "He wouldn't ever do that. Good as gold, our Kieran. He loves school, loves his friends, loves the gym. Isn't him."

He looked over the top of Jay's head, finding Margaret.

"Right?"

She didn't meet his eye, and the sudden silence in the room was suffocating.

"Right, Mags?"

"Look," said Kett. "There's really only one way to be sure."

The thought of putting them through it was unimaginably awful, but that was the truth. They had to be certain.

"I need one of you to come with me," he said. "I need one of you to take a look at the body."

CHAPTER SIXTEEN

"Got a new boyfriend, Pete?"

Porter struggled down the corridor that led to the interview rooms, glaring at the detective who'd spoken. The reason he was struggling was because he was carrying the mannequin they'd dug out of Jim Prescott's garden. Hay had brought it back to HQ with her a couple of hours ago, but a thorough examination had given up no new information. The dummy had been stripped of its clothing, but the face of the grinning boy was still glued to its head.

"What's his name?" the detective called after him.

"Mr Gofuckyourself," muttered Porter, too quietly for anyone to hear him.

He pushed through the door, almost losing his grip on the smooth plastic. A couple of constables were loitering in the corridor, and he saw one of them open his mouth.

"The next person who calls this thing my boyfriend gets a kick up the arse," he said before anyone could speak. "Where's Prescott?"

"In there," said the constable, nodding to the second room along.

Porter carted the mannequin to the door.

"Just want to say, sir," the constable went on, "I appreciate that you both want to keep your relationship on the down-low."

Porter shot the man a murderous look, but it didn't last long because the interview room door opened and PC Felicity Niven peered out.

"Thought I heard you, sir," she said. "What took you so long?"

"Wanted to wait until Hay had finished with this thing," said Porter, carrying it past her into the room. "Figured we might need it for this one."

Jim Prescott sat in a chair on the other side of the desk, as red-faced and furious as the last time Porter had seen him. When he saw what Porter was carrying, he pushed himself to his feet, as shocked as if he'd seen a real body. He knocked his chair over as he backed into a wall, his hands up to defend himself.

"Calm down," said Porter, dumping the mannequin on one of the chairs. It immediately began to topple off, and he planted a hand on its shoulder to keep it there. "Anyone would have thought you'd seen a ghost."

"I!" said Jim, and he started choking on his own spit, as if the word had poisoned him.

"You what?" said Porter.

PC Niven closed the door and walked over.

"Hold this, would you, Flick?"

"Do I have to, sir?" she asked.

"Hay disinfected it when she was finished. It's clean. Ish."

She still didn't look sure, placing a single hand on the mannequin's neck. Porter sat on the other chair, letting out a long, low groan that made it perfectly clear how he felt about being here. Prescott was still squirming in the corner, his fists clenched, a string of spit hanging from his rubbery lips.

"Sit down, Jim," said Porter. "The sooner you do, the sooner I can never see you again."

Like a scolded child, Prescott shuffled to the chair and picked it up. He plonked himself down on it as far from the desk as he could manage.

"Closer," said Porter.

The man edged forward a couple of inches, the chair letting out a squeal like somebody was dying. Porter extended a finger and beckoned him forward some more, continuing to do so until Prescott had squeaked himself all the way to the desk.

"Don't know why that thing's here," Prescott said. He wasn't even looking at the mannequin, he was staring at the scuffs and stains on the top of the table.

"What thing?" said Porter.

"*That* thing."

"What thing?"

Prescott was about to explode.

"That bloody bastard thing!" he roared, and this time he looked at the dummy. The expression on his face changed, but Porter couldn't work it out. It looked like a plastic mask in the oven, like it was melting. "Why were you digging out there in my garden? Why couldn't you just leave him be?"

"Him?" said Porter.

Prescott put both his shovel-sized hands to his face. Porter wasn't sure, but he might have been crying.

"Look, just so we're clear," he said, "you're not under arrest. We don't think you've done anything..."

He glanced at the mannequin, not quite sure what word to use.

"Uh, wrong?"

Prescott was definitely crying, a choked gargle.

"But the truth is we found this... *thing* buried in your back garden alongside a rucksack that was filled with methamphetamine, cocaine, ecstasy and angel dust. Given that there was enough there to supply about ten nightclubs, and that it was bagged and tagged for distribution, I'd think very carefully about how you want to answer my next few questions."

The contents of the bag had been going on for about twenty grand in street value. Maybe more. They'd also found a digital scale in one of the side pockets, and Hay had managed to lift a decent print from the top of it.

"It's not mine," said Prescott, his words muffled by his hands.

"The bag, or the... boy."

"Both!"

Prescott peeked through his fingers.

"It's not a boy, it's a man."

Porter glanced at the photograph that had been stuck to the mannequin's head.

"This?" he asked. "I don't know, Jim, he looks pretty young to me."

At this, Prescott slammed his hands onto the table—hard enough to make PC Niven let go of the mannequin. It slid off the chair and under the table like it was trying to get back to the man who'd made it. There was no mistaking the look of alarm on Prescott's face, and the expression of relief when Niven had wrestled the dummy back onto the chair.

"Sorry about that," she said.

"Looks like a boy to me, Jim."

"He's a man!" Prescott yelled. "He's over eighteen. I'm not one of *those*."

"One of what?" said Porter. "A paedophile?"

The word seemed to ricochet around the small room like a bullet, and Prescott reeled back like it had hit him in the heart.

"I'm not!" he bellowed. "I wouldn't! I'm not into kids, I just... I'm into..."

If he knew the answer to that, he couldn't find it. Porter took pity on him.

"Like I said, mate, you're not being accused of anything. We went through your collection of reading material, and it's fine."

Fine wasn't the word he'd normally have used for a stash of porn that size, but he was still feeling sorry for him.

"It's pretty vanilla, if you ask me," he went on. "All top shelf magazines, all over eighteen. Fairly eclectic for a man of your generation, if I'm honest. And it's your own business, so I'm not even going to ask you about it."

He rested a hand on the mannequin's shoulder, almost knocking it out of Niven's grip again.

"But it's not every day we see something like this, and I need to understand why you've got a shop dummy in your garden, and a... a chicken-stuffed cock puppet on your bed."

Prescott was deflating like an old balloon, shrinking into his chair with a long puff of breath.

"It won't leave this room," said Porter. "You have my word. Nobody will ever know."

"Nobody *to* know," the man replied with a sad shrug. "Nobody left. Barb's gone, kids never come home."

"So that's what this is?" asked Porter. "A friend?"

Prescott shrugged again, and Porter felt the man's loneliness like a kick to the gut.

"You wanted some company, so you made a pal," he said. "Right?"

"Mannequin was Barb's. She used to sew," Prescott said. "Made clothes for the girls. Weren't doing nothing after she went, so I brought it into bed with me. Nothing worse than an empty bed, is there?"

He was crying again, but much more gently now.

"Was cold at first, so I put clothes on it, used a hot water bottle. After a while I started talking to it, you know? First it was Barb, because I missed her."

He grabbed hold of his shirt, squeezing hard.

"Missed her like you wouldn't believe, even though she did nothing but get on my tits when she were alive. Then... The days are so long. When you lose someone, the days double, triple, they get so long you think all the clocks have broken and the sun's forgotten how to go down."

He sucked in a ratcheting breath, releasing it as a moan of horror.

"And the nights. Christ, man. You just wish you were dead. Better dead than on your own night after night after night."

Porter sat quietly while the man trembled and sobbed.

"And I missed Barb more for having *that* next to me," he said. "I missed her more because of that thing, so I... I made it something else. I made it something I wanted. A proper friend."

"A companion," said Porter when he fell quiet. "I get it. Nothing wrong with that."

Prescott's expression said otherwise. The ripple of loathing that passed over him made his entire body tremble.

"Nothing right with it, though," he said. "I weren't living no more, weren't doing anything but..."

He glared at the mannequin.

"Fucking thing wanted more and more of me so I... I

swore to myself, it ends here. Took it outside one night and buried it."

He jabbed a finger towards the dummy.

"Fucking buried you, and you fucking... you fucking came back!"

He looked like he was about to vault over the desk and attack it.

"Easy," said Porter, holding up a hand. "That's why it was in your garden? Because you wanted to get rid of it?"

"Yeah," said Prescott. "Why the fuck else would it be there? I thought I could get rid of it, thought it'd leave me alone, and he *did*."

He wiped his wet mouth, staring into the middle distance.

"Left me alone," he said.

"For a little while," said Porter. "Right?"

It took an age for Prescott to nod.

"Happens to us all, mate," said Porter. "The addiction never goes away. Not really. So you made another one?"

Prescott continued to nod, his eyes locked on something far away.

"And that's all it was, a companion?"

Nod, nod, nod, like a mechanical man.

"Okay, glad we got that out of the way," said Porter. "Thank you. I just need to know about the rucksack now, Jim. Is it yours?"

"It's not mine."

"And it doesn't belong to your friend, right?" said Porter, tapping the mannequin on the shoulder again. This time it tipped sideways.

"Shit, sorry," said Niven, righting it. "He's a slippery one, isn't he?"

"Course it bloody doesn't belong to him," said Prescott.

"So..."

Prescott adjusted his position on the chair, sitting a little taller. He rested the backs of his hands on the table, staring at his fingers.

"I found it," he said.

The seconds ticked by, but Porter was happy to wait.

"In my garden, this morning. Somebody'd left it there."

"You know who?"

"Course I don't fucking know who," he said. "Wasn't there, was I? Was fast a-fuckin'-sleep. Came out this morning to check the barn and somebody'd slung the bag over the hedge. Was just sitting there."

"You looked inside?"

Prescott shrugged.

"Not my business."

"You saw the drugs?"

"Don't want nothing to do with it," he said. "Or with *them*."

"Them?"

Prescott was losing his patience, baring yellow teeth and bulging eyes at Porter.

"Those fucking kids up at the park," he said, leaning over the desk. "In't the first time they've thrown shit in my garden. Actual shit, sometimes."

"Actual—"

"But it's the other stuff they piss about with, bags of this and that, sometimes knives. They sling it into my garden."

"Why?" asked Porter.

Prescott shrugged.

"Must think nobody lives there."

"Or that whoever does live there couldn't give a shit," said Porter. "Right? How many times have you called in what you found?"

"To *you*?" Prescott scoffed. "Never. None of my business, is it?"

"So you bury it in the garden?"

"Yeah, or burn it, if I've got the fire on."

Porter sat back, shaking his head in disbelief.

"So you found this bag in your garden this morning, and you went out and buried it with your... friend."

Prescott shrugged again.

"I'm so confused," said Porter. "Why not throw it back over the hedge?"

Prescott picked his yellow teeth with a yellow fingernail, then studied what he'd found.

"Don't want no trouble," he said. "They know me, they know I ain't no bother."

"No," said Porter. "Something's not adding up here, Jim. You're not telling me the truth. Drug dealers don't just throw their wares away. They don't give them up like that, because that's a pretty good way of getting yourself killed."

Prescott was still studying whatever he'd picked from his teeth.

"You know what I'm thinking?" Porter asked. "I'm thinking they throw these bags over your hedge because they know you'll look after them. Right?"

Prescott wouldn't meet his eye.

"They know you'll bury them, keep them safe, until they come back to collect them. Right?"

"Wrong," said Prescott, without conviction.

"But why would you do that for them, Jim? Why would you break the law, risk getting arrested, for a bunch of knobends who deal drugs in the park?"

"I want to go home now," said Prescott. "So you can either arrest me, or let me—"

"Jim Prescott," said Porter, leaning over the desk. "I am

arresting you for possession with intent to distribute Class A narc—"

"Alright!" the man shouted, drumming both fists on the table. "Alright, there's no fucking need to do that! They caught me..."

He growled at the ceiling, and Porter sensed another secret about to tear its way free.

"They caught me looking at them one day, up at the park. And I weren't even doing that, was I? I was just walking up the hill, minding my... But they thought I was looking at them, those young men, and they started having a go at me, calling me all sorts of names, saying they were going to call the police, or worse, call somebody to beat me up for being a..."

He wiped his leaky mouth with both hands.

"I'm not one of *them*. But the fucking pricks wouldn't let me go until they made me swear I'd look after something for them. A bag. Told me to keep it safe, told me somebody would be by to pick it up another day."

"And somebody was?"

"Yeah, they was. 'Bout a week later, just came and took it, didn't see 'em. Was in my barn."

"How many times have you done this, Jim?"

"Three, four, ten—how the fuck do I know?"

"Okay," said Porter, trying to calm him down. "So somebody gave you the bag we found in your garden, yeah?"

Prescott nodded.

"Who?"

"Fuckin' kid," he spat.

"Last night?"

"Middle of the fucking night, yeah. Showed up before dawn hammerin' on my door."

"You've seen him before?"

"No. I don't know."

"What did he look like?"

"Like a fucking walking tracksuit," said Prescott. "Hood up, collar round his face. I didn't see. Just said to look after the bag until somebody came calling. Then he fucked off."

Porter nodded. Prescott looked like a man whose every bone had been filleted. It was a wonder he hadn't slid off his chair.

"What kind of tracksuit?" said Porter. "What colour?"

"Black," said Jim. "But he had a red coat. That's all I know. Can I go now? I'm tired."

"You just admitted to working for drug dealers, Jim," said Porter. "What do you think?"

He pushed back his chair and stood up.

"You're going to a cell until we figure out what we're charging you with. And what that will be depends entirely on you telling us some more about who gave you that bag."

He walked to the door, stopping when Prescott called out behind him. The man was staring at the mannequin, his hands kneading invisible dough.

"You think I could take him with me? To my cell? It's pretty lone—"

"Lonely, yeah, we get it," said Porter, opening the door. "And no, you bloody can't."

CHAPTER SEVENTEEN

Kett leaned against the wall outside the morgue, wishing he still smoked.

It was well into the evening now, and the night had turned bitter. It felt like every single bone in his body had frozen over. One good bump and they'd all shatter.

It was still better than being inside, though.

It was better than having to see what rested there on a cold steel tray.

He glanced through the door, wondering whether Mike Spicer had made it to the body yet. They'd driven back to HQ half an hour ago, after leaving Margaret's house, Mike following Kett in his bright blue BMW X6. Kett had offered to go in with him, of course, but he'd insisted on accompanying Franklin alone.

Kett didn't blame him. Some things you didn't want an audience for.

He blew out a lungful of air, watching the cloud of breath dissipate like cigarette smoke. The cravings were as strong as they ever were, even though he hadn't touched one since he'd known Alice was on her way—twelve years ago now. They were always worse during a case. Back when he'd worked the Met, nicotine had kept him sane. Those quiet moments away from the yard, away from the blood, away from the violence.

He'd literally kill for one right now.

"Oi-oi," came a voice from the far end of the car park.

Kett squinted into the shadows as somebody walked through them, the heels of their shoes clacking. It was Porter, the big DI pulling his coat around him as he approached.

"Oi-oi?" said Kett. "How old are you, Pete?"

"Chuffin' cold, isn't it, sir?" said Porter, huddling so close that their arms touched. Kett didn't mind, the warmth of the man was welcome. "What're you doing standing out here?"

"I don't know," said Kett, glancing through the door into the stark, empty interior of the morgue. "Just hate that place."

"Me too," said Porter, shivering. "Gives me the willies."

"What are you doing here?" Kett asked him.

"Just finished up with Jim Prescott, sir. Grilled him about his wank muppets."

The laugh was out before Kett could stop it.

"He made them because he was lonely," Porter went on. "But he also confessed to working with the gangs that deal over at the park."

"What?" said Kett.

"Working with is a bit of an exaggeration," said Porter. "They caught him perving at them one day, bullied him into looking after some of their gear. He stashes bags for them."

"Like the bag we found in the garden?" said Kett. Porter nodded.

"Some kid dropped it off this morning, near dawn.

Prescott couldn't ID him, hood and mask and all that. But he had a red coat. Kid told him to look after the bag so he buried it next to his dead sex puppet. The *first* one. This was right before Kate got there."

"That's good work," said Kett. "The bag gets dropped off at the same time the body gets left in the park. Can't be a coincidence."

"Right," said Porter. He stamped his feet and patted his pockets.

"You got smokes in there, Pete?" said Kett.

Porter laughed.

"No, sir, force of habit. You feeling it too?"

"Yeah."

"It's the weather," said Porter. "Gets me every year. Like I said to Prescott just now, the addiction never leaves you."

Kett heard a door slam deeper in the morgue.

"Who's in there?" asked Porter.

"Mike Spicer," said Kett. "I'm guessing he's the father of our dead kid."

"Shit."

Kett breathed out another cloud of smoke, trying to find a glimmer of joy in the memory.

"Shit indeed."

Another clanging door, then Mike Spicer appeared in the lobby. He was almost running as he made his way to the exit, and Kett had to move quickly to avoid the doors as they swung open.

"Mike," he started, but the man barrelled past, breaking into a sprint. "Mike!"

The shadows swallowed him whole.

"Shit," Kett said, turning to Porter. "Do me a favour and go after him, will you? He looks like a man on his way to do something stupid."

"Yes, sir," said Porter, jogging off.

"Be careful, Pete," Kett yelled.

He made his way into the lobby of the morgue just as Emily Franklin was coming out of the door opposite, a bottle of Irn-Bru in her hand. The look on her face told Kett everything he needed to know, but he asked anyway.

"His son?"

Franklin nodded.

"No doubt at all. It's Kieran Spicer."

"He say anything?" asked Kett.

"Not much. He said he'd never seen the tattoo on Kieran's wrist before, the red line. Oh, and he asked if Kieran had been found alone."

"That's a weird thing to ask, isn't it?" said Kett.

"That's what I thought," she replied, taking a sip of her drink. "I said he had, and he said something else. I couldn't hear it. Sounded like 'he shouldn't have been on his own,' but I don't know for sure."

"Thanks, Emily," said Kett.

"Where's he gone?" she asked.

"Nowhere good," he told her. "You found anything else on the body?"

"Nothing worth reporting. You'll know if that changes."

He gave her a half-hearted salute as he walked out into the night. It was cold enough now that when he tried to pull his phone out of his pocket, it almost slipped from his numb fingers. It seemed to take an age for him to find Savage's name as he trudged towards the main building, and another age for her to answer.

"Sir?"

"Where are you, Kate?" he asked.

"Still at the Spicer house, sir," she said, her voice little more than a whisper. "Aaron and I are putting Peanut to bed while we wait to hear. Is it... Was it him?"

"Yeah," said Kett. "Kieran Spicer. The dad confirmed it. He stormed out of here in a hurry, looked like he was gunning for somebody. I'm going to send a couple of units to you just in case it's Margaret he's after."

"Okay, sir."

Kett stopped walking, staring up and seeing for the first time that the sky had cleared. Stars had gathered, more than he'd seen in some time. It took him by surprise, and for a few seconds he was stunned into silence.

"Sir?"

"Sorry," he said. "Mike said Kieran shouldn't have been on his own last night, or at least that's what Franklin thought she heard. What do you make of that?"

"That he should have been home?" came Savage's reply. "Or his mum should have been there?"

"Or his friend," said Kett. "Margaret said they were thick as thieves, right? If your son turns up dead and somebody was supposed to be with him, you'd be angry."

"You're thinking of Jonah?" said Savage.

"Yeah. Nobody's been out to talk to him yet, have they?"

"No, sir. I can go, but somebody should be here. Somebody needs to tell her..."

"I'll do it," said Kett. "I'm on my way now, I'll see if I can find a FLO."

He studied the stars for a moment more, patting his pockets with his free hand the way he always did when the cases got too hard, when bad things just kept on happening.

Force of habit.

"Leave the bedtime stories to Duke," he said, turning reluctantly back to the real world. "And get over to Jonah's house."

THE AUDI CRAWLED down the dimly lit street, Savage scanning the numbers on each property as she passed. They were all shabby bungalows that had seen better days, lined up in a drunken formation that made her think of *Dad's Army*. Even though it wasn't even nine yet, only a handful of them had their lights on.

She hadn't wanted to leave the Spicer house, not now, not when Margaret's life was about to be reduced to ash. In less than half an hour, she'd find out for sure that the boy who was butchered in the park was her son. There was no going back from that. No recovery. There was only before, and after—an epilogue that would haunt her for the rest of her life.

There was a chance she already knew, of course, a chance that Mike had called her. And that was the other reason she hadn't wanted to leave.

Because if Duke was the only copper in the house when that happened, he was well out of his depth.

But all had been calm when she'd left. Peanut had been asleep, and Jay had been curled up with his mum in Kieran's bed, both of them looking like they were close to drifting off. It was their final moment of calm, that beautiful place where there was still hope.

Let them have it.

"There you are," she said, finally spotting the property she was looking for.

She pulled the car up to the kerb and killed the engine. The sound of her door slamming shut echoed across the quiet street, setting off a dog inside one of the houses. She pulled her collar up against the cold, jogging to the low wall of the Whites' decrepit bungalow. The closest streetlight was way back on the corner, and the overgrown garden looked silver in the moonlight. She followed a cracked path, pounding on the flimsy door loud enough to set off a second dog nearby.

"Jonah White?" she called out. "It's the police."

She made her way to the window as she waited, cupping her hand to the glass to see that the curtains were open, the room inside pitch black. She walked around the corner and tried the next one, but it didn't seem like there was a single light on in the building. Shivering, she made her way down the side passage and into the small garden, peering through the kitchen window before trying the back door.

It was unlocked, creaking open.

"Hello?" she called out. "Is anyone here? It's the police."

The house held its breath, no sound other than those distant barking dogs.

She hovered in the open door for a moment before making a decision.

"I'm coming in," she said. "If anyone is here, make yourself known."

She couldn't see a thing in the dark, so she slid her hand along the smooth wall until she found a switch. She was inside a utility room, a washing machine tucked under the counter and, somewhat inexplicably, a toilet plumbed into the opposite wall. Past the small room was a corridor, open doors like gaping mouths.

"Hello?" she called out again, her voice too loud in the cramped space. "Jonah?"

In the kitchen, dishes were piled in the sink, a bottle of milk fast turning to cheese on the counter. The mugs on the table all had green fur in them, and she had to put a hand to her face against the stench of rot. The living room wasn't much better, two ashtrays overflowing with cigarette butts and what Savage was almost certain were mouse droppings on the carpet.

She made her way through the house, leaving the lights on as she went. It didn't take long to conclude that the place was empty, but it would take more time to search it properly because it was in such a state. All three bedrooms were piled high with junk—*literal* junk, like a whole street's worth of garden sheds and garages had been emptied in here. Mouldering deck chairs and bags full of clothes and old bikes and about fifty opened cans of paint competed for space amongst dozens of damp cardboard boxes. Only two of the bedrooms had beds, and Savage wouldn't have slept in either if somebody had offered her a million pounds.

She pulled out her phone and texted Kett:

Inside Jonah White's house, nobody here, place looks like it's been abandoned for weeks.

She returned to the bigger bedroom at the front of the bungalow. She'd spotted a few shoe boxes in the mess, piled next to the teak wardrobe in one corner. They looked new, and sure enough when she lifted the lid of one she saw a pair of mint condition Nikes. The next box down held an even more expensive pair of trainers. Both were a size 9.

She turned her attention to the bed, which was piled high with clothes. She didn't particularly want to touch them, but they seemed to be the kind of thing a teenage boy would wear: Nike tracksuits, North Face jackets, a couple of Hoodrich jumpers that didn't look like they'd ever been worn.

She crouched by the bedside table, opening the drawer to see a handful of twenty-pound notes alongside some receipts. There was more crap beneath the bed, and she pulled out her torch, clicking it on to see what had to be dozens of shopping bags plus even more clothes.

And there, just out of reach, a phone.

She wormed her way beneath the bed, the frame grating against her back like it was trying to crush her. It was too low, she couldn't get far enough to reach the phone. She squeezed in a little more, then lay still when the sound of a big engine rose up from the street. It stopped right outside, a door opening and closing.

And finally, a shout.

"Jonah!"

It was a man, his voice choked with rage and grief. He screamed the name again and Savage pushed herself out from beneath the bed. She scrambled up, running to the window and ripping open the curtains.

Mike Spicer was right there, standing on the path—just a shadow silhouetted against the faraway streetlight. In one hand he held a bottle, and Savage wondered if he'd been drinking.

"Jonah!" Mike roared. "You fucking *left* him!"

Mike lifted the bottle, just enough light on the street for Savage to see the strip of cloth that hung from the open top.

With his free hand, Mike snapped open a lighter and fired it up.

"Oh shit," said Savage.

She hammered on the window.

"Police! Mike, don't you dare!"

But the man was lost, his face a storm of emotion as he lit the end of the taper. The cloth ignited, and before Savage could say another word he'd hurled it at the bungalow.

She staggered back as the Molotov cocktail struck the front of the building, liquid fire splashing over the window.

The heat of it was instant, the glass cracking like a gunshot, the room boiling beneath the force of the flames outside.

Savage swore again, running for the door.

Stopping.

She looked back, thinking about the phone she'd seen beneath the bed.

Another bottle struck the window hard enough to shatter it, a hail of glass followed by an actual wave of fire. It spilled into the room, engulfing the boxes that were stacked by the window, gorging itself on them.

Savage dropped onto her hands and knees, diving beneath the bed again. She reached for the phone, the scene lit by firelight as the flames ate their way through the room.

She couldn't reach it.

She jutted her torch out, catching the edge of the phone and dragging it closer. It inched towards her, painfully slowly. The heat was unbearable, the fire almost touching her legs, the thunder of it the loudest thing in the world. The smoke was creeping into her lungs, impossibly hot.

Outside, another bottle smashed against the bungalow, and the entire building seemed to groan.

"Come on!" Savage screamed.

She swiped the torch again and the phone spun out, vanishing beneath a pile of bags. She pushed back, the bed doing its best to pin her to the floor, to hold her there for the hungry flames. Growling, she heaved herself out from under it, crawling to the bags even as the fire reached them.

She grabbed the phone, coughing hard as she felt her way across the room. One side was a wall of fire, the other a wall of smoke, but once she was through the door into the corridor, the cool, clear air embraced her. She stuffed the phone into her pocket, pulling out her own and calling 999 as she passed through the utility room and into the back garden.

"This is DC Kate Savage, Norfolk Police," she said when the operator answered. "I need fire and police, Kennedy Close in Dereham. Fast."

The entire front end of the bungalow was a pyre, the heat so intense that Savage had to jump the wall into the neighbour's driveway to get past it. By the time she'd reached the street, Mike Spicer was back at his car, halfway into the boot.

"Oi!" she yelled. "Mike, stop!"

He stepped back, his face dripping with sweat, his eyes burning more fiercely than the flames. Confusion creased his face, but only for a second before the fury took over again.

He was holding a fresh Molotov cocktail, the lighter still gripped in his hand.

"Put it down," said Savage. She took a step towards him, but only because the heat was blistering her back. "Put it down, Mike."

"Why?" he screamed. "So that little shit can get away with it?"

He staggered towards her.

"You protect him, and you die too."

Every line of his face showed he meant it.

"He's not even here," said Savage. "The house is empty."

She wasn't sure if her words had registered. Mike's attention was on the lighter as he flicked it once, twice. It lit on the third try, the rag in the bottle erupting.

"You die too," he said.

He cocked his arm, his body tensing.

The road suddenly lit up—not fire, but headlights. A car

gunned down the street, the engine roaring as it accelerated. Mike didn't even have time to look back before it thumped into him, slamming him off the side of the BMW and rolling him down the street.

The bottle smashed, a river of fire flowing alongside him, then *over* him. Mike sucked in a breath, and the scream that tore from his mouth was like nothing Savage had ever heard before.

Porter clambered out of the stationary Mondeo.

"Kate!" he yelled, and his voice shocked her from her paralysis. She ran down the street.

"Fuck," said Porter, clattering up beside her. The asphalt was a puddle of fire, and he grabbed Mike by his shirt, hauling him out of the flames.

Savage ripped off her coat and slung it on Mike's thrashing body, throwing herself on top. Porter dropped down beside her, smacking his big hands on the flames until the last of them guttered out. Mike lay there in a smoking heap, his face screwed shut with pain, his body curled tight. Porter was pulling a set of cuffs from his coat, but Savage didn't think they'd need them.

"Hell was that all about?" Porter said, holding the handcuffs and staring at the bungalow. The fire had found the tins of paint, the flames roaring like a jet engine, blazing green and blue. People were emerging from their houses, watching in horror.

"I have no idea," said Savage, getting to her feet. "But thank you. I think he would have thrown it at me."

Porter nodded, the flames lighting up his face. He rubbed his shoulder with his free hand.

"I think so too," he said. "You okay?"

Savage laughed.

"Is there ever a good answer to that, sir?"

CHAPTER EIGHTEEN

It was always the worst part of the job.

"I am so sorry, Margaret," said Kett. "I really am."

He stood in the Spicers' kitchen, the smell of waffles still hanging in the air, the heat unbearable. Margaret sat with her head on the dining table, her hands in her hair, her sobs almost silent. These were the reactions he found hardest. The shouting and the screaming and the wailing were bad, but there was something so natural about it, so human. Those were the songs of grief, ancient and cathartic.

The silence is what killed him.

Margaret had barely reacted when he'd told her that Kieran's death had been confirmed, but he'd seen the way her face went slack and her eyes dulled—as if she, too, had died. She had folded herself around the table, shrivelling like an insect in a fire, contracting as if to pull herself out of the world. She hadn't moved in the ten minutes since, other than those almost imperceptible sobs, the juddering of a broken machine.

Kett understood it all too well. He knew that feeling. He'd been there. If you didn't move, if you didn't speak, if you stayed bone still and dead quiet, then it didn't have to be real.

The only blessing was that the boys were asleep.

"If there's anything we can do for you, just ask," said Kett, glancing to the kitchen door where PC Jenny Scott stood—one of the force's Family Liaison Officers. She was an older woman, her face wrinkled with kindness, her eyes bright. She nodded to Kett.

"I can take it from here, sir, if you'd like me to."

There was nothing else he could do. He wanted to promise Margaret that it would all be okay, promise that the sadness would pass, promise that they'd catch whoever had done this to her oldest son.

But he didn't want to leave the house with a lie.

"Call me if you need anything," he said to PC Scott as he walked past. "Look after them."

"It's what we do," she said.

Kett nodded, but he couldn't agree. They hadn't looked after Kieran Spicer at all. The boy had been sliced into ribbons, his body paraded around the park in the middle of the night.

"How is she, sir?" asked Duke from where he stood in the front hall. He had his hat in his hands, and his face was gaunt.

Kett nodded for him to open the door and they stepped out together. Duke closed it as quietly as he could.

"About how you'd expect," said Kett when he realised the PC was still waiting for an answer.

"Gutted for them," said Duke. "You can't imagine it, can you? Those boys are going to be devastated. They both idolise their brother."

Kett nodded, trying to imagine how he'd break the news to his own daughters. He walked down the gravel driveway and onto the street, pulling out his phone as he went. Before he could look at it, he glanced at the house next door to the Spicer place, seeing the man they'd spoken to earlier—Morris Gough—staring from an upstairs window.

He wasn't sure if it was his imagination, or if he was grinning.

Kett ignored him, turning back to his phone. He'd switched on *Do Not Disturb* before speaking to Margaret, and when he swiped it off he saw a dozen or more texts and missed calls clatter onto his screen. Most were from Savage.

"What the hell?" he said as he cycled through them.

"Is that Kate?" said Duke, peering over Kett's shoulder. "She went to Jonah White's house, sir. Mike Spicer was throwing Molotov cocktails."

"What?" said Kett.

"He tried to lob one at her, but Porter ran him over."

"*What?*"

"I would have told you, but you were busy," said Duke, shrugging. "She's okay, I spoke to her."

"Jesus Christ," said Kett, heading for the road. "Will it ever bloody end?"

THEY DIDN'T NEED AN ADDRESS, because when they reached the end of the street, a fire engine was tearing past, its siren deafening. Kett followed it for less than two minutes before he turned a corner and saw the flames reaching for the night sky. Another fire engine was already there, the firefighters scrambling to get the hose into position. He couldn't see anything past it.

He clambered out into the heat and the smoke, coughing his way around the fire engine. A little way ahead, on the left side of the road, a bungalow was lost inside an inferno. It roared like a blowtorch as it burned, cannon-like snaps and cracks from inside. The heat was insane, blasting away every trace of the cold night.

A crowd had gathered at the corner to watch, their wide eyes reflecting the flames. The smokies must have evacuated the nearby houses, because the fire had already spread onto the roof of the bungalow next door. If they didn't hurry up and get those hoses working, they could lose the whole street.

"That's Kate's car, sir," said Duke, stepping up beside him and pointing to an Audi. Porter's Mondeo was there too, and Spicer's blue BMW, which was close enough to the pyre that it was in danger of going up in flames. "Can't see her."

"They're in there," said a firefighter as he ran past, a coil of hose looped over his shoulder. He nodded to a house a little further down the road, the front door open.

"Why?" Kett asked, but the man was already gone.

He crossed the street, approaching the house to see a little old man standing outside the open front door. He had to be ninety if he was a day, dressed in striped pyjamas and smoking a cigarillo.

"Hi," said Kett, fishing out his warrant card. "You got some police in there?"

The man exhaled a cloud of acrid smoke and hitched a thumb over his shoulder. Kett squeezed past him into a narrow corridor, following the sound of voices into a cosy living room. It was no small relief to see Savage on the sofa and Porter standing by the window. Both looked knackered, but unhurt, and both were holding a china teacup that looked small enough to have come from a doll's house.

Mike Spicer sat uncomfortably on a chair, his hands

cuffed behind his back. He was wheezing a little, his eyes closed. The room reeked of chemicals—white spirit and alcohol.

"You alright?" Kett asked Savage.

"I am, sir," she said. "Thanks to Porter."

"I heard. Good work, Pete."

Porter took a delicate sip of his tea.

"This dickhead was lobbing bombs," he said, giving Mike's chair a kick. The man groaned, trying to find a comfortable position. "He's lucky I didn't roll back over him."

"You actually ran him over?" said Kett. "Like... a full *smoosh*?"

Porter frowned, and Mike finally opened his eyes. One was bloodshot.

"No, sir," said Porter. "Just a nudge. I was only doing twenty."

"Busted my fucking rib," wheezed Mike, but there was no anger there. He looked like a broken man.

"What the hell were you—"

"Language," came a gruff call from the old man by the front door.

"Oh, uh... sorry." Kett moved closer to Mike. "Molotov cocktails? What were you thinking?"

Mike scoffed, digging at the carpet with his trainers.

"Wasn't thinking, was I? Just... just found out my boy died. Just... just fucking lost it."

"Language," the old man said again.

"But how did you even have them?" said Kett.

"Boot full of booze," said Porter. "Strong stuff."

"I improvised," said Mike.

"I find that hard to believe," said Kett. "You just happened to have bottles, fuses and a lighter in your car?"

Mike closed his eyes, clearly struggling with the pain. The tattoo on his neck had blistered a little, the skin raw.

"Ambulance is on its way," said Savage. "Bill and Mary kindly opened their house for us while we waited."

"I'm sure they'll make you a cuppa," said Porter.

"Already have, dear."

A woman walked into the room, a tray rattling in her gnarled hands. She was even older than the man, and Kett took the tray before she dropped it. He put it down on the coffee table, trying to ignore the heavenly scent of tea that rose from the pot.

"Thank you," he said. "Mary, right?"

"That's me," she said, studying Kett with rheumy eyes, then straining to get a better look at Duke. "Gosh," she said. "I think we're going to need more biscuits, Bill."

"We don't need biscuits, thank you," said Kett.

"*He* definitely doesn't need a biscuit," said Porter, spraying crumbs from the custard cream he was eating.

"He'd like a biscuit, wouldn't he?" said Mary, giving Duke's stomach a pinch. "Wasting away, he is."

"Maybe just one biscuit," said Duke. "Thank you."

Kett waited for the woman to shuffle away before turning back to Mike.

"Forget about the how for a minute," he said. "Tell me *why*. Why were you at Jonah's house?"

Mike sucked in a breath, then groaned it back out again.

"So fucking stupid," he said, quiet enough that it didn't earn a reprimand from Bill.

"Tonight?" said Kett when he didn't continue. "Yeah, you're not wrong."

"No," said Mike. "Not tonight. Had my reasons, I'll stick by them. Doesn't matter what happens to me now, it's over. Lost my boy, no fucking point to it."

"You've got two more sons," said Duke, enough anger in his voice to make Kett turn around and shoot the PC a look.

"Nah, I don't," said Mike. "Maggie does, not me. Those boys won't even look at me after what she's told them. Key was the only one who loved me, always did. Loved him too, so..."

His body heaved, and he actually cried out with the pain of it.

"So much," he finished, the tears rolling down his smoke-scarred face.

"What was stupid, then?" said Kett.

Mike sniffed. He looked to the ceiling, even though his eyes were closed.

"I can't tell you," he said. "Not now."

Kett was about to ask another question when Duke bustled past, heading for the coffee table. He picked up the pot in his giant hand, tea going everywhere as he tried to fill the tiny cups.

"Sorry," he said to nobody in particular. "Gasping."

"If Kieran was doing something bad, Mike," Kett said, and he had to pause again while Duke almost upended the milk jug.

"Sorry."

"Uh, if he was doing something illegal, then it can't hurt him," Kett went on. "He can't be punished for it now."

"Can't he?" said Mike. "Not by you lot, maybe, but there are different kinds of punishment."

"Like what?" said Kett.

"Like your whole reputation being trashed. Like nobody ever looking at you the same again because they found out something. He was a good kid; he doesn't deserve that. And it's not him getting punished, is it?"

"It's you," said Kett.

Mike scoffed.

"I couldn't care less what people think about me. But it would break Maggie's heart if she found out."

Duke straightened slowly, a cup in each hand, tea raining onto the carpet. Kett was close to screaming at him, but when the PC handed him one of the brews he felt his temper calming. He took a sip just so he wouldn't lose any more of it to gravity, and almost spat it back out again. It was the sweetest tea he'd ever drunk.

"You put sugar in this?" he asked.

"No, sir," said Duke, downing his cup in one gulp.

"Right," said Kett, struggling to find his train of thought. "Uh... Maggie, right. So Kieran *was* doing something bad? Something his mum wouldn't approve of?"

Mike didn't reply, his face screwed up with pain. Outside on the street, a siren bleeped. Probably the ambulance. Kett finished the thimbleful of tea and put the cup back on the tray.

"Nobody else has to find out," he said. "Not even Maggie, if you think that's best. But Mike, somebody did this to your son. Somebody killed Kieran."

Mike flinched like he'd been stabbed.

"You don't want them to get away with that. And you don't want them to do it to somebody else, right?"

Still nothing.

"Mike," said Kett. "He's gone, but you're still his dad. You can still do the right thing."

Mike sighed as well as his ribs would let him, his eyes still shut.

"He was pushing," he said, just a whisper.

"Drugs?" asked Kett.

"Yeah. With them boys over at the park. That shithead Jonah got him into it. Little runt got fuck all—"

"Language!"

"Got fuck all in his life," Mike said, ignoring the old man. "You seen where he lives, he's a piece of trash. He started pushing for them boys, and suddenly he was wearing all the good gear, all the good kicks. And he was trying to get my lad to do it."

He opened his eyes, looking at Kett.

"You got kids?"

Kett nodded.

"Boys?"

"Girls," he said. "Young, still."

"They ever do what you tell them? They ever listen?"

Kett laughed quietly, and it was answer enough.

"That never changes," said Mike, leaning forward and wincing again. "I knew if I told Key he couldn't do it, he'd do it anyway. So I made a deal with him instead, him and Joe. Said if they promised to look out for each other, to always be there for each other, and to get the fuck out as soon as they saw any sign of proper danger, then they could do whatever they wanted."

"Just so we're clear," said Kett, "you gave him permission to sell drugs?"

"No," said Mike. "I knew you wouldn't get it. It's not like that. I gave him permission to... to be safe."

That last word died slowly on his lips.

"It's okay," said Kett, trying to stop him from clamming up again. "Kieran and Jonah were working together, with the boys at the park. Can you tell me anything about them?"

"Only what Key told me," said Mike. "Local lads, but not from Dereham, from out King's Lynn way. He said they were a bunch of duds, wannabe hard men. They got their product in from somebody else, though. Some London crew."

"You know any names?" said Kett.

Mike shook his head, then frowned.

"Wait, uh, he did mention one. Uh... Nick, or Nicky, or... Niko. That was it, Niko. Probably made it up to make himself look like a gangster. Key said he was the biggest prick of them all, thought he was in charge."

"Niko ran the local gang?" said Kett. "He got the drugs from London, distributed them to the dealers, including Kieran and Jonah. Right? The lads would sell the drugs and push the money back."

Mike shrugged.

"Far as I know. It wasn't like they were slinging kilos of cocaine or anything. Heroin, any of that shit. Bit of weed to the kids, no harm in it. He always had a few quid on him, nothing major. He wasn't Scarface."

"He was slinging pretty much everything," said Kett. "Including heroin."

Mike shook his head.

"Nah, mate, he wasn't."

It wasn't worth arguing about.

"Is that what Kieran was doing last night?" asked Kett.

Mike was still shaking his head.

"Don't know," he said. "But Saturday night? Probably. He'd stay at mine when he was working, unless he was at Joe's, because I don't ask questions like his mum does. Turned up at all hours, Joe sometimes too, although I never liked the little shit."

"Language!"

"It's pretty obvious you don't like him," said Kett. "You tried to burn his house down. You thought he was inside?"

Mike nodded.

"You were angry because he should have been there

with Kieran when he was attacked? He should have helped him?"

"That was the deal," said Mike. "That's all I wanted. I wanted him to keep my boy safe. I said if they were out doing anything dodgy, stay together. It's all I asked."

He took a shuddering breath.

"Key was on his own?"

"We don't know for sure," said Kett. "He wasn't... The body was moved to the park, we don't know where he died. Jonah might have been there."

Mike shook his head.

"Sometimes you do stupid shit without thinking it through," he said.

"You don't say," answered Kett.

"Maggie okay?" Mike asked. "You told her?"

"We did," said Kett. "And no, she isn't."

"I should probably go over there," said Mike. "Check on her and the boys."

He started to get up, then seemed to remember the cuffs on his wrists.

"Oh, yeah," he said, easing himself back into the chair. "The fire."

"Right," said Kett. "The fire. Pete, can you book him?"

"Already done, sir," said Porter. "I'll ride over to the hospital with him."

Kett nodded, heading for the door but thinking better of it.

"If there's anything else, let us know," he said to Mike. "Because I want to find the people that did this. Doesn't matter what he was doing, Kieran didn't deserve to die the way he did."

Mike nodded what might have been a thanks, a fat tear rolling down his face.

Kett walked out of the room, heading for the front door. The ambulance was right outside, the paramedics watching as the firefighters battled the flames. The old man was finishing his cigarillo, putting it out in a flowerpot full of sand. He turned to Kett as he appeared.

"You lot don't half have potty mouths," he said.

"Sorry. We appreciate the hospitality."

"Tea okay?" he asked, shuffling painfully until he was facing Kett. "Mary puts sugar in the pot. Tastes like a fairy's glittery bumhole."

"Language," said Kett, and the old man laughed.

Savage squeezed through the door, standing next to him. She nodded down the street to Jonah's bungalow.

"You know who lives in that house, Bill?"

"Know who used to live there," he said. "Deirdre. Lovely old bird. Lived here almost as long as we have, since they built the bloody things. 1956. She died a couple of years ago."

"Was there a lad living there too?" asked Kett. "A teenager?"

The man's face wrinkled into a scowl.

"Yeah, right little bugger that one. Joseph, his name is. Or something like that."

"Jonah?"

"Maybe. Arrogant as they come. Don't think he had parents, not ones that wanted him anyway. Can't say I blame them. Deirdre watched over him, him and his brother Spence."

"Spence still about?"

"Nah, he moved out earlier this year. Older, he was, by quite a bit, I think."

"So Jonah's been on his own in there?" said Savage.

Bill frowned.

"Must'a been," he said. "Little young for that, come to think of it."

"It didn't seem like an adult lived there," said Savage. "Not a responsible one, anyway."

"You remember the last time you saw Jonah?" asked Kett.

Bill shook his head.

"Can't remember the last time I went for a wee," he said.

"Coming through," said Porter.

Kett stepped to the side to let Mike through, Porter steering him down the path towards the ambulance.

"Don't worry lads," the DI shouted to the paramedics. "We'll come out to you, don't trouble yourselves with a stretcher or anything, we're absolutely fine."

The paramedics hopped to attention. Bill struggled over the low step and into the bungalow.

"Goodnight, then," he said.

"I think you've still got one in there," said Kett. "Duke! We're going!"

Duke appeared, still holding his tiny cup in one hand and a packet of custard creams in the other.

"Leave the biscuits," ordered Kett.

Duke handed the cup and the packet to Bill as he passed, closing the door behind him.

"You find anything in the house before Mike burned it down?" asked Kett.

"Just this," said Savage, pulling a phone out of her pocket. "It's dead."

"Then let's bring it back to life," said Kett, watching Mike Spicer clamber into the back of the ambulance. "With any luck, all the answers we need will be on there."

CHAPTER NINETEEN

It was almost eleven by the time Kett arrived back at HQ, and he was so tired he thought he might have to crawl from his car to the building. He managed to stay on his feet, limping through the empty reception and down the corridor towards the MIT offices.

He pushed through the door to see that the bullpen was deserted. So was Clare's office, so he made his way to the Incident Room. Savage and Spalding were sitting together at a desk, a laptop open in front of them and the phone that Savage had rescued from Jonah White's place plugged into it. The room reeked of smoke from Savage's clothes.

They looked around together as he walked in.

"Fire out, sir?" asked Savage.

"Just," he said.

The fire crew had only managed to extinguish the inferno an hour ago. The bungalow—and one of the neighbouring properties—had been reduced to a smoking sculpture of charred beams and blackened bricks.

"They find anyone?"

"Inside?" he asked, pulling up a chair. "It's still too hot. But you said it was empty, didn't you?"

"I didn't check the loft," she said. "There was no time. I keep thinking what if Jonah was hiding up there?"

It was too horrific to even imagine.

"Don't torture yourself," said Kett. "You'd have heard him. He wasn't there."

She nodded, but she didn't look sure.

"Aaron with you, sir?"

"I sent him home," said Kett. "He kept telling me how much his clangers hurt. His words, not mine. There are only so many times I can have Duke's clangers in my mind's eye before I want to jump off a bridge."

"They are still pretty swollen," said Savage, and Kett shut her up with a look.

"Boss about?" he asked.

"Haven't seen him, sir," said Savage. "Been pretty quiet."

"Probably just as well," said Kett, leaning back in the chair to stretch the vertebrae in his back. "He'd only be yelling at us."

"Telling us we're not tossing hard enough!" said Savage, snorting a laugh.

"I heard that!" came a roar from the corridor, the shock of it so loud that Kett's chair almost tipped backwards. He grabbed the table, thumping back onto four legs. "For the record," Superintendent Clare continued as he walked into the room, "I only shout at you when you're *not tossing hard enough!*"

His voice was loud enough to make Kett's ears ring.

"Boss is here," said Spalding with an enormous grin.

"Yeah," said Kett. "I can see that."

"What have you got, then?" said Clare, grabbing a chair

and mounting it like he was climbing onto a horse. "Because I'll tell you what you *don't got*, you *don't got* the tosser who killed our boy."

"We're getting closer, sir," said Kett. "Mike Spicer confirmed his son was selling drugs with the gang at the park. He was working with his mate Jonah."

"Whose house you burned down," said Clare, glaring at Savage.

"I didn't burn it down, sir..."

"Mike knew about it, condoned it, even," said Kett.

"Condoned his son being a drug dealer?"

"Yeah. He was furious because he asked Jonah to keep an eye on Kieran, keep him safe. That was the deal he made with them. He thinks Jonah abandoned Kieran, left him to die. But there's no way he could know that."

Kett paused, chewing on it.

"Unless he knows more than he's letting on," he said. "Did we find out anything about Mike?"

"Yes, sir," said Savage, digging out her notepad. "He's forty-seven, owns the pub in Dillington, the Fat Monk."

"So that's why he had a boot full of booze," said Kett.

"He's known to us after a couple of assaults and affrays back in the nineties, nothing he went to prison for. Married Margaret Shepherd in 2002, bought the house two years later, then Kieran turned up in 2007. They separated in '09, but it was on and off, because they had the other two boys together. Never divorced. He's been living in the pub for the last eight years or so, doesn't see the little ones much. Nothing to suggest he was involved with the gangs or the drugs, but I checked the record and we've raided his pub a couple of times over the years, picked up a handful of punters on possession charges. Oh, and they had a lock-in on Saturday night, he was there until the early hours."

"Confirmed?" said Kett.

She nodded.

"Do we know anything about the kids in the park?" said Clare.

"We know they were dealing pretty much everything under the sun," said Kett. "They bullied Jim Prescott into—"

"Who?" said Clare.

"The sex chicken puppet guy," said Kett. "They bullied him into holding drugs for them. He admitted that but didn't give us much else, other than to say somebody dropped off a rucksack of drugs in the night. Spicer said the park lads are connected to a gang in London. County Lines for sure. Your Willy told me—"

"What, sir?" said Savage, almost choking.

"The CI, Willy Boyle, said there's a London gang called the Fulham Crew who've infiltrated Norwich and King's Lynn, big outfit. The kids bring the drugs up from London and distribute them across the county. He didn't know any names, but Mike mentioned a guy called Niko."

"I'm hoping there will be something on here," said Savage, picking up the mobile phone. "Got this in Jonah's house, but..."

She held it up. It was an antiquated Samsung, and there was a glowing padlock displayed on the screen.

"Older model, with some kind of third-party encryption software. Proving a bit of a nightmare to get into."

"Well hurry up," said Clare. "Anything else?"

"Hay analysed the ribbon we found in Prescott's cat's mouth, sir," said Savage, her tongue twisting on the sentence. "It's exactly the same as the type that was wrapped around Kieran's head."

"Shit, really?" said Kett.

"Yes, sir. It is. But when uniforms were searching the fields they found more scraps of ribbon. They probably blew away from the park in the night. The cat might have just found one and brought it home."

"That suggests the killer took the time to wrap up their victim in the park, though," said Kett. "They brought the ribbon with them. Seems risky to do that in such a public place."

Clare nodded.

"I spoke with the high school, sir," said Spalding. "Northgate, in Dereham. Kieran was a good student. Top end of all his classes, never in trouble. The head was shocked when I asked if they'd ever suspected criminal behaviour or a connection to the gangs. But..."

"I don't want to see your butt, Alison," said Clare.

"She did mention that Kieran's work had slipped in the last couple of months. He's been tired, short-tempered. They intervened, but didn't get much out of him. She assumed it was a relationship thing, although she didn't know if he was in one."

"Do we know?" asked Clare.

"Dad says no," Kett replied.

"I asked about Jonah, too," Spalding went on. "Different picture entirely. He left after failing his GCSEs. But when he was at school he was in the bottom sets, never tried, spent more time out of the classroom than in it. He was suspended twice since 2020. They were aware that his grandmother had died, but not that his brother had moved out. Not their concern anymore, they said."

"What have you been doing while everyone else has been working?" Clare asked, turning to Kett.

"Uh, plenty, sir," Kett said. "Like I mentioned, I spoke to Willy. One weird thing, when I told him about the tattoo on Kieran's wrist he almost shat himself. Told me to get out of his house."

"Did he say why, sir?" asked Savage.

"Just said that everyone was scared of the red line. That if you saw it, then you belonged to them."

"Who?" said Clare. Kett shrugged.

"You never heard of it, sir, when you were working narcotics?"

"Never," said Clare.

"He said something weird, uh..." He struggled to remember, wishing he'd written it down. The truth was he'd been so desperate to wash his hands after his visit to Boyle's piss-soaked house that he'd forgotten. "Something about following the red line."

"Wait," said Savage. "That rings a bell. Follow the red line."

"You've heard that before?"

"I think so, sir," said Savage. "I'm sure I heard Granddad mention it. I'd have to look it up."

"What else?" said Clare. "That can't be all you've got."

Nobody answered, and for a few seconds, the Super rocked back and forth on his chair like a child on a mechanical pony.

"Bloody useless, the lot of you. Where's Bollock Cop?"

Kett started laughing before he could stop himself.

"Bollock Cop?"

"Don't ask, sir," said Savage. "There's videos of him everywhere, stuck on the snails. He's a meme."

"So he's too famous to come to work now, is he?" boomed Clare.

"No, he's off duty, sir," said Savage. "There's still a significant amount of swelling in his—"

"Nope," said Kett, putting his hands over his ears and

getting out of his chair. "You need to stop putting that man's gonads in my head."

"It's no joke," said Clare. "Injuries to the crotchal area can be very debilitating. I once had a twisted testicle. Had to be blue-lighted to hospital. Looked like a giant pink kiwi fruit."

"Jesus Christ," said Kett, running for the door. "Enough! Call me if you find anything."

"Where are you going, sir?" Savage asked.

"To gouge out my eardrums," he said. "Then I'm going home."

HE PULLED into the driveway forty minutes later, guided home by the lights that were on in every room. In the years following the horror of the Pig Man—and Kett's abduction by Hollenbeck—Billie had slowly learned to heal. She'd started to accept that her home was a safe place where bad things could not reach her.

But ever since they'd linked Joseph Maynard to the witchcraft case in the summer, she'd fallen right back into old habits. The lights came on as soon as the sun went down—all of them—and they stayed on until the morning. The alarm was set, the windows secured. Their home became a fortress.

The doors got locked, too, which Kett discovered when he put his key in the lock and tried to turn it. Billie had popped up the snib on the Yale, which meant she'd also drawn the bolts, locking him out.

He tried again, then slipped his keys back into his pocket. Midnight had come and gone, and Billie and the girls would be fast asleep—probably after another gruelling evening of getting them into their own beds. He lifted his hand to knock, but decided he couldn't do that to her.

He slunk back to the car instead, sitting in the passenger seat and reclining it as much as he could. The Volvo had warmed up on the way over, but the cold had snuck in, and it was brutal. He slung his coat over his lap, pulling it up to his chin, changing his mind and yanking it back down over his knees. He texted Billie—*In the car, didn't want to wake you*—then wriggled himself into the most comfortable position he could find and closed his eyes.

Kieran Spicer was waiting for him in the dark, the boy beaming like in the family photos at his house. Here was a kid who had everything, Kett thought. A good family, even if it was a little broken; and loving parents, even if they showed their love in very different ways. If he'd wanted money, all he had to do was ask his mum or dad. If he'd wanted attention, he had friends he could call on, as well as two little brothers who doted on him. If he'd wanted respect, there were a million better ways he could have found it.

So why did a sixteen-year-old kid from the good part of the neighbourhood end up dealing drugs? Sure, his best friend was doing it, but kids weren't lemmings. They didn't throw themselves off cliffs just because somebody else led the way.

The answer was painfully clear: *excitement*. Things had been too comfortable, too good, and this was a good way for Kieran to get his heart racing.

A good way to get his heart *stopped*, too.

But that didn't explain why somebody had killed him. If he'd been dealing for the gangs then something had to have gone very wrong for them to turn on him like that. He hadn't just been murdered, he'd been assassinated, then paraded around the park. It didn't feel like a beef with a rival gang, because they wouldn't have gone to the trouble of moving the body, of pushing it down the slide and on the swings, of wrapping it in ribbon. So either Kieran had messed up monumentally, or whoever had killed him had wanted to send a message.

But to whom?

Kett sat forward, opening his eyes as a sudden thought entered his head. He pulled out his phone and texted Clare:

You don't think Kieran was working undercover, do you? Can you check?

Because what if he'd been working for the police, for the narcotics department? A crime like that certainly merited being butchered, at least in the eyes of the gangs. It was rare that somebody so young would be behind enemy lines, but it wasn't unheard of.

His phone bleeped, a message from the Super. It was so garbled it took him a moment to decipher it.

how has it taken you all day to think of that you twatting turtle tosser first thing I looked at he wasn't hurryup and do your jod

"I am doing my bloody *jod*," said Kett, resting the phone back on his lap.

So maybe Kieran had made a mistake. He couldn't exactly have been streetwise, not when he grew up in a nice house, not when he was at a good school. Maybe he got in over his head and messed up.

Or maybe he got in over his head and wanted to leave.

That was probably it, Kett realised. Good kid, dealing for a thrill, gets cold feet and backs out. That was the kind of thing that couldn't go unpunished either, and that was the kind of punishment that was used to send a message, too.

He closed his eyes again, trying not to picture Kieran's final moments, the terror, the regret.

But how could he not? How could he not feel each of those blows as they cleaved his flesh, as they cracked his bones, as they severed his ear?

He forced it away, trying to focus on something else. But the images were playing on repeat, cycling over and over until they filled every inch of space inside his skull—then, when he finally drifted off into a fitful sleep, spilling into his dreams.

CHAPTER TWENTY

Monday

He woke to a gentle tap, opening his eyes to see a blurred shape in the fogged-up window of the car. When he scrubbed away the condensation, he saw that it was Billie, dressed in her pyjamas. It took him a moment to remember where he was, and another to remember how to move. When he lifted a hand to wave, a lightning storm of pain ripped down his spine.

"Ahhhhhh," he said, feeling something in his lower back start to cramp.

He sat still until the agony had dulled, then pressed the button to wind down the window. The air outside actually felt warmer than the fridge-like chill of the Volvo. It was still dark, but only just.

"I am so sorry," said Billie. "Why didn't you just knock?"

"It was late," he said, experimenting with moving his legs. The cramp returned, everything from the waist down either buzzing with pins and needles or completely numb. "I didn't want to wake you. What time is it?"

"Nearly six," she said. "You could have frozen to death out here, Robbie."

Billie opened the door, offering a hand.

"I'm hard as nails, mate," he said, accepting her help. "Could survive for a week at the top of a mountain wearing nothing but a G-string."

"Slightly unsettling image," she said. "And patently untrue. Come on, I've made tea."

Kett swung one leg out of the car only for his back to lock up again. He grimaced, clenching his teeth so hard he thought his jaw was going to shatter. After a couple of seconds the pain passed, and he let her haul him out.

"Hard as nails? Hard as *snails*, more like. You are getting far too old for this, Robbie."

"I'm not that old!"

She kicked the door shut, practically carrying him to the house as the feeling slowly returned to his feet.

"Speaking of snails," she said, "how's Aaron doing? The poor guy was in so much pain. That safety bar was like a guillotine, he's lucky he's still got his bits and bobs."

"It is far too early for Duke's bits and bobs, Billie," said Kett as he walked over the threshold. He could hear the girls inside, a peal of laughter that thawed his frozen limbs.

"Still, he should sue them," she said, using her backside to shunt the front door closed.

The heating was on, the house a sauna. Kett shuddered like he'd slipped into a warm bath, and his muscles had about ten seconds to ease before the thunder of little feet made him tense up again.

"Dadda!" screamed Moira, hurtling out of the kitchen.

"Watch out," yelled Billie. "He's—"

Moira thumped into him like she was a copper taking down a criminal, her forehead connecting with his bladder. It took all his strength to remain on two feet, and not to scream when the cramps returned.

"Where have you been?" clamoured the five-year-old. "We looked everywhere for you! Evie said you'd been flushed down the toilet."

"I was," he said. "All the way out to sea. I had to get a bus back from Yarmouth."

"Ew!" said Moira, letting go of him. She turned, hollering loud enough to be heard back at HQ. "Evie, he *did* get flushed down the toilet, you were right!"

Evie appeared at the top of the stairs, already dressed in her school uniform.

"Dad, can I show you something?" she said.

"Oh God, Evie, not now," said Billie.

"No, *I* want to show him!" said Moira.

Evie stamped her foot, the smile vanishing.

"No, I said I was going to do it."

"Do what?" said Kett. "Can't you do it together?"

"Or not at all," said Billie. "It's not really appropriate, especially for six o'clock on a Monday morning."

Evie stampeded down the stairs so fast Kett thought she was going to fall. Moira saw her coming and dropped to the floor like a possum, both legs in the air and her tongue out.

"What are you—"

"Help, I'm stuck!" Moira yelled, her voice surprisingly deep. "Aaaaah my legs are trapped and I can't get out."

Evie had darted into the living room, appearing again a second later with a cushion in her hand. She dived to the floor as well, holding the cushion over her stomach.

"Help me, I'm crying!" she wailed, then snorted such a

powerful laugh through her nose that a bubble of snot appeared with it.

Moira was laughing too, almost too hard to speak.

"My tummy is too big, I can't get it out!" she said. "I'm going to be stuck here forever!"

"And now my willy is trapped!" Evie shrieked.

"Evie!" said Billie.

"My willy!" Moira echoed in that same deep voice, and they both erupted into uncontrollable giggles, rolling around on the floor.

Kett barked out a laugh before he could stop himself.

"Girls!" Billie said through a smile. "That's enough!"

"It's been squashed!" Evie said.

"It's been mashed like a potato!" Moira added.

"It's been pickled!"

"*Pickled?*" said Kett.

"Poor Aaron," said Billie, as the sisters descended into another fit of hilarity. "They're never going to let him forget that."

Kett stepped over Moira, then Evie. Alice was clomping down the stairs with a face like thunder. She was always at her worst on Monday mornings, because of the stress of school, but today she seemed even grumpier than usual. She looked like she'd been crying.

"Shut up!" she roared at the two little ones. "I'm sick of it! All morning you've been screaming at each other!"

She proceeded to make an angry impression of them, which descended into screams. Moira rose to the bait, screaming back.

"Shut your stupid mouth, you little shit!" Alice shrieked.

"Alice!" Kett boomed, the volume of his voice surprising him and making Alice jump.

"You shut your mouth, you big shit!" Moira said, then burst out laughing again.

Alice launched herself at her, slapping Moira's head before anyone could stop her. Moira hit her back, her face as terrifying as Alice's, and for a moment it looked like they would have happily killed each other.

Kett stepped between them, struggling with Alice's weight and surprised at Moira's strength.

"Oi!" he said, even louder. "Pack it in, both of you."

"I hate her!" screamed Alice, charging back up the stairs.

"She's going to get a ten thousand percent punch next time," said Moira, giggling like the whole thing was a joke.

"No she's not," said Kett, fixing his youngest daughter with a look. "That is not okay, Moira. We do not swear, and we do not hit. You're sisters, you have to look after each other."

"Not my fault," said Moira. "She made me do it."

"Not okay," Kett said, pointing his finger of doom at her. "I expect better from you."

Moira's face fell as she realised the seriousness of the situation

"Sorry," she said quietly. "I didn't mean to."

"You have to be kind to each other," said Billie.

"I'm kind," said Evie.

Kett was too tired to say anything else. He opened his arms and gathered Moira into a hug. When he let go, she fell right back to the floor.

"My willy! He crushed it!"

Evie started rolling too, both of them arguing about whose willy was more squashed. Kett made his way into the kitchen. The sun was awake, but it looked like it wanted to go back to bed, a weak, grey light lying half-dead by the bifolds. Two mugs of tea sat on the counter and Kett homed in on them, inhaling the fragrant steam like a man who'd just swum up from the depths of an ocean.

"I can't believe that just happened," he said, picking up a mug. It was too hot to drink, so he cradled it to his chest.

"I'll talk to Alice later."

"What's got into them?"

"The joys of having a big sister," said Billie. "A bad influence."

"Not always," said Kett. "Right?"

Billie didn't answer.

"You guys sleep okay?" he asked, changing the subject.

"We did until about twenty minutes ago," said Billie. "You got a phone call."

"A call?" he said, frowning. He pulled his phone out, seeing that it was dead. "Shit. Who was it?"

"Who do you think?" said Billie, collecting the other mug.

"Somebody from the National Lottery?" he said. "Saying I never have to work again?"

Billie laughed.

"Robbie, you and I both know that even if we were millionaires, you'd still go to work. It's the job."

"It's the job," he said, nodding. "Clare?"

"Yeah. You want me to tell you what he actually said, or just paraphrase it in a way that won't make your toes curl?"

"The second one," he said, risking a sip. The tea blasted away some of the exhaustion, the heat of it a missile that he felt all the way to his stomach.

"Dear Robert, my trusted friend and kind-hearted employee," said Billie, doing a passable impersonation of Clare's Northern accent. "I'm delighted that you're catching up on some sweet dreams, but could you possibly call me back because something important has happened and we could really use your help. Sending love and hugs, your bosom buddy, Colin."

"That does actually sound like the sort of thing he'd say," said Kett.

"That's word for word. Nice guy."

Kett laughed again, but this time there was a hollowness to it that he couldn't hide. As his body thawed, so did the memories—and once again the ghost of Kieran Spicer seemed to hang behind his shoulder, that single dead eye watching, waiting for some kind of justice.

He put his mug on the counter, shivering.

"I guess I'd better call him back, then."

CHAPTER TWENTY-ONE

THE LAST THING HE WANTED TO DO WAS GET BACK INTO his car, but thirty minutes later, after a shower and a change of clothes, then a slice of toast and jam and two more cups of tea—and finally a quick hug with Alice to make sure she was okay—he found himself driving through the quiet city streets. Even with the heater on full blast, it was hard to shake the chill that had settled into his bones overnight. His exhaustion felt overwhelming, as if he was driving through a dream.

Clare had certainly *not* sounded like a bosom buddy when he'd called him back.

"Get over to Heartsease right now, or I swear to God I'll peel you like a grape and use your skin as a cockflosser."

He'd hung up before Kett had found time to ask what a cockflosser was.

He made his way up Salhouse Road, the sun in his eyes as bright as a blowtorch. An IRV overtook him, its blues on, and when it turned down Watling Road, Kett followed it. More police cars had gathered ahead at the foot of one of two residential tower blocks, an army of coppers blocking off the street. He was surprised to see a tactical van in the middle of the fray.

Kett bumped the Volvo onto the pavement and parked it there, exiting into the frozen morning. He scanned the crowd, spotting Duke standing head and shoulders above the other constables on a small green outside the building's main entrance. Savage was beside him, her face taut with apprehension. She seemed to breathe a sigh of relief when she saw Kett walking over.

"Hi, sir," she said. "I've been trying to reach you all morning."

"Phone was dead, sorry," he said. "What's going on?"

"Digital forensics were working all night on the phone we found at Jonah White's place, sir. Finally hacked it a couple of hours ago. It's Jonah's. A burner, but there was still some good intel on it."

Kett stepped back as a line of tactical police moved across the green. Sergeant Gorski was amongst them and she nodded to Kett as she passed.

"Jonah was using the phone to communicate with his local supplier, a guy called Niko. We think that's Nikolai Spellman, who works out in King's Lynn. West Norfolk Police are looking for him now."

"Mike Spicer mentioned Niko," said Kett.

"Right, sir," said Savage. "There are texts back and forth from somebody else, too, somebody he calls Ginge."

"Ginge?" said Kett. "Somebody with red hair?"

Savage waited, and it took him a second longer to hit home.

"Ginger. It's a spice."

"Almost certainly Kieran Spicer," said Savage, nodding.

"They're mostly business texts: meeting places, amounts, warnings. There's a lot of banter. They know each other well, talk like a couple of kids. We never found Kieran's phone, and the likelihood is he had a burner as well, so it's hard to be sure."

Kett stared at the building, a brutally ugly ten-storey tombstone.

"What are you looking for here?"

"There were some texts on the phone that mentioned a stash house," said Savage, squinting at the tower. "43 Ashbourne. There's no streets with the name Ashbourne in Norwich, or in King's Lynn or Dereham. Not many people with that name either. This is our best bet."

Kett read the sign on the building's front wall: Ashbourne Tower.

"The last text that Jonah sent Niko was on Sunday morning, at 4:33 am," Savage went on.

She pulled out her phone, finding a photograph and zooming in. She passed it to Kett but he couldn't see it without his glasses—which he'd left in the car—so he handed it right back.

"It's a screenshot of Jonah's burner, sir," she said. "The text Jonah sent to Niko reads: '*Shit gone down, K merked, after me too, need to LL in AT.*' K merked probably means Kieran was killed."

"And AT?" said Kett. "Ashbourne Tower."

"Lie low in Ashbourne Tower, yeah," said Savage. "If it's a stash house it will be well protected. Hence the firearms team."

"Good work," said Kett. "It's been two days, you think he's still here?"

"We're about to find out, sir," she replied.

"On me!" yelled Gorski. "Go, go, go!"

Somebody ripped open the front door and Gorski ran in, the rest of the tactical team following. They vanished into the dark interior of the tower, their shouts echoing back.

"Let's hope he's here," said Kett.

"And that he's still alive," added Savage.

"You find any location data on the phone?" asked Kett. "Anything to tell us where they were on Saturday night?"

"It's an older model, sir," said Savage, her eyes still on the tower. "Nothing on the phone itself, but we're waiting to see if it pinged any towers. It's..."

She frowned, shielding her face from the sun as she gazed upwards.

"Is that..."

Kett followed her line of sight.

"Is that what?" he said.

"On the roof, sir."

Sure enough, there was a shape on the top of the tower, just a smudge of black that vanished as quickly as it appeared.

"Shit," he said. "Let Gorski know."

He hobbled towards the door as fast as his back would let him, entering a deserted lobby. He could hear cries of 'armed police!' from the stairwell so he took the lift instead. The doors were just closing when Savage scooted in.

"Duke's calling it up," she said. "Gorski will be on the fourth floor."

"No time," said Kett, pressing the ten instead.

The doors closed, the lift vibrating so hard his teeth chattered. It lurched up, moving painfully slowly.

"Come on," he muttered.

It seemed like an age later that it grumbled to a halt, still vibrating like it was about to explode. Kett stepped into a corridor that ran both ways, pointing to the right.

"Find the roof," he said.

He went left, passing three flats before he heard Savage call out.

"It's here, sir!"

He doubled back. Savage was standing inside an open door, one foot on the concrete stairs that led upwards. She took them two at a time, swinging around the banister and reaching the top before he was only halfway up. There was another door here, weak sunshine trickling through.

"Hang on, Kate," Kett said, puffing for breath.

Savage was already through the door, her voice echoing back.

"Oi! Don't move!"

Kett burst out of the stairwell onto the roof, so blinded by the morning sun that he lost his footing, sprawling onto his hands and knees. He swore as he got back up, squinting across the enormous expanse of the roof. Savage was standing in the middle of the space, and Kett had to move to the side to see past her.

A teenage boy stood on the other side of the roof, dressed in a black tracksuit and a red puffer jacket. His face was thrown into shadow by a wide hood, but his eyes glinted like silver pennies, full of fear. He was holding a black rucksack in one hand, the other tucked into the waistband of his trousers. He walked from side to side, as jittery as a trapped rat.

"Fuck off," he shouted, the wind swallowing his words. "Or I'll merk both of you."

"Calm down," Savage said, her hands still up. "We just want to talk."

"Fuck off," he said again, feigning a lurch forward. His

jacket hung too low for Kett to see whether there was a weapon in his trousers or not. "Let me go. Just let me go."

"You're not in trouble, Jonah," said Savage. "It *is* Jonah, isn't it?"

The boy didn't answer, his wide eyes finding Kett.

"Fuck off," he said again. "I mean it, I'm strapped. I'll do you."

"We just want to know what happened to Kieran," said Savage.

Jonah—it had to be him, Kett thought, because at the mention of his friend his body contorted like he'd been punched in the gut—groaned, taking a step back. He was a good way from the edge of the roof, but he was a lean teenager with a head start.

"I don't know anything about him," he yelled. "I don't know who that is."

"I don't think that's true, Jonah," said Savage, holding her ground. "We found your phone, at your house. We saw the text you sent Niko yesterday morning."

He stared at her, still pacing. The sweat was rolling down his face.

"I don't know anything about that," he said. "Just get out of the way."

He advanced a little, his hand still hidden beneath his jacket.

"I will fucking flatline you! Move!"

Kett heard a thunder of footsteps behind him, and a second later Gorski exploded through the door, her rifle up. Three more officers followed, a flood of noise and violence.

"Armed police!" they yelled together. "On the ground, now!"

Jonah staggered away in shock, his hand sliding out of his trousers—empty.

"Wait!" roared Kett, standing in between the police and the kid. "He's not armed."

"Get on the floor!" yelled one of the men, sidestepping Kett so he had a clear shot.

"Fuck's sake," said Kett, spinning back. "Jonah, get on the floor or they're going to shoot you."

The boy was terrified, hyperventilating inside his hood.

"On the floor!" Gorski yelled. "Now!"

Jonah dropped his rucksack, backing away.

"Stop!" Kett shouted. "Just stop, mate, and nobody will get hurt."

"It's too fucking late for that," Jonah screamed. "It's too fucking late, isn't it? He's dead."

"It's not too late for you," said Kett, moving forward. "Come with us. We can protect you, Jonah, from whoever's doing this. From whoever killed Kieran. Just come with us."

"Protect me?" he scoffed. "You're fucking mad. Key found it. He found the fucking red line, ain't nothing going to stop them from getting to me."

"The red line?" said Kett. "What do you mean?"

"Get on the floor!" came another shout.

Jonah flinched like he'd been shot, backing away even further. The edge of the roof was just feet away, only a low wall between the kid and oblivion.

"Just stop and listen to me," said Kett. "Forget about the police, forget about the guns, just listen. We *can* keep you safe."

"You think you can, but you can't," he replied, speaking through a sob. "Nobody can. It isn't just the drugs, it isn't just the parties, they're something else, something worse."

"Tell me," said Kett. "Tell me what the red line is, and we can take them down. I promise you, we'll end them."

Jonah was sobbing hard now. He pulled his hood back, staring at the sky.

"It's not what you think it is," he said. "I'm sorry."

He turned, breaking into a sprint with such force that his back foot slipped. It didn't take him long to recover, running for the edge.

A gunshot exploded next to Kett's ear, blood erupting from Jonah's leg. He spun like a rag doll, landing on his back next to the wall. His mouth opened, a moment of shocked silence followed by a harrowing scream.

"Stay down!" Gorski yelled.

She moved fast, but Savage was already on the run. She skidded down beside the boy, one hand on his chest as he tried to get up.

"You're okay," she said, but the rest of her words were drowned out by another scream—not one of pain, but one of anger. Jonah had one hand on his leg, blood spraying from it as he kicked at the floor. His other hand grabbed the top of the low wall. It looked like he was trying to haul himself over.

Gorski stowed her rifle and dropped to her knees, patting Jonah down.

"Clear," she said. "Get a medic!"

"Medic!" echoed one of the tactical officers. More police emerged from the stairwell, pushing past Kett as they ran to the boy.

Kett hobbled over, the last one to arrive. There was no room for him in the melee, or for Savage. She walked to his side, leaning on him, her breaths fast and shallow.

"Get an ambulance!" Gorski shouted. "I clipped the fucking artery."

Somebody had ripped off Jonah's tracksuit, and another

officer was fastening a tourniquet around the boy's skinny thigh. There was blood everywhere.

"Please be okay," said Savage. "Please be okay."

Kett didn't see how her prayers could be answered. He watched silently as the team worked. Jonah lay beneath them, his eyes rolled back in their sockets. His hands flailed madly, his fingers marking a trail of blood from his forehead down to his chin.

A single red line.

CHAPTER TWENTY-TWO

THERE WAS NOTHING THEY COULD DO ON THE ROOF, SO they walked in silence down to the fourth floor. Two of the tactical team were waiting outside the demolished door of a flat, laughing quietly about something. They fell quiet when Kett and Savage walked out of the stairwell, nodding a stony-eyed welcome.

"You find anything inside?" Kett asked them.

"I'm getting high just standing here, sir," one replied as they made way.

As soon as he entered the narrow hallway, Kett understood what they meant. The flat reeked of chemicals, something acrid and sharp and pissy that sat right at the back of his throat. He had to step over the remains of a metal barricade, peering through the first open door on the left. It was supposed to be a bedroom, but there was no furniture, just a stack of clear plastic boxes against the far wall. When he walked in for a closer look he saw that they were full of shrink-wrapped parcels, all of them containing various powders and bundles of pills.

"Holy shit," he said, doing some mental maths. "If that's what I think it is, there must be a million quid sitting here."

He left the room, passing a shower and a toilet on the right—the stink of an unflushed shit competing with the chemical aroma for airspace. There was another bedroom, this one with two single mattresses on the floor and a tangle of duvets. Past that was a living room lit only by the blue screen of a television. An old PlayStation whirred noisily on the floor.

"Got weapons in here, sir," said Savage, who hovered in the doorway. She nodded to the far corner, and it took Kett a moment to notice what had been propped up against the wall.

"Shotgun," he said.

There was a pistol on the coffee table too, almost buried beneath beer cans and overflowing ashtrays.

"Why didn't he take them onto the roof with him?" he asked. "Why pretend to have a gun?"

Savage shrugged, but she answered anyway.

"Because he's just a kid, sir. He didn't know what he was doing."

Kett entered the room, the cloying smell of weed taking over. He used an elbow to flick the switch but nothing happened. There was no bulb, he saw. He made his way carefully through piles of trash to the window, pulling away the blanket that had been nailed there. Dust swirled like a flock of panicked birds in the explosion of sunlight. The room looked worse for being illuminated, the beige carpet stained in numerous places, the sofa ripped to shreds by what had to have been a dog, or maybe rats. The smell was getting worse by the second.

"Christ," said Kett, wondering how long he could hold his breath.

He checked the mostly empty shelves of a bookcase by the window, then the TV unit, which was close to falling apart at the joints. Savage squatted by the table, already wearing gloves.

"Gun's a replica, sir," she said without touching it. "Air-gun, I think they've sprayed it black."

She picked up a small notepad, shaking ash from it before opening the cover.

"Jackpot," she said. "It's their ledger."

Kett looked over her shoulder as she flipped it open. Inside were columns of names and figures, all detailed in minuscule blocky handwriting. It was so small that Kett couldn't read any of it.

"Are those dates?" he asked.

"Yes, sir," said Savage. "Dates, products, initials, and a number. Not a phone number, maybe a GPS."

She navigated through the greasy pages until she found the last one. Kett leaned closer, then pulled away, trying to make the words focus through sheer force of will.

"That's Saturday, sir," said Savage, seeing him struggle. "The last entry. The 18th of the 11th, 00, RM (!!), one bag, full bag. 4k. 52.65891, uh, 0.84177."

"Those are definitely GPS coordinates," said Kett. "This is gold. I'll bet that's where they were the night Kieran was killed."

He reached for his phone before remembering it was charging at home. He clicked his fingers instead.

"Phone."

Savage handed it over, and he passed it back when he remembered he couldn't see.

"Find out where that is, Kate."

She dropped the book back where she'd found it, standing up. Kett heard the crackle of static from outside, followed by a garbled voice. He walked into the hall in time to see one of the firearms team finish speaking into his radio.

"That was the Sarge," he said. "Your boy's stable, they got the bleeding under control. Air ambulance is going to pick him up from the roof."

"Thank you," he said, a wave of relief rolling over him. He glanced at the ceiling, firing a message up through it. *Thank you*. Then he turned back to the officers. "He in any state to talk?"

"Out cold," the man said.

"Make sure he's accompanied," said Kett. "Tell Gorski he stays under armed guard, for *his* safety as much as anyone else's."

The officer nodded. Kett ducked back into the living room.

"You hear that? Jonah's going to be okay."

Savage's body seemed to untense as she let out a breath.

"Thank God," she said.

She held up her phone.

"Coordinates lead to a place southwest of Dereham. Can't be sure, but it looks like a house. A big one."

Kett managed a smile.

"This is good," he said. "We're getting somewhere. Let's go check it out."

THEY PICKED up Duke on the way out of the tower, then hit the road in Kett's Volvo. Savage took the passenger seat, Duke in the back with his legs spread so far apart his knees were almost touching both doors. Traffic coming into the city was gridlocked, but the roads were clear on the way out, and within ten minutes they were back on the A47, heading west.

"Can't find much on the place, sir," said Savage, her eyes glued to her phone. "Looks like an old estate house, a big one. Wayside Manor. Georgian. Was owned by a man called Edward De'Ath for decades, open to the public for some of that. He died in '09 and it passed to his niece. Went on the market a decade ago but I don't think anyone bought it. It's in a bad state, by the look of it."

"Derelict mansion," said Kett. "Good place to do a deal."

Savage nodded, putting her phone on her lap.

"You okay?" Kett asked her. "That whole thing on the roof..."

"Not really, sir," she said. "We shouldn't have gone up there. We shouldn't have cornered him. We didn't give him any choice."

"Yes, we did," said Kett. "He had all the choices in the world, he just made a stupid one. He's going to be okay."

"What does that, though?" Savage said. "What scares a kid so much they'd rather jump off the roof of a tower block than trust the police to help them?"

"Gangs are pretty scary," said Kett. "This London crew sounds brutal. If Jonah saw what happened to Kieran then he'd know jumping would hurt less. He said he was in hiding, didn't he? When he messaged Niko."

"Yeah," said Savage. "Lying low. You think he and Kieran tried to rip off their suppliers or something?"

"Two young lads, treating it as a bit of a game," said Kett, nodding. "Yeah, that might be it. They steal some product, or some cash, think nobody will notice. But they *do* notice. They kill Kieran, Jonah gets away."

"Maybe that's what the drop was, sir," said Savage. "In

the ledger. An ambush. They were told to bring a bag to the house—the rucksack we found—and they were jumped."

"Derelict mansion," Kett said again. "Good place for an assassination, too. With any luck, we'll find out when Jonah starts talking."

He glanced into the rear-view mirror.

"You're quiet this morning, Aaron. You okay?"

Duke opened his mouth, but Kett cut him off.

"And I do *not* need an update on your... you know."

The PC shut his mouth, massaging his crotch with one hand.

"Please don't do that," said Kett.

"What did I tell you, Aaron," said Savage. "Leave them alone."

"I can't," said Duke. "They're still—"

Kett switched on the radio, loud, and for the last twenty minutes of the journey they drove without speaking. The countryside was losing itself to the disease of winter, the trees bare, the fields barren, the greenery eaten away to shades of brown and grey. The few people they passed on the way looked just as miserable, their bodies weighed down by heavy clothes and their eyes haunted.

Eventually, Savage pointed to a lane on the right and Kett took the turn, stopping after a quarter of a mile when the decaying bulk of Wayside Manor appeared over the hedgerows. He pulled the car up to an enormous wrought iron gate and killed the engine, turning down an Aerosmith song just as the chorus was about to kick in.

The estate was surrounded by a brick wall that undulated back and forth in tight curves. It was eight feet high, and it was topped with a very modern strip of razor wire. The gate was secured with a monstrous chain and a padlock that had to be bigger than Duke's fist.

"Not sure we're getting in this way," said Kett.

He groaned out into the damp air, pushing his hands deep into the pockets of his overcoat and using his backside to shut the door. Savage got out, then opened Duke's door for him.

"Come on," she said.

Duke replied, but Kett couldn't make out what he said.

"You're fine, Aaron," Savage went on. "I'll buy you another Ribena."

"Bloody hell, Kate," said Kett, opening the other back door. "He's not five years old. Duke, out, now."

Duke gingerly eased himself out of the back seat, closing the door and leaning on the car.

"I'm okay, sir," he wheezed.

"I know you're okay," said Kett. "We've all taken a hit to the clobbers, mate, stop making such a bloody meal of it."

He set off up the lane, the only sound the scuff of feet and the endless song of the crows. The wall stretched on as far as he could see, covered by sickly strands of ivy and malignant growths of lichen. Past that, was dense woodland, the trees reaching for the skies like undead hands.

"It is bleak out here," he said, and that reminded him of somebody. "Anyone heard from Porter, by the way?"

Nobody replied.

"Can you call him, Kate? See what he's doing?"

She nodded, putting her phone to her ear.

Kett upped his speed, more to get his blood moving than anything else. The wall was meandering slightly to the left, the road following it.

"Not answering his phone, sir," said Savage.

"Keep trying."

He walked on, covering a quarter of a mile before the estate showed its first sign of weakness. A section of the wall had crumbled inwards, nature doing its best to seal the gap with a tangle of ivy. As he closed in, he saw that the vegetation had been stamped down, some of the thicker strands snapped.

"Someone's been through here," he said.

"Recently, too," added Savage, putting a finger to the ivy. "There's still sap."

Kett grabbed hold of the wall and stepped over the thick plants, treading carefully as the fronds snatched at his boots. He stumbled through the undergrowth into the wood beyond, the day growing dark and cold beneath the meagre shelter of the trees. Savage came in after him, Duke following, holding his Taser in place as he hopped, skipped and jumped past the blockade.

"Ouch," he said, doubling over.

From here, there was no sign of the estate. Kett set off along the closest thing he could find to a path, the ground rising towards the top of a shallow hill. The birds welcomed them cautiously, the drumming of a distant woodpecker like machine gun fire.

"Can't get hold of him, sir," said Savage, sliding her phone into her pocket.

Kett reached the top of the hill, breathless and broken-backed, grabbing hold of a skinny sapling for support. The view was better up here, but there was still no sign of the house—just trees and mud for as far as he could see.

"Shame Porter isn't here," said Kett. "He'd have loved this."

"What's that, sir?" asked Savage as she climbed up beside him. He had to follow her finger to see what she was pointing at.

A bright red ribbon, caught in the trees at the bottom of the slope.

"Weird," he said.

He set off towards it, doing his best not to slip on the damp ground. The ribbon had been tied in a neat bow around the trunk of a tree. It fluttered in the gentle breeze like it was trying to draw their attention.

"Red ribbon," he said as he reached the bottom of the hill. "What do you think it's for?"

"Boundary marking?" said Savage. "You see them on estates like this, where some of the land has been partitioned off to a new owner."

"Maybe," said Kett.

"Red line," came Duke's voice from behind them.

The PC was sitting on his backside, inching his way down the hill like a nervous kid on a slide.

"What on earth are you doing, Aaron?" he asked, immediately wishing he hadn't bothered.

"I'm scared I'll fall and do myself more damage, sir," said Duke, shuffling relentlessly through the dirt.

Kett turned to Savage and she grimaced.

"You're marrying that," he said.

"I mean... it's still a long way off, sir."

Duke got to the bottom and eased himself back to his feet. He was absolutely caked in mud, the seat of his trousers soaked through. He gave his crotch a gentle pat as if to reassure it.

"Unbelievable," said Kett. "What were you saying?"

"That if I fell, I'd—"

"About the ribbon."

"Oh, right. It's like a red line, sir."

He wasn't wrong.

"A warning, maybe?" said Duke.

"Or an invitation," said Kett. "Grab a photo, Kate, and bag it."

He passed the ribbon, pushing into an even darker section of woodland. It didn't take long before he spotted a building between the gnarled trunks.

"There it is," he said.

"Bloody massive," said Duke.

Massive was right. As soon as Kett walked out of the shelter of the canopies and onto the overgrown lawn, he saw that the house was bordering on palatial. There were over a dozen windows on this side alone, spread across four floors. Most of them had been shattered, looking like gaping, toothless mouths. They held nothing but darkness.

To the left was a gathering of old outbuildings, so he walked right, heading for the front. Crows scattered from the long grass, clamouring into the trees. But other than them, there was no sign of life.

People had been here, though. Lots of them.

"What a mess," said Savage.

There were paper cups in the grass, hundreds of them. Crisp packets and sweet wrappers sat amongst them, a sea of rubbish. Kett spotted the occasional item of clothing, too. T-shirts and jumpers, and even some underwear.

"What happened to them?" asked Duke from where he trailed behind.

"To what?" said Savage.

"To the people who were here. Why did they leave their clothes? You think they just... vanished?"

"No, Aaron," said Kett. "I think they probably just got undressed."

They'd reached the front of the house, the gate visible at the end of the weed-strewn drive, the Volvo still parked there. The building looked even grander from this angle, the windows bigger, although still mostly without glass. An enormous double door occupied pride of place, one side hanging off its hinges.

"That's just asking us to come in and have a look around, right?" said Kett.

"Be rude not to, sir," said Savage. "Really doesn't seem like anyone is here."

And the words had barely left her mouth when a brick came soaring out of one of the top windows, hurtling towards them.

CHAPTER TWENTY-THREE

Porter pulled his Mondeo into the gravel car park beside the playground on the hill, leaving it next to the only other vehicle. It was an IRV, and the single constable inside lifted a hand in welcome when he recognised him.

Porter waved back, opening the door and surrendering himself to the cold. The wind was as sharp as a knife, sliding into his wound and making him screw up his face in pain. He pulled his coat tight, his feet like blocks of ice as he walked to the IRV. The constable wound down his window about an inch.

"Morning, sir," he said. "Not much to report, I'm afraid. Had a few cars drive by and slow down, got their details. Nobody else has shown up."

"Good job," said Porter, and the constable wound the window back up before he could say anything else.

The park had been sealed with police tape, so he skirted around it, heading for the woods again. Temperatures had plummeted in the night and the field was still frozen solid—a minefield of hard ridges and treacherous valleys. He almost turned his ankle a dozen times before he arrived at the trees.

"Bastard bloody dirt," he muttered.

It was hard to remember which path he'd taken yesterday, and there was no smell of rabbit to guide him this time. He had to double back on himself more than once, and he was ready to give up altogether when he accidentally stumbled into the clearing where he'd met Freddy and Ben.

There was no sign of them. The tent and the chairs had gone, the fire long out.

"Shit," he said, stamping his feet to try to get some warmth into them.

He crossed the clearing and entered the woods on the other side. He wasn't entirely sure why he was here, because he trusted that the two men had been telling the truth about themselves. He'd looked them up on the system last night, both as suspects and victims, but there was no record of them. The only thing he'd found on Google was a newspaper article from nearly two decades ago about a school trip to Holyrood—both Ben and Freddy were in the grainy photo, their arms thrown around each other's shoulders, just kids with big grins.

He hadn't found anything to explain why they were living rough in the woods, surviving on rabbits, slowly freezing to death.

The trees were bigger and denser here, thick roots doing their best to trip him up. He stopped after a while, his heart thrashing, his face burning from the cold.

"Shit," he said again.

He turned around to head back, then stopped. Somebody was moving through the woods to his right, the slow crunch of broken branches. Porter squinted into the shadows between the trees until he found them—a camouflaged shape moving from right to left. He almost called out but thought better of it, moving as quietly as he could to intercept them.

Less than a minute later he was close enough to see that it was Ben Rawling. The man struggled through the crowded woodland, a spade in one gloved hand, the other grabbing the trees for support. Dangling from his belt was the same curved blade that Porter had seen outside the tent.

Both the knife and Ben's clothes were spattered with blood.

"Shit," said Porter for a third time.

He thought it had been a whisper, but Ben stopped dead, his head jerking up. He was twenty yards away, and it took him a moment to find Porter in the trees.

"The hell you doing here?" he said, taking a step back.

"Looking for you," said Porter. "Everything okay?"

Ben couldn't seem to find an answer. His face looked even skinnier than it had yesterday. His eyes were red raw, as if he'd been crying, and his nose was swollen. He planted the tip of the shovel in the ground, his other hand straying towards his belt.

"What's going on, Ben?" said Porter, his body electric with anticipation. "Where's Freddy?"

"Around," said Ben. "We're fine."

"I'd believe that more easily if you weren't covered in blood, mate," he said. "And if you weren't carrying a weapon."

Porter took a step towards him.

"I'm going to ask you again, what's going on?"

Ben flinched like Porter was running at him, grabbing the handle of the knife. He glanced into the trees for a second, his tongue running over his lips.

"Don't," said Porter. "I told you before, I'm not after

you. I'm here to help. But you have to tell me where Freddy is."

Ben swallowed hard enough for Porter to hear it. After a few seconds, his hand dropped away from the knife.

"Around," he said. "I left him on the hill."

"He's okay?"

Ben nodded, wiping his dripping nose with the back of his hand.

"Aye, of course he is."

"And the blood?"

Ben seemed to understand what Porter was hinting at, his eyes narrowing.

"You think I've done something to him?" he said. "You think I'd *hurt* him?"

"I just want to make sure he's okay," said Porter. "That you both are."

"I'm the only one who cares about him," Ben went on, the anger visible as it boiled inside him. "I'm the only one who looks after him, okay? Fuck you for thinking I'd do anything to hurt him."

He closed his eyes like he'd gone to sleep, swaying.

"Ben?" said Porter.

"I'm okay," Ben said, just a whisper. "I'm alright."

He was as far from alright as it was possible to be. Porter jogged over, reaching Ben just as his legs gave way. He grabbed his arms, lowering him to the forest floor where he sat cross-legged like a child.

"Hey, easy now," he said. "Take a breath, Ben, you're okay."

He leaned the man against a tree and pulled out his phone, remembering that there was no signal. Ben had opened his eyes—barely—his mouth shaping silent words before his voice caught up.

"Don't call anyone," he said. "Don't call anyone."

"Mate, you're in a bad way," Porter told him, returning his phone to his pocket. He felt Ben's coat, which was soaked through, then he put his hand to his head. His skin was like ice.

He pulled off his overcoat and draped it around the man's shoulders.

"I'm fucking fine," Ben said, his eyes closing again.

"What are you trying to prove?" said Porter. "Living out here like this. If you love your brother so much, you need to get out of the woods. You need help."

Porter wrestled the knife out of the man's belt, lobbing it into the bushes just in case. Ben didn't resist. Porter wasn't even sure if he noticed.

"We can't," he said.

"Can't what?"

"Can't get help. It's too late for that."

Porter crouched beside him, trying to ignore the chill that had settled in his bones. He put a hand around Ben's shoulders and pulled him close, feeling the young man's body vibrating. The smell of him was atrocious—old clothes and unwashed skin and fresh blood.

"Whatever it is, it can't be that bad," he said. "It can't be so awful that you die for it."

"They'll take him away," said Ben, his teeth chattering so hard Porter could barely make out what he was saying. "He won't last without me."

Porter looked through the trees, trying to find Freddy, and trying to remember which way led back to the car.

"Okay," he said. "Here's the deal. You listening?"

Ben didn't reply, his face pushed into the thick collar of Porter's coat.

"You and Freddy pack up your things and come with

me. Right now. You helped us out yesterday, remember? You gave us some information about the park. That makes you both witnesses, and that means I can find you a place to stay."

Ben looked like he was going to argue, but Porter spoke over him.

"It's not official," he said. "We don't even have to use your names. There are no questions, no papers to sign, no ambulances and no police, other than me. It'll be a hotel. A warm room, you get an allowance for dinner. You can wash, get a good sleep. Both of you. You can rest."

Ben shook his head.

"One night. It's one night, Ben. You'll be safe there, I promise. In the morning, if you want to go, I won't stop you."

The young man sniffed, burrowing himself even deeper into the coat.

"Do it for Freddy," said Porter. "There will be a TV. Let him have a night off."

It took a few more seconds for Ben to lift his head. His skin was parchment-thin, dirt etched into every line of his face, snot caked in his beard. His eyes were so red they could have been bleeding, crusted with sleep. He looked like he was a hundred years old.

But he looked like a child, too.

"Come on," said Porter, pushing himself back to his feet and offering Ben a hand. "We can find Freddy on the way. He'll be chuffed, I know he will. What's his favourite show?"

Ben took Porter's hand in a frozen grip, letting himself be pulled back to his feet. He could have weighed ten stone soaking wet. He let go, wiping his hand down his scraggly beard.

"Bluey," he said. "He loves him."

"The dog?" said Porter. Ben nodded. "Hate to break it to you, but Bluey's a girl."

Ben frowned up at him.

"Aye?"

"Yeah."

Porter picked up the spade and pointed it to the right.

"This way?"

Ben stared into the trees before setting off to his left. He walked like a man who was on his way to his own execution, stumbling over fallen branches. At one point he put his hand to his belt and stopped, looking back.

"My knife," he said.

"We can come back for it," Porter told him.

Ben started walking again, the trees thinning and a wide band of daylight appearing ahead.

"I was burying the rabbits," he said. "The ones we didn't eat. They spoiled. Foxes come for them if you don't bury them."

"You packing up to leave?" Porter asked.

"Aye."

"Where were you going to go?"

Ben shrugged hard enough to shake Porter's coat from his shoulders. Porter picked it up and offered it back to him, but he waved him away.

"Moving south," he said. "Trying to follow the sun."

"You're going to have to go pretty far south to keep up with the sun, mate," said Porter. He shivered his way into the coat, buttoning it up as best he could with the spade in one hand. It stank of Ben, but he was too cold to care.

"Disnae matter," said Ben. "Got to keep moving anyway, can't go back."

"Why?"

"We just can't."

They stepped from the trees together, the sun like a blade in Porter's eyes. They were at the top of the hill here, the park ahead of them. He didn't know how that was possible, given that he felt like he'd walked for miles in the other direction, but he could see his Mondeo, and the IRV.

He could see Freddy, too, the kid sitting by a tree fifty yards away next to a pile of bags. When he spotted his brother he stood up, doing a little jig of happiness and waving both hands. He was wearing the Parka but he still looked frozen, his cheeks blazing.

Ben waved back, and so did Porter.

"Alright, Freddy?" Porter called.

Freddy shouted something, but Porter didn't catch it. The kid was trying to pick up all the bags, and Porter jogged over to help him.

"How're you doing, mate?" he asked.

Freddy grinned at him, one thumb up. Porter took the bag that he was struggling with and slung it onto his shoulder. Ben took the other one, and the tent.

"This everything you've got?" Porter asked.

Ben didn't reply, his face full of shame.

"It's good," said Porter. "Less to carry. My car's over there. You okay with this?"

Ben didn't look sure, but he managed a nod.

"You want to go somewhere warm?" Porter asked Freddy. "Someplace with hot food? A TV. Maybe we can find some Bluey, yeah?"

Freddy's smile seemed too big for his face. He gave two thumbs up this time, dancing on the spot.

"Come on, then," said Porter.

Before he could walk away, Freddy reached into his jacket, pulling out a camera that was on a leather strap around his neck. It was an old Olympus, an analogue one. This was what he'd hidden yesterday, Porter realised.

Freddy waved a hand at them.

"You want a photo?" Porter said. "Of us?"

Freddy nodded.

"Sorry," said Ben. "He loves that thing. I don't even think there's any film in it."

They shuffled together until their shoulders were touching, and Freddy lined up the shot. When he pressed the button, he made a popping noise with his lip—but Porter was sure he heard the camera click and whine as well.

"You been taking photos around here?" Porter asked him.

Freddy nodded, tucking the camera back in his jacket.

"You want me to develop them for you?" Porter said. "I know a guy."

Freddy looked at Ben as if he didn't understand the question.

"Sure," said Ben, answering for his brother. "If there's anything in there."

"That's great!" said Porter. He hefted the bag onto his shoulder, gripping the spade. "My car's over this way. Let's get out of here."

CHAPTER TWENTY-FOUR

"SHIT! KATE, WATCH OUT!"

Kett grabbed Savage's arm, pulling her back as the brick thumped onto the driveway a dozen yards in front of them. It thumped across the gravel, disintegrating.

A second brick was on its way, arcing gracefully from one of the windows on the top floor. It struck the lawn by the side of the driveway hard enough to leave a crater, spraying dirt. Duke had pulled out his Taser as if shooting bricks was an option.

"Oi!" roared Kett. "Pack it in, we're police!"

He was answered by a third brick, this one well off target as it crashed into the grass.

"Inside," he yelled.

The door was closer than the safety of the garden, and he ran for it. Duke was right beside him, pushing Savage in front of him like he was her bodyguard. Kett risked a look up as he went, another brick spinning out of the window. The angle was too tight, the missile bouncing off the front of the house and exploding into fragments.

Savage shouldered her way through the broken door,

almost ripping it free of the mouldering frame. Kett ran through behind her, seeing a grand entrance hall with a marble floor and a curved staircase leading up to a galleried landing. There was debris everywhere, chunks of plaster and stone that had crumbled from the walls and a skip's worth of rubbish.

"Twats!" said Duke as he stumbled through the door. He looked at Savage, his expression furious. There was blood on her cheek, the brightest thing in the dim space. "You okay? You hit?"

Savage put her hand to it.

"No, scratched myself on the door," she said.

"That was coming from the top floor," said Duke, heading for the stairs, still gripping his Taser. He bellowed as he went. "You're dead!"

"Wait," said Kett.

The PC was already climbing, the entire staircase shaking beneath his weight.

"Bloody hell," Kett said, turning to Savage. "Call it in, get some help out here."

"Yes, sir," she said, pulling out her phone.

Kett grabbed the banister, ready to chase Duke, but a section came loose in his hand with a puff of wood rot. He hopped onto the first step and immediately thought better of it. The whole thing looked like it was about to disintegrate into matchwood. Fortunately, Duke had reached the landing, roaring like a bear as he lumbered down it.

"Wait!" Kett shouted to deaf ears.

Kett ran to his left, looking for another way up. Through the closest door was an enormous drawing room, trashed almost beyond recognition. He crossed it, doing his best not to trip on the carpet of detritus as he jogged into the corridor on the other side. Ahead was a set of stairs descending into the darkness of a basement, and past them was a grand kitchen. It had been stripped of everything except the sink and a vast wooden table, which groaned beneath the weight of what had to be a hundred or more glass bottles.

"Sir!" he heard Savage shout.

"Back here," he called, making his way across the kitchen. There were four doors ahead, and the first two were pantries. The third led to a small, plain corridor, a set of narrow stairs leading upwards.

He climbed them as quickly as he could, hearing Duke howling from somewhere overhead. By the time he'd made it to the top, Savage was right behind him.

"There's a unit on its way from Dereham, sir," she said. "ETA ten minutes. You want to wait it out?"

"That sounds like a great idea," he said, walking down the corridor and peering through the open doors into empty bedrooms. "Except your boyfriend has Leeroy Jenkinsed, and I have no idea where he is."

Duke shouted again, dust raining from the ceiling as he trampled overhead.

"Duke! Wait!" Kett shouted.

"Stairs," said Savage, pointing down the corridor to an opening on the left. Another flight of steps huddled in the dark like they were hiding there.

She took the lead, vaulting up them with impressive speed. Kett took them one at a time, his back on fire. At the top was another corridor, even smaller than the last, as if the building was shrinking level by level into a doll's house. This one was dark enough that they both pulled out their torches.

"Aaron?" shouted Savage.

Duke called back—nothing more than a noise—and they set off to their left, following the beams of their torches.

"It's the next floor up, right?" Kett said.

"I think so, sir. This place is a maze."

They checked the rooms as they passed, finding nothing but rows of beds. The sheets were crumpled but they looked new.

It had all gone very quiet upstairs.

"Aaron?" Savage called.

They reached the end of the corridor, Savage opening the door to reveal a wider landing. Light spilled from a lantern window overhead, revealing more stairs—leading up and down.

"Who built this place?" said Kett. "Escher? How many staircases do they need?"

He was answered by a soft shout from below them. He ran to the banister, careful not to touch it as he craned his head over.

Somebody was hurtling down the stairs at some pace, but it was too dark to see who.

"Duke?" Kett shouted.

"Up here!" came the reply from the floor above.

"Up or down?" said Kett, turning to Savage.

She headed for the staircase leading to the lower floors.

"I doubt you'd catch up to them, sir," she said. "Go help Aaron."

"Just be careful," Kett told her. "Do not engage."

Savage had already dropped out of sight.

Kett started up the other flight of stairs—only to stop when somebody ran around the bend in the stairwell.

It was a man in his twenties, as toned as an underwear model, his hair down to his shoulders. He wore a dressing gown that was several sizes too small for him—flimsy enough for Kett to see that he was naked beneath. He skidded to a halt, his eyes as big as saucers. He was breathing like a horse at the end of a Derby.

Lodged in his chest were two Taser barbs, the wires dangling, and in his hand was a brick.

"Do not move," Kett told him from halfway up the stairs.

The man lifted the weapon, his body tense. He was so close that it would be hard for him to miss if he lobbed the brick, and Kett held his arms in front of his face to defend himself.

"I swear to God, mate," he said, "if you throw that bloody thing, I'm going to make you eat it."

The man paused, swaying like he was drunk. He didn't lower the brick. Everything was hanging free beneath the loose dressing gown, his body slick with sweat even though it was freezing in here. Kett hadn't seen him blink once.

"Put it down," said Kett. "Slowly. I'm not joking."

"You're one of them!" the man shouted, his voice deep and powerful. Spit exploded from his mouth. "One of *them*!"

"I'm police," said Kett, torn between taking a step forward and a step back. "Put down the brick."

"Yeah?" the man said, drawing the word out for an entire breath. "So you can kidnap me? Yeah? Yeah? So you can put me on the back of your bike and cycle me to the fucking moon? Yeah?"

"What?"

The man cocked his arm back even more and Kett retreated to the bottom of the stairs. He covered his head as he went, bracing himself for the pain.

"Drop it!" came a cry of pure rage.

Duke flew around the corner of the stairwell, crunching into the man with the brick and driving him into the wall so hard it launched a cloud of plaster dust into the air. They tumbled down the steps together, Duke on top, riding the guy like he was bobsleighing. By the time they got to the bottom, there was no sign of the brick.

"Stay down," Duke said, reaching for his cuffs.

There was no way the man was getting up again. He lay with his cheek planted against the wooden floor. Beneath the mess of his hair, his eyes were wide open but not really seeing anything. A constant stream of dribble, blood, and groans poured out of his mouth.

Duke snapped the handcuffs onto his wrists.

"Tasered him," he said, panting. "He wouldn't give up. He's off his face, sir."

"That would explain the whole bike to the moon thing," said Kett.

"There was another one," said Duke, looking around. "Where's Kate?"

"Gone after him. Down the stairs."

"It was a woman," said Duke, pushing himself up and sprinting to the other set of steps. "I'll get her. Wait here with this one."

"Yes, *sir*," grumbled Kett. "Anyone else up there?"

"No."

Duke careened down the steps. The whole house seemed to tremble as he went.

Kett double-checked the cuffs to make sure they were tight, then slid down the wall so he was sitting next to the guy. He noticed that the brick was lying on the third step up and he stretched out an arm to grab it. It was old but it was solid, the edges sharp. If the man had hit Kett with it from the top of the stairs, it would have hurt.

If he'd hit somebody from the top of the building, it would have killed.

"Arsehole," he said.

The guy was coming around, his eyes roving in their sockets for a full minute before they locked onto Kett. He started to push himself up, so Kett showed him the brick.

"I meant what I said, mate. I'll make you eat it."

It must have done the trick because, with a final moan, the man gave up. Kett clutched the brick tight, taking shallow breaths to listen past the thunder of his pulse. He thought he could hear shouts from downstairs but he couldn't be sure because the building seemed to have woken up—the floorboards and rafters cracking as the day grew warmer. He reached for his phone, remembering again that he didn't have it.

"Discombobulated," said the man, speaking into the carpet.

"What?" said Kett.

"Bobcomdisculated," he mumbled.

"You want to tell me what you've been taking?" Kett asked him.

"Combomlascadisted," he said, then he erupted into a wild laughter that echoed across the landing. It lasted a second or two before it suddenly cut out. The man frowned. "I think my leg is broken."

Kett glanced at it. It did seem to be lying at a weird angle.

"Yeah, maybe," he said. "Does it hurt?"

"I can't feel a single thing," the man said.

"What's your name?" Kett asked him, and the guy laughed again.

"You already know," he said. "I'm Jesus."

"Right."

He heard the stairs creak, and a moment later Savage's head appeared. She looked flustered, and her shirt had lost its top two buttons—as well as picking up a suspicious brown stain on the front. Kett offered her a genuine smile of relief.

"You alright?" he asked.

"I mean, it's not been the best day of my life, sir," she replied. "First Jonah, then that idiot throwing bricks." She nodded down the stairs. "Then *that* idiot throwing... *different* kinds of bricks."

"Tell me she didn't throw poo at you, Kate."

Savage looked miserably at her shirt.

"She threw poo," she said. "Aaron got the worst of it. This was just an... an after-smear."

Kett suddenly felt grateful that the man had only been threatening him with a brick.

"She also gave him a pretty good kick to the nethers," said Savage.

"Ouch."

"But we got her, sir. She's out on the driveway. Duke's sitting on her."

"Backup here yet?" Kett said.

Savage shook her head.

"Who's that, sir?" she asked.

"I'm Jesus," said the man, still not blinking. "It's nice to meet you."

"Give me a hand, Kate," said Kett, every joint crunching as he got back to his feet. "Let's get our lord and saviour downstairs and see if we can figure out what the hell is going on."

CHAPTER TWENTY-FIVE

They gathered in the garden in the cold light of the morning.

It had taken the better part of half an hour for Kett and Savage to manhandle Naked Jesus down three flights of stairs, mainly because he was hopping, and because he hadn't stopped screaming about his broken leg.

Kett might have taken him a little more seriously if he hadn't been hopping *on* the leg he'd claimed was injured.

By the time they'd reached the front door, the backup units were arriving. The local constables had used an angle grinder to cut the padlock on the gate before parking their IRVs on the driveway—well out of reach of the house in case anyone else started lobbing bricks from the top windows.

Naked Jesus had been loaded into the back of an IRV, where he was currently licking the windows and bestowing divine blessings on anyone who passed. The woman that Savage and Duke had arrested sat alone on the grass, because nobody wanted to touch her. Her hands, which were caked in faeces, had been cuffed, but she showed no sign of wanting to do anything other than stare at the swaying stalks of grass, and occasionally roll back and forth, screaming.

She was young as well, in her twenties, and she looked too clean-cut to be the kind of person who threw her own shit at the police. She was wearing a long skirt and a pink bra beneath a woollen cardigan. Her fair hair was done up in a French plait that had largely managed to stay in place even after the chase. A random scattering of colourful tattoos decorated her body, a string of ornate letters reading 'never enough' along her breastbone.

In all his years on the Force, Kett didn't think he'd ever seen anyone as baked as these two.

Duke leaned against the bonnet of the second police car, his eyes puffy, his face so pale he was almost green. He kept swallowing like he was going to be sick. Savage stood beside him, looking just as gaunt. The stain on her shirt seemed worse than ever. Kett had told her to go home and get changed, but she was still here.

He idled nearby, wondering if it was too late to retrain as a teacher. Or a dentist. Maybe a vet.

Anything other than this, really.

"Got a van on the way, sir," said one of the PCs. She glanced at the woman on the grass. "We'll put her in the back, if that's okay. She really threw poo?"

"Yeah," said Kett, throwing a sympathetic glance at Savage and Duke. "She's got good aim, too."

"Nasty," said the PC. "Ambulance is inbound too."

"Good," said Duke, shuffling uncomfortably.

"Not for you, mate," said Kett. "For Jesus."

"I don't need no ambulance!" the man yelled from the back of the IRV. "I can fly!"

He licked the window again, grinning.

"Jesus blesses you, children. I do, I do, I do!"

"You know much about this place?" Kett asked the PC, doing his best to ignore the guy.

The young woman stared at the house.

"Been empty for years, sir," she said. "Me and my mates all thought it was haunted when we were kids."

"It is," said Duke, glaring at the woman on the grass. "By a couple of dickheads."

"Occasionally, we get called out to remove squatters," the PC went on. "Usually by the neighbours, who've seen lights or something. And there was a fire here a few years back, just kids messing around. But most people have forgotten about the place. I'm amazed it's still standing."

"Not everyone has forgotten," said Kett, gesturing to the grounds. "A lot of people were here recently, by the look of it."

"Probably a rave," said the PC. "We break them up every now and again, usually in fields. This place is perfect, though. I think we got some calls about music on, um..."

She turned to another of the constables.

"Derek, when were those calls about the music?"

"Saturday night," said the man.

"Yeah, a few people reported loud music into the early morning, but it happens."

"Nobody checked it out?" said Kett.

The PC arched her eyebrow.

"You know what it's like, sir. A bit of loud music gets pushed right down the job list until it falls out the bottom, especially at the weekend."

Kett nodded.

"Don't suppose you've ever seen these two before?" he said.

The PC looked at Naked Jesus through the saliva-smeared window of the car.

"Nope," she said. "Be happy to never see them again, too."

"How could you say that, Delilah?" the man wailed. "After all these years, Jesus loves you more than you can imagine! Jesus loves you even when you're naked! Delilah!"

"My name's not Delilah," she said to Kett.

"One more thing," he said. "There was a red ribbon in the woods, tied around a tree. You ever seen that before, or heard of the red line?"

She shook her head.

"Can you do me a favour?" he asked her. "Can you do a quick search of the house, see if you can find blood? A lot of blood."

She didn't look sure, but after a moment she nodded.

"This about the boy they found in the park yesterday, sir?"

Kett nodded.

"Take somebody with you," he said. "It's a big place, and we don't know for sure that it's empty."

He watched her walk away, then turned to the woman on the ground. She was lying on her side now, eating grass like a dog with a poorly stomach. Kett walked over to her—close, but not *too* close.

"You going to throw anything at me?" he asked.

The woman looked at him without lifting her head.

"Because this suit is clean, and I don't want to have to burn it."

She went back to her grass.

"Can I ask you your name?" said Kett.

He was expecting another Biblical reference, but he didn't get one.

"Izzy."

"Izzy what?"

"Mooney."

"How old are you, Izzy?" Kett asked.

She shrugged as much as the cuffs would allow.

"Do you want to tell me what you've taken, Izzy?"

She bit off a mouthful of grass and laughed. Her teeth were bright green.

"Everything," she said.

"That figures. There was a party here, right? On Saturday night?"

He was cut off by a banging from the IRV, Naked Jesus pounding his fists on the window.

"Don't talk to him, Iz, he's the devil!"

Izzy stopped chewing, looking at Kett like he'd grown horns.

"I'm not the devil," he told her. "I'm a policeman."

"The devil walks amongst us!" Jesus roared from the back seat. "Wearing a terrible suit!"

"Hey," Kett said to one of the constables. "Can you drive him down the road a bit?"

"A terrible cheap suit, that's how you know!" he cried, his eyes bulging. "That's how you know he's Satan! Look at that awful polyester!"

"It wasn't that cheap," said Kett, tugging on his jacket and feeling a little more defensive than he should have. "Got it from Marks and Spencer's."

He waited for the constable to jump into the driver's seat and pull the car away, then he turned back to the woman. She was rolling back and forth, arching her back.

"I'm itchy!" she wailed.

"I know. Izzy. You already told me."

"*Itchy*," she said, enunciating it. "My skin's on fire. I think I'm dying."

She did have a few blotches on her face, he saw. He wondered if she was having a bad reaction to the drugs.

"Ambulance is on the way. But I still need to ask some questions. Does *he* have a name?"

"Probably," she said, still squirming. "Don't know him."

"You don't know him? But you're living here together?"

"Don't live here," said Izzy, spitting out a wad of green cud. "We just never left after the party. I don't even know what day it is."

"Want to hazard a guess?" asked Kett.

"Sunday?"

"Monday," Kett told her.

Izzy stopped moving and closed her eyes. When she opened them, she seemed a little more lucid.

"I'm in so much trouble," she said.

"Yeah, you could say that," Kett replied. "Who was throwing the bricks out the window, him or you?"

"Bricks?" she said, and there was genuine confusion on her face.

"But you threw the poo?" said Kett.

"Oh God," she groaned. "I did, didn't I?"

"Yeah, you did," said Savage from the car.

"That's... that's awful," said Izzy, trying to sit up so she could see Savage. "I wouldn't... I would *never* do that. I'm so sorry. Just you scared me, all of you jumping us like that. That big ape running up the stairs with his gun out. I was clogged up and you scared it out of me and I... I caught it because I didn't want to make a mess, then you ran at me and... I didn't know what else to do with it."

"With the poo?"

She nodded.

"Right," said Kett, rubbing his temples with both hands.

"We'll come back to the poo later on. I need to know what happened here on Saturday night. The party. A rave, right?"

Izzy rested her head on the ground, closing her eyes.

"I think I'm going to be sick," she said. "I'm so itchy and I think I'm going to be sick and then die."

"Just hold it in. Saturday night. Tell me why you were here."

Izzy breathed in hard through her nose.

"Not a rave," she said. "It's not just the music. I mean, there is music, yeah, but it's different. It's... I don't even know what the word is. They call it the Masque."

"The Masque," said Kett. "Like a ball or something?"

"Kind of. I mean, most people weren't actually wearing masks or anything. But it's exclusive, you have to get invited, you can't just show up. There's security on the doors, they search you when you go in, make sure you haven't got a phone or anything. You don't fuck with them."

"And you what?" said Kett. "You just dance?"

Izzy opened her eyes and looked at him with what might have been disapproval, or pity.

"Been to many raves?"

"Uh, no," said Kett.

"Any parties?"

"I mean, a few," he said. "But not for a while. The parties I go to these days have cakes and balloons."

Izzy actually laughed. She rolled onto her back, then onto her side again when her cuffed hands got trapped beneath her. She drummed her bare feet on the ground.

"I really feel sick," she said. "It's the smell. Can you take these things off? Can you scratch me? Please?"

"I don't really want to go anywhere near you," said Kett. "Sorry. So what happens at these parties?"

"I can't tell you."

"Because it's illegal?"

"Yeah, obviously."

"I don't care about that right now. You get high, you listen to the music, what else?"

Izzy sighed, the noise becoming a gag.

"It's mental," she said, spitting more grass. "You turn up and there's everything you could want. Drink, drugs, and it's all free. And there's rooms. Like, themed rooms. Things happen in them."

"What kinds of things?"

"Musical chairs," said Izzy. "Backgammon. What do you think?"

"Sex stuff?" said Kett, remembering the beds.

Izzy laughed, but her face screwed up and she gagged again.

"Sex stuff, yeah. That's right, *granddad*."

"I'm not that old!" he protested. "I need to know what sort of stuff. Just places where people can get together? Consenting adults? Or something else?"

"It's whatever you want it to be," said Izzy. "You ask, they provide."

"Who's they?"

At this, the young woman clammed up.

"Izzy, this isn't about you, okay?" Kett said. "I don't care why you're here, I don't care that you're off your face, I don't even care that you kicked a policeman in the bollocks."

"Hey!" said Duke. "I care!"

"But we think somebody was murdered here on Saturday night."

Izzy stared at him, her mouth open, her cheeks blotchy. Kett could see grass caught between her teeth.

"A teenage boy, just sixteen years old. He was hacked to pieces by more than one person. We know he was supposed to be here, probably delivering drugs at around midnight. I need to find out what happened to him."

"I didn't do it," said Izzy.

"I know. But this was a child. He was murdered. Anything you know about this place, about the people who run it, about who else was here, it will help us. It will help *him*."

She heaved again, spitting.

"I'm going to be sick," she said.

"How did you find out about it? The party?"

She groaned, her body writhing on the grass, her bare feet kicking.

"I don't know," she said. "Alright? I was on Tinder and I hooked up with some guy. Jase. He told me he was going to a party, asked me if I wanted to come. Course I did, obviously. He said it wasn't like anything I'd ever been to, that it was like some kind of... I don't know. I can't remember half of what he said. He picked me up from the city in this big car, proper fancy thing. Made me wear my best dress."

She looked down at herself, frowning.

"No idea where that went. But we drove out in the middle of nowhere, proper dark, I thought he was going to kill me. Got here and the place was bouncing, you know? A hundred people. More. Rooms were lit up, music was mental."

She stopped, and Kett let her collect her breath.

"Course I didn't see Jase after about an hour, he fucked off into one of the rooms. But I didn't care at that point, was drunk. You've never seen so much booze, everyone was giving me drinks. Had a dance, had a smoke, had a wander. Saw some shit I probably didn't need to see. Then somebody gave me some pills and... and I don't really remember much after that."

"You didn't see a teenage boy there?" asked Kett, pulling out his phone and finding a photograph of Kieran. "This one?"

She barely looked before shaking her head.

"No kids."

"Did you see anyone in charge? Anyone who looked like they were giving orders?"

"No," she said, screwing her eyes shut as another wave of nausea rolled through her. "I mean, plenty of bouncers, all big fellas in masks. Scary. But come on, you don't go to a club and look for the manager, do you? I was just having a good time."

"So good you didn't want to leave?" said Kett. "Because it's coming up for eleven on a Monday morning and you're still here."

"I have no idea," said Izzy, looking for the IRV with Jesus in it. "I must have met *that* guy at some point, we hooked up. I think we broke through a door and climbed into the attic, no idea when but the party was still going. Must have fallen asleep up there because when I woke up everybody else had gone, apart from him."

"You stayed here together?" asked Kett. "Why?"

"Why do you think?" said Izzy. "You've seen him naked, you tell me."

"Fair point. The place was empty when you woke up, yeah?"

"Apart from all the shit everyone left," said Izzy. "Nobody else around. I thought it was still the weekend."

There was a deafening bleep from outside the gates, an ambulance rolling past on the road outside. Savage skipped off to speak with the paramedics.

"Okay," said Kett. "One last thing, Izzy. Did Jase tell you how he found out about the party?"

"No," she said. "Made it out to be this mystery that only he knew the answer to. He just wanted me to think he was royalty or something. Oh, but he did say it cost him an arm and a leg. I remember him saying that. I think he wanted me to know that I owed him something."

She spat again, moaning.

"But that guy," she went on. "Big-dick Jesus, he said he got an invite too."

"Yeah? You think he'll tell us anything?"

"Uh, not for a few days," said Izzy. "He is gone. Out of it. Maybe permanently. I think he thought I was a figment of his imagination. He spent a few hours last night, or this morning, or whenever, hiding from me because he thought I was made of squirrels."

"Made of squirrels?"

"Yeah. But he said the invite came through on his phone, I remember that much."

"He didn't have his phone on him," said Kett. "You know where it is?"

"Last I saw, it was in the attic," she said. "He wasn't supposed to have it at the Masque, they check. I don't know how he got it in. We were in the room on the left of the stairs, the one with all the blankets. I'd..."

She gagged so hard her body bucked off the ground, then a jet of orange vomit exploded from her. Kett jumped back, even though it wasn't anywhere near him.

"Whoa," he said, looking around to see the paramedics coming through the gate. "You timed that well."

"Sorry," said Izzy, retching hard. She released another torrent of puke, as powerful as a fire hose. "Oh God, I'm dying."

"You're going to be alright," said one of the paramedics. He kneeled beside her then rocked back, a hand to his face.

"That is bad," he said.

"She was throwing poop," said Kett.

"I'm sorry!" Izzy wailed.

"You were going to say something," Kett said. "Before the vomit fountain."

"I was just going to say you should probably wear gloves or something up there," she said. "Sorry. I am sorry. Sorry. Sorry."

"Thanks for the warning," said Kett.

He started to walk away, stopping when he heard Izzy calling out to him.

"Jesus gave me his code," she said. "Because he wanted me to call his dad for him."

"His dad?"

"Yeah, his heavenly father. God. I couldn't get through. It's 0007."

"Thanks," said Kett.

He nodded to the paramedics as he walked away.

"Good luck."

CHAPTER TWENTY-SIX

Izzy hadn't been lying.

They needed gloves.

The attic room was a cramped space beneath low-hanging rafters, a single dormer window covered by yellow newspapers. A mound of what Kett thought were blankets sat right beneath the window, but when he clicked on his torch and took a closer look he saw that it was a bed of foamy yellow loft insulation.

"That would explain the itching," he said.

He crossed the room carefully, the floor groaning like a living thing. Savage followed, sweeping her torch from side to side. One corner seemed to have been used as a toilet, a piss-scented stain beneath the eaves. There were some loose bricks here. A handful of empty bottles sat by the window, plus an overflowing ashtray, a bag of pills, and a mind-boggling collection of condoms—new and used.

"Ew," said Savage. "Forget the gloves, sir. I think we need to call in the bomb disposal robot."

Kett laughed, using the toe of his boot to peel away strips of insulation. It was like playing pass the parcel, except every layer he opened revealed a new item of discarded clothing. It didn't take long to find a phone amongst the mess. Kett picked it up in a gloved hand—doing his best to ignore the sticky residue as he laid it on the window ledge. He patted his pockets for his glasses before remembering he'd left them in the car.

"Nearly dead," he said, squinting at the little red strip of battery life that remained. The picture on the screen was a close-up of Naked Jesus and two other guys, all of them topless and ripped, on a beach somewhere, drinks in their hands. "0007, right?"

"Right, sir."

He tried to type the digits on the screen, but it wouldn't recognise the touch of the glove.

"Fuck's sake," he said. "Have you got any hand sanitiser on you, Kate?"

"I do," Savage said, pulling a tiny bottle from her pocket. "I've started carrying it since I met Aaron."

Kett laughed, then gave her a look.

"I really don't want to," said Savage.

"But I can't see anything without my glasses."

She puffed out a breath as she pulled off her glove, using the tip of her pinkie to type in the code. The phone woke slowly, as if it too was hungover, the icons slouching onto the screen.

"Did she say email or text?" she asked.

"Email," said Kett, leaning in.

Savage opened the email app, scrolling past a chunk of stuff.

"Nothing here, sir. Nothing in the trash, or in his messages. He might have another email app, hang on."

"You know what to look for?"

"Yes, sir," said Savage. "I'll try Proton."

She shook her head.

"Nothing, I'll try Runbox."

She typed on the screen with her single finger.

"Tuta, maybe?"

"Are you making these up, Kate?"

"No, sir. Onion."

"You're definitely making them up."

She typed some more, then grunted a noise of approval.

"Bingo. Onion. It's a tor-based app for the dark web. I'll check the search history."

She was quiet for a moment while she worked.

"There, sir," said Savage, pointing to something he couldn't see. "Mobius, it's an anonymous email app. Oh, and look."

"Can't look," he said.

"Sorry, sir. Emails, a few of them, the subject line is *2511 Masque*."

"Kate, you're a genius. What do they say?"

"They say DCI Kett really needs to start carrying a spare pair of glasses," she said. "'*The venue has been confirmed. All attendees must transfer Bitcoin prior to arrival in order to receive their ticket. A reminder, while most things are permitted, some things are not.* READ THE RULES. *Attendees participate at their own risk. The organisers accept no responsibility for your personal safety. See you at the Masque.*'"

"Anything else?"

"Hang on," said Savage. "There's an older email here, from last Monday. '*While we try to keep to our pre-established dates and times, this isn't always possible. You will be updated on the day. Disclosure of these dates to anyone will lead to immediate removal.*'"

"Removal of what?" said Kett.

"I dread to think. There are a lot of emails here, sir. They all seem to be for different parties, all called Masques. Twelve this month alone."

"Surely they can't have raves on this scale every few days?"

"Depends how much money they're making, I guess. A few hundred people paying a few hundred quid, that's thousands. And if they're selling the drugs and the drink, too, it's an easy profit."

"Izzy said the drugs were free," he said. "But that the ticket cost an arm and a leg. A buffet, you think?"

"Maybe, sir." Savage pointed to the screen with her little finger. "That's today's date. You think there's going to be another one?"

"I don't know," said Kett. "Monday feels like an odd day for a rave, and there's no way they'll be back here, now that we've turned up. Who's sending the emails?"

"Random email address, sir. Letters and numbers followed by the words *reddeath*, and ending with *.onion*."

"Red death?"

"Yeah," said Savage, leaning in. "You know the story, right?"

"Kind of," said Kett. "I remember the Hammer film. Masque of the Red Death."

"It's Poe. A guy called Prospero hides out in a house during a plague. They throw this elaborate masked ball and everyone dies. There's more to it, but that's the gist."

"Cheery," said Kett. "That's weird, though, right? Red line, red death. It's a connection. Which reminds me, did you look up the whole red line thing?"

"I did, sir," she said. "But there wasn't much. I might have imagined it, but I swear Granddad mentioned something like that years ago. There was a poem, I remember him saying it. I just can't remember the words."

"He was a copper," said Kett. "Maybe he saw it on the job."

"Maybe, sir."

"Any photos on the phone?" he asked.

"We'll be lucky to see them. We're on 2%."

Her fingers swiped the screen and she recoiled immediately. Even without his glasses on, Kett could see Naked Jesus filling the screen.

"Did not need to see that," said Savage, flicking back through the photos. "Or that. Or that. I don't even know what that is."

She kept swiping.

"There are photos of him and Izzy up here, but nothing from the party. I'm guessing they weren't allowed their phones. Nobody wants a photo taken of them at a drug-fuelled sex rave."

"True," said Kett. "Okay, this is good. Let's get this back to HQ, see if we can find out who's running the events."

"Yes, sir," said Savage. She slid the phone into an evidence bag, then proceeded to squeeze half a bottle of hand sanitiser over her little finger.

"Might want to keep hold of some of that, Kate," said Kett.

Savage frowned up at him.

"Why, sir?"

"Because we might be going to a party tonight."

FOR THE NEXT HOUR, Kett went from room to room in the giant house, finding nothing but the remains of the Masque.

Judging by the sheer number of empty bottles on the floor and the volume of litter—not to mention a charity shop's worth of discarded clothing—Izzy had been telling the truth. There had to have been hundreds of people here on Saturday night.

Despite the mess, though, he was pretty sure the place had been cleaned up.

For one, none of the clothes or bags he found had any form of ID in them. Cash, yes, but no debit cards or driving licences or even library cards. Anything with a name was missing. There were no phones either.

It wasn't a coincidence, he knew. Either people had been told not to bring anything that might identify them, or somebody had gone through the house and collected the stuff that could lead the police back to the ravers. There would be fingerprints everywhere, he knew, but processing them would be a gargantuan task and ultimately pointless. It wouldn't lead them to their killer.

If their killer had even been here.

Kett made his way out of the back door, seeing the cluster of decaying outbuildings gathered like begging paupers in the garden. They were all empty, but the biggest one—an old stable right across from the house—stank of gasoline. There were deep gouges on the concrete floor that looked fresh, and it took him a moment to work out that there had probably been a generator here on Saturday night, powering the party.

Whoever these people were, they were professionals.

As he was walking back to the house he spotted another door in the back wall, just down from the one he'd walked out of. It was open, and when he peered inside he saw a stone staircase leading into darkness.

"Hello?" he called, clicking on his torch. "Anyone down there? It's the police."

Nothing answered except the moan of the wind, a breeze reaching up and feeling his face with cold fingers. He set off down the steps, holding onto the metal handrail as he went. He stopped at the bottom because there was a length of red ribbon lying on the flagstones.

"What are you doing there?" he asked.

He stepped over it, walking through an archway into an enormous, vaulted cellar. It was largely empty, a few rotting cardboard boxes against one wall and an old bed leaning against one of the brick columns that held up the ceiling. Kett made his way from one side to the other, catching another flash of red further ahead. This wall of the cellar was occupied by wooden shelves, all of them empty. Somebody had affixed another red bow here, the ribbon stapled into the painted timber. He gave it a tug, but it didn't budge.

There was nothing else, so he made his escape and circled the house. He found Savage chatting with the local police, and she looked up as he approached.

"Anything, sir?"

"Maybe," he said. "Found a couple more red ribbons in the cellar. I'll get a Uniform to bag them up. You?"

"Nothing that can help us," said Savage. "No sign of blood, no sign that anyone was killed here."

"We've been around the estate, sir," said the PC. "No blood there either. I don't think the boy was murdered here."

"Or the killer knew what they were doing," said Kett. "They came prepared, didn't make a mess." He looked around. "Duke out in the woods?"

"He's in the ambulance, sir," said Savage. "Said his plums—"

"Got it," said Kett before she could finish.

"Clare called," she added. "He was looking for you."

"He say why?"

"Yeah, sir. They've collared the dealer that Kieran was working with. Niko Spellman. He's at the King's Lynn nick. Boss wants you to talk to him."

"Great," said Kett, heading for the road. "The joy never bloody ends."

CHAPTER TWENTY-SEVEN

In all his years in Norfolk, this was his first visit way out west to the King's Lynn police station. It was an impressive building in the heart of the town, with four brick pillars holding up the stately 'Norfolk Constabulary' sign. Above that was a bedraggled Union Jack that didn't seem to have the energy to fly even in the cold breeze, and a verdigrised clocktower that said it was coming up for five.

Kett checked his watch to see that it was only just after twelve.

"Not every day we get royalty from Norwich," said the portly desk sergeant when Kett arrived at the custody suite. His rosy cheeks boasted a set of bushy mutton chops that would have suited a Victorian bobby. "The great and mighty DCI Kett. You look smaller in real life."

"Oh," said Kett. "Right. Sorry."

"Not your fault, everyone looks bigger on the TV. Which is weird, isn't it? Because you're actually smaller on the TV." The man held his hands a few inches apart. "Like, you're about this big. Although, I guess if you've got a bigger TV that might change."

He stretched his hands out a bit, then looked at Kett like he was gauging his height.

"No, you'd still be smaller than real life."

"I'm here to see—"

"Nikolai Spellman," said the sergeant, nodding so hard his mutton chops danced. "Right you are. Prickly little shit, we've had him in a dozen times or more over the years but he always manages to wriggle out of it. He's ready. Got DC Okoro in there, she picked him up for you."

The man stepped out from behind his desk and led Kett along a series of stark corridors. He knocked on a door, waiting for a reply before opening it.

"DCI Kett for you, Stef," he said. "Looks smaller in real life, doesn't he?"

He stood to one side and Kett walked into the room. A young woman in a grey suit sat on one side of the desk, offering Kett a tight nod. On the other side was a man in his late twenties wearing a camouflage tracksuit and bright white trainers. His face was handsome but unfriendly, his dark hair and stubble perfectly sculpted. He leaned back in his chair, his knees so far apart that he looked like he was training to do the splits. Arrogance dripped from every part of him.

"Thanks, Sarge," said the detective.

The door closed, and Kett walked over to the empty chair.

"DC Okoro?" he asked as he sat down.

"Yes, sir," she said, her accent pure London. "Thanks for coming."

"Thanks for picking him up," said Kett, turning to the guy. "Nikolai Spellman, right?"

"No comment," said the man, giving Kett an impressively infuriating shit-eating grin.

"Yeah, this is Nikolai Spellman," said Okoro. "Hang on."

She started the recorder and gave the introductions, stating the date and time.

"Niko here is one of the town's finest arsebags," she went on, speaking directly to the man on the other side of the table. "If something in the town smells bad, you can be sure this one has been there."

"Not very nice, *Stef*," said Niko, spitting her name like he'd eaten something bad. "I thought we were friends."

"I've had haemorrhoids that I'm more likely to be friends with," said Okoro.

Niko laughed, but there wasn't anything nice about it. His four top front teeth were missing, replaced with a silver grille that would have looked better on a car.

"Niko here is part of a local club called the... What was it again, Niko? The Bad Ma'am Crew?"

Niko was bristling beneath his grin.

"The Sad Ham Crew?" Okoro went on.

"Bad Man," said Niko, flicking his hand out like he was holding a gun. His accent had turned a little Jamaican. "Big Bad Man from outta England."

"That's right," said Okoro, trying to hold back a smile. "The Big Bad Man Club. Because Niko loves a big, bad man."

"Gonna wipe that smile off your face one day, sweetheart," said Niko.

"You'll have to learn to wipe your own arse first, mate," she said, and this time it was Kett who had to try to keep the smile from his face. "We'll let you go back to your little club in a bit, but I have a man here who wants to talk with you. And Niko, can I just point out that this guy here, DCI Kett."

She held out a hand in introduction.

"He's actually dealt with some bad men. *Proper* bad men, not little boys like you. Ask him what he did to those men, Niko."

Niko's eyes crawled lazily to Kett, and he stared down his nose at him for a moment.

"What did you do, old man? Beat them with your walking stick?"

"Close," said Okoro. "But it was a hammer, not a stick."

A flicker of doubt crossed Niko's face, but he managed to hide it after a second or two. He shrugged, picking at his teeth like he had a million better things he could be doing.

"Come at me with a hammer, bro," he said. "See what happens."

"I'm not interested in you," said Kett. "Okoro's right. I'm not interested in little men doing little things."

Niko bristled again, his eyes full of violence.

"Kieran Spicer," said Kett. "Tell me about him."

"No idea who that is," said Niko, studying his nails.

"Sixteen years old. He was murdered on Saturday night."

Niko shrugged.

"He was butchered by more than one person. Probably machetes."

Niko's arrogance faltered again, his brow furrowing. He licked his lips.

"Don't give a shit about that ickle nitty," he said. "Never met him, don't care about him. He probably deserved it."

"You think he deserved it?" asked Kett. "You want to tell me why? We know he was working for you, dealing for you over in Dereham. You're the middleman. You get shipments from the Fulham lot. You deliver the drugs to Kieran Spicer and Jonah White and their mates, they sell them for you and kick the money back."

"Fucking hallucinating, you are," said Niko. "Nothing to do with me."

"Yeah? So it's not a problem that we found your safe house this morning?" said Kett. "The one in Ashbourne Tower? By my reckoning, there's about a million quid in narcotics sitting there."

He smiled.

"At least, it *was* sitting there. I should think by now it's safely locked up in one of our evidence lockers."

The blood seemed to drain right out of Niko's face. He closed his legs and leaned forward, pointing a finger at Kett. There were a lot of things the young man wanted to say, that was obvious enough, but he managed to lock them all in his throat.

"Cat got your tongue?" said Kett. "I'm guessing the drugs don't belong to Kieran or Jonah. I'm guessing they don't belong to you, either. I'm guessing that big ol' stash of food belongs to those Fulham fellas."

Niko sat back, shrinking.

"And tell me if I'm wrong, but those are proper bad men. Yeah? Those are the kind of bad men that will hack a sixteen-year-old boy to death."

Niko looked at Okoro.

"I want a brief," he said.

"You turned down your right to representation," said Okoro. "So just answer the question."

"Who killed him?" said Kett.

Niko spat out a laugh.

"Fuck off," he said.

"You're scared of them?"

"They scared of *me*," he said, thumping his chest. It was like watching a child.

"Niko, did the Fulham Crew kill Kieran?"

"Fuck. Off."

"What did he do to upset them? Did he steal? Was he skimming off the top?"

"Fuck off."

"Ah, I get it," said Kett, leaning back in his chair and turning to Okoro. "Kieran was gunning for the top spot. He was going for Niko's job."

Okoro nodded.

"You're right," she said, catching on straight away. "That makes sense. Niko's clearly not leadership material, the Fulham lads wanted somebody else to take the job, somebody smart."

"Somebody dangerous," said Kett. "That was Kieran, right?"

Niko laughed, that silver grille catching the light.

"That little prick wouldn't take a piss without asking for permission," he said. "Stupid little soldier boy didn't have a fucking clue what was going on. He was shook. He did what we told him, little robot, little fucking smurfer."

He clamped his mouth shut so fast his teeth clacked.

"I don't believe you," said Kett. "I think he was rising through the ranks, and I think you killed him before he could take your job."

"Ain't nobody mad enough to take me on, bruv," said Niko, thumping his chest again. "Not Kieran, little batty boy couldn't tie his own laces. Even that sket mate of his has more wise to him. He was an amateur, didn't want the money, just wanted to be in the game. Was never gonna be here long."

"So he was thinking about leaving?" said Kett.

"Why don't you ask him?" he said, flashing that malicious smile again. "Oh yeah, you can't. Dickhead got himself bare shanked. But it weren't me, I ain't got time for that shit. Weren't me or any of my fam. What we going to get out of that? Dead boy haunting us, bringing beef down on us. Bullshit."

"The Fulham Crew, then?" said Okoro.

"Never heard of no Fulham Crew," said Niko. "Even if there was one, which you can't prove, they wouldn't even know that little shit existed. He was nothing to them. People come, people go, nobody talks so long as the Ps keep rolling. Don't need no meat cleaver to put that fear into people."

"So if it wasn't you, and it wasn't the London lot, then who killed him?" said Kett.

Niko shrugged.

"If I was you, I'd be looking at that creepy wannabe bad man who hung about with him. Know what I'm saying? Little ratty."

"Jonah?"

Niko licked his metal teeth.

"Now *he* wanted to be bad, wanted to show himself to the big men, wanted to prove himself. He weren't rich like Spice, he *needed* more, always more. So why don't you ask *him* what he done?"

Kett took a moment to think, silence flooding into the room like dark water.

"On the night he died, Kieran and Jonah were doing a delivery together," said Kett. "To a rave in a house just outside of Dereham. We found Kieran's bag, with the drugs. He never made the delivery. You're saying Jonah killed him, stole the drugs, then what? Hid out in the one place where you lot were guaranteed to find him?"

Niko shrugged.

"It's air. You're hallucinating. I don't know shit about shit."

He sat back, his chair creaking beneath him. The arrogance had returned to his face, that grille beaming like a set of headlights.

"We spoke to Jonah," said Kett. "You know what he told us?"

Niko shrugged.

"He told us the red line killed Kieran."

"Now I know you're fucking mad," said Niko. "Believing fairy tales like that."

"Fairy tales?"

"Red line ain't nothing but a story. Fucking boogeymen. They talk about the line to keep you *in* line, you understand? Red line ain't real. If Jonah told you that, he for sure merked your boy. He's trying to pin it on people who don't even exist."

"He was scared of them," said Kett. "Scared enough to try to jump off the roof of the tower block."

"Being shook does that," said Niko, lacing his hands behind his head. "Guilt does too, you know? Little pagan ratty in a corner, should have let him unalive himself."

"What about the Masques, you heard of them?"

"The parties?" said Niko. "Yeah. But they're too cool for you, old man. Invite only, got to know the right people."

He sucked his teeth, stretching his arms out.

"Gonna arrest me proper or what?" he said. "Gonna come for me, big man?"

Kett would have liked nothing more, but sticking this arsehole in a cell for twenty-four hours wasn't going to do anything but leave the local coppers with paperwork and headaches. He drummed his knuckles on the desk.

"Interview terminated at 12:25," he said, standing up.

"Bye-bye, cop," said Niko, firing that shit-eating grin again. "Was nice meeting you. Bring your hammer next time, yeah?"

OKORO CLOSED the interview room behind her, and they walked a little way down the corridor before talking.

"Like I mentioned, sir," she said. "Prime arsebag."

"You're not wrong," said Kett. "You like him for the murder?"

Okoro thought about it for a moment.

"I don't doubt he's capable. I don't even doubt he's done it. He came up from London, Lewisham, and I'd heard of him when I worked the Met, him and his brothers. But killing Kieran Spicer? I don't know why. Killing a child brings a lot of heat. Killing a child like that and leaving him in the open, for everyone to see...?"

She shook her head.

"No. I don't think it's him."

Kett waited for a couple of constables to walk past, clattering through the door.

"You know much about his operation?"

"A little, sir," she said. "We've sent it all over to your Super."

"The Fulham Crew?"

"Albanians, as far as we can tell," said Okoro.

"They're the sort to use machetes," said Kett. "And the sort to send a message."

Okoro shrugged.

"But come all the way up here to kill a sixteen-year-old? Even if he was guilty of something, they wouldn't make that kind of effort. It's beneath them. They'd send somebody with a gun, or a knife, and they'd make sure nobody ever found him."

"What about the red line?" Kett asked. "You ever heard of that before?"

"I've seen County Lines operations with similar titles," she said. "But the red line? I don't think so. It's a strange name, don't you think, sir?"

She rubbed her lips, thinking for a moment.

"The red line is the place you can't come back from," she said. "The place of no return. The crossing of the Rubicon, right?"

"Yeah," said Kett, struggling to remember what that was. "I think so."

"But it doesn't just mean that," said Okoro. "The *thin* red line, you know that phrase as well, sir?"

Kett nodded.

"A thin line of soldiers against an impossible enemy," she went on. "A moment of great courage. It's a line guarded by heroes."

"Like the thin *blue* line," said Kett. "The police."

Okoro nodded.

"I think Niko might be right, sir. It sounds like a fairy tale. But if it's not, ask yourself why any group of criminals would use that name. The red line. It doesn't make a lot of sense."

"From my experience, gang names rarely do," said Kett. "I just assumed it was the name of the line they were running drugs along."

"Maybe," said Okoro.

"But maybe not. That's good thinking, Detective, thank you."

CHAPTER TWENTY-EIGHT

The drive back to Norwich seemed to take forever. The A47 was clogged with farm transports, and somewhere past Dereham Kett had to stop to tend to a seventeen-year-old girl who'd tried to overtake a tractor on a bend and ploughed her red VW Polo into a ditch.

He spent the twenty minutes they'd waited for backup and an ambulance berating the girl for being so careless, as well as detailing all the horrific things that could have happened if luck hadn't been on her side. By the time he got back in the Volvo and drove off, he was pretty certain she would never sit behind a steering wheel again.

It was growing dark by the time he arrived back at HQ, and the MIT offices were mobbed. He went to Clare's office but there was no sign of the Superintendent. He made his way to the kitchen instead and filled the kettle, leaving it to boil while he checked out the Investigation Room. Spalding was the only one there, and she barely looked up when he walked through the door.

"How's it going, Alison?" he asked. "Got the troops in, I see. Busy out there."

"You didn't hear, sir?" she replied. "Another case. Armed robbery, in the city."

"Shit," said Kett. "Anyone hurt?"

Spalding shook her head.

"But they did a runner. Your case has been demoted until we find him."

"Clare about?" he asked.

Spalding didn't answer. Kett made his way to the door, scanning the corridor outside. Then he walked to the back of the room and checked behind the rolling whiteboard to make sure he wasn't lurking there. He had to admit, he couldn't sense the Super anywhere nearby.

He returned to Spalding's desk.

"Just as well," he said, rubbing his eyes. "I am too bloody tired to be tossed—"

"You're always bloody tired," said Clare, barging into the Incident Room so hard the door bounced off the wall. "I've never known a man to do so much bloody moaning about his energy levels."

"Come on, sir," said Kett, rubbing his heart and shooting Spalding a mean look. "*How*?"

"How do I move with the stealth of a jackal and the purposeful force of a rhinoceros?" said Clare. "Because I look after myself, Robert, that's how. I make sure I take the required nutrients from a healthy diet. I drink several litres of water every day. I relieve stress with a combination of high-intensity exercise and vigorous lovemaking with my wife. And—"

"Nope," said Kett, trying to cover his eyes and his ears at the same time.

"And I don't spend my home time being jumped upon continuously by three feral children. This is why I am energised all day and all night, Detective. This is why I never nap, I never moan, I never rest, I never sleep."

He gurned at Kett, his eyes bulging.

"You should try it sometime."

"I really don't want to vigorously make love to your—"

"Where is everyone?" Clare interrupted, perching on a desk at the front of the room. "I need an update."

"I'm here, sir," came a voice from the corridor. A second later, Porter stepped through the door with four mugs in his hand. Kett groaned as the DI set them down on a table. "Don't all fight for them at once."

Kett wandered over, picking up a cup and putting it straight down again.

"It's cold, Pete," he said. "How? I literally just put the kettle on."

Porter shrugged.

"How can somebody be so bad at making tea that they break *physics*?" said Kett, slumping onto a chair.

Porter sat at the desk next to him—smelling a little funky, Kett thought—and took a sip from the cup.

"It *is* a bit cold," he said. "Weird."

"Have you finished?" said Clare. "Update, now."

"I'll start, sir," said Spalding. She shuffled a stack of papers, flipping through them. "Jonah White's in the N&N, critical but stable. He's talking, but he's doped up on painkillers so best take everything he says with a pinch of salt. Confirmed that he and Kieran were asked to run a bag of drugs over to Wayside Manor for the party on Saturday night. Niko gave the order. Full bag means a bit of everything. Meth, MDMA, weed, cocaine, and so on. This was around midnight."

"Did he say what happened?" asked Kett.

"Only that they drove out there in Jonah's Fiesta and walked through the woods to the house. They were expressly forbidden from entering through the front. Jonah says Kieran went on alone, because they were only expecting one delivery guy. Says he watched him walk to the door then he got cold feet and bolted, left him."

"Only we know that's not true," said Kett. "Because at some point Jonah took the rucksack and dropped it off with Jim Prescott."

"We know for sure that was him?" said Clare.

"No, sir, but the red coat is a bit of a giveaway."

"Can we confirm any of this?" asked Clare.

"A little, sir,' said Spalding. "CCTV from the city has Jonah and Kieran in the Fiesta heading to Ashbourne Tower, this is at about four on Saturday afternoon. They stayed there for a few hours before driving away. CCTV shows them leaving the tower at 21:15 with the same bag we found in Jim Prescott's garden. Last sighting is on the A47 back to Dereham at 21:37, still in the Fiesta."

"Good work," said Clare.

"Jonah's the last person we know to see Kieran alive," said Kett. "I spoke with Niko over in King's Lynn and he thought Jonah might have killed him."

"Convenient way of putting the blame on somebody else," said Clare. "I've met Spellman and he's a lying little arse squirt."

"Right, sir," said Kett. "But he might have something. Kieran and Jonah were friends, but that was about all they had in common. Kieran's got a solid home life, loving parents, money. He's doing well at school, he's going places. I think he fell into the drug stuff because he was bored, he was looking for a thrill. It was a game. But Jonah needed it.

He was broke, no hope of an education, no support at home at all. There's a chance he either killed Kieran because he wanted his cut of their operation, or somebody paid him to do it."

"Why?" asked Clare.

"I don't know, sir," said Kett. "Maybe because Kieran wanted out, and he knew too much. And there's another problem with that theory. Kieran was killed by multiple attackers. Jonah would have needed help."

"Maybe he grassed him up," said Spalding, scratching her face with her pencil. "He told the London players something, made it up so that the gang would attack him. That way, Kieran's out of the way and Jonah gets the whole thing."

Kett nodded.

"Could be," he said. "Maybe Jonah steals the bag of drugs as they're on the way out to the party. He blames Kieran. Kieran's murdered by whoever's running the Masque. Jonah takes the bag to Jim Prescott, tells him to hide it. He plans to go back another day to pick it up."

"Except Kieran wasn't killed on site," said Spalding.

"And he was sitting on a hundred times that much money in the safe house," said Porter. "Why not just steal that?"

"Because if Jonah did that, he'd have Niko and the Fulham Crew chasing him down for the rest of his life," said Kett. "This way, he makes a little money and gets away with it. Plus Kieran is out of the picture, Jonah's free to take on his plays as well."

"That seems like a lot of planning for a dense young lad," said Clare, shaking his head. "And a lot of wheels in motion. Remember the saying. If you feel rain, it's probably raining."

"That's a saying, sir?" said Kett.

"Yes, something like that. I mean it's not somebody tossing out of an upstairs window."

"What, sir?"

"It's probably rain," Clare went on, flapping his arms. "Not toss."

"I think the saying is, 'If you hear hooves, think horses, not zebras,'" said Spalding.

"Mine is better." Clare shot her a murderous glare. "Jonah doesn't seem the sort to be able to organise a hit like that and get away with it. Have we found his car yet?"

"The Fiesta?" said Spalding. "No, sir. He claims that by the time he got back to the road it was gone. He walked home, a good three-hour trek. He didn't sleep, just packed a bag and headed to the safe house in the city first thing, in case Kieran was there. He took the bus. We've already pulled the footage and that bit's true."

"Good," Clare said. He turned to Kett. "And what would you like to delight us with this afternoon?"

"Not sure where to start, sir," said Kett. "The party was a real thing, a rave on Saturday night in Wayside Manor. Had to have been a few hundred people there, professionally run, known as the Masque."

"Rings a bell," said Clare. "As far as I know, the Masque has been running for years all over the country. Big parties, all you can eat, drink and snort."

"And we've never shut them down?" said Kett.

"They move from place to place," said Clare. "Very secretive."

"Well, we found a couple of people who'd stowed themselves away in the loft before the house was cleared out."

"Are these the ones that threw their droppings at Savage and Duke?" asked Clare.

"What?" said Porter.

"Yes, sir," said Kett. "Puke and piss and shit everywhere, it was quite something. We got hold of a phone and found an invite to the Masque from the company that organises them. It's all anonymous, they let you know the date in advance, but hold back the location until the day of. You pay in crypto. They have events every few days, there's another one tonight. Might be worth us taking a look."

"Going to a party, sir?" said Porter with a nod of approval. "I'm up for that."

"You're not going to a party," said Clare. "Is there any sign that this is where Kieran was killed?"

"No, sir," said Kett. "Plenty of places to do it, but there's no blood. Locals are scouring the woods, though, so they might find something."

"You thinking it happened there?" said Clare.

Kett blew out a long sigh.

"It's impossible to tell, sir. The only eyewitness to the fact that Kieran was even at the house is Jonah, but if we're treating him as a suspect, then we can't trust him. There's every chance he stopped the Fiesta on the way out to the house, murdered Kieran, then never delivered the bag. He might have even done it close to the park where we found him."

"Let's say Jonah's telling the truth," said Clare. "Kieran enters the party. Why would somebody kill him?"

"Maybe they wanted the drugs," said Porter. "Bunch of punters at the rave, see a kid with a bag full of shit. Easy pickings."

"But if that was the case," said Kett, "how would the bag have got back to Prescott's place?"

"Maybe Prescott was at the party?" said Porter.

Everyone stared at him.

"I mean, it's not impossible," he said.

"It had to have been somebody connected to the gang in Dereham," said Clare. "Somebody who knew to stash the bag at Prescott's place."

"Unless Jonah found the bag after Kieran was killed," said Kett.

"Found it?" said Clare.

"Let's say Kieran wasn't killed for the drugs, sir. It was something else. He enters the house, somebody attacks him, takes his body away. They don't care about the bag, or they don't know what's in it."

"Who does that, Kett?" said Clare. "Who goes to a party and then randomly decides to hack a teenage boy to bloody chunks?"

"These parties are pretty exclusive, sir," he said. "High-end, expensive to attend. It's not just drugs and music, there's sex stuff there too."

"Sex stuff?" said Porter.

"You know, bedrooms and... sexy stuff."

"Alright, granddad," said Porter.

"I'm not—"

"Prostitutes?" said Clare.

"I'm guessing so, sir," said Kett. "The woman we found on site claimed that anything goes. You ask, the party people will provide. She didn't comment on whether those things were legal or not."

"You think Kieran was caught up in that side of it, sir?" asked Spalding. "He goes inside, he gets lost, or he gets distracted. He sees something that takes his fancy."

"Or he sees something he shouldn't have," said Porter.

"Right," said Kett. "That's good. He sees something he

shouldn't have, and they kill him for it. Plenty of rich folk there who wouldn't want any witnesses. No phones, too, so maybe he was caught with his mobile out."

"We haven't found his phone?" asked Clare.

"No, sir," said Spalding. "It's been off since Saturday night."

"These are wild nights," said Kett. "Debauched, definitely dangerous. It's the kind of thing that would attract somebody who doesn't play by the rules, the kind of person who enjoys violence, maybe. There's every chance Kieran met his killer inside the house, an unlucky accident."

"And somebody like that isn't going to be content with one kill, sir," said Porter. "They're going to go back for more."

"Right," said Kett. "Exactly. If we're going to find out what happened to Kieran, I think we need to see one of these things for ourselves."

"You're not going to a tossing party!" said Clare.

"Wasn't just tossing, sir," said Porter. "There's music too, remember?"

Clare glared at him so hard his eyeballs could have popped.

"And speaking of tossing, Porter," he said. "Where have you been all day?"

"I was back in the woods by the park, sir. Had a couple of things I needed to check on. Remember the two brothers who were camping there the night Kieran showed up?"

"No," said Clare.

"Well, I told you about them, sir," said Porter. "Freddy and Ben Rawling. They're on the run from something but I don't know what."

"Did they kill Kieran?" said Clare.

"No, sir. I think they're harmless."

"Then who gives a goblin's toss what they're doing there? We've got enough on our plate."

"I think they need help, sir. They've been living rough for a while and they're in a bad way. The younger kid's got Down's. Sweetest lad you'll ever meet."

"Oh, right," said Clare, softening. "I remember now."

"I wanted to talk to them again about Saturday night, because they were so close by. Freddy has a camera, a 35mm one. He was taking photos of everything. It had film, but I don't know if there's anything on it. I'm getting it developed as we speak."

"Thanks for that," said Clare, his face sour.

"For what?" asked Porter.

"That big bag of useless toss you just gave me. I'll treasure it forever."

"Oh, right, sir. I tagged them as witnesses, by the way. I hope you don't mind. They're staying in a hotel tonight on the allowance."

The Super looked like he was going to reply, but Porter beat him to it.

"I just wanted to get them out of the cold, sir," he said. "I don't think they would have lasted another night out there."

"You lot are really yanking my tosspipe today," said Clare. "I've got an armed robber on the loose somewhere in the county, and you lot are dossing about at raves and being Good Samaritans to lost souls in the woods. Anyone find out any more about the red line bollocks?"

"Not much," said Kett. "Some folk are terrified of it, most don't believe it."

"But it's a drug thing?"

"I'm not sure," said Kett. "Feels like more than that. But I don't know what."

"Of course you don't," said Clare.

"I might have something that helps, sir," said a voice from the corridor.

Savage jogged in, out of breath. She was wearing a clean shirt and a fresh suit, but she still carried a faint whiff of poo —enough to make Porter pinch his nose as she passed. She crossed the room, stopping at the table with the tea.

"Hang on, gasping," she said, picking up a mug and taking a sip. It lasted about a second in her mouth before she let it trickle back into the mug. She put it on the table. "Never mind."

"What is it, Kate?" asked Clare.

"I had a call from West Norfolk Police as I was driving back into the city," she said. "They brought their forensic unit to the manor after we left this morning, and they think they've found blood."

"In the house?" asked Kett.

"No, sir. In the grounds. There's a folly in the woods, it's a ruin. There's nothing much to look at, but they were suspicious because of the smell. Bleach. It's everywhere, buckets of the stuff. But the forensic team found evidence of blood as well."

"Shit," said Kett. "If that's where Kieran died, it means the killer was prepared. They brought bleach to destroy the evidence."

He looked at Clare.

"That changes everything, sir. Somebody at that rave knew they were going to kill. It was premeditated."

"And they might do it again," added Savage.

Clare checked his watch again.

"You know when this thing's going to be?"

"Tonight, sir," said Kett.

"You know where?"

"No, sir," said Savage. "But we're on the email list for attendees thanks to Naked Jesus."

"Thanks to *who*?"

Clare waved his own question away.

"Doesn't matter. Have it your way. I'll do all the hard work. You lot go to your bloody party."

CHAPTER TWENTY-NINE

Kett sat at his desk, nursing a proper cup of tea as he studied the meagre files they had for Kieran Spicer's murder. The tea was a necessity, because ever since Spalding had stolen his desk by the office's best radiator, he'd been relegated to the far corner of the bullpen where the temperature seemed to hover a few degrees above absolute zero. Even with his coat on and the tea cradled in his hands, he felt like he was close to freezing over.

He glared at the back of Spalding's head. She was so warm she'd taken her jumper off.

The bullpen had emptied out after they'd received a tip about the armed robber, Clare leading the charge. Porter was missing too. Kett had sent him to check out the folly at Wayside Manor.

He shivered so hard that a little of his tea spilled. He could have moved desks if he'd wanted to, but the truth was the cold helped focus him.

And right now, he needed all the help he could get.

No matter how hard he tried to arrange the pieces of Kieran Spicer's death into some kind of pattern, his mind wouldn't let him. It should have been an open and shut case: a teenage boy is recruited into a notorious County Lines gang, does something stupid, and pays the price with his life. It happened too often: wrong place, wrong time, and the majority of victims were young people.

But that just didn't seem to fit here.

Something was missing.

"Sir," said Savage from her desk. She tipped her chair back, looking over her shoulder. "This is really weird."

Kett was too cold to get up and walk over. He took a sip of his tea while he waited for her to continue.

"I've read through every email on Naked Jesus' account."

"Do we not have a proper name for him yet?" asked Kett.

"Liam Walton, sir."

"Doesn't have quite the same ring to it."

"Uh, no. Anyway, the emails for the parties come with a list of instructions on how to get there. Usually, if you were going to Wayside you'd drive up the A47, east or west, before taking the Shipdham Road. Or come up from Watton. Those are the only main access routes. Everything else is country lanes, a nightmare at any time, but especially in the dark and *especially* especially if they're busy."

"Right," said Kett.

"But the email for the party on Saturday gave specific directions on how to get there. And they're nuts. They told people to drive all the way to Swaffham, then take the Brandon Road south. After two miles they said to take a left onto an old farm track and follow that to South Pickenham. Then they were back on the lane all the way to Wayside."

"To avoid cameras," said Kett. "Clever. But there must be cameras in Swaffham?"

"There are, sir," said Savage. "Plenty in the centre of the town. But only one on the north end of Brandon Road."

"So check that to see—"

"Already have, sir," said Savage. "It's not working. Somebody cut the cable, it's been on the list for maintenance since Saturday afternoon."

"Shit," said Kett. "We're blind?"

"We can send out Uniforms to check for doorbell cameras, car cameras, anything like that." Savage shook her head. "But I think they checked the route pretty well. The Swaffham cams have caught a lot of traffic, but there's no way of telling which way they go when they leave town."

"Check anyway," said Kett. "Cross-reference them against anyone who has a record. The more people we can identify from the Masque, the more likely we are to find a witness."

He called across the room.

"Alison, you found anything?"

"I'm plenty warm enough, sir, thank you for asking," Spalding yelled.

Kett shot daggers at the back of her head until she turned around.

"I've raided Google," she said. "I've spent an hour searching everywhere. Social media, photo sites, directories. There's not one single mention of the Masque, of these parties, of the red line. All the stuff you asked for."

"We know they're private," said Kett. "They don't want people talking about them."

"Right, sir," said Savage. "But not a single slip? Over all the years they've been running? Naked Jesus was shouting about it. We're talking hundreds of people drunk and drugged up at least twelve nights every month, and not one of them accidentally posts a photo or leaves a comment on Facebook?"

"It is weird," said Kett. "But these are serious people, Kate. It's not a rave, they're not doing it for fun. They're making a tonne of money, and they're risking a lot. They probably make it very clear to everyone at the start that if you mess up, you pay a price."

"Like at the trampoline park, sir?" said Savage.

"Huh?"

She swivelled around in her chair to face him.

"You know, when you go to the trampoline park they make you watch this video before you start bouncing. It shows all the things you can't do, and what will happen if you do them. Broken legs, crushed heads, splintered spines. Horrific injury and then death. Really puts you in the mood for it."

Kett laughed into his tea, spraying it over his chin. He wiped his face with his sleeve.

"Those videos are terrible, aren't they?" he said. "First time we took the kids to the trampoline park in the city, Alice wouldn't stop crying. She didn't bounce once."

"Exactly, sir," said Savage with a shrug. "Maybe they issue a warning at the start of the party. A threat of death."

"You think that's what happened to Kieran?" said Kett.

"Feels a bit extreme, sir. And I checked his socials, no mention of the parties or the drugs. On the internet, he was a normal kid doing normal kid stuff."

"You find anything else?" he asked Spalding.

"Nope. No companies listed under Masque or red line, no organisations, no criminal enterprises that have used them as an alias. There's the urban legend we keep hearing about, but I think that's all it is. Nobody knows a single verifiable fact about them."

"Fuck's sake," said Kett, taking another sip of his tea.

"Oh," said Spalding. "Hang on."

She walked to the printer as it began to churn out some papers. Kett waited for her to make her way over. She shivered as she approached.

"Bloody Baltic over here, sir," she said.

He gave her a hard stare.

"You do realise, Alison, that I am your superior officer. If I ask you to give me my desk back, you have to do it."

"Then ask, sir," she said, giving him a hard stare right back. "See how that turns out."

For a moment they eyeballed each other, then Kett nodded to the paper.

"What's that?"

"Results of Spicer's autopsy," she said, laying it on Kett's desk. "Franklin just sent it over."

Savage got up, she and Spalding sandwiching Kett as he started to read. Most of it he already knew, and didn't particularly want to hear again, so he skimmed the first few paragraphs.

On the fourth, he stopped dead.

"Holy shit," he said, reading it in his head, then reading it aloud to be certain it was real. "'*Victim's blood shows significant levels of ketamine. Traces also found in stomach, which means it was ingested shortly prior to death.*'"

"He was drugged, sir," said Savage.

"He was," said Kett. "Either he took Ketamine, or somebody made him. But..."

He leaned back in his chair, and the wave of relief that washed over him was strong enough that he felt the tears prickle in his eyes.

"It means he probably didn't know it was happening," Savage finished for him. "Significant levels. Ketamine's a dissociative anaesthetic, pulls you out of your head, numbs the pain."

"He didn't feel it," said Kett. "Doesn't make it any easier."

Except it did.

"If the killer was at the party, sir, they might have sourced some Ketamine there. This might have been part of their plan."

Savage pointed to the page.

"He had alcohol in his system too. The K could have been disguised in the drink."

"So the killer drugs him at the party, lures him outside to the folly where he's got a kill kit ready to go," says Kett. "There are a couple of problems with that theory, though."

Savage and Spalding waited while he sipped his tea.

"First, the punters at the party don't know where it's going to be until a few hours before, right?"

"That's what we've been told, sir."

"But the killer must have had some time to prepare."

"Unless he had the kit in his car," said Spalding. "He gets the notice about the location at the same time as everyone else. He's got everything he needs. He drives over, parks his car with all the others, scouts the woods, stashes his kit."

"Feels risky," said Kett. "Especially if there's security there."

"Riskier than killing a kid in the woods in the middle of the party?" asked Savage.

"Fair point."

"The killer could be involved in the organisation of the Masque?" said Spalding. "They know where it's going to be in advance, it gives them the time they need to prepare."

"Right," said Kett. "Good. But there's another problem.

Whoever killed Kieran knew about his link to the playground where we found him. They had to have, because after they killed him they took him there. They pushed him down the slide, on the swings, left him on the merry-go-round. He's not a random kill, they know him."

Nobody replied, the weight of the case sitting on them, suffocatingly heavy.

"And there's still the fact that the killer's not working alone," said Savage after a moment. "There's more than one of them."

Kett finished his tea and rubbed his face, groaning into his hand.

"This job," he muttered. "All that does is pull me back to the drug links. What if a rival gang followed Kieran to the house when he made his delivery? They wait for him to drop off the bag then attack him in the woods."

It was as full of holes as everything else that had been suggested, which is why nobody answered him.

"Any news about tonight's party?" he asked.

"Not yet, sir," said Savage. "You got a plan?"

"I'm working on it, Kate."

He stared at the ceiling.

"What are we missing?" he asked.

"Not sure, sir," said Savage, heading back to her desk. "But whatever it is, maybe Porter will find it."

CHAPTER THIRTY

PORTER WAS LOST, WHICH WAS QUITE A FEAT considering he'd only left the road two minutes ago and the woods weren't even that thick. He'd followed Savage's instructions and entered through the hole in the perimeter wall, telling the constable on duty that he didn't need any help finding his way. But the bloody trees were running rings around him—*literally*, he was sure of it. The bastard things had uprooted themselves and were shifting positions, just to piss him off.

"Fucking woody bastard pricks!" he roared, a little louder than he meant to.

"Oi!" came a reply from deeper in the woods. "Who said that?"

Porter walked towards the voice, fighting his way through a bush to see a couple of constables ahead at the foot of a shallow hill. One of them was PC Niven, and she gave him a welcoming smile. The other was an older man who offered a tight nod that suggested he was as upset about being here as Porter was.

A woman stood between them, in her fifties or early

sixties, dressed in a Barbour jacket, jeans and a pair of bright pink wellies. She was as skinny as a rake, her silvering hair pulled into a ponytail beneath a yellow hat.

"Hi, sir," said Niven. "Did you just hear somebody shouting?"

"Oh, yeah," said Porter, tripping on a root as he stumbled over. He waved his arm backwards. "Some, uh, hoodlum on the road. Don't worry about it. I'm looking for the folly, you know where it is?"

"It's right around there," said Niven, nodding to her left. "You want me to take you?"

"No," said Porter, before realising he'd probably get lost again. "Actually, yeah, maybe."

He looked at the woman.

"Who are you, then?"

"Sorry, sir," said Niven. "This is P—"

"Patricia De'Ath," the woman said, offering a slender hand that Porter shook. Her fingers were like ice pops. "It's my house."

"The Manor?" said Porter. "Oh, right, you're the niece?"

"I'm a little more than that," she protested. "But yes."

"You don't live here, though?"

"Dear God, no," she said. "You've seen the place?"

"Actually, no," said Porter. "Caught a glimpse from the road, though. Looks nice enough."

"A hundred years ago, maybe," said De'Ath. "Now it's a ruin. Belonged to my uncle, who adored it, then my aunt, who detested it. No kids, so it passed to me. Not that I wanted it."

"Too much work?" Porter asked.

"Too many memories," she replied, her eyes glassy as

she stared into the trees. "I don't come here much, figure the woods will reclaim the place in time."

"You don't want to sell it?"

De'Ath laughed quietly.

"And pass on those ghosts to somebody else? That is a particularly awful form of cruelty, don't you think?"

Porter had no idea what she was talking about, so he didn't reply.

"Ms De'Ath lives over in Didlington, sir," said Niven. "Heard we were here and came over to see if she could help."

"And can you?" Porter asked.

"I don't think so," said De'Ath. "Like I say, I never come here. We've had a few squatters and teenagers in the place, nobody that you diligent folk haven't been able to remove for us. But I can't even tell you the last time we were here."

"We being?"

"Me and Margo."

"Your wife?"

"In all but name," she said. "She wants to build the place back up, can't understand why I wouldn't. She calls it our goldmine, but she doesn't understand there's no gold in these walls, only..."

"Memories," said Porter. "Yeah, I get it."

He clapped his hands together.

"Well, if you can think of anything at all that might help us, please don't hesitate to say. It really could make the difference."

He set off, twigs cracking beneath his feet.

"I can take you to the folly, if you like?" De'Ath called out behind him.

Porter looked back.

"Is it clean?" he asked Niven.

"There's no, uh, blood or anything, sir," she said. "Forensics are long gone."

Porter nodded to De'Ath, waiting patiently for her to catch up. She walked stiffly, as if she'd suffered some kind of injury to her back. PC Niven accompanied her, one hand poised as if to catch her if she fell. She didn't though, keeping her balance even on the treacherous ground, as if she'd done this a thousand times.

"You say you've had squatters here," Porter asked as they walked. "Do you know about anyone else who might have used the house or the grounds? Drug dealers, maybe?"

"Out here?" said De'Ath, limping like a machine and already struggling for breath. "Who would they sell their wares to? The earthworms?"

Porter laughed.

"You know about the party on Saturday night?"

"I do," she said, sniffing. "Your colleague here was just filling me in. Ironically, we heard the music from our house, we had no idea it was coming from here. Quite outrageous that they would use the manor like that. Or that they would even know about the place."

"That's a good point," said Porter. "How would they have known?"

De'Ath ran a hand over her wet nose.

"Maybe they, like you, simply saw it from the street," she said.

"But you didn't know anything about it?"

"I do not," she said.

"And Margo?"

She met his eye a little more fiercely than he was expecting, but she didn't reply.

"That's it there," said PC Niven.

Porter followed her finger, and it took him a moment to see what she was pointing at. About fifty yards ahead, drenched in the shadows of the woods, was a structure. It was almost invisible because most of it was draped in ivy, a handful of stone ribs poking out from the vegetation like bones in a rotting corpse. When he sniffed the air, he realised he could already smell bleach.

"What is this place?" he asked as they drew near.

"I always hated it here," said De'Ath, her voice quiet. "When we were kids I wouldn't go anywhere near it. It's got an atmosphere. Can you feel it?"

Porter did feel it, a sense of foreboding and oppression that made his scalp shrivel up.

"Don't all woods feel like that, though?" he said. "It's the trees."

"No, this place is different," said De'Ath. "But don't ask me how. My uncle told us terrible stories about the folly."

"Yeah?"

"Yes. Monsters, demons, ghosts and goblins, everything really. He told us people were killed here and offered as human sacrifices to the old gods of the woods."

"Seriously?"

"No, not seriously. He also told us a werewolf called Albert lived out here, and that if we got too close he'd knit our hair into mittens. He was just trying to scare us, nothing more."

"And yet here we are," said Porter.

The folly seemed to grow unnaturally large as they approached, stretching and swelling like a cobra that wanted to scare them away. It was far taller than Porter had originally thought, maybe thirty feet to the top. There was a break in the ivy to his right and he pushed himself through, ignoring the scuttling touch of bugs and spiders as he entered the building.

It was pitch black inside, but when he switched on his torch he saw a large circular space framed with columns. The remains of a staircase reached hopelessly towards a balcony on the floor above, and past that was a domed ceiling that was still largely intact. The mass of vegetation made it feel like a child's den, quiet and dark and hidden.

It almost felt safe in here.

Until he remembered, again, that this was where Kieran Spicer had been brought to die.

He breathed through his mouth so the bleach wouldn't burn his nose, examining the folly with his torch and finding nothing that Cara Hay and her team wouldn't have already spotted. But the truth of it was in that stench. You didn't bring a gallon of bleach into the woods to make the trees shine.

"I heard about the boy," said De'Ath. She had followed him in, pressing so close behind him that he could feel the heat of her breath against his neck. "Is it true?"

"We don't know," said Porter. "It's an ongoing investigation, sorry."

"What a place to meet your end," she went on. "Give me any ground but here for my eternal rest. For here, rest you shall not find."

"Huh?" he said.

She didn't say anything else, peeling away from him and retreating through the curtain of ivy. Porter waited a moment more, hoping to find something that might explain what had happened, hoping to find the thing that ended this case, which would get him out of the woods.

Finding nothing.

He shuffled out backwards until there was room to turn, brushing more creepy crawlies from his hair as he retreated into the woods.

"Bastard buggy pricks," he muttered, his skin rippling.

De'Ath had walked away a little, staring into the skeletal canopy. PC Niven was waiting for him, though, her face miserable.

"How far away is the house, Flick?" Porter asked, feeling like there were ants beneath his shirt.

"Uh..." She got her bearings, pointing to the way they'd walked. "I'd say as far as we came, then that again, sir. Maybe 400 metres?"

"What's that in normal distances?"

"Uh... like, a quarter of a mile?"

"Is that a guess, or a fact?"

"A fact?" she said, pulling a face.

"Because you sound like you've got a question mark at the end of every sentence."

"Sorry, sir?"

"Never mind."

Porter turned to the trees, seeing the bristling walls of bare branches, the minefield of vegetation.

"Can you see somebody dragging or carrying a teenage boy a quarter of a mile through all of this shit, Flick?" he asked. "It would have taken all night, especially if he was fighting back."

"Unless he knew his killer, sir," said Niven. "And he went willingly."

Porter nodded.

"Or unless they didn't pass through the woods at all," said De'Ath, who must have had the hearing of a cat to have listened from where she stood.

She turned, the shadows of the trees dancing on her frown.

"You do know about the tunnel, don't you?"

DE'ATH LED them past the folly, stopping more than once to get her bearings. It was only when her pink welly landed on the ground and a dull clank echoed out that she threw her hands up.

"I knew it was around here somewhere," she said.

Porter stepped up beside her, kicking the ground with his shoe until he found the edge of a thin metal plate. It was buried beneath a carpet of vegetation, and when he scuffed some of the leaves away he saw that it was painted brown and green to better camouflage it.

"Trapdoor?" he said.

"My uncle was a professional amateur at everything he did," said De'Ath.

"Flick, give me a hand getting all this shit off it, will you."

PC Niven kicked her way over the top of the trapdoor, clearing the vegetation with her feet. It was easier than Porter had expected, mainly because much of it looked like it had been recently cut—thick branches neatly severed.

That could only mean one thing.

"Somebody's used it recently," he said.

He spotted a handle, flapping his arms at Niven to move her out of the way. He wrapped his hands in the sleeves of his coat and grabbed it. The door was cumbersome rather than heavy, and the way he had to lean over made it harder than it should have been. But after a couple of good tugs, the metal hatch lifted. Niven grabbed the other side, her face slick with sweat as she struggled to heave it over. After an age, gravity kicked in and the plate fell away, sliding down the slope.

"Well, that's definitely a tunnel," said Porter.

There was a hole in the dirt, maybe two metres wide and crudely dug. He clicked on his torch and aimed it inside, finding nothing but loose soil, tree roots and a much deeper darkness at the bottom.

"Yeah, there's no way I'm going down there," he said. "Where does it lead, Patricia?"

"To the house," said De'Ath, peering past his shoulder. "There were tunnels already here when my uncle bought the place. He became a bit obsessed with extending them. This is the only one he finished, as far as I know. I never went in them. Too many scary stories about what might be inside."

"Albert the werewolf, yeah," said Porter. "Where does it end up in the house?"

"In the cellar," she said. "In the back."

She frowned at them.

"You do know about the secret room, don't you?"

AS FAR AS secret rooms went, it was a doozy.

Porter and Niven followed De'Ath to the back of the house, gathering an escort of constables as they went. She stopped outside an open door, took a breath, then plunged into the dark. The steps that led into the cellar were so worn by time and use that Porter almost buggered over on the way down, coming close to taking out De'Ath on the way.

"Bastard steps," he muttered, and he thought he'd said it

beneath his breath until De'Ath's disapproving scowl caught the torchlight.

"It's this way," she said, clicking her fingers. "I'll need to see where I'm going."

Porter handed her his torch and she set off into the dark cellar. More lights followed, wavering from left to right between bare stone walls, from the dirt floor to the low, vaulted ceiling. The cellar was pretty much empty, and the chill was worse down here than it had been outside.

"It's there somewhere," said De'Ath as they approached the back wall. A row of wooden bookcases had been built into the alcove, every shelf empty.

"You sure?" asked Porter.

She reached beneath one shelf, feeling for something.

"I am, although it's been fifty years since I was last down here so I don't know if I can—"

The shelf clicked, loud enough to make Porter flinch.

"Beautiful," said De'Ath. "I need a strong pair of hands, please."

She moved out of the way and Porter took hold of the shelf.

"Here?" he asked, and she nodded.

He gave the shelf a tug and felt the entire bookcase slide out towards him. It didn't want to come but he pulled again and it finally relented, trundling across the floor on squeaking rollers. It came out about a foot, then stopped, bringing a breath of cold, dead air with it.

"Roll it to the right," said De'Ath.

He tried, but nothing happened.

"Your other right," she said.

This time the shelf obeyed, gliding alongside its neighbour and revealing a hole in the wall. A few beams of torchlight had already strayed inside, revealing a room maybe ten-foot square.

Porter didn't want to go in, but it wasn't like anyone else was dying to do it.

"Fine," he grumbled, taking his torch back from De'Ath before stepping over the threshold. "But if anyone closes this door while I'm in there, I'll eat you."

"You could always take the tunnel out, sir," Niven offered.

She was right. Directly across from the hidden door was a sheet of corrugated iron, and when Porter peeked behind it, he saw the tunnel opening. This end was bigger, its walls brick and its ceiling vaulted. The air was damp, but it carried the freshness of the day and the old smell of the woods.

"Bloody bastard tunnels," he muttered, swinging the torch back the other way. There was no furniture here, no decoration of any kind.

But there was writing on the wall.

He approached it, shining the light on the giant letters that had been neatly drawn there in crimson paint.

Or blood, he thought.

THE RED ROOM.

Beneath that was a single red line of paint, followed by a row of smaller letters that simply read: *Follow the red line, find the red room, make a red wish.*

Porter shivered in another gust of cold wind, the knife wound in his shoulder crying out. He pushed the back of his knuckle against one of the letters and felt the tackiness of it as he pulled away.

"Shit on it," he said as he took a photograph of the wall with his phone. He tried to send it to Kett, but he had no signal down here.

"You find anything, sir?" said Niven, peeking her head through the gap.

"I think so," he said. "I mean it, Flick, do not close that bloody door. Don't even lean on it."

He took another photo, then beetled towards the exit, only breathing again when he'd left the secret room. The little huddle of constables stared back at him, seven of them now.

"Right, pop quiz," he said. "Who here likes Country and Western music?"

The older constable who'd been outside when he'd first arrived put his hand up, and so did a younger one.

"Great," said Porter. "And your punishment for that is that you get to explore the tunnel."

They started to protest, but Porter silenced them with a raised finger.

"Just map where it goes, and if it gets complicated come back. Don't get lost in there. I only want to know if it leads to the folly."

They traipsed into the room with their torches out, grumbling beneath their breath.

"Somebody get Cara Hay out here again," Porter said. "The rest of you, go back to whatever you were doing."

They seemed more than happy to be given the excuse to leave, clattering out of the cellar. Dust rained from the ceiling as they trampled up the stairs. Porter wiped it from his eyes, turning to see that Patricia De'Ath had wandered inside the secret room.

"Sorry, Ms De'Ath," he said. "That's a crime scene. I really need you to come out of there."

She didn't answer, staring at the painted wall like she'd seen a ghost.

"Ms De'Ath?" he said. "Please."

Finally, she turned to him.

"Do you know what they mean, those words?" she asked, her quiet voice seeming to fill the whole cellar.

"This way," he said. He didn't want to walk back inside, so he frantically beckoned her instead. "Out you come."

She still didn't move, studying him with an odd expression.

"You do know about the red room, don't you?"

CHAPTER THIRTY-ONE

"I really don't see why this is necessary, Kate," said Kett.

Savage was reversing her Audi into one of the few remaining parking spaces at Chapelfield shopping centre, and she didn't reply until she'd pulled up the handbrake and switched off the engine. Even then, all he got was, "Huh?"

"I said, I don't see why we need to do this," he repeated. "Can't we just go as we are?"

Savage gave Kett a once over, then opened her door.

"What?" he said, chasing her out. "What was that look for?"

"Sir, when was the last time you went to an illegal party fuelled by dangerous drugs and sex?"

Her voice echoed across the quiet car park. A woman was walking past on the other side of the aisle, pushing a pram. She gave Savage a look of horror, scuttling away at double-speed.

"If we're going to do this, sir," Savage went on, "you need to look the part."

She set off towards the lifts, Kett checking his suit as he walked after her.

"It's Marks and bloody Spencer's, Kate," he said. "It's not like it's from Primark or anything."

The woman with the buggy had already pushed the button for the lift, and she watched them warily as they walked over.

"That's not the point, sir," said Savage. "The point is not to look like you're a police officer. These are serious people. They'll get violent if they find out who you are. And remember, whoever killed Kieran could be there. We can't risk them making us."

The woman pushed the button more urgently.

"I'm not even sure I should go," said Kett. "Somebody might recognise me. Everyone knows I was the guy who put the hammer through the Pig Man's head."

The lift doors opened, but the woman with the pram didn't move.

"After you," Kett told her.

"I'll get the next one," she squeaked.

Savage and Kett walked in together, watching her frightened face disappear behind the closing doors.

"I always forget normal people don't live in our world," said Kett.

Savage laughed.

"You're right about the disguise," he said. "And about being careful. Too many of us and they'll realise something's up. We need two inside, no more. Definitely you."

"You're probably too old anyway, sir," said Savage as the lift doors opened into the noise and bustle of the mall.

"I'm not too old, Kate," Kett told her as they glided into the channels of moving people. It was only mid-November, but the place was bedecked in lights, the shopfronts sagging beneath the weight of Christmas joy. "I'm sure plenty of people my age go to illegal rave parties."

"Of course they do, sir," said Savage. "All the cool folk go to *illegal rave parties*. And that's what they all call them, too. Illegal rave parties. There's Duke."

Kett looked, but couldn't see him.

"Where?"

"There, sir," said Savage, pointing.

The PC was hiding in the crowds, dressed in a black tracksuit, with a white hat pulled down over his eyes and a red scarf wrapped up to his nose.

"Oh yeah," said Kett.

They cut through the seating for Costa Coffee, meeting Duke on the other side.

"Didn't recognise you there, Aaron," said Kett, raising his voice to be heard over the dull roar of chatter. He noticed that the hat was crocheted in the shape of a happy little snowman, complete with two arms that stuck out to the sides and a wonky carrot nose. He had no doubt at all that the big PC had made it himself. "What's with the outdoor gear? It's roasting in here."

Duke mumbled something that was lost behind the scarf. When he saw their blank faces, he pulled it down, leaning in.

"People keep saying things to me," he said. "They keep calling me..."

He looked left and right and leaned in even more.

"Bollock Cop."

Savage snorted a laugh that she quickly covered with her hand.

"That's so unoriginal," said Kett, trying to keep the smile off his face. "I can think of a hundred better names."

He considered it for a second or two.

"Dicksquashed of Dock Green?"

Savage snorted again. Duke looked deeply unimpressed.

"Sorry," said Kett. "But honestly, mate, don't worry about it. It will blow over."

"You did the right thing, coming out," said Savage, giving Duke a playful punch on the shoulder. "Facing it head on. You're Aaron Duke, Britain's Bravest Copper. Never forget it."

Duke pulled the scarf back over his mouth without another word.

"I think it might be a bad idea putting Duke undercover too, sir," said Savage. "Given all the memes and stuff."

"Memes?" said Duke, pulling the scarf down again.

"We might be okay," Kett said. "I barely recognised him when we walked up. It's a masked ball, right?"

"Masks aren't compulsory, sir," said Savage.

"But they're permitted, and we already know they don't check your ID when you go in."

He popped his lips, studying the various shops.

"Let's get you both kitted out anyway, we can decide on who goes in later. What kinds of things do people wear at these illegal rave parties?"

Savage started to answer, but his phone was ringing and he pulled it out.

"Porter," he said, reading the name on the screen. He looked at Savage. "You two okay to shop?"

"We are, sir," she replied, looping her arm through Duke's and leading him away.

Kett answered the call.

"Pete, any news?"

"Yeah, sir," said Porter. "Couldn't call you from the house, no signal. Did you get the photo?"

Kett checked his messages, then put the phone back to his ear.

"No, what did you find?"

"A secret room, sir, down in the cellar. Linked to a tunnel that runs right to the folly where Kieran was murdered."

"Wait, the cellar of the house? I was down there, didn't see anything."

"Yeah, that's what I said, a *secret* room. Behind some shelves."

Kett thought back.

"That's where I found the red ribbon," he said. "On the shelves at the back, another one on the stairs, both tied in bows. They were taken for evidence."

"Weird," said Porter.

Kett sat on a chair, using the back of his hand to push an empty cup to the other side of the table.

"How'd you find the room?"

"Owner showed up, Patricia De'Ath. She knew about the tunnel and the room. The photo arrived yet?"

Kett checked again.

"No, Pete, just tell me what it was."

"Small room, nothing in there except some words painted on the wall. I say paint, it looks like blood. I don't know, Cara's on her way."

Porter stopped for breath, and Kett felt his phone buzz. It was a message, and when he opened it he saw the room that was being described. He could just about read the biggest line of text without his glasses.

"The Red Room," he said.

"How did you... Oh, the photo arrived? Yeah, The Red Room in big letters, then under that it says, *follow the red line, find a red room, make a red wish.*"

"There's nothing else in there?" asked Kett.

"No, sir. But get this, Patricia De'Ath knew—"

"Who?"

"Patricia De'Ath, sir, I just mentioned her. She owns the house but doesn't live there. She knows about the red line and the red room. Said her uncle used to talk about it fifty years ago. He always told her if you found a red line in the woods, string or ribbon or something, you could follow it and it would lead you to a red room. It's almost impossible, apparently, but if you do find the end, and you reach the room, you can make a wish. Any wish."

"You can make a wish?" said Kett.

"Right," said Porter, his voice fading out for a second.

"And it comes true?"

"Yes, sir."

Kett waited for a moment.

"I mean, I'm not saying it's *actually* true," said Porter. "But it's weird, right?"

"If this woman knew about it, and she said her uncle knew about it, then maybe one of them wrote it on the wall years ago?"

"She says it wasn't her, sir," said Porter. "And it's fresh. I mean, it's dry, but it's still sticky. It's recent. Honestly, it feels more like blood than paint."

"You said there was a tunnel?" said Kett.

"Yeah, splits in the middle. One branch goes to the folly in the woods. Other side doesn't go anywhere, just ends. Uniforms scoped them out, but there's nothing there. No blood, nothing that links to Kieran. But it's definitely been used recently."

"Okay," said Kett. He nodded to the waitress as she collected the cup from his table, waiting for her to walk away. "Did Patricia say anything else about the red line and the room?"

"I mean, yeah," said Porter. "But none of it made any sense."

"She there now?"

"No, sir. She had to go. Tried to get her to stay, but I couldn't exactly cuff her."

"So do your best to explain it," said Kett. "A red line, hidden somewhere, if you follow it you find a room, and you get to make a magic wish, is that right?"

"Right, sir. But she said those wishes are tainted. No, not tainted, poisoned. That's how she..."

His voice faded into static.

"Pete?"

"Sir? You there?"

"Poisoned," said Kett. "How?"

"Same as with all these stories," Porter went on, fizzing. "Like genies and shit. You can make a wish, but it always comes back to bite you."

"She said that?"

"Yeah, but not exactly like that. She said you make a wish, but it isn't free, something along those lines. You make a wish and you end up paying more than you can ever imagine. I don't know, I can't really remember. It was all pretty weird, and my shoulder was hurting. I think I stopped listening after a while."

"That's really useful, Pete," said Kett.

"No problem, sir," Porter replied, missing the sarcasm completely. "Oh, but she said that's why it's red."

"Why?" said Kett.

"Why it's red," Porter said again, fading.

"Yeah, but *why* is it red?"

There was a moment of silence before Porter realised what Kett was asking.

"Right, sorry, sir. I mean the line is red because that's the colour of blood. You pay for your wish with blood."

"Okay," said Kett, drawing the word out. "Did Patricia De'Ath seem a little... Was she drunk, Pete? Because this is all sounding pretty far-fetched."

"Definitely not drunk, sir," said Porter. "At least, I hope not. She was driving."

"Right."

"It's an old wives' tale, sir. I don't believe it, but... I don't know. Some people do believe this shit, don't they? Look what happened in the summer because Aggie Clegg believed in demons."

Kett didn't reply, taking a long, deep breath instead.

"I've got Ms De'Ath's number," Porter went on. "She seems happy enough to talk about it. She's a proper local, says the red line's been a Norfolk myth for as long as she can remember. I'll text it to you."

"Thanks, Pete," said Kett.

"You know who'd be able to tell us more, right?"

"Balls?" said Kett. "Nope, not happening."

He rubbed his eyes until fireworks exploded against the dark.

"Listen, I'm going to need you back soon. We should plan this undercover job, at the illegal rave party."

"They really aren't called that, sir," said Porter. "I'm on my way, see you back at HQ?"

"Yeah."

He hung up, searching the crowds for Savage and Duke and seeing no sign of them. He was halfway to getting out of his seat when the waitress returned, a paper cup of tea in her hand. To Kett's surprise, she placed it on the table in front of him.

"Oh," he said. "I didn't order one, sorry."

"I know," she said. She couldn't have been much older than eighteen, and with her broad smile and her kind eyes, she reminded him of Alice. "You just looked like you needed one."

"That's really kind of you," said Kett, his own smile warming his face. "You may have just saved my life."

"That's what we're here for," she said, walking away and collecting rubbish as she went.

Kett wrapped his hands around the cup, breathing deeply, losing himself in the smell of it. He genuinely felt a hundred times happier for this unexpected kindness, so much so that he was still grinning five minutes later when Savage and Duke reappeared. They sat down on the other side of the table, dumping a collection of shopping bags on the floor.

"Done?" Kett asked them.

"Yeah, sir," said Savage. "I think we're good."

"We're definitely not good," said Duke from behind his scarf. "I've told you, I'm not wearing them."

"We'll see," said Savage, giving Kett a wink. "Shall we go back to HQ? I think it's time for a fashion show."

CHAPTER THIRTY-TWO

There was little in the way of developments waiting for Kett when he walked into the Incident Room, although a handful of new photographs had found their way onto the wall. He saw Kieran's father there, Mike Spicer, a copy of the police report from his arson attack pinned next to him.

Margaret, Kieran's mother, was next, a family photo with the three boys, taken in the park where he had been found dead. Kieran was a couple of years younger here and he could have been a different person entirely, his face alive with delight as he pushed his youngest brother on the swing—far too high, by the look of it. Jay watched from the top of the slide, slightly out of focus.

Their mother was halfway between them, a smile on her face but an anxious look in her eyes. It was the same expression Kett wore when Alice pushed her sisters on the swing, he realised—the knowledge that broken bones were only a careless shove away.

There were a few photos towards the edge of the board: what looked like school portraits of four teenage boys, as well as a mugshot of one more. With their dead eyes and dull smirks, none of them looked like the kind of person Kett would want to meet in a dark alley.

He slid his glasses on and leaned in for a closer look. Only when he pulled away again did he feel the breath on his ear.

"Welcome back, Detective," whispered a voice that was almost entirely drowned out by the scream that ripped its way out of Kett's mouth.

He spun around, the Superintendent's face just inches from his own, his eyes bulging, white flecks on his lips. He was holding a long roll of paper like a sword.

"For the love of God, sir," Kett wheezed, feeling a stab of pain in the left side of his chest. "You *have* to stop doing that."

"No," said Clare. "I've decided it's my mission in life."

"To kill me?"

"To train you. It's disgusting how easy it is for me to sneak up on you, Robert. Imagine if I was a criminal, by the time you realised I was there you'd already have a knife in your back."

"Comforting," said Kett, finding the nearest chair and collapsing into it, still rubbing his aching chest. He nodded to the photographs of the boys on the board. "Did we get anywhere with those other lads from the park?"

"Dead ends," said Clare. "All accounted for on the night Kieran was killed. They admitted to being at the park, but they all left before eleven. Seemed spooked by something but wouldn't say what. Jonah and Kieran were the last two there. Toerags, all of them, but their story is consistent and they have alibis."

The Superintendent dumped the roll of paper on the desk at the front of the room.

"Where have you been, anyway? Spalding has been looking for you."

Before Kett could answer, the door opened and DS Spalding walked in, carrying an armful of papers.

"I was looking for you," she said.

"See," said Clare.

"Sorry," said Kett. "I was..."

The door had almost closed when Porter shouldered his way through.

"Alright?" he said to nobody in particular.

"*Alright*?" echoed the Super. "What am I, Porter? Your friend? Your chum? Your friendly Uncle Dave? You will address me appropriately, Detective."

"Sorry, sir," the DI said as he took the seat next to Kett. When he was sure Clare wasn't looking, he rolled his eyes.

"I saw that," said Clare, who absolutely could not have done. "Where are Savage and Duke?"

"On their way," said Kett. "They're getting ready for the undercover job. Any news on that?"

"That's what I wanted to talk to you about, sir," said Spalding, sliding her pen into the top of her ponytail while she sorted through her files. She pulled out a sheet of paper and handed it to him. "An email came through to Liam Walton's Mobius server while you were out. It's from the reddeath.onion address."

"We've got a location," said Clare.

Kett studied the sheet of paper Spalding had given him. It was a commercial estate agent's listing for a warehouse: a square concrete building that looked like it had been empty for decades.

"This is Hampton Court," said Spalding. "No connection to Henry VIII's old place. It's a few miles out of King's

Lynn. A few miles out of anywhere, really, just farmland and woods in every direction."

"Perfect place for an illegal rave party," said Clare.

"I told you they were called that," Kett said to Porter. "You've got the email?"

Spalding handed him another sheet of paper, a short email from the .onion address they'd found on Naked Jesus' phone. He scanned it, then read the relevant parts out loud.

"'*The standard rules apply. Attendees must make payment via Bitcoin before the event begins. All travel rules must be followed. A single guest is permitted per person on receipt of an additional payment, at their own risk. Absolutely no phones must pass the gates. You may not bring your own refreshments, these will be available on site. The management reserve the right to expel attendees and their guests with appropriate force.*'"

"It's a tight operation," said Clare. "Read on."

"'*You may not discuss this event with anyone, before or after. Any attempt to do so will be met with severe punishment.*'" Kett laid the paper on the table. "They're not messing around."

The door opened again, just a crack. Kett had to lean forward to see Savage's face peering through.

"What are you doing, Kate?" said Clare. "Get in the bloody room."

"I'm not sure I dare, sir," she said. "You promise not to laugh?"

She didn't wait for a reply, pushing the door open all the way.

"Bloody hell," said Porter. "Who are you?"

Savage walked into the Incident Room, her face tight with embarrassment. She was wearing a sleeveless, rainbow-sequinned dress that barely came past her backside, gold tights, and a pair of bright pink boots with two-inch heels. A yellow handbag hung from one shoulder. Perched on top of her head was a carnival mask, and when she pulled it down over her face, Kett saw that it was a grotesque punch doll with a swollen nose and cruel eyes.

"Too much?" she said, wincing.

"It's perfect, Kate," said Kett. "You look like a different person."

She lifted the mask back onto her pixie cut, frowning a little.

"I can be fun, you know, sir," she said. "I used to go clubbing all the time when I was younger."

"What about Duke?" Kett asked.

Savage's expression shifted into something unreadable.

"He is still going, isn't he?" barked Clare. "He's not gone home to fondle his crotchal area? I've planned this operation for the two of you."

"Oh yes," said Savage. "He's still coming."

"I'm not," came Duke's voice from the corridor.

Savage waved him forward.

"It's not as bad as you think, Aaron," she said.

Porter was craning over his desk, his eyes alive with anticipation. He had his phone out and ready.

"Please be as bad as he thinks," he said.

"Get in here now, Duke," Clare roared, stamping his foot like an angry child.

"I don't want to be a police officer anymore," Duke shouted back. "I quit."

"You can't quit," Clare bellowed. "Ever. Move it along, Constable, or you'll be going to this party with a size twelve brogue lodged in your colon."

"Come on, mate," said Porter. "We won't laugh."

Kett could hear Duke's reluctant, shuffling footsteps

from outside. Savage entered the room first, geeing Duke on like he was a stubborn donkey until, finally, he slouched around the door.

"Holy shit," said Porter.

Kett might have said the same thing, if he hadn't been speechless.

Duke stood there, framed in the doorway. The giant PC was wearing a fluorescent yellow fishnet vest that revealed every single jutting abdominal muscle and sculpted pectoral in all its glory. There were more fishnets on his enormous arms, from elbow to wrist, one green and one pink. His bushy beard was drenched in pink glitter.

Barely covering his lower extremities was quite possibly the shortest pair of leather hotpants Kett had ever seen. They looked like they'd been painted on.

"Holy shit," Porter said again, and there was a click as he took a photo on his phone.

"What's wrong, sir?" said Duke. "Why aren't you laughing?"

"I mean, I *should* be," said Porter, crashing back into his chair. "But I'm just... I'm just horrified, mate."

"It's bad," said Duke, trying to retreat through the door. "I can't do this."

"You can, and you will," said Clare, giving the PC a grim smile. "You look bloody fabulous. Have I ever told you lot that I had a run as a burlesque performer back in my uni days?"

All eyes swivelled to the Superintendent.

"I was Mellow Miss Muffins for one whole summer semester," he said. "Wore an outfit not a million miles away from yours, Aaron, although it was a skirt, not shorts. And I was a lot rounder in the middle than you are. Mellow Miss Muffins played some seriously chill jazz flute on stage for the annual leaver's ball that year. It was an immensely liberating experience."

"I think I'm having a nightmare," said Porter, rubbing his eyes.

"But enough about that," said the Super. "You've got a mask?"

"But then you won't see all the glitter," said Porter.

Duke ignored him, pulling on a rubber mask that covered his whole head. The features were so distorted that it took Kett a moment to realise he was a sad clown.

"Don't even ask," said the PC from inside.

"Sit down, the pair of you," said Clare.

Savage walked over, rummaging inside her yellow bag. She pulled out two more bright orange fishnet T-shirts, passing one to Kett and one to Porter.

"Not sure what the plan is yet, sirs," she said, "but just in case you need to be undercover, here you go."

Kett unrolled the T-shirt. It looked like something Rab C. Nesbitt might have worn if he'd supported the Netherlands.

"Uh, no," he said.

"I said sit down," barked Clare, and Savage obeyed.

"You've seen the email?"

"Yes, sir," said Savage. "A warehouse, this time."

"Right," said Clare.

He unfolded the roll of paper he'd walked in with, using pins to fix it to the board over the top of the crime scene photos. It was a blueprint.

"This is..."

Clare had to stop as a series of squeaks echoed around the room. It was Duke, Kett realised, his leather hotpants chafing on his monstrous thighs as he walked to a desk.

Everybody waited as he lowered himself painfully, and noisily, onto a chair.

"You sure you should be wearing them after... you know?" asked Porter, nodding to his groin.

Duke had gone a little pale.

"Focus," said Clare, snapping his fingers. "You can talk about Duke's testicles in your own time. This is Hampton Court. Built in 1972, it's an old grain storage unit that forms part of a disused farm. It's immense, nearly 300 feet long and a third of that wide. Fortunately for us, Spalding managed to find the original architect's drawings. You want to run us through it, Alison?"

Spalding pulled her pen from her hair and tapped it on the blueprint.

"The main building is almost entirely one open space," she said. "But there's an elevated metal walkway around the perimeter and a room that leads off from this. An observation space, we think. There are three more storage rooms on the ground floor, all smaller."

She moved her pen to a huddle of relatively tiny structures scattered around the warehouse.

"This is the farm. We've got a five-bedroom house here, pretty standard. There are six stables right outside the warehouse, and a couple of smaller barns to the north. There are three acres of meadow that lead into barren farmland, and a natural perimeter of woodland that stretches almost all the way to the Hunstanton Road."

"There's no electricity or running water, as far as we can see," said Clare. "Based on what we saw before, at least one of these areas will be used to run the generators."

"I'm guessing the stables, sir," said Kett. "It'll be the closest space to the warehouse."

"They'll probably host the more... unsavoury stuff in the

house," said Savage, tugging on the hem of her dress as it threatened to ride up. "Back at Wayside Manor, they used the bedrooms. They'll want them to be cosy, and away from the dancing."

"Makes sense," said Clare. "We're looking for the people who are running the event. My guess is they'll be somewhere they can keep an eye on everything."

He tapped the blueprint with a long fingernail.

"This room on the first floor, off the walkway, is our best shot. They'll have a bird's-eye view of the whole shebang from there."

"That's what I was thinking, sir," said Savage. "But they'll also want somewhere with an easy exit. Do we know if there's a fire escape?"

"There is," said Spalding, circling something that Kett was too far away to see. "External steps, right here."

"Then that's where they'll be," said Clare. "Did your two witnesses say anything else about the party?"

"Not really, sir," said Kett. "Only that there was a pretty free-flowing supply of drugs."

"*So* many drugs," said Savage.

"One question, sir," said Porter, raising his hand like he was in a classroom. "You have to pay to get into the party, right? In Bitcoin. How are we going to do that?"

"Already done," said Spalding with a sly grin. "We have Jesus' phone, and his passcode, and his Bitcoin wallet. He's authorised a dozen transactions to the *reddeath* planners over the last two years, he won't notice another one."

"Not sure that's entirely legal," said Kett. "How much is it?"

"Zero point zero five Bitcoin per ticket," said Spalding.

"What?" said Kett. "That's nothing? Why is it so cheap?"

"That's nearly £2000, sir," she said. "Double if you're bringing a guest."

"*What?*"

"Naked Jesus and his girlfriend also mentioned security," said Savage. "They're pretty obvious, I think. Uniformed and masked. They want to make their presence known. And they search you on the way in."

"How many?" asked Clare.

"I don't know, sir."

"Okay. Just be vigilant." Clare stroked his face for a moment, deep in thought. "I put the word out about illegal rave parties that call themselves the Masque. Almost every Force in the country knows about them, but so far nobody's shut them down. They bounce from place to place, never long enough to be a real issue. By the time they've moved, they're somebody else's problem, and they get pushed back down the list. They're clever, they know what they have is valuable, and my guess is they'll go to some lengths to protect it."

He took a breath.

"The only solid intel we have comes from Merseyside Police. They seemed quite impressed that we'd found a way in. An ongoing investigation there linked two suspects to the Masque, a couple of old-school hardmen out of Toxteth. Martin Capper and Warner Hobbs. They're notorious. Used to be part of the Liverpool Mafia but split in 2003 when Tommy Comerford died. Both have done time. We don't know if this intel is good, and even if it is, we don't know if Capper and Hobbs will be on site. But take a look at their photos just in case."

Spalding dealt sheets of paper to Savage and Duke, then slid one onto Kett's desk. Two of the ugliest, meanest bastards he'd ever seen in his life smirked back at him from their mugshots. One was completely bald, his face like a ballsack, the other was thinner with grey hair and a matching goatee. They were both in their fifties.

"This is an information-gathering mission, Kate," said Clare. "I want to know who's running these events, and what kind of services they're providing. Most importantly, I want to know if they had anything to do with Kieran Spicer's death, and whether an opportunity for murder might have presented itself during Saturday's party. But Kate, Aaron, it is imperative that you remain safe. Do not engage, even if your cover is blown. And do not partake."

"Partake, sir?" said Savage.

"Don't do the drugs."

"Why would I—"

"Or drink the drink."

"Sir, I would never—"

"Or get involved in the sexy stuff. This is undercover, not under *the* covers."

Savage seemed lost for words.

"Our primary goal is to identify the ringleaders. Once you do, give the order and the rest of us will move in."

"It's going to be hard to get numbers out there, sir," said Kett. "It's a big operation, tight security. It wouldn't surprise me if they monitored the area."

"They probably use drones, sir," said Savage. "For early warning."

Duke said something—or at least Kett thought he had, but it turned out to be another squeak as he adjusted his legs beneath the desk.

"I'll have units on standby in King's Lynn," said Clare. "Tactical, too. Upside is, they're too far away to cause a panic. Downside, it's a twelve-minute drive to the warehouse. If the shit hits the fan, that's going to be a long wait."

"Pete and I can be closer, sir," said Kett. "You know where they'll park?"

"I'm guessing anywhere there's space," said Clare. "Probably the yard in front of the warehouse, and up the hill into the meadow. If it's cold, they might use the field, but unless it hits zero and freezes over, the cars will sink in the mud."

He stared at Kett.

"What are you thinking?"

"We stay in the car, sir," said Kett. "Kate can park on the edge. It will be dark. If it kicks off, we can help."

"You can help?" said Clare, looking Kett up and down.

"Yeah," said Kett.

"By hobbling over to the warehouse and... and what, exactly?"

Kett sat up a little straighter.

"You know," he said. "Help get them out of there."

"I can't tell you how reassured I am by that," said Clare, turning back to the blueprint.

"I don't *hobble*," muttered Kett.

"Okay. You and Porter will be on site, but you'll remain hidden unless you hear a direct order from me. That means no wandering about, no..."

He shot another look at Kett.

"No *just taking a looks*."

"As if," said Kett, waving the words away.

"Sir," said Porter, putting up his hand again. "What about the red line stuff? Did you get my photo?"

"I did," said Clare, perching on the edge of a desk. "I'm still trying to make sense of it. Anyone care to enlighten me?"

"There was a secret room in the cellar at the other

house, sir," said Porter. "The red room. I think it's part of the Masque, but I can't figure out how it fits."

"Follow the red line, find the red room, make a red wish," said Clare.

"That's the poem I was trying to remember," said Savage. "The one I heard from Granddad. It's not really a poem. It's a fairy tale he used to tell, about finding a red room in the woods and making a wish, but the wish backfires. It's not well known, I don't think, I'd completely forgotten it. But there are versions of the story everywhere."

She shrugged.

"And you think this red room is where Kieran was taken from the house?" asked Clare.

"I don't know, sir," said Porter. "Looks that way, though. He went through the tunnel to the folly, and that's where he was killed."

"I found ribbons in the cellar," said Kett. "They led from the woods, almost like a trail. It fits what we've heard, the legend of the red room."

"If you find it, you get to make a wish," said Porter.

"A wish?" said Clare.

The DI nodded.

"A real one?"

"No, sir," said Porter. "I don't think so. Whatever you wish, it will backfire. That's what the story says."

"So Kieran was in that room," said Clare. "He found it?"

Nobody answered.

"He made a wish?"

"And it backfired," said Kett. "Something went wrong, and they took him into the woods and killed him."

"Which makes no sense at all," said Clare. "But you're right, Pete. If the red room is a part of these parties, and we have no reason to doubt that, then something extremely messed up is happening in there."

He turned to Savage.

"That's your second priority. Find out if there's a secret room, find out what happens in there, and find out if it's related to our victim's murder."

Savage nodded. Duke squeaked.

Clare rubbed his face again, shaking his head.

"I don't like this," he said. "But I can't see any other way of getting to the truth. You say they search people on the way in?"

"That's what we were told, sir," said Kett.

"Which means you can't carry protection, and you can't carry a radio. I can give you a panic button, we'll find a way to keep it hidden. Press it, and we'll come running."

He glanced at Kett.

"Hobbling, anyway."

"I don't hobble!"

"I mean it. Stay safe. Do not put yourself anywhere you feel uncomfortable."

The Superintendent checked his watch, and Kett saw that his arm was trembling slightly.

"We've got four hours until we roll," he said. "Go learn everything you can about this place before we move in. I want you to be as ready as it's possible to be. And Kett."

"Sir?"

"We had a call from Kieran's mother a little while ago. She wants to talk to you."

"About what?"

"She didn't say, but she asked for you specifically. Go out there, will you? It might be important. Just make it quick."

"Sure, sir."

"Good. Now, off you all toss."

There was a collective shuffling as everyone got out of their chairs—plus a long, drawn-out squeak from Duke's leather hotpants.

"Aaron, come with me," said Clare. "I have just the thing to make you feel more comfortable."

Duke had a moment to look relieved before the Superintendent finished.

"There's an old jar of Vaseline in my desk. Let's grease up those glorious gams."

CHAPTER THIRTY-THREE

"It's going to be another late one?"

Billie's voice crackled through the hands-free as Kett drove out of the city, making her sound even further away than she actually was. He could hear the kids in the background, possibly laughter, probably screams, and he found himself pining for them the way he always did—especially when the nights drew in so early. His fingers twitched on the wheel as some part of him tried to rebel against his conscious mind, tried to turn the car around and drive it home.

One day, he knew, he wouldn't be able to resist it.

"I'm sorry," he said, picking up speed. "We don't have a choice."

"It's about the boy who was killed? The one on the news?"

"Yeah," said Kett.

"Then go and get them, Robbie. Go and make sure they can't do it again."

"I'll try," he said, but there wasn't a lot of conviction in his voice.

"Just be safe, yeah?" said Billie. "I've got a bad feeling tonight. I don't know why."

"I'll be safe," he told her. "Don't worry, it's a big operation. The scariest thing out there tonight will be Duke in his undercover hotpants."

"His *what*?" said Billie, and her laughter was a welcome sound. "Hotpants? Can you take a photo?"

"You want a photo of Duke in his hotpants?"

"Yeah," she said, still laughing. "You know, just for... research."

"Research," said Kett, and he laughed too. "Sure, Billie. I'll take a photo. Are the girls there?"

"They are," said Billie. "But I've had to separate them. They won't stop fighting, and Moira's still copying everything Alice does. They were lobbing shoes at each other earlier. Alice has a bruise on her cheek."

"God, that's not good."

"No. It's making her lose her mind. You should have heard some of the things she was calling her little sister, and Moo-moo was yelling them right back. I was worried the neighbours were going to phone the police."

"Sorry," he said.

"Don't be, Robbie. We're fine."

She sighed so deeply that it rattled down the line.

"We'll see you tonight. Ring the doorbell, okay? Do not sleep in the car again."

"I will," he said. "Sleep tight. Give them a cuddle from me."

"If Moo-moo stops calling her big sister a twat-faced shitbag long enough for me to get a word in edgeways, I will."

She hung up, and Kett settled in for the drive. The rush hour traffic had thinned, so it didn't take him long to get out to Dereham. For a little while he couldn't get his bearings in the knotted mess of roads that made up the outskirts of the town, then he spotted Jonah White's burned-out bungalow and remembered the route, parking outside the Spicer house.

He didn't get out straight away, taking a moment to appreciate the lights that twinkled on the front porch, the soft glow that poured from every window. To anyone passing, it would look like any other home getting ready for the Christmas season.

Nobody would guess the horror of what had happened to this family.

He eased himself out, his back screaming. The lights were all off in Morris Gough's house next door, although he thought he could see a morbidly obese shape shifting in the dark glass.

He was halfway up the Spicers' driveway when he realised he *was* hobbling, and he did his best to straighten out. There was nobody in the living room, although the TV was on, throwing ghostly light over the sofas. It was well after eight, and he didn't want to risk waking anybody up, so he rapped his knuckles gently on the glass.

It turned out he had nothing to worry about. As soon as he'd knocked, he heard one of the boys yelling for their mum, echoed by the second, and then the first again. This went on for almost a minute before a shadow appeared in the textured glass and the door opened.

Margaret Spicer stood there in the same clothes he'd last seen her in, her face flushed and her eyes red raw. Still, she managed a smile when she saw Kett, and stood back to let him in.

"It's still chaos," she said, sniffing. "Sorry."

Kett walked past her, feeling like he'd stepped out of a

freezer into an oven. He shook off his coat, draping it over his arm.

"I can take that, if you like?" she said, closing the door.

"Don't worry," said Kett. "It's a flying visit, I'm afraid. How are you holding up?"

Margaret sniffed again, her eyes searching for an answer she couldn't possibly find.

"We're putting everything we have into finding out what happened," said Kett. "We've got some good leads."

She looked up at him, sniffing again. It was taking all she had not to cry. He could see the effort in every line of her face, every clenched muscle. She managed a nod.

"It's—" Kett started, and he clamped his mouth shut as the smallest Spicer boy, Peanut, came tearing down the stairs. He stopped on the bottom one, beaming, his eyes bright beneath that mop of sandy hair.

"Are we making more waffles?" he said. "I'm hungry."

"It's bedtime," said Margaret, running a trembling hand over his head. "You can have waffles for breakfast."

The boy's smile vanished, replaced by a playful pout.

"Do you want to see my Lego?" he asked Kett. "I finished the Batmobile today. Just the little one. Jay helped me, though, because I can't do the fiddly bits, they always go the wrong way round. Key usually helps me. Have you found him yet?"

Kett glanced at Margaret as she smudged tears from her face.

"I... I can't," she said to the question that Kett hadn't asked. "I can't do it."

"Maybe in a minute, Peanut," he said. "Why don't you go get it ready, and give me a second with your mum?"

"Sure!" said the kid, and he went tearing up the stairs so fast Kett was amazed he didn't fall.

He held up his hands.

"No judgement, Margaret. I can't imagine how hard it is. But he's going to find out sooner or later, and it's better if it comes from you."

The woman was swiping at her face with both hands, but she couldn't keep the tears off her cheeks. There was a choking noise in her throat as she strained to hold back the violence of her grief. If she went on like this for too long, Kett knew, she would simply break.

And the worst of it was, there was nothing he could do to help.

"You mentioned on the phone there was something important you needed to tell me," he said, keeping his voice low.

Margaret nodded, wrapping her hands around her chest like she was trying to hold herself together.

"I need to show you," she said. "It's upstairs. I..."

She swallowed hard, and Kett wondered if she was about to be sick.

"Jay knows," she said. "I had to tell him. He was getting so angry. He's..."

She seemed to run out of words, starting up the stairs instead. Her arms were still locked around her body, and she pressed her hip against the banister to keep her balance, the entire staircase creaking. Kett walked after her, studying the gallery of framed photos as he went. Some were missing, just spectral outlines on the wall, and it didn't take him long to realise that he couldn't see a single picture of Kieran.

It was the same on the landing, a handful of absent frames. Only Jay and Peanut grinned back at him, as if somebody had tried to erase Kieran from the house entirely.

Grief did that, he knew. Sometimes the only way of dealing with the pain was to do everything you could to forget. How much of Billie's stuff had he left in their old house when he'd moved? How many photos of her had he sealed with tape in cardboard boxes, just so he didn't have to see her face every day?

Just so he didn't spend every waking second wondering what had happened.

Peanut was scrabbling around in the smaller room, but Margaret headed for Jay's. His door was closed, and she knocked a couple of times before turning the handle. Like before, it opened a few inches and stopped.

"Jay," she said. "It's me, let me in."

Something clunked on the other side of the door, and it creaked open. Jay stood there in a set of Spider-Man pyjamas, his hair damp and his face fresh like he'd just come out of the bath. He looked years younger than he had last time Kett had seen him. His eyes were still dark, though, and they didn't hold much welcome when he looked up.

"Hi, Jay," Kett said, trying to sound as friendly as possible. He glanced back to make sure Peanut wasn't there, then leant a little closer. "I'm really sorry about your brother."

The kid didn't reply, he just turned to his mum, glaring at her.

"Do you want to tell the policeman, Jay?" asked Margaret.

Jay shook his head. Margaret tried to rest her hand on his shoulder, but he slunk back.

"It's okay," she said. "I can do it. I told you, you haven't done anything wrong."

Jay didn't look like he believed her.

"Last time you were here," Margaret said to Kett, "you thought Jay might have taken something from Kieran's drawer, when you were looking through his room."

"I wasn't sure," said Kett, speaking to the boy. "And I

wasn't accusing you of anything. I just wanted to make sure we weren't missing something that could help us."

"You were right," said Margaret. "Jay did take something, didn't you?"

He didn't reply, his eyes never leaving Kett. If the boy was ten years older, he thought, that look might have scared him.

"Can I see it?" Kett asked.

"It's... it's bad," said Margaret. "I couldn't believe it when I realised what it was. I... I don't know what else to say."

"Whatever it is," Kett said, still speaking to Jay, "I know it's not yours. I know it was Kieran that brought it into the house. And I know that you were only trying to help him. That's what brothers do, they help each other. You did a good thing. And telling me is a good thing too, okay?"

At long last, a crack appeared in the boy's stony demeanour. He looked at the floor, his bottom lip trembling as he took a breath. His eyes were filling up, and Kett wanted to save him the embarrassment of crying.

"It's in your room?" he asked.

"It's in mine," said Margaret. "I can show you."

Kett moved out of the way so she could squeeze past, then he followed her to the smallest room. She approached the wardrobe, stretching onto her tiptoes, struggling to reach.

"You need some help?" Kett asked from the door.

"I got it," she said.

She found what she was looking for—a shoebox—hefting it down from the wardrobe and dropping it onto the bed so fearfully that there might have been live scorpions inside. She scrubbed her hands down her dress, then wrapped them around herself again, as tight as a straitjacket.

"It's in there," she said. "I put it all in when I found it."

Kett used a knuckle to lift the lid, toppling it onto the quilt. Inside the box was a crumpled stack of banknotes held together with a hair bobble—maybe a grand. There were also four baggies of white powder, the size of conkers. The last thing was a folding knife, the blade probably six inches in length.

"I'm sorry," said Margaret. She was swaying from side to side like a tree in a storm, ready to collapse.

"Don't be," Kett told her. "None of this is your fault. You didn't know about the drugs? The money?"

She shook her head.

"He was just Kieran," she said. "He was a good boy. I... I can't believe he'd do this."

Kett put the lid back on the box and picked it up, carrying it onto the landing. Jay watched from his open door, his face now full of fear.

"Hey," said Kett. "You didn't do anything wrong. I promise. You're not in any trouble."

The kid breathed out slowly, his eyes full of tears. Margaret pushed past Kett and walked to her son, and this time when she reached out he folded himself into her, hugging her as tightly as his skinny arms would let him.

"I told you," said Margaret, stroking his hair. "I told you it would be okay."

"Can I ask you one thing?" Kett said. "This is really important, Jay."

The boy peeked out from his mother's hold, his face wet.

"Did Kieran ever ask you to look after this stuff? Did he tell you to move it if anyone ever came looking?"

Jay didn't look like he wanted to say, but Margaret stroked his hair.

"It's okay," she said. "Tell the truth."

The boy nodded.

"Did he ever ask you to do anything else?" said Kett. "Anything to do with the money, or the white powder?"

Another nod.

"I didn't know," said Margaret, a flash of anger crossing the ruin of her face. "I didn't know, or I would have done something."

She sniffed, and a sob finally tore its way out of her. She buried her face in Jay's hair, shouting.

"It's not fair!"

There were more questions he could ask, but this wasn't the time. He held the box to his chest, crossing the landing just as Peanut walked out of his bedroom. The kid grinned as he lifted his Lego Batmobile, but the smile faltered when he saw his mum crying.

"That's ace," said Kett, his heart shattering like it, too, was made of Lego. "You've done a great job, Peanut."

"Mum?" said the boy, walking past Kett like he didn't exist.

Margaret opened an arm and gathered him up, the three of them closing around each other like the petals of a tulip.

I'm sorry, Kett thought.

And with nothing else to say, he let himself out of the house.

CHAPTER THIRTY-FOUR

Kett was getting back into the car when he felt his phone vibrate in his pocket. He closed the door and started the engine so that he could ramp up the heat, then he answered it.

"Sir," said Savage. He could hear the sound of a car behind her. "You still Dereham way?"

"Yeah," he said, a powerful shiver running through him —one that had more to do with what had happened in the house than the relentless cold. "The middle Spicer brother, Jay, was holding drugs and money for his brother. Kieran was making him do stuff. I don't know what, exactly."

"That's awful, sir," said Savage. "Is he okay?"

"I don't think so," said Kett, picturing the boy's sunken eyes, the haunted look on his face. "I—"

"Hang on, sir," said Savage. "Boss wants in on this."

The phone hissed, then Savage spoke again, her voice fainter.

"You're on speaker, sir. We're in the Superintendent's car."

"Say all that again," barked Clare. "I couldn't hear any of it."

"Kieran was making his little brother an accomplice, sir," said Kett. "I don't know how much Kieran shared with him. I don't know if he ever took him up to the park when they were dealing. The whole thing's a mess. He's only ten; it's going to scar him for the rest of his life."

"And now his brother's dead," said Savage. "Talk about a double whammy. Is that what he was hiding from you yesterday, sir?"

"Yeah," said Kett, glancing at the shoebox on the passenger seat. "About a thousand pounds in cash, a knife, and four bags of powder. Probably cocaine or meth. There's not a huge amount, but it's not tiny either."

"You thinking that's what he stole, sir?" asked Savage.

Kett hadn't been thinking that at all. He leaned his head against the seat.

"That's a good point, Kate. That makes a lot of sense. Kieran skims a little of whatever he's dealing. Not much, just a small amount every time. Keeps it at home ready to sell on whenever he gets the chance."

"Only he never gets the chance," said Clare.

"Right. Somebody finds out. And he's expecting somebody to find out, because he asks Jay to take the drugs and the money out of his room if anyone comes calling, tells him to hide them someplace."

"Only he forgets that drug dealers don't need proof," said Clare. "They just need to suspect you enough to take you out."

"Do you think... Sir, can you slow down a bit, this is a fifty."

"Fifty my arse," said Clare.

"Can you at least stay on the right side of the road?"

"Close your eyes if you don't like it, Kate," said Clare. "What were you saying?"

"Uh... I, uh..."

"Drug dealers," Kett prompted.

"Oh, yeah. Do you think they found out, or suspected him? Maybe Jonah grassed Kieran up. They give Kieran one last job to do, then they kill him. Afterwards, Jonah takes the bag."

"Maybe," said Kett. "But that doesn't explain why he was in the red room in the house."

"We don't know that for sure, sir," said Savage. "The blood in there, and in the folly, hasn't been ID'd yet."

"Good point."

He rubbed his face to try to wake himself up a little, the dark evening pouring into his skull like an anaesthetic.

"It's looking like our best theory, though," said Kett. "We need to put more pressure on Niko and Jonah. One of them must know who ordered the hit. You on your way to the illegal rave party already?"

He checked his watch.

"Yes, we are," said Clare. "There's no point you coming back to the city. We're using an old gravel yard in Pott Row as a base. Savage will text you the details. Get your lumpy arse over there now."

"Lumpy?" said Kett, but Clare had already ended the call.

HE PULLED off the pitch-black country lane half an hour later, seeing Clare's Mercedes parked in the middle of an empty yard. The engine was off but the interior lights were on. Clare and Savage sat in the front. It was hard to tell because of the tinted glass, but he thought it was Duke and Porter crammed into the back. All four of them looked like they were having a heated argument about something, the windows almost completely fogged up.

Kett drew the Volvo alongside them, allowing himself another few seconds of warmth before cranking open the door. Nobody seemed to be paying any attention to him, so he knocked on Clare's window.

"Get in," said the Super, his words muffled.

"Get in?" said Kett. "There's no room."

"Get in!"

Duke opened his door and Kett started to clamber into the back of the Mercedes.

"Faster, you badger shagger, you're letting all the heat out!"

Clare reached over from the driver's seat and grabbed his coat, hauling him inside.

"Close the door!"

Kett did as he was told, almost trapping his foot. With Porter and Duke taking up most of the back seat, there was no room for him. He was practically sitting on Duke's lap, a fact made infinitely worse by the fact he was still wearing his hotpants.

"Budge up, mate," he said.

"He can't budge up," Porter yelled. "There's no space over here."

Kett noticed for the first time that Porter was wearing the T-shirt that Savage had bought him—bright orange and full of holes. Kett knew he hadn't been working out as much since Bobby had been born, but he was surprised at how skinny the DI's arms had become, and how portly his middle was. Porter seemed to notice, doing his best to flex his biceps and accidentally elbowing Duke.

"Can you *both* budge up?" said the PC, who looked like he was in quite a bit of pain. "I need to open my legs, my walnuts are—"

"It would help if you put your chair forward, sir," said Kett, his knees up to his chin.

"No," said Clare. "Quit your bloody moaning, all of you. You're worse than my kids."

"Because none of your kids are the size and shape of a fridge, sir," said Porter, shooting Duke a look of disgust.

Kett wedged himself as close to the door as he could. Only when he'd found a comfortable spot did he notice the stench inside the car. He put a hand to his face, accidentally elbowing Duke in the process.

"What *is* that?"

"That is the aroma of fine young Clare men," said Clare, smacking his hand on the forest of air fresheners that hung from the rear-view mirror. "BO, Lynx, flatulence, and a toxic cauldron of hormones. You get used to it."

"You don't," said Savage.

"Can I open a window?" Kett asked.

"Only if you want to lose a hand," said Clare. "If I have to breathe it, so do you."

"We're going to be high as kites before we even get to the party," said Savage.

"Or dead," muttered Duke, still trying to find space for his legs.

"That was a good find at the Spicer house," said Clare, ignoring them. "It fits what we thought about why Kieran was killed. Now, we need to know who did it. The rave starts in about an hour, but we don't want to be the first people there. The road you drove up on is the road they're telling people to take, so we wait until we've seen a few cars pass before we make our move."

"Same plan, sir?" asked Kett. "Kate and Aaron in the house, Pete and me in the car?"

"That's right," said Clare. "You're taking my car, because you'll be harder to spot in the back."

"Not with this thing on, I won't," said Porter, smoothing his hands down his shirt like he was trying to rub it off.

"Park as far from the warehouse as you can, and keep watch. You only leave the vehicle if I give the order."

He put his hand back and clicked his fingers.

"I'll take your car, Robbie. We'll be down the road and ready to roll if you Kett this up."

Kett handed him his keys.

"Kate has a panic button in her bag, disguised as a rape alarm," said Clare. "It will send a signal to me. But other than that, you're on your own."

Savage opened her mouth as if to say something, then closed it again. She caught Kett's eye for a second before looking away, something hidden in her tight expression.

"You've got Walton's phone, fully charged," Clare went on. "The fee is paid. We received QR codes, which will be your tickets: one for you, Duke, as you'll be posing as Walton. One for you, Kate, as his guest. There's no mention of bringing ID, so we should be fine, but if they ask, tell them you forgot it."

"Not exactly room for a wallet in those shorts, Aaron, is there?" said Porter.

"You ready for this?" said Clare, looking at them all in turn.

Nobody replied, and it didn't seem to bother him.

"Good luck," said the Super, opening his door and launching himself into the cold. He didn't even bother to close it before diving into Kett's Volvo.

"Fuck's sake," grumbled Kett, opening his own door. He

slipped on his way out, planting a hand on Duke's leg and recoiling immediately. "Why are you so *moist*, Aaron?"

"It's the Vaseline, sir!" Duke protested.

"Out."

Duke got out, running around to the driver's seat. Savage had already climbed over the gear stick to claim it, so he scooted to the other side. Kett got back into the rear seat, all three of them closing their doors together. There wasn't a scrap of warmth left in the entire car, and Kett pulled his collar around his neck, shivering so hard it hurt.

"Sorry, sir," said Savage, pulling something out from beneath Duke's feet. It was the fluorescent orange fishnet T-shirt.

She winced apologetically at him.

"Super's orders."

CHAPTER THIRTY-FIVE

There was no doubt at all that it was a party.

They spotted the first car at a quarter past ten, a bubble of light that sped past the entrance to the gravel yard, quickly swallowed by the dark. The next followed four minutes later, music blaring from open windows.

Soon there was a constant stream of traffic moving east along the narrow lane, a glowing artery that led towards a world-shaking heartbeat that had begun to pound in the night.

"Here we go," said Kett, feeling his pulse echo the thump of distant music. "Everyone ready?"

"Yes, sir," said Savage.

"As I'll ever be," said Porter.

"No," said Duke.

"Let's move out," said Kett, buckling up.

Savage started the car, the Mercedes' enormous engine spluttering to life. She eased it to the open gate, waiting for two more cars to pass before pulling onto the road. They had directions to the warehouse, but they wouldn't need them. It was a pilgrimage, the sheer number of cars slowing traffic to a crawl. The glow of their brake lights set fire to the night, the world burning.

"I really hate to be pushy, sir," said Savage, glancing at him in the mirror. "But if anyone sees you in the back, they're going to know you're police."

Kett looked down at his suit with a sigh.

"Fine."

He shook off his coat, then his jacket, looping his tie over his head before unbuttoning his shirt. Porter was watching him like a hawk.

"Little privacy, Pete?"

"Why?" the DI asked. "We shared a locker room for years when we were in uniform. Nothing I haven't seen."

"Yeah, but everything's got a little... saggier since then."

"Happens to us all, sir," said Duke. "Well, not me. But everyone else."

"You just focus on those hotpants, Constable," said Porter, but he turned away while Kett pulled off his shirt. He replaced it with the orange T-shirt, not sure whether he should laugh or cry when he saw his reflection in the dark window.

"You look spectacular, sir," said Savage.

"My nipples are literally poking through the holes," said Kett. "This can't be what people wear?"

The music from outside was getting louder, a fast, bassy thump that could surely shake the stars from the sky. There were lights on the horizon, too, waves of blue and red and pink that swept over the bony canopies of a distant woodland.

"They must be bright enough to be seen from space," said Kett, leaning between the front seats. "How have we never heard about these parties before?"

"Because by the time we get to them, they're over," said Porter.

"And they move on," added Savage. "They head somewhere else. Nobody makes them a priority."

"Because they become somebody else's problem," said Kett, nodding. "It's clever. Look, they're turning."

The cars were funnelling off the road through a gap in the hedge, and Savage followed them, steering the boat-like Mercedes over the low verge. Ahead was a track that led into the woods, the traffic still single file and painfully slow as it negotiated the potholes. The trees closed in on either side like security guards, branches scraping the windows as if searching for illicit goods.

It wasn't long before the track opened up again, leading into a wide field.

"That's it," said Kett, pointing down the slope of the hill. A large, boxy building squatted in the valley, drenched in colour from the roving lights. Free of the trees, the music was loud enough to rock the car.

"They're parking here, sir," said Savage.

The cars were spreading out, some already stationary. There was no rhyme or reason to it, so Savage steered right, avoiding the densest clusters and skirting around the edge of the field.

"Bit further," said Kett. "We need a good view of the site."

She trundled over the frozen peaks of soil, everyone jiggling up and down. The warehouse really was enormous, more like an aircraft hangar. It dwarfed the other buildings around it, the farm reduced to a doll's house.

People were getting out of their cars, the air full of whoops and cheers as they made their way down the hill.

There were more of them than Kett had anticipated, and half already looked off their faces.

True to Savage's predictions, they weren't wearing a lot of clothes, and the things they were wearing were painfully bright.

"Here will do," said Kett, as they approached an oak tree on the outskirts of the field. Savage stopped the car beside it and switched off the engine. More cars pulled up beside them, and behind. It would make it impossible to get the Mercedes out in a hurry, but there wasn't much they could do about it.

"Your first job is to stay safe," said Kett. "Okay? It's going to be wild in there, and for all we know, there's a killer on site. More than one. Stay safe, stay together, and if you sense anything dangerous, press the button."

"Yes, sir," said Savage, nodding. She looked nervous, clutching her yellow handbag to her chest.

"We're right here, Kate," he said. "You're not on your own."

Somebody smacked a hand against the car window as they walked past, a chorus of laughter. Savage waited for them to move on before opening her door. Duke pulled on his sad clown mask as he got out, giving Kett and Porter a front-row view of his squeaking, leather-clad arse as he went.

"I never want to see anything ever again," said Porter, rubbing his eyes.

They closed their doors together, walking into the flow of people, hand in hand. A second or two later, the car's internal lights cut out, plunging them into darkness. Only for a second, though, before a bright flash lit up the Mercedes like a firework, followed by a click.

Kett whirled around as the car fell back into darkness.

"Did you just take a photo of me, Pete?"

"Absolutely not, sir," said Porter.

Kett watched Savage and Duke until they were swallowed by the bright lights and the roar of music.

"You think they'll be okay, Pete?" he asked.

"I think Duke's going to get eaten alive," Porter replied. "But it's Savage, sir. She's going to be fine."

CHAPTER THIRTY-SIX

SAVAGE HAD NEVER FELT SO OUT OF HER DEPTH.

Somehow, the trickle of people moving towards the house had become a river of bodies; men and women barging into her from every direction. The night was full of their laughter and their shouts, reduced to a whisper by the sheer volume of the music that pounded from the warehouse—loud enough to be the voice of God, she thought.

The revellers drank from bottles as they went, they smoked cigarettes and spliffs, the air toxic. They were all ages, but mostly in their twenties and thirties, with a scattering of older men; all shapes and sizes, all united by the excitement in their faces, by the gleeful anticipation in their eyes.

She clutched Duke's hand all the way to the end of the field. There was a shallow ditch here and people were vaulting over it into the open yard beyond, some of them falling with peals of laughter. Duke was tall enough to step over it, and he reached back to help her. He said something, but thanks to his mask and the music, she had no idea what it was. She shrugged, and he lifted his mask so she could see his mouth.

"Tickets?" he bellowed.

She dug into her bag as they crossed the yard, pulling out Naked Jesus' phone. Everyone was heading to the left, a queue forming outside a door on the building's flank. Two men in long, black coats, each as big as Duke, were checking phones and ushering people past. A third security guard stood a little way off, speaking on his phone.

They were all wearing crimson masks.

Savage unlocked the phone, scrolling to the QR code they'd been sent. There was no text with it, no instructions, no way to know if it was the right thing, and the heat of her growing panic was enough to chase off the chill. She tugged the hem of her skirt down with her free hand, watching the last few people in front of her pass security and walk through the open door. Then she grabbed Duke's hand again, squeezing his fingers and feeling him squeeze back.

The nearest bouncer snapped his gloved fingers at her until she held out the phone, and he used a handheld scanner to read it. It seemed to take an age before he waved them through, holding up two fingers to the second guard.

They walked on, almost at the door when the second security guard stopped them, gesturing with his fingers until Savage passed him the phone. He slung it into a box beside the door, handing her a raffle ticket stub. He asked for her bag next, peering inside and running his fingers around the interior. Only when he handed it back did she release the breath she was holding. There was literally no place on her person she could be smuggling anything, because her dress was so tight, so he gave her the nod to move on. He patted Duke down, recoiling when he touched his slimy hotpants.

"It's Vaseline!" she heard Duke shout through his mask.

They moved down a short stretch of dark corridor, crushed in the crowd. Savage's fear was a living, thrashing thing inside her. The noise was like nothing she had ever heard before, every beat powerful enough to crush her organs into jelly. There were so many people that she couldn't have turned back even if she'd wanted to. She was pushed slowly, inexorably forwards, feeling like a scrap of food being forced along the throat of some monstrous creature.

Until, at last, she fell through a set of internal doors into the vast interior of the warehouse. It was quieter here, more space to spread out. Maybe a hundred people were already dancing, bathed in colourful lights and drowning in sound. Others were making their way to a door on the far side of the room, another masked security guard stationed there. Savage pulled Duke along with her, taking hold of his waist like they were about to dance.

"You okay?" she asked.

There was no way he could hear her through the thick, rubber mask. She wondered if she should pull her mask down as well, but she felt claustrophobic enough without it.

Spinning Duke around, she peered past his shoulder and scanned the metal walkway that ran along the wall maybe twelve feet overhead. The lights did their best to blind her, but after a moment she spotted a set of large, slanted window frames that overlooked the dance floor. There was no glass in them, but the observation room was too dark to see if anyone was watching.

She spun Duke a little more until she found the stairs that led up to it. Another bouncer stood sentry there, his eagle eyes watching the crowd through the holes in his mask. His hand rested on something that was tucked into the waistband of his trousers, but his coat stopped her from seeing what it was.

They were carrying weapons, though, of that she had no doubt.

Her pulse ratcheted up another few degrees, her mouth dry. The space was filling up fast as more people were vomited through the door, so she pulled Duke along the edge of the room, doing a circuit of the space. Vast speakers sat in all four corners, the kind you saw at music festivals. Flashing lights were fixed to the walkway, and there were heaters too, glowing red and radiating warm air. Cables as thick as her arm snaked along the floor, all leading to the back of the room.

She hoiked her handbag onto her shoulder, reassured by the weight of it, then led Duke through the churning sea of wild-eyed dancers towards the other door. She was halfway there when somebody stepped up to her, a young woman dressed like an angel, feathery wings sprouting from her back. Her face was hidden by a glittering gold mask, but her eyes were bright.

She held a tray that was suspended on a strap around her neck, like a theatre confectionary salesperson. She wasn't offering popcorn and chocolate, though. The tray was laden with bags of powder and paper pill cups, plus several plastic shot glasses filled with a liquid Savage couldn't identify.

"Uh, no thank you," she said, her voice muted by the music.

She moved on, reaching the door where a swell of people had gathered. She had to let go of Duke in order to push through them, her panic going through the roof as she felt herself compressed in a fist of warm bodies.

On the other side, thankfully, the corridor was much

emptier. She made her way along it, seeing three doors that she recognised from the blueprint. Each one opened into a smaller room illuminated by green lights, pockets of brightly dressed people already growing there like fungus. Some were smoking, the smell of weed so thick she felt like she couldn't breathe. Others were openly snorting powder from tabletops.

Two more young, masked women dressed as angels circled the rooms, offering drugs and booze to the punters. Nobody seemed to be paying for anything.

Savage glanced back at Duke to make sure he was still there, shocked to see that he was holding a plastic shot glass in each hand—the liquid inside bright yellow.

"What are you doing?" she asked.

He mumbled something beneath the mask, shrugging his broad shoulders. She took the drinks from him, discarding them on the floor. The corridor bent to the left ahead, and when she made the turn she saw a fire exit. Another masked bouncer stood there, and he opened the door for them as they approached, letting them out into the night.

They were at the back of the building, the farmhouse twenty yards away on the other side of a stone terrace. Only a few souls braved the cold out here, but there was already a crowd outside the front door of the house. The music was quiet enough on this side of the building that Savage could finally hear herself think.

"Please don't drink the booze, Aaron," she said as she led the way across the terrace.

"But I'm thirsty," he replied.

"I can promise you, mate, that isn't Ribena."

They joined the back of the queue that was heading into the house. It was mostly men here, Savage noticed, all fidgety with excitement. Two more black-jacketed, red-faced guards stood abreast of the door, but they didn't seem to be checking anything. The windows of the house were lit up, the curtains drawn. More music spilled from inside, as well as a symphony of laughter, and more intimate sounds that made Savage's skin crawl.

"I've got a bad feeling about this," she said.

"I can't feel anything," Duke replied, tugging at his hotpants. "These shorts have cut off my circulation."

They reached the door and were ushered into an interior that was thick with smoke and perfume. Strings of pink LEDs lay on the floor, leading the way like runway lights. The punters pushed and shoved each other, barking like dogs or whooping like monkeys. Some had stripped to their underwear, a few were completely naked.

There was a different kind of energy in here, something animalistic, something hungry.

Something dangerous.

Savage tried to turn around, but people were pushing her from behind. She reached for Duke's hand, only to find that he wasn't there anymore. He'd been swallowed by the crowd, lost in the churning smoke. Somebody grabbed her backside in an iron grip, twisting—a grinning jester's mask looming up in front of her.

"Get off!" she screamed, giving the man a shove and resisting every urge she had to tell him he was under arrest.

The guy howled with laughter as he shunted past her, but more followed, all of them eyeballing her like she was meat being offered for the taking. She held onto her bag, pulling on the hem of her dress, which wouldn't stay down, letting herself be driven forward by the crowd until she reached a door.

Another angel stood here, staring through her glittery mask with the dead eyes of a doll.

Savage looked through the door, and immediately wished she hadn't. The room beyond was a sea of bedding on which naked shapes bumped and ground in sickening rhythms. The sound of them rolled out, audible even over the music, and she shuddered so hard she almost lost her grip on her bag.

The angel leaned forward and shouted something that Savage couldn't hear.

"What?" she said.

"I need to see your ticket," said the girl. "If you paid for the pink rooms?"

"The pink rooms?" Savage said.

A man ground his body into hers, one hand on her waist, the other holding out a stub of pink paper.

"She can come in with me," he said.

Savage wrenched herself free, watching as the angel waved him through. He was naked in seconds, throwing himself into the melee. Savage watched with growing horror, so engrossed that it took her a moment to realise the angel was speaking to her.

"What?"

"I said don't," the girl repeated. "Don't go in there."

"I won't," said Savage. "I'm looking for something else. That's the pink room?"

"What?" said the young woman, leaning even closer.

"The pink room?"

She nodded.

"I'm looking for the red room," Savage said. "Do you know where it is?"

The woman leaned back and shook her head so hard her mask almost came off. Her eyes seemed to boil with panic, and her free hand rose to a cord that hung around her neck. It was a panic button, Savage realised.

She didn't press it, but she didn't lower her hand.

"It's here?" asked Savage.

"No," said the girl. "No."

Another man piled into Savage's back, this one grinding his crotch against her dress. His fingers dug into her ribs, his breath hot on her neck.

"Get off!" she roared, twisting out of his grip as she turned to face him.

This guy wasn't wearing a mask, but he might as well have been. His face was warped with delight, his eyes sunken and his pupils huge. He lunged for her again, his rubbery lips parting, and she'd driven her knee into his crotch before she could stop herself.

He didn't even seem to feel it, the drugs muting the pain. She grabbed his arm, twisting hard and shoving him into the line of men that had formed behind him. A cry of outrage filled the corridor, more hands reaching for her. She ducked beneath them, pushing through the mob.

Another hand on her arm, the grip like a vice. She tried to pull herself loose, then looked up to see that it was Duke. He'd lost his mask, his face taut with worry as he hauled her down the corridor. They fell through the front door, people spilling out of their way with raucous laughter.

Only here, in the cold air, in the relative quiet, did Savage's panic start to thaw.

"You okay?" asked Duke. He reached for her again, but she pulled away instinctively, rubbing her bare arms like they'd been poisoned.

"I'm fine," she snapped, glaring at the farmhouse, at the ever-growing line of men who waited to enter. If it wasn't for the fact there were innocent people in there too, she'd have happily nailed the doors shut and set fire to it.

She forced herself to breathe slowly, taking Duke's hand and looking up at him. He stared back with such concern, and such compassion, that she almost started crying.

"I'm okay," she said.

He hadn't just lost his mask, she realised, he'd lost his T-shirt too. Other than the strips of colourful fishnet on his arms and legs, and those awful hotpants, he was naked. He scrubbed at his face, rubbing his eyes like he had grit in them.

"Are *you* okay?" she asked.

"No," he said. "I got pulled into a room. They... they were like piranhas, Kate. They were literally tearing my clothes off. Somebody blew something at me, dust or something. I think I breathed it in."

He let go of her and wrapped his big arms around his chest, looking utterly miserable.

"I want to go home," he said.

She gave him a sympathetic smile before walking away, heading around the side of the house. There were more outbuildings here, huddles of people outside and each door guarded by a masked bouncer in a black coat. Portable halogens blazed, their fierce light making every expression look demonic, forming swarms of squirming shadows that danced on the walls.

"That's what this place reminds me of," she said as they walked along a gravel drive. "You know that painting, *The Garden of Earthly Delights*?"

"No," said Duke, his wary eyes on the crowds.

"It's a portrait of hell," she said. "Insane people doing horrible things. That's what this place is like."

He didn't argue with her, he just moved a little closer.

At the end of the path, out of the reach of the lights, was the back of what looked like a stable block. Savage heard the grumble of engines over the throb of music, like the generators that powered a funfair. There were no partygoers here, no sign of anybody at all in the shadows. She crept along the wall, peeking around the corner to see a gang of lorries sitting in a courtyard. There were five of them, all running, the air thick with exhaust fumes.

Another man in a black coat leaned against the nearest one, somewhere in his late forties. He had taken his mask off so that he could smoke a cigarette, revealing the face of a boxer—his nose broken, his ears puffed up.

Savage ducked back behind the wall.

"I guess we're not going that way," she said. "Let's double back, try to find a way up to the—"

"Oi!" yelled a voice.

Savage looked past Duke to see another guard walking down the path they'd just taken, heading right for them.

"What are you doing down here?" he said, his voice muffled by the red mask.

"Oh," said Savage, then Duke gathered her in his arms and kissed her. "Oh!" she said again, speaking into the warmth of his lips.

"Oi!" the man yelled. "Pack it in."

Savage pulled free. The guard had almost reached them, thrown into silhouette by the lights. She couldn't see his face, but he sounded older, and out of breath. He stank of cigarette smoke and old BO. The other man had walked out of the courtyard, his mask back on, his hand hovering inside his jacket.

"This area's out of bounds," said the first guy.

"Sorry," said Duke. "Sorry, sorry, sorry. We were just looking for a quiet place, you know? To do... rude things?"

"This ain't it," the man said, hooking a thumb over his shoulder. "Fuck off."

They ran away like children, hand in hand, and the giggle escaped Savage's lips before she could stop it—pushed out by another wave of adrenaline.

"Rude things?" she said when they were out of earshot.

Duke laughed, and there was something almost hysterical about it.

"I didn't know what else to say."

They walked around the farmhouse into the crowd—at least two hundred people out here now, most of them dancing in the hellish light. The warehouse seemed to have swollen with the sheer mass of life inside it, the ground trembling as the music continued to pound.

"You remember where the fire exit was?" asked Duke.

"Far side," said Savage. "This way."

They cut across the courtyard, through the sweaty swell of dancers. The end was capped by a brick wall that was too high to see over, but a metal gate sat open halfway down. Savage walked towards it, faltering when another guard stepped into view—this one shorter and rounder than the others, his head shaved. He clapped his gloved hands to warm them up, stamping his feet, oblivious.

"There are so many of them," she said, pretending to dance.

Duke started dancing too—at least something that *might* have been dancing. Savage wasn't sure. He looked like a possessed chicken, sweat breaking out on his face and his chest.

"There's no way up to the room from inside," she said. "This is our best shot. How do you feel about being a distraction?"

"I don't want to split up," said Duke.

"I'll be okay," she told him. "I'll be safe."

"It's not you I'm worried about," he said.

Savage laughed.

"All I need is five minutes to get up to the room, just to see who's in there."

"Five minutes?" said Duke, doing a frenzied Macarena.

She nodded.

"Hey, sweetheart!" came a voice from the courtyard. The man from the house, the one who'd ground himself against her, was walking over, dressed in his pants and his socks. He was off his face, barely able to walk in a straight line. "Why'd you leave me? Why'd you break my heart like that?"

"A distraction?" said Duke, cracking his knuckles. "I think I can manage that."

He smiled at Savage. It might have been her imagination, but his pupils looked huge.

"Are you—"

Duke kissed her again, and strode away.

"Sweetheart!" the man called. "Don't make me chase you."

The guy was so busy ogling Savage that he didn't notice Duke until he was looming over him. He flinched, almost falling, and Duke scooped him up like he was a child, throwing him over his bare shoulder. The man's fists drummed against Duke's back, his skinny legs kicking at the air.

"Hey!" yelled the bouncer at the gate. "Put him down!"

"Stick it up your arse!" Duke roared back.

Then he was off, running into the crowd with the man still slung over his shoulder.

"Oi!" the guard shouted again, bolting from his post and holding his mask in place as he ran. "I said put him down!"

Savage took her chance, moving swiftly to the gate and slinking through it. Compared to the bright courtyard, it was pitch black back here. She had to stop to let her eyes adjust, resting her hand on the back of the wall. A few screams erupted from the crowd as Duke cut through it, more shouts fighting with the bass thump of the music.

Be safe, she thought, trying to beam the message to him.

The side wall of the warehouse towered over her, the windows painted black and only leaking a trickle of light. She set off towards it, tripping on the rubble-strewn ground. To her left were the woods, the trees creaking in the wind like they wanted to join the party.

The fire escape was almost invisible in the night, a spiral staircase that jutted from the ground like a skeletal arm, reaching for the top floor.

Nobody was guarding it.

Savage jogged over, holding the strap of her bag to stop it from slipping off her shoulder. The fire escape groaned as she put her weight on the bottom step, flakes of rust landing in her eyes and mouth.

She didn't hesitate, because she knew she'd lose her bottle if she waited too long. She climbed as fast as she dared, looping in circles, the staircase rattling and wobbling like it was ready to crumble out of the wall and crash to the dirt.

A million years later, she reached the top—a small landing connected to a solid steel door. She paused to catch her breath, creeping forwards. The window in the door had been painted over, but pearls of golden light beaded around the edges, and when she put her eye to the glass, she found that she could see inside.

A large room drenched in red light, a collection of sofas arranged in the middle. Two men sat there, dressed in jeans and thick black coats. One—in his early fifties, maybe, his hair mostly grey—smoked a cigar, looking like he was halfway through telling a joke. The angle of his head made it hard to identify him, but there was a good chance it was one of the men they'd been told about: Warner Hobbs.

The other guy seemed like he might be asleep, but he had his back to the door, so she couldn't be sure. His head was completely bald, reflecting the light.

Capper, she thought.

She reached for her phone automatically before remembering she didn't have it. Then she turned her back on the room and retreated to the stairs.

Whatever was going on in there, she couldn't do a thing about it by herself.

She'd only just dropped onto the top step when she heard the click of the door behind her. By the time she'd looked back, it was swinging open.

A security guard burst out of it, this one not wearing a mask. He was the size of King Kong and just as angry.

"Shit," said Savage.

She broke into a run, but the man was too fast. He leaned over the railing, grabbing a fistful of her hair and wrenching her back onto the platform. The pain was unreal, her scalp tearing away from her skull.

"Shit is right," he said, swinging her around. "Get the fuck in here."

He hurled her into the half-open door and she bounced off it, her body on fire. She tripped on her heels, dropping hard, screaming as she hit the floor. Her bag went flying, the panic button skidding away.

"No!" she said.

She tried to get up only to feel a boot in the middle of her back, crushing her into the freezing concrete floor. The two men on the sofa were both watching like they didn't have a care in the world, the bald guy laughing.

It was Capper and Hobbs, there was no doubt about it.

"What did I tell you?" said the guard. He applied more weight to her back, so much that she thought her spine might crack. She tried to cry out but couldn't, her lungs empty. "She's police."

The man with the beard, Hobbs, took a long drag on his cigar before blowing out a cloud of smoke. He leaned into it, looking every bit the devil as his mouth peeled open into a grin. When he spoke, it was just a whisper against the deafening beat of the music.

"Good evening, little piggy."

CHAPTER THIRTY-SEVEN

"I don't like this," said Kett.

He fidgeted in the back seat of Clare's Mercedes, trying to make sense of the dark world through the tinted windows. The engine was off and the cold had crept in. Even though he'd slipped on his suit jacket again, and draped his overcoat across his lap, he was still numb.

"Not one bit," he said. "You see anything, Pete?"

They were locked in a grid of parked, empty cars, no headlights to illuminate the scene—just a half-eaten moon low on the horizon. Vehicles were still arriving, but they were all heading to the far side of the field where there were still empty spaces. Aside from the music blaring out of the warehouse, every note of which could be heard from here as if it was coming from the car's speakers, the world had fallen silent.

"No, sir," said Porter, cupping his hand to the window.

Kett checked his watch, seeing that midnight was approaching fast. It had been nearly an hour since Savage and Duke had left the car.

"You think they're okay?" he asked.

"Probably drunk," said Porter, his words steaming up the glass. "And dancing."

"I don't like it," Kett said again.

The panic was gnawing at him, the uncertainty driving him crazy and the cold making everything ten times worse.

Not to mention the god-awful stench of the Superintendent's car.

Porter looked at him, his orange vest glowing in the dark.

"Don't, sir," he said.

"Don't what?" snapped Kett.

Porter's raised eyebrow was barely visible.

"I just want to take a look, Pete," he said. "Make sure everything's okay."

"Clare told us that under no circumstances were we to leave the car without a direct order, sir," he said.

"Well, he's not here, is he?" said Kett, rubbing his hands together to try to get some feeling back in his fingers. He had the sudden urge to check the boot to make sure the Super wasn't lurking in there ready to surprise him, but he managed to resist it. "We're not doing anyone any good stuck here," he said. "A quick look, just to see what's going on."

"You heard anything else from him?"

Kett pulled out his phone, nothing on the screen.

"Nope."

Porter shrugged.

"Your funeral, sir."

Kett thought about it for all of five seconds, then opened the door. The air outside seemed warmer than the chill of the car, and he shivered his way into it.

"You coming?" he asked, leaning back in.

"No thanks," said Porter. "I'm going to stay right here,

like I was told to. That way Clare won't jam something spiky up my arse."

He rubbed his shoulder through the vest.

"Also, I'm still injured. And the cold's killing me. And I'm tired."

Kett slammed the door, muttering darkly as he passed the oak tree and set off towards the warehouse. He was well aware of how ridiculous he looked in his orange vest and jacket, but it was dark enough for him not to care.

He rubbed his arms as he went, seeing a handful of revellers walking towards the warehouse up ahead and wondering how anyone could be out in short skirts and sleeveless tops without freezing to death. The youth of today were insane.

"You really are starting to sound like a granddad," he told himself, managing a quiet laugh.

The warehouse was a hive of activity. A line of people stretched from the front door as they waited for security to let them in, more men in long, black coats and featureless red masks patrolling the perimeter. It looked more like a military operation than an illegal rave party, a thought that was reinforced when he saw one of the security guards adjust something on his belt—a flash of yellow that might have been a Taser.

He took cover behind another gnarled tree, breathing out a cloud of breath as he tried to figure out what to do. Without a ticket, he wasn't getting anywhere near the party, and he really didn't fancy getting Tasered if they spotted him roaming around.

He set off to his right, struggling in the dark and on the rough terrain as he made for the woodland that fringed the site. The moon hung over the trees, painting them in yellow light, making them look like ghosts. It was as bright as a searchlight as he jogged across the open meadow, making him visible to anyone who might be watching. The waist-high grass snatched at his legs, trying to trip him, but when he crashed into the trees thirty seconds later, he didn't hear a cry of alarm, didn't hear the thunder of footsteps.

He waited for a moment until the fire in his lungs had died out. It was dark enough that he had to pull the pencil torch from his pocket. He cupped it in his hand before clicking it on, the light pooling on the ground in front of him. He could hear the music from the warehouse, but the silence of the woods felt even louder.

"Right," he said.

He had no idea what he was doing, but at least he wasn't twiddling his thumbs in the car. And maybe the woods were a better place to start looking. Whatever had happened inside the red room at the last Masque, he was pretty sure Kieran Spicer hadn't been killed inside the building.

He'd been taken into the woods to be butchered.

Kett wove his way through the trees, keeping the light low so it wouldn't be seen from the party. It was hard going, the undergrowth dense and full of roots, his boots sliding into channels of water and mud. After a while, he couldn't see the warehouse anymore, although the music played relentlessly.

He wasn't sure how much later it was that his phone buzzed. He pulled it out to see a text from Clare.

You'd better still be in the car.

He forced his numb fingers to write back.

I am.

Clare's reply was immediate.

Prove it.

"Fuck's sake," said Kett.

He put the phone on *Do Not Disturb* mode and slid it into his pocket, trudging deeper into the trees. There was nothing here, no sign of human life at all, but he couldn't have found his way back now even if he'd wanted to. Without the warehouse to orient him, he didn't even know which direction he was moving in.

"You're a bloody fool," he said, wishing he'd taken Porter's advice.

He stopped again, heaving in a lungful of frozen air and lifting the torch to get his bearings.

There was a flash of red in the trees, maybe twenty yards away.

He had to walk a little closer to work out that it was a ribbon tied around the bole of a beech tree. And he had to walk all the way to make sure it was real. He touched it with his free hand, tugging. It had been tied tight, and recently, too, because it was bone dry, not a trace of mould or moss or lichen.

He circled slowly, illuminating the trees, searching.

Another burst of crimson in the distance, as bright as a gunshot wound.

He moved towards it, his teeth chattering from the cold, his legs so stiff that it took him nearly five minutes to walk fifty yards. The ribbon had been tied in an identical fashion, a careful bow and two neat ends.

Exactly the same as the ones he'd found at Wayside Manor.

He thought about texting Porter, but he was so cold he didn't think he'd be able to get his phone out of his pocket. Besides, he couldn't exactly call for backup—he had no idea where he was. He swept his torch again, finding nothing this time. But he had two points to work off, and he set off in the same direction, his boots slipping on the frozen ground, his feet so cold they felt like they were burning.

The third ribbon was nearly a hundred yards away from the last, and it was pure luck that he managed to find it. This one was tied to a tree like the others, but one end dropped all the way to the ground and kept going, trailing into the woods. In the torchlight, it looked ridiculously clean and bright, an impossible red line that belonged inside a fairy tale.

"Follow the red line," he said, his teeth chattering like a joke shop toy.

He did exactly that, trailing the ribbon through the dirt and around the bushes, deeper and deeper, until the music from the warehouse was just a distant memory. Here, even the moon had deserted him, the woods as dark as a grave, so oppressive that even the light from his torch seemed to cower into nothing.

Not enough for him to miss it, though.

Not enough for him to miss the house that was nestled in the trees.

It was a stone cottage, so green with moss that it was almost invisible. The roof had partially caved in, tiles scattered on the ground like broken teeth. The windows didn't even have frames, let alone glass.

The red ribbon led right through the front door.

Kett retrieved his phone and took a photograph, the flash lighting up the trees for a fraction of a second. He texted it to Porter.

Found the red line, he added. *Going in.*

He slipped it into his pocket before Porter could write back to tell him what an idiot he was. He pulled his torch out instead, crossing the patch of open ground that served as the cottage's front garden. The air seemed to grow even more frigid as he approached the building, a draught leaking from the open door.

He braced his free hand on the rotting frame and aimed the torch down the cottage's throat, seeing a corridor that led past two doors and ended at a third.

He leaned in, clearing his throat.

"Hello?"

The building gobbled the word down before it could so much as echo back.

"Anyone in there? It's the police. I found your ribbon."

The red line snaked along the hallway, vanishing beneath the closed door at the end. It might have been his imagination, but there seemed to be a soft glow spilling through the crack, a whisper of light pooling on the stone.

Red light.

"Here I come," he said, more to himself than anyone else. "Ready or not."

He stepped into the cottage, the damp chill making him feel like he'd sunk underwater. Shivering hard, he passed the first two doors, finding empty rooms.

He stopped at the last one.

His heart thrashed, its frenzied beat surely audible to whoever sat on the other side of the door. His chest was aching again and he rubbed it, wondering what he'd do if his heart packed in while he was in the middle of the woods.

"Knock knock," he called out.

He twisted the handle and pushed, the swollen door resisting for a few seconds before surrendering. The light flooded out like it had been desperate for release, a crimson bulb in the corner blinding him. He threw up his free hand, blinking away the glow, looking again.

There was a table in the middle of the room, and on the other side of it sat a figure in a crimson robe.

Their face was obscured by a featureless, blood-coloured mask, their eyes drenched in the shadows of their hood. Their gloved hands rested on the table, fingers intertwined.

The fear filled Kett from head to toe.

The anger, too.

"Who the fuck are you, then?" he asked.

He stayed in the doorway, his body tense in case the person made any sudden movements. There were words painted on the wall to his right, he noticed.

The Red Room.

Beneath that was the same riddle they'd seen before. *Follow the red line, find the red room, make a red wish.*

"You followed the red line," said the person at the table, seeing where he was looking. It was a man's voice, the accent somewhere from the Northeast.

"You found the red room," said a second voice, a woman.

Kett twisted his head to see somebody standing behind him at the end of the corridor. She was dressed identically to the first, her hooded robe reaching the floor, her mask revealing nothing.

She pulled the front door of the cottage shut, the sound of the bolt slipping closed like a gunshot.

"Don't move," Kett told her. "I'm police, and I'm not on my own."

He turned back to the man in the room.

"Take the masks off," he said.

Only, they weren't masks. The man's head had been wrapped in red ribbon, just like Kieran's—two slits for him to look through, another for his mouth.

"No," the man said.

Kett pulled out his phone, holding it up.

"One call from this and an army will descend on this place. Take off the fucking masks."

"You're not going to do that," said the man.

"No?"

Kett unlocked the phone, finding Clare's number.

"Because we know why you're here," said the woman. Her accent was the same as the man's, only softer.

Kett turned to see that she'd moved closer, her hands lost somewhere inside those robes.

"Uh-uh," he said, retreating into the room. "Stay where you are."

"We know what you want," said the man.

He pushed himself up from the table, his seat scraping back. He was so tall that the top of his hood pressed against the ceiling. A handle jutted from the waistband of the filthy jeans he wore beneath his robes: a machete, maybe.

"Sit down," said Kett.

"We know you want answers," said the woman, still advancing.

"Fuck this," said Kett, and he thumbed Clare's name.

"So ask your questions, Robbie," said the man.

The last of the warmth drained out of Kett. He cancelled the call.

"How do you know my name?"

"Because we know everything," said the man, and even beneath his shroud of red ribbon, Kett could tell he was smiling. "So go ahead. Make a red wish."

CHAPTER THIRTY-EIGHT

SHE'D BEEN RIGHT.

This place was *hell.*

Savage lay face-down on the floor, the security guard's boot grinding into her back, crushing her. All she could hear past the roar of blood in her skull was the relentless drum and bass from the dance floor below—the entire building vibrating with the force of it—but she could see the laughter on the faces of the two men. They howled their delight, their eyes bright and cruel as they watched her squirm.

Hobbs, the man with the beard, sucked in a mouthful of smoke from his cigar as he squatted down beside her. He blew it into her face and she had no choice but to breathe it in, her crushed lungs spasming. A high-pitched whistle broke out in the middle of her head, as if her brain was screaming.

"You lot finally found us, then." Hobbs was close enough that she could make sense of his shout, could hear his Liverpudlian accent. "Took you fucking long enough."

"I'm not police," she tried to say, but she didn't have the strength to speak.

"How many of you are there?" he asked. "Just you and that gorilla you came in with?"

She tried to push herself up but the guard must have weighed eighteen stone, and all of it was right on top of her.

"Because we know there aren't a lot of you," he said. "There aren't reinforcements in the woods, or down the road. There's no choppers up there."

He sucked on his cigar again, Savage's eyes burning as he breathed his poison onto her.

"We know the closest you can be is King's Lynn," he went on. "What's that, fifteen minutes?"

He laughed again, holding the red-hot tip of his cigar an inch or two away from her eye.

"It's fifteen minutes unless some cunt has left his truck in the middle of the B1145," he went on. "Because then it's at least twice that. You think about that when you were planning your shitty little raid?"

He stood, walking to where she'd dropped her handbag. He collected it, and the panic button, carrying them back.

"Let me guess," he said. "You press this, the cavalry comes?"

Hobbs held the panic button over the glass coffee table between the sofas, then let it fall into his drink. The inferno of Savage's fear grew even wilder, spreading fast. He carried the bag over, crouching beside her again.

"How'd you find out?" he said. "Who told you?"

She couldn't have replied even if she'd wanted to. There wasn't enough air, the darkness falling from the ceiling like soil. She felt like she was sinking into her grave.

"Get off her, Brian," said Hobbs to the man on her back.

The weight was released from her spine and she rolled over, clawing in a desperate breath. She grabbed the collar of her dress, pulling it away from her neck, kicking her legs against the concrete floor until she no longer felt like she was dying. Lights exploded in her vision, a lightning storm of frightening intensity.

"I'm not..." she started, then coughed so hard she thought she was going to lose a lung.

"You're not what?" asked Hobbs, leaning against the arm of the sofa.

Savage rolled onto her side, then onto her hands and knees, her forehead pressed to the cool floor. The adrenaline did its job, numbing the pain.

"Police," she said. "I'm not police. You've got it wrong."

The security guard grabbed her hair again, hauling her up onto her knees.

"No!" she said.

He let go and she put both hands to her head, her scalp burning. She couldn't think straight. She didn't know what to do. If Hobbs was telling the truth, if they'd blocked the roads to the warehouse, reinforcements weren't going to get here in time. Kett and Porter were in the car, she had no way of alerting them, and for all she knew Duke had already been caught.

Nobody was coming to help her.

If they wanted to, these men could kill her right now. They could lose themselves in the crowds, melt into the night, long gone before anyone found her body.

Capper, the bald guy, was struggling out of the sofa. He yelled something at Hobbs, but the music was too loud for Savage to catch what he said. Hobbs yelled something back, both of them agitated.

Savage took advantage of their distraction. Her yellow handbag lay at her feet, and she leaned forward on her knees to pick it up, taking small comfort in its weight.

"Don't even fucking think about it," said the guard behind her, grabbing her hair again.

"It's empty," she said, holding it open. There were tears on her face, and they weren't fake. "I just don't want to lose it. It's my mum's."

He gave her hair a violent shake, jerking her head back and forth. The pain was unreal.

"Please stop!" she screamed, the sob exploding from her. "Please!"

"You're lying," said Hobbs, walking back over.

Savage clutched the bag to her chest, her fingers exploring the seam at the bottom.

Finding the zip that Duke had stitched there earlier that day.

"How did you find out about us?" said Hobbs, leaning so close that she could smell the smoke on his breath. "Who told you?"

Savage tugged the zip as slowly as she could, feeling it glide open. Her fingertips met with cold metal and her heart seemed to do a somersault behind her ribs.

"Get her up," said Hobbs, his patience gone.

The guard hauled her to her feet using her hair, and a current of rage surged through her like nothing she'd ever known. Her mind was fizzing, her body charged with something she didn't even have a word for. Her dress had ridden up past her waist, and Hobbs looked her up and down, the pink worm of his tongue running over his lips.

He began to loosen the knot of his tie.

"Let's see if we can't work the truth out of you, eh?" he said with a dead-eyed smile. "See if we can't warm you up a little."

It was too much. Savage wrapped her fingers around the bar of cold metal that had been hidden inside the lining of her handbag. She locked eyes with Hobbs, and when she spoke, it felt like the words were screamed by a million different voices at once.

"Fuck! You!"

She ripped the baton from the bag, extending it in one smooth motion.

Then she swung her arm back with all the strength she possessed, twisting her waist, every muscle in her body working in perfect harmony.

The weighted head of the baton struck Hobbs' cheekbone like a hammer meeting glass. His head snapped to the side and he spun, a spiral of blood seeming to hang in the air as he dropped onto the sofa.

The guard yanked her hair again, his roar of rage drowning out the music. He dragged her backwards and she almost fell, only just managing to keep her balance in the heels. She spun to face him, feeling her hair rip out of her scalp.

His other hand clamped around her throat, as tight as a noose.

He squeezed, hard, and the world went faint. His face gurned, his eyes bulging, his yellow teeth bared—nothing but hate.

Savage almost dropped the baton, but she didn't. She swung it again, cracking it into the man's shoulder. He didn't even seem to feel it through his coat, crushing her throat, lifting her so hard she felt her feet come off the ground.

She hit him again, catching him on the temple. Then she brought the handle of the baton down on the bridge of his nose, again, and again, until he cried out in pain and let go of her.

She landed lightly, adjusted her weight, and drove her

foot into the soft joint of the man's knee. He was already struggling, and his leg folded inwards like a stork's—a crack that she could feel as much as hear. He grabbed for her as he fell, knocking her backwards. She tripped on Hobbs' prone body, landing on the sofa. The baton flew out of her hand, rolling beneath the coffee table.

Capper was lumbering to the corner of the room, his chins swinging like a turkey's wattle. He was calling for help, but the music was just too loud. He ducked down beside a bag that had been stowed by the wall, reaching inside.

"Oi!" Savage yelled, forcing herself back to her feet. "Stop! Police!"

When he stood up again, he was holding a gun.

Savage dived behind the sofa, hearing the crack of the pistol. Capper fired again, a hole appearing in the leather just feet from where she was crouching, an explosion of foam from inside.

"Stop!" she screamed, crawling away.

Two more shots punched through the sofa. She couldn't work out if the man was moving, she didn't know where he was. She kept crawling, stopping only when Capper stepped into sight.

He pointed the gun, his finger on the trigger.

But he didn't have time to take the shot.

The fire escape door crashed open, Duke standing there in his hotpants, his face like a rampaging bull, his eyes wild. He spotted Savage—just for a second, but long enough to see the fear on her face, the pain, the horror of what had just happened.

Capper started to turn, swinging the gun.

Duke roared as he charged into the room, slamming into

Capper like a wrecking ball. He grabbed him by the scruff of his neck, one hand holding his gun arm. He drove him across the room before hurling him into the far wall—or the place where the wall would have been if it still had windows.

Capper went straight through the empty frame, tumbling over the metal railing of the walkway. His gun barked, a single flash of light, then he vanished into the seething mass of people below.

"Shit!" said Savage, running to Duke. "You hit?"

She wasn't sure if he could hear her, because he didn't reply. She couldn't see a wound, though.

She ran to the railing and looked down. People on the dance floor were scattering from where Capper had landed, falling over themselves as they tried to get away. He'd hit badly, his body twisted at an unnatural angle, but he was still moving. She couldn't see the gun anywhere.

Duke took hold of her gently so that he could look at her face, his mouth shaping words she couldn't hear until, with a crunch, the music suddenly cut off.

For a second Savage thought she'd gone deaf. Then the screams filtered through the ringing in her ears, a serenade of chaos and panic from below as people bolted from the warehouse. If there were guards down there, she couldn't see them. But she knew it wouldn't be long before they found their way up.

"Are you okay?" Duke asked.

She managed a nod.

He looked over the railing.

"Is he... I... whoops. I didn't mean to do that, I just saw you and I... I lost it, Kate, I lost it and I..."

"I'm okay," said Savage, taking his hand. "I'm okay."

It wasn't entirely true, of course. She could feel her

pulse in her scalp where her hair had been torn out, and her entire body ached from being thrown to the floor.

All of that paled, though, to the knowledge that in another life, with different choices and a lot less luck, she could have easily been killed.

"Find a phone," she told Duke. "Call Clare. Tell him he'll need air support if the roads are blocked."

She crossed the room, heading for the security guard. He was lying on his back, his bad leg stretched out in front of him, the bottom of his face caked in blood. He was shaking like a cement mixer with a brick in it, and he looked like he'd have happily torn her head off if he'd been able to.

"Stay down," Savage told him, like he had a choice. She had to fight the urge to rip his hair from his head.

She ducked down beside Hobbs instead, her stomach churning as she checked his motionless body for a pulse. The left side of his face had swollen like a balloon, his eyes half open and full of blood. He looked dead.

Which was why she almost sobbed with relief when she found the weak flicker of a heartbeat in the damp hollow of his throat.

She rolled him into the recovery position in case he started choking, patting his pockets. He had a phone and a wallet, as well as a key fob for a BMW. The phone was locked, but the wallet had everything she needed. She pulled out his driving licence, seeing the name Warner Andrew Hobbs.

She used the phone to call 999, relaying her situation to the operator.

"I need you to contact Superintendent Colin Clare. Tell him to call me back on this number. This is an active operation, and an emergency."

She made sure the operator understood before hanging up.

"Can you keep watch, Aaron?" she asked as she waited. "Make sure they're not coming up."

Duke nodded, heading back across the room. Hobbs' phone started to ring, and she answered it.

"Check on the guy you threw off the walkway," she yelled to Duke. She lifted the phone. "Sir?"

"Please tell me I didn't just hear the words 'threw off the walkway,'" said Clare.

"It's a long story," she said.

"Well, we're not going anywhere in a hurry," he said, the anger audible in every word. "Some prick cut off the roads. So tell the bloody story."

"Uh, we found the organisers," she said. "It's Capper and Hobbs, plus a security guard. There's a gun, sir. I, uh, overpowered two of them. One's unconscious. Duke took out the third. I think he's out cold too."

She frowned.

"I guess it wasn't that long of a story," she said.

"You've got Capper and Hobbs there?" said Clare.

"Yes, sir. Kind of."

"You're safe?"

"Kate," said Duke, who was still on the walkway. He looked back into the room. "Security inbound, a *lot* of them."

She could hear their shouts as they crossed the warehouse floor, the pounding of feet as they started up the stairs. Duke was retreating, offering her a hand as he passed.

"We've got to go," he said.

She took his hand, letting him haul her up. She held onto the wallet, the phone to her ear.

"Negative, sir," she said. "We're outnumbered. How long will you be?"

"Not long," said Clare. "But air support is on its way, they're minutes out."

It wouldn't be fast enough. Duke opened the fire escape, cold air rushing in like a slap to the face. Savage was halfway out when she heard a shout from the security guard on the floor.

"You're fucking dead," he said, tilting his head back so that he could see her. "I know your faces. Both of you. You're fucking dead." He drew a breath, hollering. "In here! They're getting away!"

Savage ran through the fire escape, closing it behind her just as the first of the guards ran past the glass windows. Duke was clattering down the steps, the whole frame shaking like a carnival ride. She didn't have a free hand to hang onto the railing, and barely made it to the ground on her feet.

Duke grabbed her again, pulling her away from the warehouse into the night. There was a stretch of woodland ahead, the trees beckoning them into the welcome dark.

"Kate?" Clare was yelling. "Are you okay?"

"I'm okay, sir," she said into the phone. "We're heading for the woods to the, uh, west of the site. We—"

The fire escape door crashed open, two guards running onto the platform. Savage ducked down, feeling Duke do the same. She covered the phone with her hand again to mask the glow, holding her breath even though there was no way they could hear her from up there.

After ten seconds or so, they vanished back into the warehouse.

There was another shout from nearby as somebody came crashing through the gate in the courtyard wall—a young woman in party clothes. More people followed as the warehouse was evacuated, all of them swarming across the meadow into the trees.

"Kate?" said Clare on the phone, beside himself with worry. "Talk to me."

"I think we're safe, sir," she said. "We can hide out in the woods until we see you. But Hobbs and Capper are going to get away unless you hurry up. Can you tell Kett and Porter to watch out for them? We might be able to follow—"

"Porter's on his way down from the car," said Clare. "But Kett's gone AWOL."

"What, sir?"

"He tossed off. Last I heard, he was going into the woods."

Savage looked over her shoulder at the creaking trees, the fathomless dark between them no longer so comforting.

"He thinks he's found something," Clare went on. "He thinks he might have found the red room."

Savage knew what was coming before the Superintendent said it, and the chill of the night seemed to settle inside her aching bones.

"Get in there and find him, Kate, before he ends up dead."

CHAPTER THIRTY-NINE

"Follow the red line, find the red room, make a red wish."

The man stood behind the table, his hands interlaced in front of him like he was praying. His eyes were dark and glassy through the holes in the ribbon—*dead eyes*, thought Kett. He could have been a mannequin if it wasn't for the flutter of movement every time he blinked.

"Make a red wish," he said again. "Anything you can dream of."

There was a crunch of breaking glass as the other masked figure stepped closer. She was shorter than Kett, but she wasn't exactly small, and her hand still hovered inside her robes. Like the man, her mask was made from layers of coiled ribbon, the colour of blood.

She moved even closer, her head cocked to one side like she was studying him.

"Stop," he told her, but his voice was a croak. He clung to his phone, ready to use it as a weapon if he needed to.

He moved across the room to get away from her, backing

to the far wall so that he could keep them both in his field of vision. There was another door here, he saw with some relief. It was open, leading into a corridor that was ink black.

"I mean it," he said. "Stop moving."

"Time is running out," said the man. "We are not renowned for our patience."

The woman came to a halt next to the table, both figures side by side as they watched him. He wondered if he could take them if he needed to, if he could rip those masks away to see who was under there.

The woman seemed to read his mind, peeling back her robe to reveal the handle of a knife tucked into her waistband.

A *big* knife.

The man did the same, pulling the machete out a little to reveal the blade.

Kett licked his lips, eyeing the door to his left.

"We cannot keep you here," said the man. "We have no interest in imprisoning you."

"Or hurting you," added the woman.

"Unless that is your wish."

They laughed softly, not a shred of kindness in the sound.

"Leave, if you must."

"But this is a gift, from us to you," said the man. "You have earned it. We can grant you anything. Any wish."

"Any desire," said the woman.

"We can gift life."

"Or death."

"But I sense you want none of those things," said the man. "I sense you want something else from us, Robert Kett."

They turned to each other, as if they were sharing an unspoken thought, before looking back.

"We sense that you want information," said the man. "You want to *know*."

Kett's blood was boiling, his thoughts a chaos of fear and confusion. A tremor had started deep inside him, one that shook his whole body.

"So ask us," said the man. "Ask us your question, make your red wish."

"Find out the truth," said the woman.

Kett licked his lips.

"Who are you?" he asked.

They began to laugh again—an ugly sound that made Kett's skin crawl, that made his scalp shrivel.

"We are nobody," said the woman.

"And everybody," added the man. "This is not your question."

Kett hesitated for a moment before trying again.

"What happened to Kieran Spicer?" he said. "On Saturday, at the other party. He found you, didn't he? Somehow he found the secret room, and he met you. Tell me what happened to him."

"He did not find us," said the woman. "He did not follow the red line."

"But we did kill him," added the man, his voice so matter of fact that at first Kett couldn't comprehend what he'd said.

"What?"

"We hacked his body into pieces," said the woman. "We had no choice, it was our burden, not our wish. But this still isn't the question you really want to ask."

"No," said Kett, pointing his finger at them. "That's exactly the question I want to ask. You killed him?"

They didn't answer him this time, a mirror image of each other.

"You're both under arrest, you hear me? You're under arrest for the murder of Kieran Spicer. You do not have to—"

"You're running out of time," said the man. "If you want to know the truth, ask us now."

Kett opened his mouth, but nothing came out. He could hear distant thunder, the soft, pulsing roar of a helicopter.

"You're fucked," he said. "You hear that? You're the ones who are out of time."

He moved towards the second door, keeping his finger pointed at them.

"Wait there."

But before he could step through it, the man called to him again.

"If you leave the red room, you lose your wish."

"And you won't see us again," said the woman. "It's now or never."

Kett hesitated, one hand on the door frame. His stomach boiled like a kettle. He thought he might be sick.

The man and the woman simply watched him. No sign that they were going to attack, no sign that they were going to run, even though the helicopter was closing in.

"Anything?" he asked.

He might have imagined it, but he thought he could see a shudder of delight ripple through them.

"Anything," they answered together.

Kett walked back into the room.

"This bullshit: the robes, the masks. I've seen it all before."

They didn't say anything, they just waited.

"I saw it with the Pig Man, Schofield, when my wife

was taken. I saw it when Hollenbeck took me, when they made me fight for my life in Hell House. I saw it this year when Joseph Maynard convinced Aggie Clegg she was summoning a demon, when he killed all those people."

Still nothing, but they knew what was coming.

"You're working with Hollenbeck, aren't you?" he said. "You're working with Joseph Maynard."

He jabbed his finger at the man, the tremor making his arm shake.

"*You're* Maynard?"

And the sudden thought of it was like an injection of nitrous oxide, almost propelling him across the room. Only the woman's hand on the hilt of that machete stopped him from moving.

"You're him."

The woman laughed, a childish giggle that made goosebumps break out on Kett's arms.

"Wrong," she said.

"But we know the truth," said the man. "We know about Maynard."

"We know where he is," said the woman.

"So prove it," said Kett. "Where is he?"

"Is this your wish?" they said together.

"Yes," said Kett. "It's my wish, for fuck's sake. Tell me where he is."

"Cold Iron," said the man. "You'll find him there by a different name."

"Luan Agolli," said the woman.

"This is your red wish," said the man. "May it bring you much pain, and much sorrow."

"May it bring blood and horror," said the woman.

"May it—"

"Shut up," Kett said, his temper fraying. "Shut the fuck up, both of you."

The sound of the helicopter was fading as it passed, heading towards the warehouse. There was no way for them to know where he was. He pulled out his phone, calling Clare. The Super answered before the first ring had finished.

"At last! Where the toss are you, Kett?"

"In the woods," he said. "A cottage. There's a man and a woman here. They've confessed to killing Kieran. The chopper just went over, sir, I need it back. They're armed."

"They're running?" asked Clare.

"No, sir," he said. "They're..."

They still weren't moving, standing as still as statues on the far side of the room.

"They're not doing anything," he said. "I'm going to go outside. Tell the chopper to look for me."

Clare grunted before hanging up. Kett walked to the door and stopped there. He knew the moment he walked out of the room, they'd run—they'd be insane not to, after what they'd told him.

"Sit down," he told them. "Both of you."

To his surprise, they obeyed, lowering themselves onto two of the chairs beside the table.

"There's no point in running," he said. "You won't make it. They'll be able to track you through the woods."

"We know," said the man.

"You're fucking mad, you know that?" Kett said.

He walked through the door, finding a long corridor that led towards the back of the house. The air shook with the arrival of the helicopter, and when he walked out of the back door into the woods it was right there, suspended over the tops of the trees maybe fifty yards away. A spotlight scoured the forest floor, as bright as day.

"Here!" he yelled, waving his arms. "Over here!"

There was somebody else in the woods, he realised, caught in the glare from the helicopter—a young man dressed up for the rave. He looked terrified, his arms cradling his head as he bolted through the trees. More people followed, a couple of young women struggling in the dense undergrowth.

"What the..."

The woods were crawling, he realised, a stampede of people tearing west. Two more ran right past him, using their phones as torches.

"Shit," he said.

He waved at the chopper again before realising it was pointless. Then he ran back through the door of the cottage, tripping his way along the corridor towards the red room.

It wasn't red anymore.

The light had been switched off, the room as dark as pitch. Kett clicked on his torch, sweeping it frantically from side to side until he found them.

The man and the woman were sitting exactly where they had been before, hunched over, defeated.

"Stay there," he told them. "Don't move."

They didn't respond, their heads slumped. Their robes drooped as if they'd deflated.

"Fuck," he said.

He saw the impossible shape of them, the sagging shoulders, the lifeless hoods. When he walked over and took hold of the man's robe, it came away from the chair and fell into a puddle of empty cloth. The woman's robe held on for a little longer, and he pushed his free hand into it, searching for a body.

"Fuck!" he said again, ripping the robe away and hurling it to the floor. "Fuck!"

He bolted to the front of the house, smacking his shoulder on the door as he ran through and almost dropping the torch. The helicopter was right overhead now, the spotlight so bright it looked as if the sun had risen. People ran through the glare, eyes wide with fear, mouths twisted in panic.

"Stop!" Kett yelled to them, stepping out into the madness of the crowd. "Stop! Police!"

But his voice only drove them away, scattering them deeper into the trees.

He spun in mad circles as he looked for the man and the woman from the red room, screaming as loud as his lungs would let him when he understood that he'd lost them.

Beneath his feet, two coils of unspooled red ribbon twisted like snakes in the downdraught from the helicopter.

CHAPTER FORTY

Tuesday

KETT MADE HIS WAY TO THE WAREHOUSE LIKE HE WAS moving inside a dream, his body too heavy, his mind exhausted. He'd scoured the cottage and the surrounding woodland for half an hour, until the first uniformed coppers had scampered into view and secured the site. But the man and the woman had gone. They'd melted into the surge of frightened ravers, swallowed whole by the dark.

Even if Kett managed to corral every single person from the party, he still wouldn't know for sure who had stood in that room, who had grinned at him from behind those blood-red masks.

It was easy enough to find his way back. He just moved against the trickle of people that still trampled through the woods in search of safety. Some moved in a panic, but most were laughing now—high on adrenaline and narcotics as they ran from whatever had scared them.

He didn't bother trying to arrest them. He didn't even tell them he was police. What was the point? They were kids, thrill-seekers, not guilty of much more than enjoying a fun night out.

Besides, there weren't enough cells in the county to hold them all.

He was nearing the edge of the woods when he heard Porter calling his name. The DI was up ahead, standing in a puddle of torchlight.

"Sir? I thought that was you. Where have you been?"

Kett didn't have the energy to answer him. He walked over, Porter meeting him halfway, his face etched with concern. He shrugged off his overcoat and offered it to Kett, and when he didn't take it, he draped it over his shoulders. It was filled with Porter's body heat, beginning the long job of thawing Kett's bones.

"Let's get back to the warehouse, sir," he said, shining the torch ahead. "You find anything out there?"

"Yeah," said Kett, but he couldn't manage any more than that.

"Well, whatever it was, it can't have been worse than what happened to Kate and Aaron," Porter said as he walked across the meadow. The warehouse squatted in front of them, surrounded by police. It seemed smaller from this angle. "You heard?"

"No," said Kett. "They okay?"

"Kate raided the party command centre by herself," he said. "Took out Hobbs and a security guard. Guard's got a broken leg, Hobbs is out cold."

"Shit," said Kett. "What did she do to them?"

Porter grinned.

"Smuggled a baton in her handbag, sir, almost took Hobbs' head off. Martin Capper came at them with a gun. Duke took him out with extreme prejudice."

"Christ," said Kett.

"They're round the front," said Porter, leading the way through an open gate in a brick wall.

Huddles of coppers occupied the terrace beyond, maybe two dozen miserable partygoers sitting on the cold ground. A couple of the men were in handcuffs.

"Few charges of affray and possession," Porter explained. "But I don't think the boss is too bothered about bringing them in."

The night was still full of flashing lights, but when Kett walked around the front of the warehouse he saw they were coming from a sea of IRVs and ambulances. More of the ravers had been penned against the warehouse wall by a cordon of police, and Gorski's tactical team occupied the centre ground, their weapons stowed but their eyes alert.

Kett allowed himself a long, deep breath, but he didn't feel much relief.

"There's the Super," said Porter, putting a gentle hand on Kett's back and steering him through the crowd.

Clare stood beside a row of four ambulances, drowning in his monstrously ugly Big Tossing Jacket. Savage was next to him, wrapped in a foil blanket. There was no sign of Duke until Kett got close enough to see him inside the ambulance, sitting on the stretcher with a vacant look on his face—even more vacant than usual, that was. He had a blanket over his shoulders too, but other than that, and his hotpants, he was naked.

"Sir," said Porter as they walked up. "I found him."

Clare turned around, a prize scowl on his face.

"Well take him back," he said. "I don't want him."

Kett turned to Savage.

"You alright, Kate? I heard what happened."

She nodded, but didn't speak, and there was nothing in her face but exhaustion.

"Aaron okay?" Kett asked.

"I'm fine," said Duke, jittering inside the ambulance. "Fine, fine, fine, absolutely fine, nothing wrong with me at all, raring to go, get me out there, I'm fine and dandy. Dandy, dandy, dandy."

He grinned, and even from here Kett could see how enormous his pupils were.

"Are you *high*?" he asked.

"Not high, no, nope, no siree, no way Jose," said Duke.

He gagged like he was going to be sick, then burst out laughing.

"Somebody blew something in his face," said Savage. "Powder. They're not sure what it was."

"Sherbert," said Duke. "Sher-bert. That's all. Sher-bert. Sir Bert. Sir Bartholomew, Knight of the Realm. That's me."

He grinned again.

"Bloody hell," said Porter. He pulled out his phone, but before he could take a photo, Clare slapped it out of his hand. It skittered beneath the ambulance.

"Pack it in," roared the Super. "Have you lot got any idea how much you've Ketted this thing up?"

"Bit unfair to say we *Ketted* it up, sir," said Kett. "It wasn't just me."

"Well I'm blaming you anyway, you tadpole's tosshole. What part of 'stay in the car' wasn't clear enough for you?"

"Sorry, sir," said Kett. "I just wanted to take a—"

"The only thing you'll be taking a look at is my fist, Kett, when I ram it up your arse."

"That doesn't make sense on any level, sir."

Clare pointed a long fingernail at him.

"You call yourself the Extreme Crime Task Force? Extreme Fuck-Up Task Force, more like. You want a case fucked up? Call in the EFU…" He had to pause for a second to work it out. "TF. The Efutf."

He rubbed his eyes with the heels of both hands.

"I give up," he said, staring at Kett. "Go on then, tell me what happened to you in the woods. You lost them?"

"Lost who, sir?" asked Savage.

Kett took a deep breath, trying to recall exactly what had happened, trying to separate the facts from the mad dream of what he'd found in the woods.

"I followed the red line," he said. "I found the red room."

He shook his head.

"And I made a red wish."

"What?" said Porter.

"I found a cottage in the woods," he said. "A ruin, really. There were two people inside. A man and a woman, I think. Red robes, and red ribbons wrapped around their faces, just like Kieran. They both had knives. Machetes."

"Like the ones used to kill our victim?" asked Clare.

"Right, sir. And I asked them if it was them. I asked them if they'd killed Kieran on Saturday night. They admitted it."

"What?" said the Super.

"They said it like I'd asked them if they'd had chips for tea, like they didn't have a care in the world. They told me they'd hacked him into pieces."

"And you didn't arrest them?"

"Like I said, sir, the knives. They didn't look like they wanted to kill me, but they could have. There were two of them. I didn't want to risk it."

"Pfft," said Clare. "So you let them get away?"

"Yeah," he said, a deep and awful sickness rolling through him. "They bolted when I went out to check on the helicopter. I was only gone a few seconds, figured air support would be able to track them through the woods if they ran. Didn't count on the stampede."

"My fault, sir, sorry," said Savage, putting her hand up. "When Duke threw Capper over the walkway and the gun went off, all hell broke loose."

"Wheeeeeee..." said Duke, using his hand to imitate somebody falling to the ground from a great height.

"They left their robes, though," Kett said, "and their..."

"Eeeeeeeee..." Duke went on.

Everyone turned to look at the PC, and he opened his fist in an explosion.

"Splat," he finished.

"Their masks," said Kett. "The ribbon. There must be some DNA on there, prints. I don't know. We might get lucky."

"Hay's on her way out," said Clare, but he didn't look hopeful.

"They knew who I was," said Kett. "Knew my name. But more than that, they knew about Hollenbeck. It's the same tricks, sir, the masks and the robes and all the arcane bullshit. It's like they were waiting for me to find the place."

He shook his head, once again convinced that it had all been a dream.

"They're killers, that much is clear. They have to be involved with Hollenbeck somehow."

"Except Hollenbeck is finished," said Clare.

"Maynard's still out there, sir. He was in deep with them. This is what they did. They recruited psychopaths, they competed to see who could get the most kills. They tried to recruit me, too. Remember? That night in Hell House. This has Maynard written all over it. And I asked them. That was my wish."

"Maybe your wish should have been for them to turn themselves in," grumbled Clare.

"I'd have wished for a burger," said Duke.

"You asked about Maynard, sir?" said Savage.

Kett nodded.

"My wish was to know where he was."

"They told you?" asked Porter.

Kett nodded, opening his mouth to relay what they'd said before closing it again. One of the paramedics had appeared, clambering into the back of the ambulance. She shot Kett a nervous smile as she went, then pulled a thermometer from the shelf.

"I'll tell you later," he said. "I don't want to say it here. Maynard's got eyes and ears everywhere."

"It's a steaming pile of dung," said Clare.

"You're a steaming pile of dung, sir!" yelled Duke, pointing at the Superintendent and bursting into wild laughter again.

"It's a game," Clare said, ignoring the PC. "Did you take a look at this place?"

He stuck his hands in the air, whirling them around.

"It's a carnival. It's all empty theatrics. Whoever you found in the woods, whatever they told you, it's as useful as a cup of pigeon toss."

"You're a cup of pigeon toss!" echoed Duke, still pointing at Clare.

"Did you think to ask your mysterious masked strangers *why* they murdered Kieran Spicer?"

"I did, sir," he replied. "They wouldn't say much, only... They told me it was their burden, not their wish. I don't know what that means."

"Of course you don't," said Clare. "Because they knew you were Chief Fuck-Up in Charge of the Extreme Fuck-

Up Task Force. The high and mighty CFU... IC...OT... EF... Fuck it, you know what I mean. They gave you nothing, then they gave you the slip."

Kett rubbed his lips, numb from the cold, and nodded.

"I'm sorry, sir."

Clare thrust his hands into his pockets, groaning at the night sky.

"It wasn't a complete bust," he said. "We got the two men in charge of the Masques. Capper and Hobbs. Sooner or later, they'll talk."

He glared at Savage.

"Providing the doctors don't have to wire their jaws shut. They'll know about the people you met in the cottage, Kett. We'll find them."

One of the ambulances was pulling away, heading for the road. Two IRVs followed. Clare watched them go before turning back.

"You lot look absolutely tossed," he said.

"You look tossed!" said Duke, and this time Clare eyeballed him.

"I don't care how much angel dust you've snorted up your bellend, Duke. If I hear one more word come out of your mouth, I'm going to pump your stomach myself. With a rake."

Duke pretended to zip his mouth closed.

"Go home," said Clare. "All of you. Or go to the hospital. Go anywhere that isn't here. We'll meet in the morning and see if we can sort this mess out."

He gave them all a look in turn, one that wasn't entirely unfriendly. Then he made his way to the warehouse.

"Right," said the paramedic who'd taken Duke's temperature. "This one's coming in for a detox. Anyone want a ride back to the city?"

Savage put her hand up, and Porter nodded.

"Yeah," said Kett. "That would be great, thank you."

Duke grinned.

"Welcome aboard my spaceship, you sexy arse muffins! Let's fly!"

KETT DIDN'T REMEMBER MUCH about the ride home, mainly because after five seconds in the passenger seat up front, bathed in hot air from the vents and gently rocked by potholes, he'd fallen asleep. He was woken sometime later by a rush of cold air and a gentle hand on his arm.

"Come on, sir," said Porter when he'd opened his eyes. "We can share a cab."

They rode away from the hospital in a taxi that smelled of doner kebabs, arriving at Kett's house first. The lights were on, as always, but it was way past two in the morning, and he didn't think there was much chance of him getting in.

"Can you wait for a second?" he asked the driver.

He hopped out and crunched over the drive, sliding his key into the lock.

Please, he thought, feeling the pull of everything he loved right behind the door, knowing that the comfort of his own bed and the warmth of his wife were just an unsnibbed Yale and a sliding bolt away.

The key didn't turn.

"Please," he said, resting his head on the door. His finger hovered over the bell, but he didn't press it. He felt too guilty at the thought of waking Billie, of bringing the stench of every foul thing he'd encountered that night into their home.

He pulled the key free and started back towards the street, stopping when he heard the door opening behind him. He turned to see Billie framed in soft light, one hand stifling a yawn, the other beckoning him inside.

"Thank you," he said.

He waved to Porter before walking inside. Billie closed the door behind them and drew the heavy bolt across. She looked at the orange fishnet vest beneath his jacket, at the green stains on his trousers, at the exhaustion on his face.

"Do I want to know?"

"No."

She wrapped her arms around him, her eyes closed as if she'd sleepwalked down the stairs. He held her tight, breathing her in.

"You smell terrible," she said. "Where have you been?"

"At a party," he told her. "Booze, drugs, sex. The works."

"At your age?" she said.

"I'm not that old!"

She peeled away, yawning again.

"Come to bed," she said.

"I will," he told her. "I'm absolutely knackered. I just need a cuppa to settle my nerves. You want one?"

She shook her head, checking the bolt again before traipsing upstairs.

Kett waited until she'd gone before heading into the kitchen. He filled the kettle and switched it on, finding the biggest mug he could before adding a couple of teabags. He made the mistake of closing his eyes while he waited for the water to boil, losing himself to the roil and the bubble, feeling consciousness start to slide out of his skull.

He slapped his cheeks to wake himself, pulling out his phone and opening a browser. He thought about the two people he'd met in the woods, their featureless crimson faces, their robes, the blades that were tucked inside their belts.

Make a red wish, they'd said.

And he had.

He typed four words into Google.

Cold Iron. Luan Agolli.

Then he leaned against the counter, clicked search, and began to read.

CHAPTER FORTY-ONE

It came as no surprise to Porter that he was the first one to arrive at HQ the next morning.

He walked through reception just after eight, finding the MIT offices empty. Clare's door was closed, but the distinct lack of snoring from within meant the Super wasn't there—either that or he'd finally succumbed to his sleep apnoea.

He walked to the Incident Room, just in case anyone was hiding there, but that too was deserted. It was freezing here, and the cold air had caused one of the photographs to peel away from the wall. Porter collected it, seeing Kieran Spicer smiling back at him.

Kett had met the boy's killers last night—or at least two people who'd confessed to his murder—but he'd left the woods empty-handed.

"Sorry," he told the boy, fixing the photograph back to the wall. "We'll find them, mate. I promise. It won't have been for nothing."

He returned to the bullpen and slung his coat over his chair. There was a stack of mail on his desk and he lifted the biggest package, opening it to find a pack of photographs inside. He had to tip them out before he remembered what they were: the shots that Freddy Rawling had taken on his camera.

"Oh yeah," he said, sitting down.

He flicked through them, finding a completely random selection of shots, almost all of which were selfies of Freddy's out of focus, rosy-cheeked face—lighting up the room even as it blocked most of whatever he'd been trying to take a photograph of.

Porter focussed on what he could see behind the young man: a cowpat, another cowpat, then the bony rear end of the cow that had dropped them. The next load were of trees, and it was only when Porter reached the seventh one that he noticed a robin in one of the branches. Ben was in the next two, building a fire in the first and waving to his brother in the second. He looked exhausted, like a sapling holding up the weight of the world, ready to snap.

He was still smiling, though.

Porter stopped at the next photo, leaning in. It was taken from a little way down the hill, after dark, looking up at the little playground. Freddy grinned at the camera, and past his head Porter saw five figures in the park. All but one was wearing black, the last in a red coat that he recognised as Jonah White's. They were too far away to identify—their faces little more than pinprick smudges beneath their hoods.

He flicked to the next, Freddy's face again, lit up by the flash. He must have been closer to the park, because it took up most of the remainder of the shot. The five figures were ghostly shadows in the night. There was a weird pattern of light on the right of the image, like the photo had been taken through a kaleidoscope. Porter couldn't figure out what it was.

He turned to the next photo to see the campsite he'd found in the woods, the fire roaring. Ben was hunched over near the tent, butchering a rabbit with the knife that Porter had seen. The next three snaps showed almost the exact same shot—including one where Ben was looking back at his brother, the slightest hint of annoyance creasing his features.

Then Freddy was back at the playground in the dark, shooting it from a different angle: closer to the road, Porter thought. It was hard to make out much because a set of headlights had thrown their glare over the scene, sabotaging the shot. Freddy wasn't in this one, and he wasn't in the next, either, which had been taken from almost the same place.

Porter squinted at it, trying to make sense of the shapes. It looked like there were two figures inside the park, a third walking towards the car. It was too dark to ID the make or model, or the driver, and the licence plate was hidden behind the low fence.

He tried the next, another selfie of Freddy inside the park at night. He looked like he was on the swings, his face red from the effort, his smile bigger than ever.

Porter moved the photograph into the useless pile, surprised to see two familiar faces close up in the next snap. The first was Kieran Spicer, easily recognisable even with the hood of his Canada Goose coat pulled up and a scarf over the lower half of his face. Next to him was Jonah White in his red puffer, not the slightest trace of kindness in his eyes. Both lads leaned back, scowling at the camera, their arms extended like they were posing as gangsters.

Jonah was holding a carving knife, the blade easily ten inches long.

This photo went right into the useful pile.

The next snap was the same, only Freddy was in it too, caught mid-laugh as he posed for the selfie. Jonah was out of sight behind his head, but Kieran was there, the scarf pulled down, a laugh on his face as well.

Porter flicked to the next shot to see a fence post, then a close-up of the slide.

"Come on," he said, flicking through another six photographs of the playground before stopping again.

On the left was the corner of the park. On the right was the road. Another car was in shot, a Fiesta that seemed to glow silver in the light from the flash. Freddy had taken three shots of it, two of them selfies that obscured anything useful. In the last, though, half of the plate was visible.

"Jonah White's car," Porter muttered to himself.

He turned to the next one, a shot of the empty road, and the next, the same road from further up the hill. There was no sign of the Fiesta, or anyone else.

He pulled another one close to see the same road, a set of headlights tearing through the dark. He couldn't make out much detail, but he was pretty sure the shape of the car wasn't a Ford. He held it up, tilting it to find a better angle.

"Who are you, then?" he asked, laying the photo in the useful pile.

The rest of the shots must have been from the following morning. Freddy either hadn't returned to the playground, or he hadn't taken any photos of it. There was just the campsite, the fire still roaring. A dead rabbit in close-up. Another robin. Porter was in the next two, one taken from a distance and one smiling. His face looked twice as large here as it did in real life, he was sure of it.

Past that was a distant swarm of police, *another* robin in the tree, and a muddy field—all with Freddy's face front and centre. Finally came Porter and Ben, standing together on the edge of the woods right before he'd driven them to the hotel. Ben was smiling, but he had his eyes closed.

Porter pushed the pile of photographs away, studying the one of the two lads in the playground. Even on paper, Jonah's knife looked wickedly sharp.

"Not good," he said.

He looked at the mystery car again. The photo gave nothing away, the vehicle a smudge, the driver a stain behind the glare of the lights. He didn't know who it was, or what time of night the shot had been taken, or if it had anything to do with Kieran's death.

But he knew how to find out

He grabbed the photos and his coat, and ran for the door.

"SO, YOU GUYS HAVE A GOOD NIGHT?"

Ben Rawling had opened the door of the Travelodge room, and he moved aside to let Porter through. It was absolutely roasting in there, Porter breaking into a sweat almost instantly. He shrugged off his coat and draped it over his arm as Ben closed the door behind them.

Freddy was lying on one of the two single beds, so lost in a Marvel film on the TV that he didn't even look over. The volume must have been cranked up to the top, it was deafening, the explosions loud enough to make the glass rattle in the windows.

"Aye," yelled Ben, walking to the bed. "Hang on. Freddy, I said turn it down!"

Ben leaned over his brother to grab the remote, lowering the volume close to zero. If Freddy minded, he didn't say anything. He just smiled at his brother, then at Porter, offering a wave.

"Hey, Freddy," said Porter, waving back. "You sleep okay?"

Freddy gave him a thumbs up.

"Aye, it's braw," said Ben, standing between the beds. He seemed like he'd shaken off the cold he'd had yesterday, some of the colour back in his face, his eyes a little brighter. But he still looked wary. "It's what we needed, thank you."

Porter nodded, noticing that Ben's bed had been stripped, the blankets and pillows wedged in the gap between the bed and the wall. Ben noticed him looking and breathed a quiet laugh through his nose.

"Been a while since I've had a proper bed," he said. "Couldn't get used to it. Too soft."

He shrugged apologetically.

"You sleep wherever you want to sleep, mate," Porter told him. "It's your room."

"You want a tea or something?" Ben asked, gesturing to the kettle. "Coffee? Freddy ate the biscuits, sorry."

"I'm fine," said Porter. "It's a flying visit. I just wanted to ask you some questions, if that's okay?"

Ben nodded, the tightness returning to his features. He rubbed his hands together like he was trying to scrub them clean, and Porter noticed the raw skin between his fingers, the dirt beneath his well-chewed nails.

"You're not in trouble," he said. "This isn't about you, or Freddy. Okay?"

He pulled the packet from his pocket, spreading the photographs on the empty bed.

"I got your photos developed, Freddy," he said. "They're great."

Freddy bounced himself off the bed, walking to Porter's

side and leaning on him as he perused the photographs. The weight of him there was strangely comforting, a different kind of gravity. After a second or two, the young man turned his innocent face—the same face that appeared on so many of the images on the bed—to Porter, his smile triumphant. This time he stuck up two thumbs, and Porter mirrored the gesture.

"They really are good," he said. "You've got a proper eye for it, mate."

Ben studied the photos, still looking uncomfortable.

"Didnae ken there was film in there," he said. "Half the time he uses that thing, it's empty."

"You didn't put the film in for him?" asked Porter.

"No, but we always grab a roll if we find anywhere that sells it. He can do it himself. I can't remember the last time we got actual photos. Not since we left home. Most of the rolls are in his bag."

He looked at Porter over the top of Freddy's head.

"What's so special about these?"

Porter wiped his mouth, thinking about the best way to answer the question.

"I don't suppose you know when Freddy took these? I'm thinking Saturday night, because this one..." He pointed to himself. "Was Sunday morning."

Ben perused the photos for a while.

"Could have been Saturday, could have been earlier. We got to the woods on Thursday. Might have taken them anytime."

"Can I ask him?"

"Knock yourself out," said Ben. "But he won't know how to give you what you need. Time's... Time doesn't matter to Freddy, he's lost in it. One of the reasons I'm so jealous of him."

"Hey, Freddy," said Porter. He pointed to the image of himself again. "Do you remember taking this?"

Freddy put his hands to his face like he was holding a camera, clicking his tongue as he took a shot.

"Right. Do you remember the day?"

Freddy took another imaginary photograph, jumping up and down with excitement.

"Do you remember these two men?" asked Porter, lifting the photograph of Kieran and Jonah.

"When did you take that?" asked Ben, his forehead creasing into a frown. He picked up the selfie that Freddy had taken with them. "What did I tell you about talking with people we don't know? Is that a *knife*?"

Freddy gave his brother a thumbs up.

"This must have been after ten," said Ben. "I didn't know he'd left the camp. I hit the hay about then, out like a light. I didn't wake up until..." He blew out slowly, shaking his head. "I don't know. Must have been one, two. Woke up because Freddy was coming back into the tent, thought he'd just been for a piss."

He took his brother's arm gently, turning him so they were face to face.

"Who are they?" he asked. "Friends?"

Freddy replied with a word that Porter couldn't catch.

"Friends," said Ben. "He's saying they were friendly. But he doesn't always know when people aren't being friendly, you know? Another reason he's so lucky."

"Did these friends drive this car?" Porter asked, holding up the photo of the silver Fiesta.

Freddy stuck his thumb in the air.

"Yeah?"

"Yeah," said the young man, nodding.

"What about this one?" Porter asked, holding up the

photograph with the mystery vehicle. "Do you know who was driving this one?"

"He's not going to know that," said Ben. He took Freddy's hand in both of his, holding tight. It was an act of brotherly love that put a lump in Porter's throat.

"Can you tell me anything else about this car?" Porter said, feeling increasingly desperate. "A colour? A size? Who was driving? How many people? Anything. It could really help me."

"He just photographs things," said Ben. "Anything. Everything. It's what he does. He doesn't... It's not like he remembers it. It's not like it means anything."

Porter waited while Freddy looked at the photo. He was making a noise like the whine of an engine, a little *brum brum*.

"Right," said Porter. "A car."

Freddy spoke another word that wasn't fully formed.

"What's that?" asked Porter.

He said it again, then again, and only then did Ben suddenly nod.

"He's saying brown."

"Brown?" Porter asked Freddy, and he stuck up his thumb again.

"Own ar," he said, struggling with the shape of the words.

"Brown car?" said Porter.

Freddy did another jump in celebration. Porter grinned at him.

"Brown car. That's amazing, Freddy. Thank you."

He packed the photos into a stack and returned them to the inside pocket of his coat. For the first time since he'd arrived, the young man's smile fell away.

"I'll bring them back," said Porter. "All of them. I just need to hang onto them for another day or two."

He gently squeezed Freddy's shoulder as he eased past the brothers, heading for the door.

"Thanks," he said. "I'll be in touch."

"So that's it then?" said Ben as he turned the handle. "You've got what you need. What about us? They've already told us we've got to be out by eleven."

Porter looked back, seeing the men on the other side of the bed. Ben held Freddy's hand, Freddy rested his head on his big brother's shoulder. He was still making the engine sound, moving his free hand through the air like he was holding a toy car.

"I'm going to sort it," said Porter. "I'm going to find a place for you both. I promise. Just don't go anywhere, okay?"

Ben didn't reply.

"Trust me," said Porter, and he closed the door.

CHAPTER FORTY-TWO

"Moral of the story," said Kett, "don't do drugs."

He stood at the foot of a hospital bed in a private room at the Norfolk and Norwich. Duke lay in it, shivering quietly even though the blankets were pulled up to his chin. His eyes were bloodshot, his skin clammy, but he seemed like he was on the way home from whatever trip he'd taken last night.

"He didn't *do* drugs, sir," said Savage, who sat next to him, dressed in a black tracksuit. "It was more like the drugs did him."

"Exactly," said Duke. "It wasn't my fault."

He groaned.

"I don't remember any of it, sir," he said. "Nothing after I put that man on my shoulders and ran away with him. I didn't do anything stupid, did I?"

Savage met Kett's eye, trying not to smile.

"No," said Kett. "You were... I mean, you guys made some good arrests. *Great* arrests. That's what we should focus on."

"Right," said Savage with a nod. "You should focus on the fact you saved my life."

"Not the fact that you called me a sexy arse muffin," Kett said.

Duke's mouth opened in shock, and he shook his head.

"I'm so sorry, sir," he said. "I didn't—"

"Or the bit when you called the Superintendent a cup of pigeon toss."

Duke looked like he was close to having some kind of fit.

"Forget about it," said Kett. "Just get better. That's all I came in to say. You did good, Aaron."

He left the room, Savage following him out.

"How are you doing, Kate?" he asked her when she'd closed the door.

"I'm okay, sir," she said, watching a couple of nurses walk by. She rubbed the top of her head, and Kett saw the bald patch there, the raw skin beneath. "Lucky all I lost was some hair."

Kett nodded.

"You never should have been put in that position. I'm sorry."

"Where else would I have been?" she said with a shrug. "It's the job."

"This bloody awful job," said Kett. "Clare around? I heard he was here."

"You heard that, did you?" said a voice, right in Kett's ear.

He managed to choke the scream down his throat as he turned around, seeing Clare looming over him like some kind of vampire.

"Jesus Christ, sir," wheezed Kett, doubling over and feeling another stab of pain in his chest. "I am far too fragile for that."

"Tough titties," said Clare. "And why are you fragile? I gave you a lie-in."

That was true. Clare had waited until nine before calling. Not that it mattered. It had been after four by the time he'd put down his phone and turned in, and the kids had woken him an hour later. Just the thought of it made him yawn, Clare waiting until he'd finished before continuing.

"I've just been up to visit the men we arrested last night," he said. "Kate, you did a real number on Warner Hobbs; he's still concussed. The one that Duke hurled off the walkway is awake, by some small miracle."

"Did you ask him about the red room, sir?" asked Kett. "About the two people we found there?"

"No, of course I bloody didn't," said Clare. "I asked him what he wanted for breakfast, and whether he likes his balls to be tickled during intercourse. Yes, of course I did, you great dildo. He said he didn't know anything about it. Same thing he said about the drugs, and the guns, and the sex stuff."

"Right," said Kett.

"But he'll talk sooner or later," said Clare. "Duke up and about? I might need him to throw the arsehole off another balcony."

"Not yet, sir," said Savage.

Clare snorted his disappointment.

"Well, we made seventeen arrests in total last night, including nine members of the security team. They're already climbing over each other for a deal. Give it time. Porter got hold of you yet?"

"No, sir," said Kett.

"He's back at HQ. Go find him. He says he's got something."

KETT FOUND Porter in the Incident Room, pinning a sheet of paper to the wall. When he walked up beside him, he saw that it was a photograph. Porter tapped it.

"What do you see, sir?"

"Absolutely nothing," said Kett. He slipped on his glasses and leant in, but there still wasn't much to be found: a road at night, a car, the glare of its headlights. "What am I supposed to be seeing?"

"Freddy Rawling took this photo, sir," said Porter.

"Freddy," said Kett, racking his brain. "Uh..."

"Young lad in the woods, was living rough with his brother."

"Oh, yeah. Freddy. He took this? When?"

"Saturday night," said Porter. "Probably. That's the road right outside the playpark. Ben said Freddy went for a wander sometime between ten and one. He must have bumped into Kieran and Jonah because he's got a photo with them."

"Seriously?" said Kett. "They let him take a photo of them?"

"Freddy's harmless, sir," said Porter. "He's got the sweetest smile you can imagine, a proper charmer. I don't think they thought he was a threat. He caught some of the other lads too."

"Wait, Clare said he spoke to the lads, said they got spooked by something around eleven. It's why they went home. You think it was Freddy and his camera that scared them?"

"Maybe, sir. Freddy took a photo of Jonah's car, too. It's over there on the desk. Silver Fiesta."

Kett walked to the desk and rifled through the collection

of photographs—most of which were of the young man's face. He saw what Porter meant about his smile. It was contagious.

"This photo came towards the end of the night," Porter went on. "The one after was taken in the morning. It's a long shot, sir, but what if this has something to do with Kieran's death?"

"That really is a long shot," said Kett.

"But maybe not that long. This road is in the middle of nowhere. Nobody really uses it unless they're running up to the park to get drugs from Kieran and his mates."

"Okay," said Kett, returning to the photo on the wall. "But that doesn't really help us, does it? This could be anyone; it's just a smudge."

"It is. But Freddy told me it was a brown car."

"Brown?" said Kett. "He's sure?"

Porter shrugged.

"He struggles a bit with words, but he seemed pretty convinced. Brown car, that's what he said. I've been looking at makes and models. There aren't many brown vehicles of any kind in circulation, because nobody wants to drive a shit-coloured car, right?"

"I had a brown Volvo once," said Kett. "But yeah, it was pretty grim. You don't see them much. So you think it's an older model?"

"There are a few new cars in brown. Mercedes has one, Nissan, even the Range Rover Velar comes in a kind of toffee colour. But I had a look at them all and none of them have headlights this shape. See how they're square, and there's this lip here?"

Kett couldn't see it at all, but he nodded anyway.

"I could only find one car with these lights that also had a brown model."

Porter beamed at Kett like a kid presenting his coursework to his parents.

"A Citroen Ami."

"A what?" said Kett. "I've never heard of it."

"They haven't made them for years, they're classics. I've printed out a picture, hang on."

Porter legged it from the room, returning seconds later with a sheet of paper. He slapped it down on the desk next to the photographs.

"I think this is it, sir."

On the paper was one of the weirdest cars Kett had ever seen, a square monstrosity whose headlights and front grille made it look like some kind of robot. It was white, not brown, but the sudden stab of recognition took his breath away.

"Wait," said Kett. "I've seen this car before."

"Where, sir?" said Porter.

He couldn't remember, so he closed his eyes and reached back. It took him longer than he'd have liked, but eventually it came to him—the image of a car peeking out from beneath a tarpaulin.

"Morris Gough," he said. "The man who lives next door to the Spicers. He's got a car just like that."

He looked up.

"Except his is brown."

CHAPTER FORTY-THREE

They rode out in Porter's Mondeo, an IRV chasing them down the A47 and back into Dereham. Porter took a couple of wrong turns before finding the right street, parking the car up the road from the Gough house so as not to ruin the element of surprise. A fine drizzle had begun to fall, but it must have been heavier than it looked, because after a few seconds Kett's hair was soaked, torturous drips running down his face.

The constables were unpacking themselves from the IRV—three of them, two with Tasers—but Kett waved them back in.

"Stand down," he said. "He's an old man. We just want to talk with him."

"But if he makes a run for it on his Zimmer frame, take him out," added Porter.

They walked to the gate, but Kett didn't stop there—taking a few more steps so that he could look up the Spicers' driveway. There was no sign of life behind the dark windows, no noise from within. He hadn't had any reports from the FLO, which usually meant there was nothing to worry about. All the same, he thought he'd make time to check in with them once they'd finished with Gough.

Porter had wandered up the drive towards Gough's garage. The old car sat where it had when Kett had first seen it, half hidden beneath its blanket. It looked like the same model that Porter had found online, and when Kett held up the photograph that Freddy Rawling had taken, it was painfully obvious.

"Has to be it, right, sir?" said Porter.

"Yeah," said Kett.

He walked to the front door and hammered his fist on it.

"You've spoken to him already, sir?" asked Porter while they waited.

"The other day, yeah," said Kett. "First thing he told me was that Kieran should be shot."

Porter stared at him.

"He had a problem with the youths in the area," said Kett. "I didn't think he meant it."

He knocked again.

"If Kieran left from here on Saturday night, in Jonah's Fiesta, it would have been easy for Gough to go after them," said Porter. "He tails them to the park, watches them for a while, and follows them over to Wayside Manor. Waits for them to go into the woods..."

He left it hanging.

"In theory, I guess," said Kett. "But why wouldn't he attack them in the park, if he wanted to hurt them? Why follow them into the arse end of the countryside?"

"Maybe because there were other kids in the playground, sir? He didn't want witnesses."

Kett knocked a third time, keeping his voice low.

"There were literally hundreds of potential witnesses at the party. More importantly, why would Gough murder a child? Plenty of old folk moan about the kids, about the crime, but it's a big jump from there to slicing somebody to pieces."

Kett went to knock again, then changed his mind and tried the handle instead. The door was unlocked, opening smoothly on oiled hinges.

"Mr Gough," he called, his voice echoing down a neat hallway that was the exact mirror opposite of the Spicers'. "It's the police. Are you home?"

The reply came in the shape of a rasping snore from somewhere downstairs.

"Mr Gough? Hello?"

"We should probably go in, sir," said Porter. "Check he's okay."

"Yeah, that breathing doesn't sound right at all," Kett said, hearing another round of snores. "We'd be neglecting our duty to the public if we didn't make entry."

He walked through the door and along a brown carpet, stopping beside a mirrored sideboard. A dish held an assortment of keys, and Porter used his pinkie to hook a fob with the Citroen logo. He dropped it back in the dish, and they followed the choking snores into the large living room.

Morris Gough, dressed in his pyjamas and a dressing gown, was fast asleep in an armchair, his legs resting on a pouffe. His mouth was a gaping pit aimed at the ceiling, the sound of his breathing like a jumbo jet with its engines on fire. There was an empty bottle of cheap scotch on the coffee table, another two on the sideboard. The air was so heavy with fumes and flatulence that a lit match could have taken out the entire street.

"Crack a window, Pete," said Kett. He walked over to the man, giving the pouffe a solid kick. "Morning, Morris."

Gough sucked in a wet breath that might have been a

death rattle, ejecting a long, equally wet fart from the other end. He sat bolt upright, his eyes swimming in lunatic circles as he tried to make sense of what he was seeing.

"How?" he bellowed.

"Police," said Kett, holding out his warrant card. "The door was unlocked, we entered because we feared for your health."

"I'm still afraid for his health," said Porter, a hand over his nose. He'd opened the window and parted the curtains, a shaft of weak light entering the room. "What is wrong with your bowels, man?"

The smell had hit Kett as well. He felt like he could taste it with his eyeballs.

"Jesus," he said, recoiling. "Open another window, Pete."

"There aren't enough windows in the house, sir."

"What the hell are you doing in here?" said Morris. He was trying to get up from his chair, but he couldn't shift his enormous bulk. The way he was running his words together made it obvious he was still drunk. "Get out!"

"Not before we've asked you some questions, Mr Gough," said Kett.

"Questions my arse," he yelled back.

"About your involvement in the murder of Kieran Spicer," Kett finished.

The words were like a gag, choking the man into silence. Kett took advantage of it to hold out Freddy's photograph. Morris stared, but there was no sense he understood what it was.

"This was taken on Saturday night," said Kett. "Sometime between ten and one. You recognise this car?"

Morris grunted, mired in confusion.

"It's a Citroen Ami," said Porter, taking over. "A brown one."

"So?" said Morris, squinting at them each in turn.

"Do you know how rare they are?" said Porter. "Nobody drives them. There are only a handful registered with the DVLA."

"So fucking what?" said Morris, the fug of sleep slowly leaving him. He was definitely drunk, his breath carrying the acidic reek of half-digested scotch.

"So why were you driving it on Saturday night next to the playground where we found Kieran's body?" asked Kett.

Morris sat back, wiping the drool from his jowls.

"What?" he said eventually, much more quietly.

"When I first met you, you told me you thought Kieran should be killed," said Kett. "You remember that?"

He clearly didn't, wiping his absent face again.

"Because he's a little shit," said Morris. "Always has been. You don't live next to him. You don't have to listen to him through the walls, screaming at his mother, screaming at his brothers. Should have heard him this weekend, worst I've ever known it. Him and his mother both."

"Arguing?" asked Kett.

"Arsehole, he was," said Morris. "Proper puckered, festering arsehole."

He leaned forward as much as his enormous stomach would let him.

"You know he was a drug dealer?"

"We do," said Kett. "But he was also a child, and he didn't deserve to be killed."

Morris laughed, sinking back, his head resting on the cushion of his chins.

"Well, you have to say that, don't you? Because you're a copper. But I know you're as glad of it as I am. One less scumbag out there. You should find out who did it and give 'em a job."

"Are you saying you'd like the job?" Kett asked. "Is that why you followed Kieran to the park, and then to the party? Is that why you hacked him to pieces and slit his throat?"

Morris' eyes peeled open in surprise.

"Because that's what happened to him, Morris. That's how this sixteen-year-old child died, alone and crying for his mother. You think he deserved that?"

Morris didn't answer, his yellow tongue sliding over his lips.

"What were you doing out there on Saturday night?" Kett asked. "Because unless you tell me, I'm going to drag you out of that chair and down to the police station, and I'm going to lock you in a cell until you're sober enough to give me the truth."

"Hold on," said Morris, lifting a chubby hand. "Just wait a minute. It wasn't me. It wasn't me driving the car."

Kett didn't reply, he just waited.

"I haven't driven her in months, not past the end of the road. I don't have it in me anymore."

"Have what?"

"Have *it*," said Morris, shrugging his hefty shoulders. "It. Anything. I don't have anything in me anymore."

He glanced at the coffee table with nothing short of hatred.

"Aside from *that*," he spat. "Nothing in my blood but whisky and spite. Haven't stopped since my hip went. Fuck all else to do, is there? Can barely walk, can barely drive, can't do nothing."

He gestured at the wall behind him, the one that was attached to the Spicer house.

"And you've got arseholes like him, don't even know

they're born, fucking wasting every second God gave them. Why do they deserve it, eh? You tell me that."

"You're telling us you didn't drive the car on Saturday night?"

"No!" said Morris. "I was out of my face on Saturday, and Sunday, and last night n'all. Every fucking night. I start drinking at breakfast and I don't stop. But I don't ever die, I just keep going."

He made a noise unlike anything Kett had ever heard before, tears clustering in his puffy eyes.

"What a fucking waste," he said, shaking his head until the tears scattered. "What a fucking, awful waste."

"Morris, if it wasn't you driving the car on Saturday, who was it?" asked Kett. "Because it had to have been your car."

"It weren't," he said. "Nobody ever drives her, nobody goes anywhere near her. It weren't my car."

Morris was trying to get up again, exerting himself so much that another fart exploded from his backside.

"Stay there," said Kett. "It's okay. We're done."

"Help me, man," said Morris, his face contorted with panic. "Or I'm going to shit myself."

Kett took the man's clammy hand and hauled him out of his chair, watching him waddle from the room.

"See yourselves out," he yelled as he went.

"We need to check the car," Kett called after him.

The only reply he got was a series of soggy arse parps as Morris struggled up the stairs.

"Pretty sure those were yesses," said Kett. "Grab the keys, Pete."

They exited through the front door, heading for the car. Kett grabbed the tarpaulin and pulled it away, revealing the squat brown Citroen in all its glory. However ugly it might have looked, there was no doubt it was well maintained. There wasn't a scrap of rust on it, the chrome trim polished, the seals around the windows intact. There was mud on the body, though, hard to see against the dull paint, and the wheels were filthy.

"Somebody's taken it for a spin," said Kett. "And not just down the street, either."

Porter worked on a forensic glove before opening the driver's door. He tossed the keys to Kett, but they pinged off his fingertips and onto the driveway.

"Sorry, sir," said Porter.

"Don't bloody mention it," Kett grumbled, doing his best to ignore the pain in his back as he bent down to collect them.

He opened the boot to find that it was full of boxes—mostly vinyl records, he saw when he opened them. They'd been there a long time, leaving an imprint in the soft lining of the boot.

"No blood, sir," said Porter. "Bit of mud in the footwell on the driver's side, but nowhere else."

Kett swore silently as he closed the boot.

"There's no way this thing was used to bring Kieran's body to the park," said Kett.

"You think Gough's lying, sir?"

Kett shook his head.

"I don't know anything right now, Pete. This case is a mess."

Porter nodded, using his hip to close the door.

"I'll get a truck out, sir," he said. "We can take the car back to HQ, see if Cara can find anything."

Kett nodded, heading back down the driveway to the street. He stopped again outside the Spicer house, and this time he saw the two younger brothers standing in the living room window. The little one, Peanut, gave Kett a friendly wave, but there was no smile on his face. Jay had his arm around his brother's shoulder and he pulled him away, shooting Kett a dark glance.

Now wasn't the time to pay them a visit, he thought.

But the image of their faces behind the glass stayed with him as he walked back to the car, something in their expressions that unsettled him. They'd lost their brother, yes, but Kett had seen the same look on Jay's face *before* the boy had known about Kieran's death.

It was the look of somebody haunted by the truth, the look of somebody who'd been dragged from childhood far too quickly and far more violently than they should have.

It wasn't a million miles from the expression he'd seen on his own daughters' faces recently, especially Moira.

"You shut your mouth, you big shit," he said quietly to himself as he opened the passenger door of the Mondeo. It's what Moira had screamed at Alice yesterday morning—a twisted mirror image of her oldest sister.

He sat down, leaving the door open, trying to make sense of the cyclone of his thoughts. His kids were front and centre, the way they often were at moments like this. He didn't push them away, he knew better than that. A long time ago, Superintendent Clare had asked him why his children always led him towards the truth of a case, and he'd given the only answer he could.

Because they're everything.

And here they were again, Moira imitating the very worst of her sister's behaviour: the swearing, the disobedience, the violence, and the secrets. Losing her innocence to them, losing *herself* to them.

"You shut your mouth, you big shit," he said again.

"Sorry, sir?" said Porter, who was walking up to the door. "Did you just tell me to—"

"Hang on," said Kett, holding up a hand to silence him. "Hang on, give me a second."

You did everything to keep your children safe, he knew. But at what cost? What lines were you willing to cross as a parent to protect those dearest to you?

All of them. Every single red line.

Even the biggest of them all.

He thought about the gangs and the park and the party, he thought about the car, and about that awful red room—and with a click that could have been a key turning in a lock, he felt the last tumbler of this tragic mystery fall into place.

"Shit," he said, climbing out of the car. He clutched his hands in his wet hair. "I think I know what happened to Kieran."

CHAPTER FORTY-FOUR

DEEP DOWN, SHE MUST HAVE KNOWN THEY WERE coming for her.

Margaret Spicer's shape filled the textured glass window of the front door as Kett and Porter walked up the driveway; statue still, barely human. Kett didn't bother to knock, he just called her name.

"Maggie, it's the police. Can you let us in?"

Like a wind-up toy, Margaret moved slowly and clumsily, turning the Yale. She pulled the door open all the way, standing there in the clutter of the front hall. Her face was puffy, her eyes ringed by dark circles, her lips chewed to bloody shreds.

"Can we come in?" Kett asked when she didn't speak.

She didn't have a chance to answer before Jay thundered down the steps, his face full of furious uncertainty. He glared at Kett like he wanted to twist off his head, his knuckles white as he throttled the banister. Margaret didn't look back.

"The boys are home," she said. "Can it wait?"

"No," said Kett. "I don't think it can."

He walked inside without waiting for an invitation, giving Jay the biggest smile he could muster.

"Don't worry, mate," he said. "I just need to talk to your mum quickly. Is that okay?"

The answer was clear enough.

"My friend Pete here is going to come upstairs, hang out with you and Peanut for a bit. We'll be in the kitchen, okay? We're not going anywhere."

Porter headed for the stairs.

"Don't let them come down, Pete," Kett said quietly.

"I hear you guys have got some great Lego up there," Porter said, the bottom step creaking beneath his weight. "I love Lego."

With Porter filling the stairs, Jay didn't have much choice. The DI swept the kid onto the landing, floorboards groaning as they walked into one of the bedrooms. Kett heard Peanut chattering away, a high-pitched giggle.

And his heart broke beneath the weight of what he was about to do.

He put a hand on Margaret's arm, steering her into the kitchen. She didn't resist, she didn't complain. She still moved like a mechanical toy, struggling to the table where she began to chew on her fingertips.

Deep down, she knew. She must have been waiting for this moment since her son died.

"I saw you next door," she said, not looking at him. "I saw you with the car."

"Right," said Kett, leaning on the counter to release some of the pressure in his back. "That's some set of wheels. You don't see many of them around."

"I know," said Margaret.

"But you didn't have a choice, did you?"

She had started shaking, that mechanism inside her pushed to breaking point.

"Sit down, Margaret," said Kett. "Will you do that for me? Sit down, and tell me what happened."

She resisted, still staring at the floor.

"Tell me what happened to Kieran."

It was her son's name that robbed the strength from her legs. She collapsed into a chair and doubled up.

"I didn't kill him," she said.

"I know," Kett told her. "But you were there, weren't you? You were at the party, you followed the red line."

She curled deeper into herself, her head between her knees.

"You found the red room," he went on. "You made a red wish."

"Don't," she said, just a whisper. "Please. Don't say it. It wasn't real. It was just a dream."

"You had an argument with Kieran on Saturday, didn't you?" said Kett. "Your neighbour heard it. What was it about?"

Margaret straightened, bracing an elbow on the table, every part of her trembling.

"You don't know what he was like," she said, the words punched from her throat like she was vomiting them. "You don't know what he did."

"We know enough," said Kett.

"No, you don't. You didn't see him... You didn't hear the things he said to me. He was..."

Her mouth flexed, searching for a word.

"Evil," she said eventually, and she sobbed into her hand, finally turning her frightened eyes to Kett. "I didn't mean that," she said, speaking through her fingers. "Not evil, that's the wrong word. He was my Kieran, always. But..."

Kett gave her time, but she'd stalled, her throat clicking as she tried to speak.

"He'd changed," said Kett. "Right? The drugs, the people he was hanging around with. He changed."

She nodded.

"And his brothers were changing too."

Her tears came faster and harder.

"He was like a virus," she said. "What happened to him, it was infectious. He... he asked Jay to look after the drugs, because he knew nobody would ever suspect him. Peanut, too. I found..."

She sniffed, shaking her head until her hair fell in front of her face.

"I found bags of it in Peanut's room, hidden in his board games. That's what we were arguing about, me and Key. Peanut knew they were there. He'd put them there after Kieran gave them to him. He touched them. What if he'd *taken* them?"

"I get it," said Kett. "You were worried about them. You had every right to be."

"You don't get it," she snapped. "I wasn't worried about the drugs, or the weapons. That's not it. It's... I don't even know how to say it other than what I just said. He changed, and he was spreading it to them. The same change. He was a disease. I could see it in Jay, see it taking hold in him, see it in his eyes, in the way he looked at me, in the way he walked and talked, in the way he slept. Everything. This illness was taking him over just like it took over Key. I was going to lose him. Peanut too, even him, even though he's just a baby. You can see it in them."

She drew in a ragged breath like she'd surfaced after a deep dive, looking at Kett with pure panic in her eyes.

"You could have come to us," he told her. "We could have helped."

"No, you couldn't," she said. "Not with this, not with what he was doing to them. You wouldn't have done anything."

She shook her head.

"I almost called you, so many times. I would have done it. I just wanted him gone, I didn't care where. But..."

She broke into a sob, one that she couldn't escape for almost a minute. Kett stood and watched, the horror of it turning him to stone.

"I wanted him to know," she said when she'd found her voice again. "I wanted him to know how much I... I *hated* him, so I followed him."

"On Saturday?"

"After we argued. He'd been gone all afternoon, didn't come home until nearly ten. Him and Jonah said they needed to collect something, head out again. That's when we fought. He left in Jonah's car, but I wasn't done. I wasn't finished. I knew they'd go to the park, so I took the car from next door. Morris always leaves his door open, too pissed to do any different. He didn't even know I was there. I took the car and drove to the park and..."

She sobbed some more, frantically wiping away the tears.

"And I waited for him. I wanted to see where he was going, what he was doing. Wanted to see if there was any way to... to fix him. Because even then, even with all the hatred, I thought maybe I could get him back."

Her lips curled in a snarl of disgust.

"But I could hear them in the park, him and Jonah. I

could hear them talking about what they were doing. Talking about me. Talking about how they were going to use his brothers, talking about how Jonah's life was better now his gran was dead, about how Key's life would be better if I died, if... if his brothers died."

Her expression tightened, her eyes boiling in their sockets.

"So I waited in the car, and I followed them. Drove into the middle of nowhere till we got to this house. This party. People everywhere, but Key didn't go where they were. He went into the woods, him and Jonah. They didn't know I was there."

She paused for a moment.

"Maybe I was right before. Maybe evil is the word. That's what I thought when I was listening to them. That's what was in my head. That these two are evil."

"What happened next?" Kett asked, when she didn't continue.

"I don't know," she said, her eyes glazing over. She lifted her hands as if the truth was right in front of her, as if Kett was an idiot for not being able to see it. "Kieran and Jonah split up. I followed Key to the house, to the cellar door. He went in, and I got too close. I must have got too close, because he started running and he... he fell."

"Down the steps?" asked Kett.

"I saw him fall, but he got up and he ran and... I couldn't find him down there, in the cellar. I looked, but I couldn't see him."

Her eyes swivelled, as if her mind was coming loose.

"I found something else."

"You found the room," said Kett. "The red room."

"Just a dream," she said. "It wasn't real."

"Who was there, Margaret? Who was in the room?"

She looked at him as if he might be able to answer the question for her.

"These people," she said. "Two of them, in masks. They... they asked me to make a... a wish. But they already knew what I wanted. They..."

She took hold of her face, twisting it.

"They could read my thoughts, they knew. But I didn't wish it. I know that's what you're thinking, and I didn't wish *that*."

"What was your wish, Margaret?" asked Kett.

She shook her head like she couldn't remember, then she spoke it aloud.

"I wished for my little boys to be safe. I wished for my little boys to be safe, that's all. And for Key to be a child again. That's all I asked. I swear. But then they started saying horrible things, saying that my wish would be, uh..."

She let go of her face, turning it to the ceiling.

"May it bring pain and sorrow," said Kett. "Right? May it bring bloodshed and horror."

She stared at him like he was part of her dream, like he'd bled through into the real world.

"You did it too," she said. "You made a red wish."

He didn't reply, but she read the answer in the tight lines of his face.

"Did you see Kieran again?" asked Kett.

She shook her head.

"Did the people in the room say anything else?"

"No. I walked out, left the house, must have driven home, although I don't remember it."

Incredibly, her face broke into a smile.

"But I knew it was going to get better," she said. "I knew the worst of it was over, and don't ask me *how* I knew, because I can't tell you. I knew that I'd paid what I needed to pay, that they were going to take care of me and the little ones, that they were going to keep us all safe. Just a dream, you see. Just a dream."

She clasped her hands together like she was six years old, still smiling. The anger boiled inside Kett, surging up his throat, igniting in the middle of his skull. The red line of his rage scared him, because for a moment he felt as if he might lose himself to it.

But he did what he always did, he clamped down hard, he closed off every single part of him until the explosion had died away.

Even so, he was still shaking as he pushed himself off the counter.

"Margaret Spicer," he said, and she held up a hand to silence him.

"Don't say it. I won't let you say it. I made my wish, I *paid* for my wish. You can't break it."

"I am arresting you—"

"Don't take me away from them," she said, slamming a fist on the table. "They're safe now. Don't take me away."

"For conspiracy to murder," Kett went on. "You do not have to say anything, but it may harm your defence if you do not mention when questioned something that you later rely on in court."

"Don't do this," said Margaret, her face crumpling.

"Anything you do say may be given in evidence," he finished. "Do you understand what's happening?"

"I understand what will happen if you take this away from me," she said. "I understand what they'll do to you. This is their wish to give, it's not yours to take away."

"Get up," Kett told her, and when she didn't, he took hold of her arm and pulled her out of the chair. "Don't fight it. They've been through enough."

She must have heard him, because she made the journey down the hallway to the front door as quietly as a mouse. He opened it, passing her to the constables who waited on the driveway.

"She's under arrest," he told them.

One of the constables cuffed her hands in front of her.

"Can you talk to Mandy, down the street?" she asked. "Number seven. She can take the boys, until I come home."

Kett nodded.

"One last thing," he asked, glancing back to make sure neither of the brothers was in earshot. "Do you know why they took Kieran to the park after they'd killed him? Why they played with him there?"

"They did?" said Margaret, fresh tears pooling in her wide eyes even as she laughed. "They made him young again, that's all. It was my wish. It came true."

She smiled again, the expression of somebody lost inside a terrible fantasy.

"Just a dream," she said as the PCs led her away. "Just a dream, just a dream, just a dream."

CHAPTER FORTY-FIVE

"You, Robert Kett, are a giant pile of hippopotamus tossings."

Kett looked up from the dining table as Superintendent Clare walked through the front door of the Spicer house. Savage was there too, both of them soaked from the rain, which had grown heavier in the hour or so since Margaret Spicer had been taken away. They joined Kett and Porter in the kitchen, Clare shaking himself like a wet dog.

"A steaming pile of tossings," the Super said again. "That's exactly what you are. How the hell could you make this case even more twisted than it already was?"

"To be fair, sir, none of this is my fault," said Kett. "I didn't kill anyone."

"You're going to kill me," said Clare, dumping himself into a chair. "My coroner's report will say: 'Ketted to death after five years of relentless fuckery.' Where are the kids?"

"With a neighbour," he said.

"Because they're practically orphans now," said Clare. "Between their dad trying to set fire to a house, and their mum..."

He paused for a moment.

"Are you sure she's guilty of this, Kett? Are you sure you didn't dribble this sad little theory out of your leaky toss-hole? Because it sounds insane."

"It *is* insane, sir," said Kett. "But it's true. She confessed to it."

"That's not what the desk sergeant is telling me," said Clare. "Mrs Spicer must have had time to think about things on the ride over, because she's denying everything. She's claiming you coerced her into saying it, that you filled her head with this red room bullshit. She says she'd never heard about it until you told her, until you told her that *you'd* made a wish too."

"That's not—"

"Did you hear her confession, Porter?"

"No, sir," said the DI. "I was upstairs. Playing with the Lego."

Clare's look was murderous.

"It doesn't matter what she says, sir," said Kett. "There's evidence. Her prints will be all over Morris Gough's car, and there must be cameras on the route she took over to Wayside Manor. We've got a photo of the car outside the playground."

"It doesn't matter," said Clare. "Because at no point did she wish her son to be dead. And even if she had, no jury is going to find her guilty. This isn't Fairyland, Kett, this isn't some Genie's wet dream, this is the real world. It's not even a wish. She asked a couple of psychopaths to keep her children safe, and they killed one instead. That's like the opposite of a wish. It's the anti-wish."

"I think that's the whole point, sir," said Kett. "Whoever's running this red room, whoever's granting wishes—"

"They're not granting wishes!" Clare shrieked, banging his fist on the table.

"They're playing a sick game," Kett went on. "It's a joke to them."

"You're telling me their idea of a joke is killing a young man, driving him to a playground, and pushing him on the swings?"

Kett sat back, rubbing his face.

"It's all connected, sir," he said.

"Connected to what? Your arse?"

"Connected to Hollenbeck," he said. "To Joseph Maynard. You remember Hell House, when they took me? You remember the Pig Man. These are the same kinds of games. Masks, murder, mayhem, they thrive on it."

"You don't know there's a connection," said Clare.

"I do, sir," he said. "I can feel it."

"In your arse."

"In my *gut*. They knew who I was, they knew what I was going to ask. They knew about Maynard and where he's hiding. Hollenbeck had their fingers in everything. Their gatherings were just like the Masque we broke up last night. Their whole purpose was to find killers, to train up murderers. You remember what Mo told us when we arrested her after Hell House? She said they've been doing it for years. *Decades*. Championing psychopaths and serial killers, making bets on whose pet monster would claim the most victims. This is the same thing. These two people, the ones in the red room, they're part of it. Someone's giving them what they need to kill, and what they need to get away with it."

"It could have been Maynard right there, sir," said Savage.

"Yeah, I thought so too," said Kett. "I asked."

"And he said no," Clare said. "What a surprise that is. You know, I think you're making the red room thing up, Kett. I think you and Duke snorted some PCP and imagined the whole evening. Am I right?"

Kett didn't answer.

"I'm right," said Clare. "I'm always right."

He bared his teeth at Kett, looking like the bogeyman.

"Except your bastard red room visit paid off," he said.

"What?"

Kett leaned over the table, his pulse hammering in his ears.

"Cold Iron. We've got a lead. Spalding found it. It's an old paintball facility near Thetford, been closed for two years now. The business is registered to a Luan Agolli."

"It's an alias?" said Kett. "For Maynard?"

"We won't know until we raid the place," said Clare. "But I'm going to need more than the testimony of two twats in masks to make it happen. I need evidence, Kett. I need a watertight case if we're going to catch this guy."

"I can give you that, sir," said Kett.

Clare nodded.

"Every last devil," the Superintendent said, flashing a grim smile. "We don't rest until they're all dead and buried."

"Right, sir," said Kett.

Clare's smile dropped away.

"By which I mean in prison, Kett," he said, hammering the table again. "Because we're not tossing vigilantes."

"Right," Kett said again. "That's what I meant too, sir."

Silence fell, everybody taking a moment to study the kitchen, the photographs on the wall of two happy boys and their mother—Kieran still absent from the pictures. Kett wasn't sure if Margaret had been guilty of loving her children too much, or not enough. But that one wish had shattered this family into oblivion.

"It never ends," said Clare. "The world burns, and every time you pull somebody out of the fire, two more tumble in."

It was the truth, and nobody knew what to say to it.

Nobody except Porter, that was, who held up Freddy Rawling's photograph of the car.

"Yeah, it's a shit sandwich for sure," he said. "But I do have one suggestion for how to make it better."

IT WAS GETTING dark by the time Kett pulled the Volvo up the long lane that led to Superintendent Clare's static caravan in Elsham. It had been over four years since he'd last been to 'Clare Castle'—when they'd stayed here during the Whip Crack case—but the park hadn't changed at all, nestled close to the cliffs beneath the endless Norfolk sky.

He pulled up behind Porter's Mondeo and Clare's Mercedes, allowing himself to tune back into the real world.

"And then we put custard on it!" Evie was yelling in the back seat. "And then poo, and then jam, and then marmalade, and then poo, and then—"

"You already said poo," Moira interrupted. "I don't want extra poo on my sandwich."

"You mean you do want *some* poo?" said Evie, cackling with laughter.

"Just the regular amount though," said Moira, entirely serious.

"Nobody is getting poo on their sandwiches," said Billie from the seat next to him. "We're having fish and chips."

Both Evie and Moira groaned.

"No fair!" said Evie. "I want poo!"

"I do not understand these kids at all," said Billie.

"It's better not to even try," Kett told her.

He leaned over to give her a kiss, which generated a chorus of disgust from the back. Then he got out, the freezing coastal wind like a slap to the face.

"Yikes," he said. "It's horrible out here. Come on, girls."

"Hurry up!" came a yell from the caravan. Superintendent Clare stood in the open door, waving them on like he was expecting an air strike to hit the lane. "Before my bollocks turn inside out."

"Before his what do what?" asked Evie as Billie bundled her out of the car.

"Nothing," said Kett. "Absolutely nothing. Run inside."

The two little ones clattered up the steps, ducking under Clare's arm. Billie was next, giving the Superintendent a peck on the cheek as she squeezed past. Alice didn't seem to want to leave the car, her headphones on, her face glum.

"Come on," said Kett, giving her a smile. "It's not for long. It'll be nice to see everyone."

"I just want to stay in here," she said.

"Fish and chips?"

She looked away, lost in the sound of her music. All he wanted to do was reach out and pull her close, to remind her that they always loved her, that they always *would* love her, even on the bad days. It was unconditional, and unshakeable, and eternal.

But he found himself thinking of Maggie Spicer instead.

"You know where we are if you change your mind," he said, and he closed the door.

Another car was coming up the track, and it stopped right behind the Volvo.

"Give me a hand, sir," said Savage as she hopped out. "Got the whole chip shop here."

She passed him a tower of boiling hot paper parcels, the smell of batter and vinegar making his stomach growl.

"Girls here?" she asked. "Because I ordered, like, fifty little sausages."

"That will be enough for Evie," he said. "What about the rest of us?"

"Stop yammering!" Clare roared, still in the door. "You're letting all the heat out!"

Kett ran up the steps with the food, entering the caravan. It was absolutely mobbed, and unbearably hot. He dumped the parcels in the kitchenette where Porter had prepared the plates, then turned to the two men who sat side by side on the sofa in the living space. They both held PlayStation controllers, engrossed in a racing game. The girls were kneeling on the floor in front of the little TV, both demanding to have a go.

"Who's having what?" asked Savage, putting the rest of the food on the dining table. "Or maybe I'll just open them up and you can serve yourselves?"

"As long as nobody steals my battered brie," said Clare.

"Trust me, sir," said Savage. "Nobody is going to want that. Aaron says hi, by the way."

"How's he doing?" asked Kett.

"He's back on earth, sir, but the hangover has kicked in."

"Some excuse," said Clare. "I once did an entire four-hour jazz flute set in St Andrew's Hall dressed as Mellow Miss Muffins, the day after drinking fourteen bottles of wine."

"That cannot be true, sir," said Kett. "*Any* of it."

"Let me introduce you guys," said Porter, bustling between Savage and the Super and stealing a chip as he went. He led the way to the sofa. "Robbie, this is Ben and Freddy Rawling."

"Hey," said Kett.

"Hi," said Ben.

The young man let go of the controller to offer his hand. In the second or two it took Kett to shake it, Evie had snatched the controller from him, giggling her way across the room. She managed to hold onto it for a moment or two before Moira grabbed it, the pair of them wrestling on the floor. On-screen, Ben's car flew into a tree and exploded.

Freddy threw his hands into the air with a cry of victory.

"Oh," said Ben, crestfallen.

"Sorry," said Kett.

"Don't be. I'll win the next one. Hey, Freddy, you want to shake hands?"

Freddy beamed a smile at Kett as he stuck out his hand, and Kett pumped it enthusiastically.

"You're settling in okay?" he asked them.

"Aye," said Ben, getting off the sofa and running his hand through a mop of hair. "Aye, this place is... It's so kind of your friend to let us stay here."

"I'm not his friend," said Clare from the table. He had something in his mouth and was spraying crumbs over the unpacked food. "I can't stand him. He's an arsehole."

"Bit harsh, sir," mumbled Kett.

"But I am *your* friend, Ben, and you can stay as long as you like. Nobody's ever here in the off-season, the freezer is full of my wife's juicy meat patties, and Elsham's got everything else you need. Porter's agreed to check up on you."

He leaned in to Ben, glaring at the DI.

"Just don't let him make you any hot drinks. He's a tea pervert."

"A tea pervert?" said Ben, worried.

"But you've earned it," said Clare. "You did solve the case, after all."

Ben grinned, giving Freddy a friendly elbow.

"I didnae do anything," he said. "It was all Freddy. You hear that, pal, you solved the mystery. You're a hero."

"I mean, he definitely *helped*," said Kett with a bigger frown than he'd intended.

"Nope," said Clare, as he headed for the bedrooms. "It was single-handedly Freddy. That's what's going in my report. The rest of you just tossed it up."

"Fair enough," said Kett once the Super had gone. "They were some great photos, Freddy. You've got a detective's eye."

He wasn't sure if the young man understood him, but his smile was brighter than ever. Freddy stuck up his thumb, and turned back to the TV. Moira had somehow managed to set fire to another car.

"Good luck," Kett told Freddy. "And don't forget your chips."

He made his way into the kitchen area, taking the plate that Porter offered him and grabbing a handful of chips from one of the boxes.

"Don't worry about cutlery, sir," said Savage. "Just get in there with your fingers, really try to touch every single chip."

"Sorry," he said. "Hungry."

He put a chip in his mouth and immediately pulled it out again. It was like trying to swallow a hot coal.

"Nice lads," he said, nodding to the sofa.

"They're lovely," said Porter, keeping his voice low. "Turns out their mum died earlier in the year, they lost their house. Been living rough for a few months, gradually moving south. I don't know how they've managed to do it. They wouldn't have lasted much longer out there."

He leant in.

"I did some digging. Ben matches the description of a guy who tried to knock off a betting shop in Falkirk in September."

"Shit," said Kett. "That's why they were on the run?"

"I don't know. But I'm not planning on grassing him up. Nothing was taken, and he didn't have a weapon."

"I'm not sure that's for you to decide, Porter," said Clare as he stepped out of the toilet.

"Bloody hell, sir," said Kett. "How do you move so quietly?"

"I'm a phantom," said Clare. "I float soundlessly.

"Like a fart," Kett muttered.

"Silent and deadly," added Porter.

Clare eyeballed them both for a second, then mellowed.

"I'm not planning on turning him in either," he said, looking at Ben and Freddy on the sofa. "I know good men when I see them."

"You're a good man too, sir," said Porter.

"Go stick a toss in it, Pete," Clare snapped. "I'm a hideous old bastard, and I won't have anyone say otherwise."

He picked up a plate but didn't move away.

"Just so you know, Kett, we're planning a raid on Cold Iron later in the week. There's credible evidence that Joseph Maynard is there."

"Then we should move now, sir," said Kett. "The longer we leave it, the more chance there is that he'll know we're coming."

"There's no we," said Clare, lobbing a chip at Kett. It

bounced off his forehead before falling to the floor. "You stay well out of this."

"No, sir, I should..."

Clare threw another chip, this one slapping Kett on the cheek.

"... be there, sir, I know Maynard better..."

He took another chip to the face, this one dangerously close to his eye. The grease was so hot it burned.

"... than anyone, I should..."

Clare lobbed a fourth chip.

"Stop throwing food at me!" said Kett, almost shrieking.

"You'll do what I tell you, Detective," said Clare. "Which is stand down."

There was no point in arguing.

"You've done enough," the Super went on, and it didn't seem to be a criticism. "You've done enough, Robbie. Let us do this for you."

Kett nodded.

"Now stop dropping chips and start eating," Clare finished, walking away.

"I don't know whether I hate that man or love him," he told Porter as he collected the food from the carpet. The DI was too busy eating to answer him.

Kett picked up his plate, and was halfway to the sofa when he heard a gentle knock on the caravan door. He opened it to see Alice there, her face rosy from the cold.

"I'm hungry," she said.

"Well get in here then," Kett replied. He handed her his plate. "Here, you have this one. I'll get another."

"Is there ketchup?" she asked.

"Plenty," said Savage. "It's on the table. Good to see you, Alice."

Alice walked to the sofa, throwing the two new men a

wary look that melted away when she saw what they were playing.

"I love this game!" she said. "Can I have a go?"

"No!" yelled Moira. "It's mine!"

"Stop setting all the cars on fire!" said Evie. "Give me it!"

Evie wrenched the controller out of her sister's hands, and threw it to Alice.

"You drive!" she said. "I'll hold off the baddies!"

Moira piled on Evie, the pair of them howling with laughter as they rolled back and forth on the rug. Alice had abandoned her chips in order to play, her face alive with delight as her car tore down the racetrack.

"Bloody loons," said Billie, sliding her arm through his. "They're as bad as each other."

"No," said Kett. "Look at them. They're as *good* as each other."

In his mind's eye, he saw Kieran dead in the park. He saw the younger Spicer brothers looking out of the living room window, saw their mother being taken away in handcuffs.

It's all a dream.

But his heart had been broken too many times to bleed again.

"Come on," he said, giving Billie a squeeze. "Let's eat."

PAPER GIRLS
ALEX SMITH
BAD DOG
ALEX SMITH
THREE LITTLE PIGS
ALEX SMITH
WHIP CRACK
ALEX SMITH
RUN RABBIT RUN
ALEX SMITH
STONE COLD DEAD
ALEX SMITH
EVERY MOTHER'S SON
ALEX SMITH
SWEET BRIAR ROSE
ALEX SMITH
JAW BREAKER
ALEX SMITH
KNOCK KNOCK
ALEX SMITH
KING RAT
ALEX SMITH
KNUCKLE BONES
ALEX SMITH
LUCKY NUMBER SEVEN
ALEX SMITH
UNHOLY SAINTS
ALEX SMITH
TRULY MADLY DEADLY
ALEX SMITH
EVERY LAST DEVIL
ALEX SMITH
READ THE FIRST SEVENTEEN BOOKS NOW!

ABOUT THE AUTHOR

Alex Smith wrote his first book when he was six. It wasn't particularly good, but it did have some supernatural monsters in it. His latest books, the DCI Robert Kett thrillers, have monsters in them too, although these monsters are very human, and all the more terrifying for it. In between, he has published fourteen novels for children and teenagers under his full name, Alexander Gordon Smith—including the number one bestselling series Escape From Furnace, which is loved by millions of readers world-wide and which is soon to become a motion picture. He lives in Norwich with his wife and three young daughters.

Find out more at alexsmithbooks.com

RELENTLESS
MEDIA

Printed in Dunstable, United Kingdom

64146640R00262